PARANORMAL MISDIRECTION

SASHA URBAN SERIES: BOOK 5

DIMA ZALES

♠ MOZAIKA PUBLICATIONS ♠

Copyright © 2019 Dima Zales and Anna Zaires
www.dimazales.com

Published by Mozaika Publications, an imprint of Mozaika LLC.
www.mozaikallc.com

Cover by Orina Kafe
www.orinakafe-art.com

e-ISBN: 978-1-63142-469-4
Print ISBN: 978-1-63142-470-0

CHAPTER ONE

WITH FLUFFSTER AT MY SIDE, I review the map-meets-Venn diagram on my phone for what feels like the hundredth time.

Then I tell him about it, and he agrees with my assessment: depicted on my screen is a path through the Otherlands. A path that will take me to Rasputin—my biological father, whom I'd finally spoken to in Headspace.

"So you're really going to go after him?" Fluffster asks in my head.

"Yes," I say. "As soon as I can."

Fluffster sits up on his haunches. "It'll be dangerous."

"I know. But I'm going anyway."

The chinchilla sighs in a very human-like fashion. He knows me well enough to realize that his fantasy of me living at home like a shut-in is just that—a fantasy.

"Who do you think is torturing him?" he asks. "If we knew that, we might be better prepared to deal with it."

"Sadly, I have no clue," I say, a shudder rippling through me as I recall what I saw and felt in Rasputin's memories during our Headspace joining. Even now, my knee aches with ghostly pain from the torturer's excruciating blow. "All I know is that he's my father and he's suffering," I say. "And though he thinks he deserves it for abandoning me at the airport, I'm not about to abandon *him*."

I'm going to save my biological father, and in doing so, I'm going to meet him—a prospect that fills me with a jittery mixture of fear and excitement.

"I still wish you wouldn't go, but I understand why you want to," Fluffster says. "And though this might be selfish, I'd like to meet him myself. We knew each other once, when I was his cat, and since I got some of my memory back, I've thought about him from time to time."

"Oh yeah, of course," I say, grinning at the thought of Fluffster as a cat. Standing up, I start heading for my bedroom door, adding over my shoulder, "I have to tell Felix about this."

"He and Kit left to take Ariel to rehab," Fluffster reminds me.

That's right. They're going to Gomorrah. They mentioned that at breakfast—which now feels like a lifetime ago.

Well, since Nero excused me from work today, I might as well put my free time to good use and explore what would happen if I entered the first world on this map.

A combination of things I learned at Orientation and seer intuition tells me that going into these worlds might be tricky—but that's why it's so nice to be a seer. I don't have to actually risk my hide when I know a threat is coming.

Instead, I can do a little vision-based reconnaissance.

Explaining my plan to Fluffster calms him a little, and he goes to play with Lucifur—Rose's cat, who's now our feline mistress—while I get ready to leave.

A few minutes later, I exit my apartment, and as I approach the elevator, my seer intuition sends a tingle of warning.

Crap. Is someone about to try to kill me yet again?

No.

I don't think it's that.

A part of me even has an idea of what the issue is, but I better check to be sure.

With my finger on the elevator button, I concentrate, evening my breathing. A moment later, I find myself floating in Headspace.

As I look around, I realize that I've gotten so fast at this process that I don't even feel the seer lightning going into my eyes.

If I channeled my intention correctly, the pyramid-like shapes that surround me by default should show me my near-term future. Judging by the music they emit, they're not scary, which is good, as I didn't really expect them to be.

Here we go.

I reach out to the nearest one and fall into a vision.

———

I RIDE the elevator down and exit the building through the front door.

"Excuse me, miss?" A huge guy in a bespoke suit—without a Mandate aura surrounding him—steps into my path.

Warily, I stop.

"Mr. Gorin asked me to take you anywhere you need to go." He nods at a limousine parked nearby. "Where are we headed?"

"Actually, I'm just going for a stroll," I lie, frantically thinking up a way to ditch this unwanted distraction.

"I guess I don't mind a nice walk," the guy says. "Where are *we* headed?"

Damn it.

I can't take him with me to the gates hub at JFK. Showing that to a non-Cognizant would probably cause the Mandate to kill me, but even if not, the guy will undoubtedly report to his boss what I'm doing, and Nero might puzzle out that I've discovered the map—something I'm not ready for him to know yet.

———

I FIND myself back on my floor, my finger still on the elevator button.

It's as I suspected. Nero replaced Thalia with some rent-a-guard, and I won't be able to shake him once he sees me.

Well, as it just so happens, there's another way out.

Grinning at my deviousness, I take the stairs and exit the building in the back—where the super takes out the garbage.

The ploy works. No one stops me.

I summon a ride with my phone. If I hurry, I might even catch up with Kit, Ariel, and Felix before they enter the gate to Gomorrah.

Sadly, I don't come across my friends at JFK, nor do I see them in the hub.

Oh well.

That's not why I'm here anyway.

My target is the yellow gate.

With great trepidation, I approach the start of the path to my father.

I'm not really going to go right now, alone and unprepared. But I *can* see what would happen if I did go in—similar to what I just did with Nero's guard.

At least I hope I can.

Convincing myself to enter the gate takes a bit more effort than telling myself to exit my building—especially given what Hekima told us about the dangers of the Otherlands at the last Orientation.

It takes a while, but eventually, I believe I'm about

to step into the gate. My foot practically itches to step forward.

That's when I go into Headspace instead.

The ellipsoid shapes that surround me now are scary—proving that I did the right thing by doing this via a vision before going for real.

Overflowing with excitement, I reach out to the nearest shape.

CHAPTER TWO

BRACING MYSELF, I leap into the bright yellow shimmer of the gate, and my breath catches as I emerge on the other side.

If someone had built a large theme park on Jupiter and then blown it all up with a nuclear blast, this is what the ruins would look like a few thousand years later.

The ground under my feet is cracked and covered with multicolored slime—as is the jagged half of the Ferris wheel in the distance. Same with the ruins of the other rides.

I try to suck in a breath.

What passes for air sears my respiratory system like a hot iron.

My throat and lungs are in agony, and there's an explosion of pain in my stomach.

"Must go back," I think, but my legs buckle under me as I faceplant on the ground.

The fall knocks out what little air I had in my lungs, and my nerve endings combust like fireworks on the Fourth of July.

Unable to control a single muscle, I convulse on the ground.

A copper-flavored liquid fills my mouth and lungs, and with one final burst of agonizing pain, I fade into darkness.

CHAPTER THREE

I COME to my senses in the hub and back away from the yellow gate, my heart hammering frantically.

That was awful. Beyond awful.

Suppressing the urge to vomit from remembered agony, I turn and start walking back through the labyrinthian corridors.

Thank goodness for my instincts and Dr. Hekima's Orientation lessons. If it weren't for his dire warnings about the dangers of the Otherlands, I might not have had the foresight to have this vision.

Walking briskly, I ponder the implications of it, the key one being how I'm going to get to my father given this new information.

Maybe I need to get myself a Hazmat suit? Will that help me survive whatever killed me in that vision?

I guess I can buy one, then approach the gate and have another vision to find out.

But what if there's radiation, and I end up dying from cancer a few months or years later?

At least I have some savings to invest in this venture—Nero recently awarded me a hundred grand for punching him in the face.

Speaking of Nero, should I bring him into this?

I dodged his guard because I didn't think he'd help, but maybe I can get his help without his willing participation? After all, he has the map. Maybe he knows how to get to my father's world through the path depicted on it. At the very least, he could tell me if the Hazmat suit idea is doomed.

Or maybe he *would* help me?

Sure.

Nero helping me.

Right after someone sells me the Brooklyn Bridge.

Still, it's worth a try.

Exiting the secret section of the airport, I get a taxi to Nero's office.

"Wait for me," I say to the driver when we arrive.

He agrees, and I step out of the car and stare up at Nero's building.

I'm about to implement the same strategy as I did at my building and the yellow gate.

Step one: decide to go talk to Nero. Step two: see a vision of how that would go.

"I'm going to talk to Nero about the map," I tell myself determinedly, over and over. When I feel convinced that I'm indeed about to go face my boss, I take in a calming breath and focus on getting into Headspace instead.

Once there, I reach out to the closest shape.

———

NERO'S blue-gray eyes widen when he spots me.

"Here on your day off?" he says. "That's a first."

"Yes, and I also managed to sneak by your Thalia replacement," I say instead of a hello. "But don't kill him," I add hastily. "I'm just *that* sneaky."

He stands up and stalks toward me, his expression grim.

"Don't blame Felix for allowing me to leave, either," I say nervously. "He relayed your wish for me to take it easy, but something urgent came up and I had to come see you in person."

"Oh?" Nero stops and lifts an eyebrow.

"I'm here to talk about this," I say and show him an image on my phone. "The map that leads to my biological father."

CHAPTER FOUR

NERO'S FACE turns darker than the sky during a Category 5 hurricane.

I step back and nervously check the time as I've trained myself to regularly do.

He comes after me and grabs my wrist—preventing me from escaping. "I didn't realize you got a chance to look at the map, let alone snap a picture," he growls, and with the speed of a striking cobra, he snatches my phone from my hands.

An angry squeeze later, the phone crumbles into tiny shards of plastic, silicone, and glass.

"I have the image printed," I croak out. "It's also in the cloud. I've also emailed—"

"You will not go there," Nero says, enunciating every word. "It's too dangerous."

"But he's my father. What wouldn't you risk for *your* family?"

Something like sympathy flashes in Nero's eyes for a moment—that and pain. Then it's replaced by grim determination. "You're here on Earth for a reason," he says. "He wouldn't want your help."

I open my mouth to reply when Nero moves with preternatural speed. Before I can get a single word out, I find myself draped over Nero's shoulder.

"How dare you? Put me down!"

Nero readjusts his hold and walks toward the exit, carrying me like Santa Claus lugging his bag of gifts.

Or more like Krampus, Santa's evil opposite.

I spice up my screams with some kicking and punching.

Infuriatingly oblivious to my blows and escalating protestations, Nero walks out of his office.

His assistant Venessa stares at the spectacle in speechless horror, and I can almost see the words "harassment" and "lawsuit" swirling through her brain.

In a few strides, Nero reaches the elevator.

Stepping in, he presses the button that would take us to the basement, and I triple the kicking, punching, and screaming, using all my remaining strength.

But it's to no avail.

He carries me into the safe-like cell in the basement.

"You owe me a hundred-and-thirty-five work hours." He plops me on the soft cushions of the couch. "I want those to be consecutive. Meanwhile, I'm going to post guards in every hub on the planet."

Turning around, he smashes his fist into the passcode screen I'd used to escape this place, and it joins my phone in technology heaven as he steps out.

"Wait," I yell, but the metal door to my prison screeches into place.

CHAPTER FIVE

I COME to my senses next to my work building and back away from it as though it were infested with leprosy-carrying bedbugs.

My intuition was spot on again. I can't talk to Nero about the map—or let him find out that I know about it.

I get back into the cab, and the ride home is a blur of angry ruminations where I imagine all sorts of cleverly scathing things I could've said to Nero in my vision.

By the time we arrive, I calm down enough to sneak back into the building from the back, so that the nameless new bodyguard doesn't learn that I was gone.

When I walk into the apartment, Felix and Kit are back. The two of them, along with Fluffster, stampede to the door to greet me. Lucifur, however, glances in my direction and instantly loses interest. Not that I can blame her; proverbially, curiosity is pretty deadly for her kind.

"Fluffster said you have something major to tell us, but he wouldn't say what—said we have to hear it from your lips," Felix says with a worried frown. He looks to Kit for support, but the shape-shifting Councilor merely shrugs and makes herself look like me.

"Right." I take off my shoes and grab Fluffster from the floor to further calm my nerves. "Let's go to the living room, and I'll fill you in."

Once we're comfortably seated, I tell them all about my Headspace encounter with my father and my realization that I have a map that (probably) leads to him. I then go over my deadly "what if I go" vision and conclude with Nero's potential reaction to the whole thing.

"I wonder if it was the lack of oxygen alone that killed you?" Felix muses as the cat jumps onto his lap. "A simple scuba suit could help then, unless there are toxic agents in the air. Could you tell?"

"I have no idea," I say. "It could've also been radiation—given the way the world itself looked."

"A Hazmat suit then." Felix scratches behind Lucifur's fluffy ear, making the creature purr. "Or even—"

"Can we first talk about the elephant in the room," Fluffster states loudly in my head.

The couch creaks.

Kit has turned herself into a small elephant and is scratching her floppy ear with her trunk.

"Huh," Felix says, looking at Kit's form. "You're not just in the room. You're also the elephant of surprise."

I roll my eyes at the awful pun. "Right. Just like that famous movie, *The Fifth Elephant.*"

Though I can't see the white in Fluffster's rodent eyes, I get the distinct impression that, like me, he's rolling them with the expertise of a teenage girl. "As I said before, you shouldn't go," he says to me, pointedly turning away from the elephant/Kit. "Nero might have a good reason for wanting to stop you."

"Out of the question." I place the chinchilla on the carpet. If Fluffster is going to take Nero's side, he can rub his own chin. "If you want to help, think of a way I can survive the trip."

"A spacesuit." Felix mindlessly strokes the cat's belly.

"NASA doesn't sell that stuff." I pinch the bridge of my nose. "Please don't say you want to fly to Houston and rob a museum."

"I'm talking about a cosmonaut suit," Felix says. "After the Soviet Union collapsed, a black market sprang up for the gear used in their space program. I happen to know a guy. I used a few parts he gave me when I built Golem." He looks wistful at the memory of the destroyed robot. "The only problem with this idea is that it's going to be costly."

"I have money," I say. "How much are we talking about?"

"Probably upward of seventy grand per spacesuit." Felix stops stroking the cat, but she nudges him with her paw and he resumes his duties. "So that's over two hundred thousand if you, me, and Kit go together."

Fluffster's eyes bulge at the insane expenditure until he looks on the verge of turning into his monstrous form.

"See if you can get your guy to give us a lower price," I say quickly. The last thing I want is for my pet chinchilla to eat my roommate. "I don't have enough for *that*."

"Right." Felix gives Fluffster a worried look as well. "Hopefully, he'll consider a bulk discount. If not, maybe I can use my powers to pay at least part of the cost in trade."

"Shady favor for shady people?" I resist the urge to bite my nails. "How about you invest in a stock I recommend instead? Just make sure Nero doesn't find out I gave you the tip; I'm not supposed to be investing on my own or through friends and family."

Fluffster's scary expression is replaced with a curious one.

Good.

In the future, we'll have to make sure to have money conversations outside our apartment.

"That actually sounds like fun." Felix attempts to stop stroking the cat, but she forces him to keep going once more. "I have some savings I can dedicate to this. What company did you have in mind?"

Pretending I'm doing my job for Nero, I let my intuition (or whatever it is) pull a stock from the ether.

"Cedar Fair—the amusement park operator," I say. "Their ticker is FUN."

"You sure?" Fluffster narrows his eyes. "I refuse to have this household live in squalor."

"When I do the same thing for Nero, he claims to make bank," I say defensively. "Why shouldn't it work for Felix?"

"I'll invest later today." Finally setting the cat aside, Felix takes out his phone and types something—no doubt adding FUN to his to-do list (possibly for the first time).

Lucifur gives him a baleful glare but lets him live. For now.

"I also have some spare cash I've been meaning to deploy," Kit says as the cat starts grooming herself. "Can I jump in on this transaction if I let you keep half the profits?"

"So long as you don't blame us in case of a lack of profits," I say.

"And chip in for the rent," Fluffster adds.

"Deal," Kit says.

Felix puts down his phone, looking thoughtful. "Even if we get a spacesuit, we'll probably need to retool it for the unique dangers of the world you saw in your vision—that and somehow figure out the exact nature of those dangers. I'll have to get some help from an engineer, and we'll have to pay this person as well."

"If you let me keep all my FUN profits, I can help you with that problem," Kit says and makes herself look like a round-cheeked young woman with the dorkiest smile I've ever seen. In a nasal voice that sounds like a spoiled (but then later rehabilitated) princess, she adds, "A gnome owes me a favor."

"A gnome?" Felix and I say in unison but with different intonations. Mine is "now you're telling me there are gnomes?" while Felix just sounds like Christmas came early.

"A gnome." Kit turns back into her usual self.

"You have a deal," Felix says to Kit, then looks at me. "Gnomes are amazing with technology. Especially hardware—which is exactly what we need."

"Gnomes," I repeat slowly. "I thought they'd be good at growing beards and gardening."

"I suspect that Itzel will educate you about gnomes," Kit says in that same goofy voice. "The trick is to make her shut up about it."

"I didn't think gnomes were allowed on Earth," Felix says. "I've only met a few while visiting Gomorrah."

"Being on the Council comes with many perks." Kit sits straighter, her voice back to its usual anime-character pitch. "We have access to all sorts of secret maps to the Otherlands, and we're allowed to bring over any Cognizant, even those that are typically forbidden on Earth. We just have to use proper precautions."

So this is how Nero got the orcs here, and the proper precautions in that case included making them wear makeup to cover their green skin. I suppress a shudder as I recall how viciously Nero killed said orcs for bruising me.

Pushing the gruesome images away, I say, "Great. When can we get the spacesuit and meet this gnome?"

"My spacesuit guy will need a few days." Felix steeples his fingers. "I'll also need some time for your suggested investment to pay off."

"I'll be too busy to get Itzel until I'm done planning the funeral," Kit says. "Afterward—"

She stops talking. She must've realized everyone is staring at her with varying degrees of open-mouthed shock. "Did I forget to mention the funeral arrangements I was tasked with?" she asks guiltily.

We keep staring at her, though I have a strong urge to get up and shake the information out of her—but the memories of her turning into a gator (and a drekavac) stop me from doing so.

"Nero and I petitioned the Council to dedicate a Farewell Rite to Rose," Kit explains. "Once everyone agreed, I was tasked with the bulk of the administrative work—no good deed goes unpunished and all that."

Felix whistles. "A Farewell Rite? Wow. Of course, if anyone deserves such a great honor, it's Rose. I bet Vlad will be pleased."

"Assuming he attends." Kit turns into Vlad, and her face looks like a mask of grief. "No one has been able to get in touch with him."

"I'm sure he'll be there," Felix says.

Kit turns back into herself and opens her mouth to reply, but her phone chirps. She looks at it, then leaps to her feet. "Funeral duty calls," she says. "I have so much to do. I'm not sure when I'll be back."

She heads out of the room, but then she turns and says, "I think it would be nice if you gave a eulogy at the event."

Blood leaves my face. "Are you talking to me or Felix?" I ask as the sinking feeling spreads through me.

"You, of course." Kit frowns at me in confusion.

"And is this going to be a big event?" I do my best to swallow my rapidly pumping heart back into my chest.

"Huge." Felix gives me a pitying look, then conspiratorially mouths to Kit, "Sasha isn't a fan of public speaking."

Not a fan of public speaking. That's like saying arachnophobes aren't fans of tarantulas.

"She was fine when she spoke in front of the Council." Kit turns into me—but a version brimming with impossible levels of confidence and determination, kind of like Wonder Woman.

She's right. I did speak to the Council without freaking out—at least on my second go at it. In my vision, I fainted from the anxiety.

Taking in calming breaths, I consider that. Could it be that I have conquered my biggest fear? But if so, why do I feel like rabid skunks are trying to chew their way through my intestines?

Then again, this is for Rose.

"I'll do it," I hear myself utter. "I'll say a few words."

"Great," Kit says and leaves.

I sit there, staring blankly at the turned-off TV.

"I'm going to get a head start on the spacesuit," Felix says from somewhere. "That and investing."

"Sure," I say numbly. "You do that."

Felix leaves with the cat on his tail, but I just sit there, trying to convince myself that public speaking is not the equivalent of facing the gallows.

"Hey," Fluffster says in my head. "I just wanted to say that if meeting your father means this much to you, I won't get in your way."

"Thank you." I focus on the concerned-looking chinchilla.

Picking him up, I stroke his heavenly fur and immediately feel soothed.

"Let me know if there's anything I can do to help," Fluffster says.

"There is something, actually," I tell him, deciding not to think about that speech for now. "I'd like to learn Russian."

"Russian?" The domovoi looks up at me.

"I need a way to communicate with my father," I explain.

"I can speak Russian." Fluffster straightens his whiskers.

"I know that, bud." I smile down at him. "I was hoping you'd help me with this."

He puffs up like a feisty kitten. "Of course."

"Great." I pull out my phone and download every app for learning Russian, then a few ebooks on the same subject.

Then I tell Fluffster my plan. I will go into

23

Headspace and get a vision of me using all these tools, one after another—which should allow me to choose the one that fits my learning style best and will give me a decent head start.

Thus decided, I concentrate and find myself in Headspace.

CHAPTER SIX

I TOUCH the shapes around me all at once and receive an onslaught of Russian education, hours and hours of it, until eventually, I run out of my seer power.

Back in my living room, I assess my prodigious progress. I learned a lot from all the apps and books, and I remember most of it.

Where was Headspace when I was cramming for finals in college? I could've aced any test like this.

Interestingly, though Russian has a reputation for being a hard language to learn, I'm not finding that to be the case. If anything, the opposite seems to be true for me. Granted, the alphabet is a little wonky—H isn't an H, and P isn't a P, but overall, it feels extremely natural to me. I especially like how the alphabet lets you read pretty much right away—Russian spelling is more or less phonetic.

"*Nu kak?*" Fluffster asks me in Russian.

"I didn't learn that yet," I say sheepishly, though I

feel like I'm on the verge of understanding. "What does it mean?"

"Approximately, 'so how goes it?'" Fluffster explains, confirming my unvoiced guess. "I probably should've instead used a more common, '*kak tvoi dela?*'"

I smile. Despite the way it sounds, "*kak*" doesn't mean rooster or male genitalia. It's the Russian word for "how," so I reply with, "*Horosho.*"

"Wow," Fluffster says. "Your pronunciation is *really* good. Surprisingly good."

"I had hoped it would be." I beam a hundred-megawatt smile at him. "After all, I learned it as a child —during the critical time in your life when you form the muscles involved in speaking."

As I say this, it occurs to me that the same reasoning might explain why I'm finding these lessons so much easier than most people do. I'm relearning instead of picking up from scratch—and that's always easier.

"Why don't we watch some movies you've already seen but with Russian voiceover?" Fluffster suggests. "I know a good website for that."

I nod, excited, and we download *The Illusionist, Now You See Me 1* and *2, The Prestige*, and a few of my other favorites.

Because I've seen the films many times, I find the Russian easy enough to follow—or maybe I find it easy to follow because they use vocabulary I've just learned and/or picked up as a kid.

When Fluffster gets tired of watching, I force him

to listen to me practice speaking Russian until it's time to go to bed.

Except I can't sleep. Now that I'm not focusing on learning my father's language, my mind keeps coming up with what I'd say during Rose's eulogy.

Eventually, I give up, get out of bed, and write down what I think will sound good.

And then I can't sleep because I dread delivering the speech in front of a huge crowd.

After hours of tossing and turning, I get up, grab my phone, and study Russian for the rest of the night—probably making more progress than a graduate student would in two years.

———

WHEN THE SMELL of fried goodness wafts into the room from under the door, I trek into the kitchen.

Felix, Lucifur, and Fluffster are eating breakfast. The chinchilla's bowl with hay is on the table next to Felix's plate, and the cat's saucer with Fancy Feast is on the floor.

The cat looks up at me with an expression that seems to say, "Dare come near our Majesty's meal, and I will eat your face."

Felix's gaze is much warmer than the cat's as he examines my sleep-deprived self.

I check his plate, spot the fried eggs and hash browns, and spy more in the skillets on the stove.

Score.

"Morning," Felix says as I rush to put a heaping portion on my plate. "I hear you're learning Russian now."

"*Da*," I say, grinning. "*Eto pravda.*"

"You weren't kidding," Felix says to Fluffster in Russian. "That's great pronunciation."

Fluffster looks up from his hay and gives me a wink.

I put my plate on the table and sit down. "Yeah. It's not as hard as I feared," I say in Russian.

"I imagine the three-gender thing will be tricky." Felix gesticulates with his utensils. "This fork is female, this table is male, but an egg is neuter."

"*Da*," I say. "But the good news is that there are rules that help me figure out what gender something is." Shoving food into my mouth, I chew hungrily.

"Sasha will be fine on that score," Fluffster chimes in. "Even in English, there are a few gendered nouns. Like a ship is a she. Spanish and French also have something like this. And besides, even if Sasha messes those up, she can still be understood."

"Yeah. She'd just sound silly." Felix gives us an evil grin. "Even sillier than usual, that is."

Since my mouth is too full for a proper retort, I pinch his forearm instead.

"Hey." He jerks his arm away. "After all I did last night?"

"About that," I say through the food. "How did it go?"

"I got us a deal," he says excitedly, the pretend injury

forgotten. "The guy has a bunch of parts from Orlan, Sokol, and Birkut suits and can give us a bulk discount. I figured with a gnome on the team, we can put those together better than the Soviet engineers."

"Good," I say. "When do we get the delivery?"

"Working that out still," Felix says. "Not long, though."

I want to ask him how much it all costs but decide to do so when Fluffster is out of earshot.

"I also got us some Hazmat gear and other things I think we will need," Felix says. "And Kit helped me decide where our makeshift lab will be."

"Oh?" I spear more eggs onto my fork.

"Yep, in JFK," Felix says.

I raise my eyebrows.

"Did you picture yourself waltzing into an airport wearing a spacesuit?" Felix's unibrow attempts an answering arch.

I picture the looks on the TSA agents' faces.

He's right. It would not be a good idea, even on Halloween.

"We could bring the suits in some kind of bags, like luggage," I say.

"You're close," Felix says. "The parts can go in suitcases, but the finished product will be built in one of the underground rooms—the one you get to if you take the wrong turn right before the hub corridor."

"I didn't realize there were rooms there," I say. "I pictured pits with hungry crocodiles, or a post-apocalyptic H&R Block office with cannibalistic accountants."

Felix chuckles. "There may be those there too. But according to Kit, there is also a suitable room that we will use. She says it's best to keep the gnome as close to the gates as possible, so this kills a bunch of birds."

"Fair enough," I say. "Anything else?"

"I made the FUN investment last night," Felix says and pulls out his phone. "Wow. It's already up."

Fluffster scuttles over to look at the screen and appears pleased.

"I want to practice some more Russian on you guys," I say when they look back at me. "Why don't you say something, and I'll try to reply?"

"*Horosho,*" Felix says, grinning, and launches into rapid-fire Russian. Now that he's speaking so fast, comprehending him is harder. Still, I'm pleasantly surprised at how much I catch.

"You'll be fluent in no time," Felix says as we're wrapping up the meal. "You've made a lot of progress already."

"I have, haven't I?" I say, and strain my brain for something to reward myself with.

Of course.

There's something that always cheers me up—magic.

Of the performing kind.

Especially when I'm the performer.

Yeah, that's it. I've been thinking of ways to impress the Cognizant with something besides a card-cheating demo, and in this very moment, a whole branch of magical arts comes to mind: escapes.

"Before you go, can you help me with something?" I ask Felix as I jump to my feet in excitement.

He glances at his phone with a frown. "Sure. Let's just make it quick."

"In my room," I say and rush ahead with a bounce in my step.

Before Felix can catch up, I locate the hardest-to-crack straitjacket that I own—and I own too many—and pull it out.

"A straitjacket?" Felix looks at me as though I've gone insane enough to actually need one.

"Yep." I put the thing on. "I'm trying to build a repertoire that would impress the Cognizant, and it occurred to me that escaping this can't be explained by any powers."

"Not really." Felix walks up to me and examines the locking mechanism of the strange garment. "If you had Kit's power, you could—"

"Impress Cognizant who know what my power is." I narrow my eyes at him.

"Even with your powers, you—"

"Dude." I turn my back to him and get into the classic straitjacket position. "I don't need your opinion. I just need you to lock me in this thing so I can practice my escape. It's been ages since the last time I've done it."

I inhale deeply and hold it in.

Grumbling under his breath, Felix pulls my arms behind me—a bit too roughly.

I tense all the muscles in my body and overall try to make myself as big as I can.

"How long is this going to take?" Felix asks when he's done. "I need to be at work."

"You can go," Fluffster says. "If Sasha can't escape, I'll help."

Felix looks down worriedly. "Are you sure—"

I tune them out and start my work.

First, I exhale.

Next, I relax my muscles, creating some slack in the bindings. Then I manipulate the slack toward my left shoulder and proceed with the rest of the escape.

Four seconds later, I'm free.

Both Fluffster and Felix look impressed—and Felix is one of my toughest customers.

"I guess I'm a little rusty," I say as I drop the straitjacket on the floor. "It usually takes me three and a half seconds."

"It's good. Add it to your repertoire." Felix picks up and examines the cloth of the straitjacket for any funny business—and finds none. "If you had this on and hung yourself by your feet over some fire, almost anyone would be impressed if you escaped alive."

"I think I'll work out something like that." I take the straitjacket from him and start folding.

"Now I really have to go," Felix says.

"See you later." I wave at his back.

When he's gone, I put away the straitjacket and

resume studying Russian. I'm at it for what feels like hours, until my phone rings.

Grabbing it, I see that it's 12:30 p.m., and that the caller is Nero.

What could he want?

My heart rate speeds up as I accept the call. "Hello?"

"Sasha," Nero says in his super-deep voice. "Did you eat yet?"

I blink. "No. I'm starving, actually."

"I'm downstairs," Nero says. "Come down, and we'll grab lunch."

Before I can reply, he hangs up.

I stare at my phone incredulously.

Lunch with Nero?

Is this a prank?

Mind spinning, I dress in some presentable clothing and even put on some makeup—a rarity for me.

As I make my way down, I keep wondering what this could be about.

Is this a social call, and if so, am I glad?

Or is Nero merely planning to impart some Mentor wisdom?

Well, whatever his intentions, I always have a million questions I can ask him, so it would be crazy to turn down such an opportunity.

Yeah, that's why I'm so eager—because I want to pose pointed questions.

And to eat.

It must be hunger behind the strange fluttering of

butterfly wings in my stomach. Hunger combined with sleep deprivation.

Stepping out of the elevator, I stare at Nero.

Broad-shouldered and tall, he's practically oozing testosterone, and the unnaturally thick limbal rings in his blue-gray eyes are out in full force. He gives me a look that makes the stupid hunger butterflies increase their flapping to hurricane levels.

"How are you?" he growls.

"I'm okay," I manage to say and feel like I should be given an award for not tripping over my own feet.

Nero cares about my well-being now?

I *knew* hell was freezing over. There have been many signs.

"You're not okay." He runs his hand through his hair. "Why does everyone always forget they can't lie to me?"

"I didn't sleep last night. I bet that's why your lie detection activated. When you asked your question, I figured you meant 'how are you coping with having nearly been killed by Baba Yaga,' and in that regard, I'm okay."

"I see," he says and starts walking south. "Why didn't you sleep?"

"Kit told me about the funeral." My breath quickens as I hurry to keep up with his long strides. "She suggested I give a eulogy."

"Wait, she already told you about the funeral?" Nero sounds displeased.

Interesting. Did he come here to tell me about it in person? If so, that's a nice gesture.

"Yeah," I say as we turn onto a narrow, one-way street. "She mentioned that you were instrumental when it came to getting Rose this honor." I look over and catch him staring at me intently. Feeling awkward, I look away and mumble, "Thanks for that."

"Of course." He stops. "If you'd like, I can speak in your stead. I'm sure Rose would—"

I also stop and look up at him. "No." Instinctively, I touch his forearm, then yank my hand away, realizing what I'm doing. "I should do this for Rose. That it's hard for me just makes it more important. Besides, I think I want to. It feels right."

"I understand." He gazes at me with an unreadable expression.

I take a step back. "Anyway," I say with forced cheerfulness. "Where are we going?"

"Nowhere. We're here." He points at the large window behind me.

"This place?" We're standing next to the best restaurant in New York City—and, by transitive property, the world.

Though a short distance from my apartment, it might as well be on the moon. The waiting list for mere mortals like me is rumored to be *years* long—and if I decided to go for, say, my thirtieth birthday, Fluffster would eat me alive once he saw the astronomical bill.

"After you," Nero says and pulls open the ornamental glass door.

Swallowing my awed disbelief, I step inside. As soon as the host sees Nero, he fawns over us as though we were royalty, leading us to a well-positioned table by the window.

Before I can blink, our glasses are filled with wine that probably costs more than I make in a year.

As Nero orders the food, I take a sip of the wine and examine the impeccable tablecloth in front of me. Then I study all the movers and shakers at the other tables and the giant ice sculptures in the shape of doves by the bar.

The place is fancy.

Too fancy and romantic to take someone if you merely wanted to tell her about a funeral.

Holy estrogen.

Is this a date?

CHAPTER SEVEN

A DATE WITH NERO.

The idea is more intoxicating than the divine wine.

I must find out; else I will lose my mind. Fortunately, there might be a way—apart from simply asking.

Relaxing into my chair, I let my eyes focus on the traffic outside the restaurant as I try to get into Headspace.

To my huge relief, it works right away.

AS I FIND myself floating in Headspace, I feel silly.

Is this really the best use of my powers—to figure out why my boss took me out?

I could, for example, use the seer-juice for something more useful—like another Russian lesson.

But no. I have to know what Nero's intentions are.

I focus on the default shapes—those typically show me the immediate future.

Wait a second.

The surrounding shapes are playing music that's a lot more frightening than I'd expect from a vision of a date.

In fact, they seem like they will show me something deadly.

My ethereal wisp metaphysically trembling, I touch the scariest of the shapes and prepare for a vision.

———

"AND WHAT CAN I GET *YOU*?" The waiter smiles, but it doesn't touch his eyes.

A wave of anxiety spreads through me.

A police car passes by the restaurant, and I half expect the cops to pull up to the door and arrest me for some unknown reason.

But no.

They turn the corner and disappear.

I pick up my menu.

Am I worried about food poisoning? This place does specialize in raw delicacies like oysters and caviar —but at these prices, I figure they use the freshest ingredients in the world.

A large black van slowly rolls down the street outside.

As soon as I see it, I realize *that* is the source of my malaise.

"Is everything all right?" Nero asks. He must've noticed all the blood leaving my face.

Before I can reply, the windows of the van slide down.

I glimpse a killer clown mask before a large gloved hand pulls out a machine gun from the window.

I scream.

Everyone in the restaurant looks at me with a mixture of annoyance and concern.

With a deafening *rat-a-tat-tat*, bullets hit the glass window, shattering it into tiny shards.

My shoulder feels like it's been torn away, and the leftover stump cauterized with hot iron.

I've been shot.

The spray of bullets hits the screaming and scattering people around us.

Face twisted with fear, Nero leaps across the table, grabbing me in a tight embrace and covering me with his body as we fall.

My breath vacates my lungs as we hit the floor, but I'm glad to be down because I feel like I'm about to faint from the agony in my shoulder.

On top of me, Nero jolts, as if struck by a bullet. However, there's no pain on his face, just fury of frightening intensity.

Whoever these shooters are, they would be crazy not to finish him off. If he lives, he'll make them regret being born.

More gunfire. It sounds like either the ice

sculptures or people's heads are exploding around us, and Nero's body jerks again and again.

The tiny corner of my brain that's not screaming in terror keeps repeating one thought over and over: Nero is taking bullets for me.

The machine gun goes off again.

Nero tenses, and my ribs shatter with apocalyptic pain.

A bullet must've gone through him and into my chest.

Blood fills my lungs and bubbles up my throat as my heart stops beating.

CHAPTER EIGHT

I'M BACK in the restaurant just as Nero finishes his order.

"And what can I get *you*?" The waiter smiles his fake smile at me, just as he did in my vision.

"Run!" I shout at Nero and leap to my feet.

As I sprint for the restaurant exit, the same wave of anxiety spreads through me—only now I know what's behind it.

To my relief, Nero is on my tail.

I screech to a halt in the middle of the road—just as the police car pulls onto the street and heads my way.

Making eye contact with the officers, I wave my arms like a psychotic cheerleader.

Nero steps in front of me protectively.

If the cops decide to ram someone with their car, it would be him, not me.

I wonder what would happen if he was hit?

Something tells me Nero is harder to kill than even a vampire.

"Did you see a vision?" he asks over his shoulder.

"Yes," I hiss. "Someone with machine guns is going to shoot up the whole restaurant. It'll be from a black van that's about to turn onto this street."

The police car stops.

Nero takes that as his cue to rush to the sidewalk and stare intently at the oncoming traffic.

Only now do I realize how crazy I must look to the police—but not as crazy as I would sound if I told them the exact truth.

Not that I can tell them about a vision—or anything supernatural-sounding—without the Mandate turning me into an orifice-bleeding mess or worse.

"I heard a gunshot," I lie and point in the direction where the van is to appear.

The cops pepper me with questions, and I expand on my lie with all the earnestness of an expert magician.

Toward the end of my explanation, I spot the black van. It stops a few feet behind the police car.

This was my plan—to have the cops block their path and provide discouragement.

Hopefully.

They may have enough firepower to take on these two officers.

Just like in my vision, the van windows are tinted—yet despite the lack of visibility, I can feel the malevolent gazes from behind the dark glass.

Nero moves as though he's about to run after the van. Then he looks back at me, then at the van, then back at me.

I can practically see the gears turning in his mind.

Catch the would-be shooters or stay with me in case of danger?

Making a swift decision, I act as scared as I'd be if I saw a hungry drekavac. "In that van." I point with a shaking finger. "There's a guy with a gun inside. I just saw him."

As if trying to buy me credibility, the van's tires screech as it speeds backward.

"Quickly, they're getting away," I urge the confused officers.

And the Oscar goes to Sasha.

Telling me to stay put, the cops rush back into their car, turn on the siren, and back away after the van.

I exhale a breath of relief I didn't realize I was holding as Nero comes toward me.

"Let's take you home." He grabs my elbow.

I nod mutely, letting him drag me away at a rapid clip.

Our semi-jog turns into a sprint, and before long, I find myself in my building elevator, panting like an overheated dog.

Nero frowns, and I see a promise of cardio training in my future in his gaze. Not waiting until I catch my breath, he sternly asks, "What happened?"

I explain about my vision as we enter my apartment and go into the kitchen.

"Okay. Now let's go over it again." Nero sits down at the kitchen table across from me. "You say they wore a mask, but did you see the eyes?"

Fluffster walks into the kitchen, eyeing us worriedly. "Did I just hear you say you've been shot at?"

I explain that it was a vision and describe as much detail as I can.

"So no, I couldn't see the eyes," I say in conclusion. "It all happened too fast."

Nero and Fluffster look upset, each in their own way.

"Someone is trying to kill you *again*," Fluffster says. "Why do you insist on leaving the apartment so much?"

"Given the nature of this attack, I'm not sure she'd be safe even inside your domain." Nero's jaw flexes as he looks at the chinchilla. "If they rang the bell, then shot up the door with a machine gun, even you wouldn't be able to stop Sasha from catching a bullet."

"We'll have Felix make a robot to open the door," Fluffster says. "Or better yet, ignore the stupid doorbell altogether."

"Yeah, live like shut-ins without ever opening the door," I say sarcastically. "At least until we starve."

"Every time you leave, you almost get killed," Fluffster counters.

"We don't know that this was targeting me." My stomach rumbles, and I walk over to the fridge to grab cheese, ham, and mayo. Vision bullets don't seem to mess with my appetite. "The last time I assumed someone was

44

after me, they were really trying to kill Kit. How do we know it's not the case this time? Maybe this was Nero's enemy. Or maybe it was someone trying to kill one of the people at that restaurant—there were plenty of VIPs there. Or it could've been one of those crazy shooters from the news—some guy who decided to thin out the top one percent. You know, a kind of Occupy Wall Street, but turned violent?" I pointedly look at Nero.

"The human shooter theory stretches credibility," he says tersely.

"And who would dare go after Nero?" Fluffster looks at my boss with a mixture of awe and respect.

"Someone suicidal?" I grab the bread from the drawer, open the bag, and start spreading the mayo on two slices—one for Nero, and one for me.

It's no oyster and caviar, but it's food.

"That's why I was asking about their eyes." Nero's own eyes look the least human I've ever seen them. "You sure you didn't spot their limbal rings?"

It finally dawns on me what he's implying. "Your enemies are the same kind of Cognizant as you?"

"No one else is worth concerning myself with." He frowns. "But I'm the only one of my kind who knows about the location of this world. So no. If this were another of my kind, I doubt they'd stoop to hiding their faces. Or using guns."

"And what is that kind of Cognizant?" I ask, holding my breath in anticipation. "What should I be on the lookout for?"

Nero gives me an unreadable look, then says, "Don't put cheese on my sandwich. I'd rather get extra ham."

I violently plop ham and cheese on one slice of bread, then slap triple the usual ham on another. It takes all my willpower not to throw the finished snack at Nero's stubborn face and to simply hand it to him.

I thought he'd open up to me just this once, reveal a single one of his precious secrets.

But of course, he didn't. The man is insufferable.

I rip into my sandwich so fast I accidentally bite my cheek.

Fluffster looks at me. "Assuming this *was* someone after you, Sasha, who would it be?"

I ponder that. "I don't have a lot of enemies left, as far as I know. The only person I can think of who's still alive is Chester."

Nero looks like a lightbulb just lit up above his head. Finishing his sandwich in a single bite, he reaches into his pocket to get his phone.

A couple of taps later, Nero's video app is playing a connecting tune while he sets up the screen so that the person on the other end can see the three of us—assuming they pick up.

The video call connects.

A man sits in a chair in front of his camera, his satyr-like face a mask of amused curiosity.

It's Chester, the former Council member whose machinations nearly got me killed by a crazy necromancer and her zombies.

Then I take in the full scene and blink a few times.

Sitting next to Chester is an enormous white lion—the kind Siegfried & Roy would make appear and disappear in their magic shows.

"Ah." Chester strokes his frightening friend behind the ear like one would a cat. "If it isn't my favorite couple." I half expect the lion to chomp on Chester's hand, but the mighty creature seems to be enjoying the attention. "Nero." Chester grins mischievously. "Sasha." He looks me over. "I didn't realize you were at the stage of your relationship to jointly own a pet." He looks Fluffster up and down. "Unless that's lunch?"

Following his master's gaze, the lion takes in Fluffster and hungrily licks his lips.

"I'm calling to ask some questions," Nero says, oblivious to the lion. "Did you try to kill Sasha today—personally or via proxy?"

"No." Chester looks genuinely surprised. "I did not."

"Did you use your power on her?" Nero asks. "Change the probability that someone would make an attempt on her life?"

All amusement disappears from Chester's face. "Why would I do something like this?" He absentmindedly rubs the lion's fur. "I told you both that when I hired that necro before, it was to mess with Darian—Sasha was just a means to an end."

"You could've learned about me and Roxy," I say on a hunch. "That would make it personal."

"I don't get involved with my daughter's shenanigans." A chunk of bloody meat shows up in

47

Chester's left hand as if by magic, and he tosses it to the lion.

"So you expect us to believe you don't care that she submitted to Sasha?" Nero narrows his eyes. "I want to hear you say that as a sentence."

"She did what?" Chester nearly falls off his chair. "Submitted, as in the werewolf mumbo jumbo? She hasn't told me about that. *That little—*"

"He's telling the truth," Nero whispers into my ear. "Both when he said he wasn't after you and now when he claimed not to know about the submission."

"Great," I whisper without looking at Nero. My eyes are glued to the sight of the lion devouring the chunk of meat. "He knows about it *now*."

Louder, I say, "You never answered Nero's question about your powers. Did you use them on me?"

Nero's hands ball into fists as he glares at the screen expectantly.

"I haven't done so recently." Chester looks at his pet beast for support, but the lion is too busy munching. "Besides, it wasn't misfortune that I tried to send your way. Perhaps the opposite."

"Truth, but a vague one." Nero leans toward the camera. "Explain."

"Before I do, I just want to remind you two about free will. You both possess it." Chester looks from Nero to me, then pleadingly back at Nero. "My powers can't override that. Nothing can."

"You're stalling." Nero's eyes are almost completely black now.

"Do you know how I spy on Darian?" Chester asks.

"Dream walker," Nero says. "Tell us something we don't already know."

I want to object and say that I *didn't* know Chester used a dream walker, but then I realize that I might've had at least a clue about it. When I saw Darian's memories relating to Matilda—Chester's wife and Darian's lover—she learned about Darian's visions of her daughter's fate by using a dream walker, so it *is* reasonable to assume her husband has access to one also.

Oh, and Chester's admission finally reveals something I've never figured out for sure: how Chester originally learned about Darian's plans for me.

At the Jubilee, Felix's theory was that Chester used a spy—and it looks like he was at least in part correct. Chester indeed deployed a creative spying method: getting information from Darian's own dreams.

I realize something else also—the dream walker in question is probably Bailey Spade, a.k.a Freda Krueger.

At least, that's who Nero works with when he needs one.

"Did you know Darian was the reason I lost the woman I love?" The grief looks foreign on Chester's usually cheerful face.

"Yes." Nero's voice softens slightly. "It's hard to lose those you love."

"Right." Chester reaches for the lion, and the beast licks his hand reassuringly. "That means you might understand why I did what I did." He takes in a deep breath and quickly rattles out, "I learned that Darian's worst nightmare is seeing the two of you together, so I used my power to bring that about."

Nero's mouth gapes in disbelief, and my brain feels like a computer that tried to divide by zero.

He said "bring that about."

Me and Nero.

Together.

To spite Darian.

A part of me knows Chester means that he used his control of probabilities to somehow increase the chance of me choosing Nero over Darian, but every other part of me finds the idea incomprehensible.

And disturbing.

And wrong.

CHAPTER NINE

"HOW CAN you have any say in how I feel toward Nero?" I hear myself ask as if from a distance.

"I can't." Chester strokes his lion's pale mane. "You both have free will. All I did is make it so you'd bump into each other more often than normal, and perhaps under circumstances that could ignite a spark, should one be in place already."

What?

Is this why Nero caught me picking through his safe while he was wearing nothing but a towel? Or why Nero was there for me at just the right moment so many times, like when I was grieving Rose's death? Or when I was—

"You will never use your power on either me or Sasha again." The menace in Nero's voice seems to scare even the lion.

"You got it," Chester says quickly. "Never again."

He must not have lied, because Nero unclenches his fists.

Shocked, I try to process Nero's anger—and what it means.

Is Nero saying he felt something for me? And if so, is the anger a sign of his disapproval of those feelings? Also, if there are feelings, are they simply the result of Chester's machinations, or are they real?

And what about me? Would I be pining after Darian if Chester hadn't done his thing?

That's assuming I admit that I'm "pining" after Nero, which isn't a fact.

Still, there's some attraction, to say the least. Plus, I still have to process the fact that he took the bullets for me in my vision. That means something.

"I need the phone numbers for the parents of the other two girls in Roxy's clique," I hear Nero say through my haze. "The assassination attempt could've been their doing."

"I highly doubt it." Chester pulls out a phone and starts tapping the screen repeatedly. "But I texted you their numbers anyway."

"Good." Nero glances at his phone to make sure he got the text.

"Are we good?" Chester asks warily. "Or do I need to be looking over my shoulder from now on?"

"We are not good," Nero says grimly. "If you want to keep on breathing, stay out of my sight."

He hangs up, and I sit in stunned contemplation as he calls each of the numbers Chester provided and asks the parents point blank if they tried to kill me. They deny it, and his power doesn't detect falsehood—so I guess they all get to live.

"Thalia?" Nero says after dialing another number. "How are you doing?"

His phone pings a text. He reads it, nodding, then says, "That's good to hear. I could use your help." He then proceeds to tell her about the recent events and how he'd feel better if she worked as my bodyguard again.

She replies via another text.

"Great," he says after reading it and hangs up. Looking at me, he says, "Thalia is back on duty later today; meanwhile, you're coming with me."

"I am?"

"I want you where I can keep an eye on you." Nero stands up. "In the meantime, I'll have bulletproof windows and an extra-secure door installed here." He glances down at Fluffster—who gives him a small nod that probably implies the domovoi won't kill Nero's contractors on sight. Looking back at me, Nero almost imperceptibly smirks and adds, "Don't you think it's time you started working off those hundred-and-thirty-five hours you owe me?"

"He's talking about the penalty work allotment hours I accumulated while escaping his makeshift prison to save Vlad," I tell confused Fluffster, then pin Nero with a glare. "If I were you, I would not remind people about that day. I barely survived while you just sat there in your comfy limo and cowardly waited for others to do the dirty work."

Nero's smirk goes away, and his nostrils flare. He looks like he's on the verge of snapping back at me, but he doesn't. Instead, he just stares at me grimly.

I almost want to take my words back—except why should I? He did indeed wait in his limo as I said.

But then he took bullets for me in my vision.

That's the opposite of what I just accused him of.

"Let's go," he says, his voice devoid of emotion. Without waiting for a reply, he leaves the kitchen.

With a shrug at Fluffster, I chase after Nero and catch him by the elevator.

On the way down, Nero looks broody, reminding me of Vlad.

How *is* the vampire doing?

I feel guilty that I haven't checked on him recently. I better do so soon. Actually, why put it off?

Taking in a calming breath, I go into Headspace and focus on Vlad.

The shapes that surround me aren't scary, but they aren't friendly either.

Choosing one at random, I touch it and the vision begins.

———

I'M bodiless as is the norm for visions where the events happen without my physical presence.

A giant fist smacks Vlad in the jaw with the force of a wrecking ball.

Following basic laws of physics, Vlad flies backward, but at the last moment, he somersaults in the air and lands on his feet, like a cat.

The crowd in the surrounding colosseum claps and screams in excitement.

Undaunted by the punch, Vlad wipes a trickle of blood running down his split lip and whooshes forward.

His opponent looks down at him with a mixture of awe and respect.

The guy is huge. So big, in fact, that I suspect him to be a literal giant—as in, a type of Cognizant.

Though no one has explicitly told me that giants exist, I assumed they do after I saw the behemoth dude who performed the Rite on me.

Vlad dodges the giant's punches, then strikes him in the chest.

The huge guy reels back.

The crowd goes wild again.

———

I COME to my senses in the elevator.

Nero is examining me intently.

"I just had a vision," I say preemptively, then tell him what I saw.

"So *that's* where he went." Nero shakes his head

disapprovingly. "Don't worry. Those fights rarely end in death."

"Great," I say sarcastically. "Rarely. What a relief."

"Think of it as Vlad blowing off some steam," Nero says. "We all have different ways of dealing with grief—and his is as good as any."

The elevator arrives and we exit, with me muttering something impolite about the stupidity of machismo and Nero pretending not to hear.

"Sit in the back. I'll go up front," he says when we walk up to the limo.

He opens the door for me, and I grudgingly get in, then pointedly raise the partition thingy between me and where Nero is about to sit.

"I'll check on Vlad if that makes you feel any better," Nero says before closing the door. "I have to invite him to the funeral anyway."

Before I get a chance to ask when the funeral will be held—not to mention why Nero is extending an olive branch—he closes the door.

Oh well. That's fine. There are a few more Headspace-related errands I'd like to take care of, and now is as good a time as any.

Reentering Headspace, I try to get a vision featuring my biological mother, going under the assumption that she was the woman I saw in Rasputin's memories the other day—the lovey-dovey memory, that is, not the one with Nero or the one that featured someone torturing my father.

The woman in that memory had pale shoulders and

a graceful back that reminded me of a ballerina, and Rasputin had called her unpredictable.

That's not a lot to go on, but I dwell on these things as if they were her essence.

Nothing happens.

That must not be enough information.

Next, I try to reach Rasputin.

Not surprisingly, this doesn't work either. He must be dodging my calls.

Since I'm in a summoning mood, I ping Darian next.

Another failure.

Almost as an afterthought, I remember the bannik.

Yes. He's definitely worth checking on. There might still be seer lessons he can provide.

I focus on Yaroslav's bearded handsomeness, and how he helped me escape Baba Yaga even though he probably knew he'd lose a finger over it. When I can almost picture his sad eyes, a familiar Headspace entity appears in front of me.

It worked.

That's him.

The Yaroslav shape pulses in excitement, and I get the impression he's reaching for me just as I make my own connection.

Headspace swirls around us as we fall into each other's metaphysical embrace.

CHAPTER TEN

SURROUNDED by the scorching heat of the banya, I'm massaging pale feminine shoulders with honey.

That is, Yaroslav is doing this in a memory, not me.

The memory must be fairly recent because he/I lack an index finger.

"You're trying to distract your therapist yet again," Lucretia moans. "I want to know how the newfound freedom makes you feel."

Not in the mood for therapy, Yaroslav slides his hands from her shoulders to her breasts, then licks off some of the honey.

Why do I always get the erotic memories? Am I somehow drawn to them?

The banya heats up—both literally and in terms of what Lucretia and Yaroslav proceed to do.

"You can bite me if you wish," the bannik whispers into Lucretia's ear as he nibbles on her neck.

I was right. This is a very recent memory. Lucretia just became a vampire.

"I'm not ready for that yet," she murmurs, but there's a lisp to her speech that indicates her fangs are extended. "I need to learn more about the consequences before I take that step."

"I've seen all the consequences," Yaroslav croons. "We're happy together in pretty much *every* future. No one can—"

———

JUST LIKE BEFORE, all around us is absolute emptiness.

And like with Darian and Rasputin, in front of me is a synapse-hologram of Yaroslav, with his visage attached to the uncanny shape-entity that is his Headspace representation.

I'm a hologram too—one connected to the entity that is me, which in turn is interwoven with the bannik on the Headspace level.

"Sasha." He floats up and down. "I'm glad you reached out. There are some things I wanted you to hear from me first." He looks at me intently. "Unless Nero or Lucretia already told you?"

"Told me what?" Though my chest is see-through in this place, the sensation of my heartbeat speeding up is as real as in the outside world.

"The deal Nero and I made." Yaroslav looks down at

his hologram-like feet. "What I had to do to free myself from Baba Yaga."

I'm beginning to have an inkling of what he's about to tell me, but I still say, "No. Please explain."

"Right." He looks at his missing finger, then at me. "Long before we met, I knew we would, thanks to my visions. I also knew I'd have to let you go free in order to be free myself one day—no matter the cost. There was only a small handful of futures where Baba Yaga would be defeated, you see, and you played a key role in pretty much all of them."

I cross my arms, waiting for the worst of it. What he's said so far, I'd pretty much guessed.

"You have to believe me when I say that what happened to you was the best possible outcome." He floats down, then rises again with effort. "Had I not meddled, things would've been so much worse…"

"You used Nero to free yourself," I guess.

"He gets to use my services as a seer." He strokes his beard. "A case can be made that he got the better end of the deal."

"Let's not dwell on semantics," I say. "What did you do?"

"I asked Lucretia to take a message to Nero." He pointedly avoids my gaze. "In it, I outlined the path to the outcome I wanted. To train you in martial arts. To encourage your use of your powers. To build a jail-like room for you—and to stick a passcode keypad into it—just so that you could escape at the right moment using the technique I taught you. I told him not to stop you when you broke free to attack Baba Yaga with your friends—something he only agreed to when I assured him that you would live through the ordeal. I even told him when and where to bring the healer to you in the end, so that you wouldn't suffer needlessly."

I float down five feet as I fully register what he said.

He told Nero to put me in that cell?

"What about the attack on the pier in Staten Island?" I ask numbly. "When Nero didn't want to help me to save Vlad that time—was all that an act?"

"I didn't see that in my visions, so I didn't give him any instructions regarding that," Yaroslav says, his gaze still trained on his holographic feet. "The only charade he put on was when he didn't want you to go deal with Baba Yaga. He knew that you'd go no matter what he said or did."

My transparent head hurts from parsing all this, but what he says fits the facts—like why Isis came into Nero's building just as I was running out to deal with Baba Yaga.

He must've had her ready to heal me before I even escaped.

It had bothered me that Nero had simply sat in the limo on the threshold of Brighton Beach the other day, waiting for Baba Yaga's death to release him from the contract. A part of me had wished that he'd ignored the contract to come to my rescue.

Turns out, it didn't matter.

He knew I would be safe.

Darker implications occur to me. "Did you foresee Lucretia turning into a vampire?" I ask.

"It was inevitable," he says tightly. "But yes. I knew. She says she forgives me, but I—"

"What about Rose?" My ghostly body tightens. "Did you foresee *her* death?"

"No," he says earnestly. "I swear on everything that is holy. Just like with Vlad, I didn't even think to look at her future." He appears as miserable as is possible for a hologram to look, but it could all be an act; he knows that if I were to tell Vlad that he let Rose die, the vampire would rip out his heart.

Then I realize he might be telling the truth. If he'd looked at Vlad's future, he would've seen *him* kill Baba Yaga instead of me. Vlad had his own plan to do so and it would've worked, except he would've died in the process—

"What ended up happening really *was* the best possible outcome as far as I could tell," Yaroslav says. "It's the only one I've seen where your friend Ariel survives and lives a full life. It was the only way Lucretia wasn't going to become Gaius's slave for a—"

"Stop. You're doing a good job showing me why people dislike seers so much."

"One of the most important lessons we seers learn early on is that you can't save everyone you love," he says sagely. "None of us are powerful enough for that."

"I'm done with this conversation. I want to disconnect."

"I understand." He starts flying toward the entity

that is himself and says, "If you touch that version of yourself at the same time as I do, our meeting will be adjourned."

Too overwhelmed to enjoy the zero-gravity-like flight, I float to my Headspace representation and touch it.

He does the same, and I spiral out.

CHAPTER ELEVEN

THE REST of the limo ride, I pillage the snack bar and digest the morsels along with the bannik's revelations.

By the time we park next to Nero's building, I decide that nothing is all that different after everything's said and done.

Yes, Nero is a manipulative bastard, but I already knew that. And obviously, the bannik wanted to be free. Can I really hold that against him?

The one interesting tidbit about this is that Nero now has access to another seer—meaning he shouldn't need me as much.

Yet he shielded me with his body.

Why did he do that? Is there some small speck of goodness in him?

The door opens up, and I stare at my boss as though for the first time.

"We're here," he says, offering me his hand.

Ignoring it, I climb out of the limo on my own.

Nero shrugs and leads the way.

When we get inside the elevator, he surprises me yet again. Instead of pressing the button for the basement—as he did in my earlier vision—he takes us to the top floor instead.

Once the location of executive offices, the floor currently has only one office that's occupied—Nero's.

"You have a choice to make," he says as we come out of the elevator.

"Oh?" I catch up to him when he stops next to Venessa.

Nero gestures at the two offices on either side of his. "Which one do you want?"

Venessa's beady eyes seem ready to jump out of their sockets.

I gape at the luxurious rooms.

"That one," I mumble after a moment, pointing at the one with a view of the Empire State Building.

"Please set up Sasha's new office," Nero orders Venessa. "Her computer is in storage. The table and chairs are about to get delivered."

I'm not sure if Nero catches the sour expression that flits across Venessa's face, but I do.

Great. I can already see that working on this floor is going to be fun.

Not.

Venessa rushes off—presumably to get my computer.

As soon as she's out of earshot, I catch Nero's gaze and say, "How interesting. You're not bothering to keep me in that basement prison. It's almost as though you don't need to do so anymore..."

"The bannik squealed already?" Nero looks anything but apologetic.

"You should've told me that the whole thing was—"

"No. If I'd given you any hint of what the future held, you could've changed it. Tell me that isn't true."

He has a point. The more information I have about a future event, the easier it is to change. On the flipside, without foreknowledge, things do happen exactly as in the visions. I wonder what that says about free will, after all. Then again—

"I'd like you to see Lucretia," he says, pulling me out of my metaphysical ruminations.

I frown. "I'd rather not. I need to work off that ungodly debt of hours that I owe you."

"How about a deal then?" Nero leans in, making my heart rate speed up. "Though seeing Lucretia should not, by all rights, count as work time, I'll make an exception today. In fact, I'll count every minute you spend with Lucretia as two work ones."

"Quadruple that, and you have yourself a deal."

"Triple. And that's my final offer." To punctuate his words, he heads for his office without waiting for my reply.

"Fine," I say to his back. "I'm going."

Without turning, he gives me a thumbs-up sign.

I head for Lucretia's office and am not surprised when I find her waiting for me.

Nero's pawn once again. Maybe I should just relax and let him do with me as he pleases.

Lucretia clears her throat.

Crap. Did she pick up on my thoughts using her empath powers?

"Seems like your new state of being doesn't impede your job," I say instead of a hello. "Is it distracting, wanting to eat your clients?"

"My empath abilities are intact—and make me a lousy predator." Lucretia gestures at the chaise with her delicate pale hand, and I try not to think about what I've seen that hand do in the bannik's memories. "Nero is able to get me fresh blood from many donors," she continues. "So I don't feel any desire to, as you so crudely put it, eat my clients."

I sprawl on the chaise, grab a nearby doll, and do my best to relax.

"So." Lucretia lowers herself into her throne-like chair. "What would you like to talk about?"

"First, full disclosure. I talked to the bannik today and learned about his deal with Nero."

"Oh." She crosses her legs, her face unreadable. "And how does that make you feel?"

"Like I want to punch Nero in his smug face." I squeeze the toy's neck. "Maybe your boyfriend too."

I've got to hand it to Lucretia. Her expression doesn't so much as flicker at the mention of "boyfriend."

Sagely, she says, "I understand."

"You do?"

"You like to be in control." She steeples her fingers. "In control of your destiny. And emotions. And other people's actions."

"So what?" I sit up straighter. "Who doesn't like to be in control?"

"We're here to talk about you." Lucretia smiles, and I can't help but notice that her teeth look completely normal right now.

All righty then.

Talk about me.

Where do I start? Should I talk about how I felt seeing Bentley's burned body or witnessing Baba Yaga getting killed by a drekavac?

Nah. Though disturbing, those things didn't end up keeping me up at night as I feared—the prospect of public speaking did that.

Maybe we should talk about my insomnia priorities?

Then again, the topic that most interests me is the meeting with my father, but that's tied to the map and my desire to go on a rescue mission—something I don't want Nero to learn about, given his reaction in my vision.

"There's not much to talk about," I finally say. "But I'm game to sit here as long as you'll let me. Nero and I have this deal—"

"The funeral is two days from now." Lucretia looks at me intently.

I stare back at her in shock.

Is this a standard therapist trick?

The back of my throat throbs, and I nearly rip the leg off the poor doll.

Taking a deep breath, I close my eyes.

"I'm sorry," Lucretia says soothingly. "I figured you knew."

Though Kit has already told me about the funeral date, the pain at the reminder is just as sharp. I curl my hands over the doll and do my best to even out my breathing. When I think my voice will be calm, I say with my eyes still closed, "I did know."

"For what it's worth, you've learned to calm yourself well," she says. "Now that this is out in the open, would you be willing to talk about your feelings?"

I open my eyes and try to get to the source of the anguish choking me up inside. "I think I'm worried about the eulogy," I say. "Didn't sleep all night thinking about that."

"Is that all?" Lucretia studies me intently, her blue eyes so hypnotizing I half expect them to turn into mirrors.

"What else is there?" I set the doll on my lap and rub my chilled palms together.

"How about the guilt?" Lucretia suggests gently. "I'm sensing a lot of that. I think—"

"Get out of my head." My hands tense. "What gives you the right to keep invading my privacy like that?"

Lucretia's gaze softens. Her face is a mask of patience as she sits there, saying nothing.

I move the doll off my lap, cross my arms, and prepare to sit here, also without speaking.

Lucretia's body language mimics mine.

I take in a breath, then another.

When I feel calm enough not to blurt out something I might regret, I say, "Her death was my fault."

"But it wasn't," she says. "She was in the way of Gaius's ambition. Baba Yaga got Koschei to do Gaius's dirty work. How is any of that your fault?"

"Because Baba Yaga was *my* enemy. I should've foreseen that she might go after people close to me."

"But she didn't," Lucretia says. "You know—rationally, you know—that she went after Rose for Gaius. It had nothing to do with you."

I take in another breath. "Maybe, but I should've still foreseen it. I should've saved her. If I'd been a better seer—"

"And we're back to your need to control everything," Lucretia says. "Even the best seers can't always protect those they care about."

I roll my eyes. "You sound like your boyfriend."

"Well, he *is* a seer."

At the reminder of Yaroslav's nature, I recall our Headspace encounter, and the image of Lucretia covered in honey pops into my head.

Crap. I have to keep these free associations in check —or else Lucretia might catch on to what I just felt with her empath mojo.

Oops. I think she did. Her cheeks are suddenly pink. She must've sensed something.

Again.

"Listen, Sasha," she says after a small pause. "I want to remind you that this is a safe place. You can talk to me about any urges you want." She looks over her shoulder to make sure we're still alone and adds, "No matter who's causing those urges."

"It wasn't Nero I was thinking about," I say quickly. "It was Yaroslav. I mean, not like that. When we met in Headspace, I gleaned his memories, you see, and—"

"You saw a memory of a vision where the two of you were intimate?" She looks at me as calmly as if she's talking about the weather. "Yaroslav told me about those. He had them before either of us had even met him. Once he committed to me, they stopped, but—"

"Wait. Hold up. What?" I search her face for any sign of humor, but she looks as serious as taxes. "You're not joking? He had visions of us? As in, me and him?"

She shrugs. "Sexual urges are perfectly natural."

"Right. Except Darian had those visions also. My hypothetical future self really gets around in the seer community."

"I wouldn't worry about that." She uncrosses her legs. "Whereas a normal person would have a fantasy, for a seer, it can play out as a vision. The trick is to have an intention of getting together with that person —and being able to see far into the future. Yaroslav has admitted that he's had visions like that featuring every attractive female he came across—until he met me, that is. That's when he had a vision of the two of us

71

together and realized that was it for him. I'm still wrapping my brain around it, but I think it's romantic."

I ponder this. At the core, it's a little bit like the visions I've experimented with—the ones where I make a choice (say, to tell Nero a secret), then see a vision of how that choice plays out (Nero locks me up in a cell with no way out).

Is that what Darian did also? Did he experiment with seeing visions of a number of women until he fell in love with the future of the two of us?

Lucretia drums her fingers on the arms of her throne, reminding me of her presence.

"Interesting," I say. "Does this mean that if I were determined to date Michael Fassbender and Matthew McConaughey, I could get a vision of a threesome with them?"

"Probably not." Lucretia smiles. "I think your choice needs to be more rooted in reality. It would work better if you decided to be with someone you already know. Someone who might be willing to be with you. The question is, are you brave enough to try?"

Is she daring me to see a future where I hook up with Nero?

If so, I'm probably not brave enough. Or crazy enough.

But the idea isn't bad.

A part of me is curious about what would happen if I tried such a thing with Nero as the target suitor—and another part of me wonders about that future with Darian, especially in light of Chester's interference.

Also, am I giving up on celebrities too quickly? Maybe I should buy a ticket to Criss Angel's Vegas Show and see if that prompts a sexy vision.

No wonder other seers do this. If I go down this path, I might end up with a whole harem of hypothetical vision lovers.

Except, for whatever reason, I keep coming back to the idea of doing this with Nero.

Stupid Nero. Ever since that kiss, he's been stuck in my head.

Does it matter if Chester made the kiss more likely? The key is how it makes me feel. Except it takes two to tango, and I doubt Nero—

Lucretia clears her throat.

Oh, right. I got lost in embarrassing thoughts again. It seems to be becoming a therapy tradition.

"I just realized, you still don't have the Mandate aura," I say to change the subject.

"Oh, that." She looks down at herself. "After a pre-vamp turns into a vampire, the Mandate needs to be reapplied. I'll have another Rite when I'm ready. Speaking of which—I'd love it if you were there for the ceremony. It's not as fancy as the very first time, but—"

"Of course," I say. "I wouldn't miss it."

It suddenly occurs to me that I've been a self-centered nincompoop. Lucretia was under Gaius's control—made to kill someone—and I haven't even asked her how she's feeling.

Well, better late than never.

"Listen, Lucretia," I say, trying to think of the most

tactful way to approach this. "We've talked a lot about me. Can we talk about you?"

Her jet-black eyebrows travel almost to the middle of her pale forehead. "During *your* therapy session?"

"How about lunch?" I suggest, mentally activating "smooth-talking magician mode." "I know you don't have to eat in the traditional sense, but you still need to take breaks—and we can go outside."

She smiles. "That sounds wonderful. When would you like to go?"

I grin. "How about now?"

———

"THERE ISN'T REALLY much to talk about," Lucretia says once we're sitting on a bench in the park, with me eating a burrito and her feeding the pigeons. "I don't consider myself responsible for any lives Gaius made me take."

"I get that," I say. "But what was it like to not be in control of your body?"

"Horrible," she says quietly. "I can't tell you how glad I am it only lasted for a short time. I guess I have you and your friends to thank for that."

And her manipulative boyfriend—but I don't say that, deciding instead to move on to safer topics.

As our impromptu meal proceeds, I learn that Lucretia knew the big names in psychology personally. At one point, she had discussed dreams with Freud and human needs with Maslow. I even get the sense that she might've influenced some of them but is too humble to admit it.

As I listen to her, it occurs to me that I actually do feel better after our therapy session. Maybe Nero was right to force me into it.

In fact, now that I've eaten, I feel so relaxed I can't stop yawning.

Lucretia yawns herself, then says sternly, "Stop it. I don't need to sleep anymore but can still catch a yawn, apparently."

"I'm sorry," I say and yawn again. "Why doesn't America adopt the practice of siesta?"

"Shortsightedness," she says. Then she smiles mischievously and gets up. "Come with me. I have an idea."

We walk down the block until we reach the mattress store.

"Watch this." Lucretia's eyes turn into mirrors as she walks up to the store manager and says, "My friend is thinking about getting that Tempur-Pedic—but she wants to try before she buys. Let her sleep on it and make sure she's not disturbed."

The guy robotically nods and mumbles that it would be his pleasure to let me sleep on the mattress for as long as I want.

Lucretia walks me to the bed in question and turns on the heat and massage features. "I consider this part of your therapy," she tells me. "You need the rest."

I plop down. "Hey, you don't have to ask me twice."

"Will you come see me next week?" she asks.

"Only if you agree to do lunch with me again." I close my eyes as the vibration and the warmth combine with my food coma and the weight of my sleepless night.

"That's a deal," she says. "See you later."

She walks away, and I smile like the Grinch. I'm going to make a dent in Nero's stupid "allotment hours" by napping.

Still smiling, I let sleep drag my consciousness away.

CHAPTER TWELVE

I WAKE up in the mattress store with a start.

In my sleepy state, I completely forgot about the shooters from before.

Someone could've easily killed me in my sleep.

I also realize I never told Lucretia about what happened today. She probably would've taken me somewhere safer to nap if I did.

I look at my phone and nearly fall off the bed.

It's almost 8 p.m. My little siesta turned into an all-day affair.

Jumping up, I run for my office, only stopping in the gym to brush my teeth.

Then I text Nero that I'm done with therapy and take the elevator to the top floor.

"That must've been a hell of a session," Nero says when I step out of the elevator.

"Yeah," I say carefully. "I feel much better."

No need to make Mr. Polygraph realize I was slacking.

"You even look better," Nero says. "Lucretia is worth her weight in gold."

"Did I not look my best before?" I ask, half-jokingly.

"Your office is ready. Come."

Nero leads me in, and I struggle not to gape at the stunning view.

"I'll let you get acclimated," he says. "Talk to Venessa if you need anything."

"Sure," I say. And I will—as long as it's not food or drink she can spit into.

Nero leaves, and I log on to my computer.

As I feared, I kept getting work emails throughout my computer-less incarceration in the basement. I deal with them for the next couple of hours until I realize how late it is.

I walk over to the door and sneak a peek inside Nero's office.

He's hammering away on his keyboard, looking like he's not planning to leave today at all.

Okay, so that's going to be the not-so-fun part of being on the same floor with my boss. He'll know when I come and go—and realize just how much of a slacker I am.

Not that I care.

At least, not *really.*

Then I spot Venessa gathering her things and decide this is a sign from the corporate gods.

I lock my computer and walk over to the elevator.

Venessa has already summoned it, so I just stand and wait.

She looks at me disapprovingly, then casts an admiring look at industriously working Nero.

The elevator doors open.

She pushes me with her shoulder to step inside ahead of me.

Dude. It's not like she'll get down sooner if she enters the elevator first.

Following her in, I press the bottom floor and face away from her.

"I have to say," she mutters under her breath as the doors begin to close, "I've never seen the 'sleep your way to the top' cliché quite so literally."

The doors slide shut, and the elevator starts moving.

I stand there openmouthed.

Is this what *all* my coworkers think about my relationship with Nero, or is it just her?

Maybe she has a crush on Nero, and this is jealousy talking.

Or—and I shudder to think this—is she speaking from experience? Did *she* sleep with Nero at some point to get her spot on the top floor?

Those beady eyes aside, she's attractive, if plastic blond bombshells are your thing—which I didn't think was the case for Nero. Then again, maybe it was wishful thinking when I decided that my boss was into very intelligent (and equally modest), black-haired, pale-skinned women who are good with playing cards.

Violent scenarios flit through my mind—most of them reminiscent of Nero and Thalia's martial arts training, except with Venessa's face as the punching mitt.

My anger grows with every millisecond.

Turning around, I face her. "What did you just say? Say that again. To my face."

She opens her mouth to reply, but the elevator doors open and something she sees over my shoulder makes her swallow her words.

I spin around and fight the urge to rub my eyes.

It's Nero.

But how?

He was in his office when we got inside the elevator, so how is he down here? Did he run down the stairs?

Then I notice the thickness of his limbal rings, and my insides grow cold.

I've seen him like this once before—just prior to the orc massacre.

Staring at the quickly paling Venessa, he growls, "You will apologize to Sasha. *Now.* After that, you're fired."

Holy crap. Did he overhear her softly spoken insult as the elevator doors were closing? Just how good is his hearing?

Venessa's chin comes up, and some color returns to her cheeks. "If I'm fired anyway, why—"

"If you say anything besides an apology, you will never work anywhere again," Nero cuts in.

I wonder if Venessa realizes this isn't a hyperbole or a bluff. When I tried to leave this job, Nero ensured that no one else would hire me.

Apparently, Venessa does understand. "I'm sorry," she mumbles, and before either of us can critique the sad excuse of an apology, she rushes out of the building as though a monster might give her chase.

Given Nero's expression, that might've been a real possibility.

"I'm sorry as well." Nero looks at me, those dangerous limbal rings shrinking. "I hope you know that you've earned that office. You've made this fund more money than all the other analysts combined, and the traders know it. Anyone with half a brain will see that this promotion was merit based."

I guess this is the day to stand openmouthed because I'm doing it again.

Nero apologizing and praising my work? And this was a promotion? I thought the office thing was so that he can keep a closer eye on me.

"I have something I need to finish back in my office," Nero says and walks into the elevator. "Thalia is already waiting for you outside."

The elevator doors close, and I do my best to reboot my overwhelmed brain, so I can head out of the building.

As promised, Thalia is standing outside.

Though I didn't think it possible, the nun is even thinner now. The grieving process hollowed out her eye sockets, and her cheekbones look like they could cut grass. Worse, the usual twinkle is completely absent in her gaze.

Something must've been going on between her and poor Bentley. Why else would she take his passing so hard?

"How are you doing?" I ask carefully.

She demonstratively shrugs, then turns and walks to the illegally parked limo.

Oh, right. Vow of silence. I almost forgot.

"I can take a cab if you're not ready to get back to work," I say as I follow her. "We can tell Nero that you drove me."

She shakes her head and jabs her finger at the limo door.

"Fine," I say and get inside.

———

AS NERO PROMISED, my apartment has a new door that looks thick enough to withstand a nuclear blast.

Except someone left it unlocked—which kind of defeats the whole purpose.

When I enter, I lock the heavy-duty lock behind myself, and soon I see why they left it unlocked. There's a new key on the shoe rack and a note that it's for me.

Pocketing the key, I walk in and find everyone in the living room, watching a movie.

Fluffster is on Kit's lap, and the cat is on Felix's.

"Honeys," I say. "I'm home."

Felix pauses the movie and eyes me curiously. "Working late for a change?"

"Working off a debt," I say. "Any news on all the projects?"

"I got the first overnight shipment from the spacesuit guy." Felix scratches under Lucifur's chin. "It's already at our JFK lair."

"Itzel, the gnome, is there too." Kit strokes Fluffster's belly. "Already working on your problem."

"Can we get back to the movie?" Fluffster mentally complains.

"I'm sorry to be such a bother," I tell him and stalk to my room.

Behind me, the movie resumes.

Oh well. I'd rather sleep.

Except sleeping doesn't work out. Between my super-nap and the eulogy worries, I feel like a coked-out banker from the eighties.

So, I spend a couple of hours rehearsing what I'll say at the funeral, and for the rest of the night, I learn Russian with the aid of my powers.

By morning, I'm fairly confident that if my Wall Street or illusionist-for-Cognizant careers don't work out, I can always become a Russian translator.

Bleary-eyed, I head to work, where my day goes as was usual before the cell days. Nero asks me to research a few companies, and I do it as well as possible on what little sleep I had.

At seven, I get a text from Felix.

The gnome and I need your help.

I agree, and he explains how to find the "secret lab."

Jason—not the hockey-mask killer, but Nero's Venessa replacement—enviously watches me as I depart for the day.

Though Nero himself isn't looking my way, I'm not fooled.

He knows that I'm leaving at seven p.m.—also known as early for a hedge fund.

Who am I kidding? Nero can probably hear me thinking these thoughts.

"To JFK," I tell Thalia when I make my way downstairs. "Let's try to beat the traffic."

———

BEATING traffic and JFK are not compatible, as usual, so I thank the stars for the buffet in Nero's fancy limo as I stuff my face during the long drive.

When I finally get there, the secret lab isn't hard to locate. As Felix said, the path is exactly like going to the hub, but with a different turn at the very end.

When I step into the room, I find it to be like every depiction of a mad scientist's lair jammed into one. Cables and computer parts are everywhere, as are high-tech gizmos and power tools. The air smells like ozone and a faint hint of perfume—the latter wafting off a person I've never met before.

Presumably, she's the gnome.

Though she's short—the tip of her spiky black hair is below Felix's chin—she's taller than I'd expect a gnome to be. The weirdest part about her, though, is the breathing apparatus.

She has on a metallic mask that covers the bottom of her face, and as she breathes through it, she sounds like a miniature Darth Vader.

Catching me looking at the contraption, she says, "One of the few downsides of my kind are respiratory problems. It's what initially drove us to explore technology."

Though her voice is distorted, it's familiar. Kit used this nasal, rehabilitated-princess tone when she first mentioned the gnome. Come to think of it, thanks to Kit's random shapeshifting, I've even seen this woman's face without the mask.

Yep, the same round-cheeks are peeking out—and it's probably safe to assume the gnome is smiling the same dorky smile under the mask.

"Sasha, this is Itzel," Felix says. "Gnomes are also not big on civilities, so I figured I'd introduce you two."

I walk forward and extend my hand to the woman. She looks at it in fascination but keeps her hand at her side like a germaphobe.

"Unlike your friend, *you* could pass for a gnome," Itzel says after she gives my face a thorough examination. "A young and exceptionally beautiful one, but a gnome."

"Thanks," I say, lowering my hand. "I think."

"Gnomes grow tall in adolescence and then shrink as they grow older," Felix chimes in. "Itzel must be a few centuries old—though she refuses to tell me how many."

"What did I tell you about asking women their weight and age?" I mutter to him under my breath. "It's not just gnomes who lack civility."

"As I was saying," Felix continues, unruffled, "the very old gnomes eventually get to their garden namesake's size—and that's part of the reason they can't live on worlds with humans. Beings that tiny are hard to explain."

"Our growth cycle is another reason we had to get inventive." Itzel walks over to a large table covered with books and looks at Felix. "You know a lot about my kind. How come?"

"Orientation," he says. "Plus, I've met one of you before, and he would not shut up about what's it's like to be a gnome. Well, that and space exploration."

I notice the books on the table also deal with space exploration, but I don't say anything.

"Why shouldn't we talk about ourselves?" Itzel lifts her chin. "We're the most interesting and powerful of the Cognizant. Also the most—"

"Prideful?" Felix suggests. "Pompous?"

"He's just upset because I'm much better at dealing with technology than he is," Itzel tells me conspiratorially. "And because unlike him—who's a one-trick computer pony—I, as a gnome, have tons of useful attributes."

"Sasha, don't do what I think you're about to do,"

Felix hisses at me theatrically. "If you ask her what gnomes can do, we'll be here for a week."

"Sasha, unlike some, looks like a woman with intellectual curiosity," Itzel tells him, then looks at me. "We're immune to the many influences from other Cognizant. Vampire glamour doesn't work on us, tricksters can't influence our fate, and it is said that even the legendary thought readers and pushers couldn't access our minds—"

"Thought readers?" I interrupt. "Pushers?"

"There's no proof they're real," Felix says. "Let alone that gnomes would be immune."

"Oh, they're real." She wrinkles her nose. "They're two races of Cognizant that were extremely dangerous —and that waged open war with each other that put the rest of us at risk." She stacks a book about Elon Musk on top of the recent Neil Armstrong biography. "The gate makers joined with us gnomes to banish all the readers and pushers to a backward human world not unlike this one, but *without* a gate to get back. And with memories of their origins wiped for good measure."

Overwhelmed, I blurt out the first question that comes to mind, "Gnomes and gate makers worked together in the past?"

"Of course." She puffs up. "Even the gates themselves are part gate makers' powers and part gnome technology."

"You make it sound like you worked on that personally, but we both know that's not even remotely the case," Felix says. Looking at me, he explains, "As a thank you for their help in creating the hubs, the gate makers gave gnomes an Otherland with gates that lead back out but not in. That means any gnome you see here—as in, outside that world—was exiled for whatever reason."

"In my case, it was my grandparents who were exiled," Itzel says defensively. "The sins of the fathers do not extend to their offspring and all that. Either way, all that ancient history is boring compared to the full list of gnome attributes."

Felix rolls his eyes.

"We're more intelligent than any other Cognizant type," she says, pointedly ignoring Felix. "We quickly understand every technology we come across." She waves a rocket science textbook in front of her, then puts it down and picks up a French dictionary. "We have a knack for languages—both computer and spoken." She swaps the dictionary for a programming textbook. "But of course, it's not our mental prowess your friend is most jealous of. It's this." She puts the book down and extends her arms forward, as if miming the action of holding a small sphere.

A ball of lightning the size of an egg escapes her palms—like a Hadoken move in the *Street Fighter* video game.

The thing floats and crackles—and the smell of ozone goes up exponentially.

"Is this ball lightning?" I ask reverently. I've read

about the rare phenomenon and have always wanted to see it with my own eyes.

"Even better," she says. "Because it's under my control, it can protect me and be the power source for devices, even—"

"I told you she would brag all day," Felix butts in. "Sasha is here for the test, remember? It was your idea."

The ball lightning takes a sharp turn and flies right at Felix's face.

Felix gasps, eyes widening, but the projectile dissipates right before it would've singed his unibrow.

"Fine." Itzel walks over to a corner, and I realize they've dressed a mannequin in the gray-green spacesuit. "Let's do the test."

They put me into the body portion of the suit—a process eerily reminiscent of getting inside a straightjacket. The helmet goes on next, and it smells chemical-y, like the box from a new phone.

I patiently wait while they fasten everything together. The whole process takes longer than I expected.

Itzel then picks up a small microphone from the table, presses a button on the suit, and says, "Can you hear me?"

The sound is sharp and crisp, as though played through a high-end surround sound system.

"Yes, I can hear you." I cautiously move my arms and legs.

Whoa. This is going to be an adjustment. Assuming any of it works, that is.

"Good," Itzel says and presses something on my back. "Turning on."

Before I can ask how an article of clothing can be turned on, a digital display appears inside the spherical visor, as though it were a screen.

I guess it *is* a screen. Stats such as air pressure, gravitational pull, oxygen content, toxicity, radiation measurement, and temperature are listed in my peripheral vision.

"I'm pretty sure this isn't standard spacesuit functionality." I grin. "I feel like Master Chief or Samus Aran, not an astronaut."

"Cosmonaut," Felix corrects me. He then looks at Itzel and explains, "Master Chief is a hero from an Earth video game named *Halo*, and Samus Aran is a heroine from another game called *Metroid*."

"I had to modify the primitive tech I was provided, or the test would be useless," Itzel says to me, pointedly ignoring Felix. "The sorry excuse for a space program on this world is pitifully backward—especially when it comes to sending actual people into space."

Felix groans. "Not this again. Can we focus on the test, please?"

"Right." Itzel waves her arms and looks at me. "Do that."

I do as she orders.

More movements and gestures follow.

"Good, now let's go to the hub room," Itzel says, and we walk out of the lab.

When we arrive in the hub, I look down at the mirrored floor.

Yep. I look like a spacewoman, with my face completely hidden by the gold-tinted visor.

"The test is simplicity itself," Itzel says when we approach the yellow gate we'll need to take. "See a vision of yourself walking in, pay attention to the monitoring equipment, and tell us what you saw when the vision is over."

I recall my last vision and cringe. "Couldn't you have put together a robot rover instead of making me experience a possibly traumatic event? A gizmo that goes in, takes the readings you need, and then automatically backs out of the gate?"

"The gates don't allow that," Itzel says with obvious disappointment.

Felix nods. "The gate makers probably worried about one Otherland sending a world-buster bomb to another and made sure unmanned technology can't arrive on the other side."

The idea of something going into the gates and not coming out is a scary one. I wonder if there are conditions that would make a Cognizant disappear as well?

"Wrong," Itzel says in a condescending tone. "You can strap any bomb you wish onto a useless Cognizant." She looks him up and down. "After that, you can push him in and voila—world blown up. My guess is that gate makers actually feared human technology or that of my kind—who, even then, were close to unlocking the secret of putting a gnome mind inside a robotic body."

"Robot gnomes?" I turn my helmeted head toward Felix, then look back at Itzel. "Did I hear that right?"

"Leaving biology behind is a milestone for true space exploration," Itzel says. "Gnomes have a bigger vision than the rest of the Cognizant kind. Yes, the gate makers made many habitable worlds accessible to all, but what about the whole universes that surround those worlds? We want to reach for the stars and—"

"The test," Felix says. "Let's get to it before the establishment of the Gnome Federation." He smirks at Itzel. "Or is it the Gnome Empire?"

Itzel narrows her large hazel eyes at him. "Remind me why you're here?"

Felix glares back at her. "I got the spacesuit parts. And did you forget who put together the backend for the helmet UI?"

"I was just keeping you out of my hair." She touches the tallest spike on her head. "In the time it took you to write that code, I—"

"Guys, please," I say. "This getup is very uncomfortable."

"Sorry." Itzel demonstratively turns her back on Felix.

"Right, let's do this," Felix says. "Start your vision and try to remember all the readings."

"Hopefully, you won't die this time," Itzel chimes in. "Or if you do die, let's hope you don't die so fast that you can't gather the data."

"So we want me to die slowly?" I take a shuffling step toward the gate and do my best to convince myself that I'm about to enter it for real. "That sounds like a blast. Unless I die of a blast—that would be too fast."

"Actually, since the suit is—"

I'll never know what Felix was going to say because Itzel pinches his shoulder and he yelps.

I can guess what he was going to say, though. The suit is fireproof, so even an explosion should make my vision death long and painful.

Great. Can't wait.

Evening out my breathing, I launch myself into Headspace.

The shapes that surround me aren't scary enough for the "painful death scenario."

Maybe the suit is flawless?

Encouraged, I eagerly reach out with my ethereal wisp and start the vision.

CHAPTER THIRTEEN

I'M STANDING in the hub wearing a spacesuit.

"Phew," Felix says. "I thought she'd never leave."

———

THE VISION STOPS, and I find myself back in the real hub.

"Well?" Itzel asks eagerly.

"Don't get your hopes up." I turn away from the gate. "No painful death for me yet. I just saw Felix here, outside the gate. I don't think *you* were there in my vision. Maybe—"

"Of course." Itzel smacks herself on the forehead. "If your vision is supposed to start with you standing here in the hub, I have to leave before the test starts."

"You do?" I look down at her.

"Our immunity to Cognizant powers extends even to your kind," she explains. "A seer can't have a vision of a gnome's future, so if I stay, you'll have trouble seeing this hub."

"Wow," I say. "You weren't kidding. Gnomes *are* a force to be reckoned with."

"You should go so that the test can commence," Felix tells Itzel. "We'll come find you in the lab when we're done."

She walks away slowly, and as soon as she's gone, Felix says, "Phew. I thought she'd never leave."

So much for Felix's free will. Even his intonation is the same as in the vision I just had.

Gathering my focus, I leap into Headspace again.

This time, the shapes that surround me play music that would make a good score for a horror movie.

My wisp metaphysically quivering, I touch the nearest vision shape.

———

I LUMBER into the bright yellow shimmer of the gate.

The other side looks the same as when I saw it last: like a large theme park on Jupiter that had been nuked a few thousand years ago.

I take a step and say, "That's one small step for a woman, but one giant leap for Cognizant kind."

No one replies.

The ground under my feet is again cracked and covered with multicolored slime—as is the jagged half left of the Ferris wheel in the distance. Same with the ruins of the other rollercoasters.

Carefully, I suck in spacesuit oxygen.

The strange odor is there, but otherwise, I'm fine.

The stats in my peripheral view are going berserk. This place is radioactive as hell, and the air pressure is almost nonexistent.

Remembering my destination gate, I walk in its direction.

I make it halfway when the stomach pain begins.

It's not as severe as when I died here in my vision, but similar.

I rush for my destination—and trip over a slime-covered plastic container.

It's heart-warming to know that trash can survive whatever Armageddon happened on this world.

Faceplanting on the ground, I curse the future for its attachment to certain patterns.

The fall knocks all air out of my lungs, and like in my previous vision, the pain explodes into fireworks.

Doing my best not to let the agony make my mind go blank, I watch the stat readings—

———

I COME BACK to the hub and almost step into the gate when a hand grabs me from behind.

"Does that mean the test was a success?" Felix asks me.

"No." I turn to face him. "The suit needs more work."

"Then why did you almost walk in?" He glances at the gate behind me.

I shrug. "I must've done too good of a job convincing myself I have to walk in there."

He frowns. "Good thing I was here to stop you. Let's go tell Her Nerd Highness."

"Talk about the pot calling the kettle black," I mutter as we start walking.

"I know," Itzel says crisply inside my helmet. "And *His* Highness forgets I can hear everything from your helmet."

"I knew she heard," Felix whispers defensively, but he doesn't insult the gnome for the rest of our walk back.

When we reach the lab, they take off my gear, and I do my best to explain the different readings I saw throughout my misadventure.

"At least her blood didn't boil this time," Itzel muses and writes something on a notepad in front of her. "We're close, but we might as well be on a different planet given the tech limitations I have to—"

"Hold on," Felix says. "Blood boil?"

"The pressure in that world is low." Itzel waves at her notes. "That moves the boiling point of fluids in her body below—"

"If you expect me to convince myself to walk into that gate ever again, you might want to stop there," I cut in.

"Assuming you have anything to test," Itzel says. "As I was trying to say, based on these readings, this test is a huge letdown. I think we pushed this primitive technology to its limits. It would take gnome-powered tech to survive in that world."

"And if only we could somehow locate a gnome for that," Felix says sarcastically. "Unless you're saying we need a *better* gnome?"

"You don't understand." Itzel looks at me. "Gnome tech requires a gnome to power it over time." She produces another ball lightning between her palms, looks at Felix as though considering tossing it in his face, then makes it fizzle away. "It would mean I'd have to join your expedition, and as much as I like to explore, I have a huge debt I need to focus on repaying and—"

"Please, Itzel." I step toward her. "It's not like I'm going exploring for the fun of it. This is all so that I can meet my biological father. It's the only way I can get to him."

"I'm sorry, but I have to put my debt first," Itzel says, not unkindly. "Kit only paid me enough to—"

"Is your debt in cc?" Felix cuts in. Seeing my confused stare, he explains, "That's what they call their crypto cash on Gomorrah."

"You're from Gomorrah?" I look at Itzel with renewed curiosity.

"I don't live there permanently, as that would strip me of my power, but I do spend a lot of time there. A lot of my kind do, on the account of the cool tech." Itzel spikes up her hair.

"Is that how you met Kit?" I ask.

"Yes," Itzel says. "I'm a consultant at Tranquility rehab. They're trying to replicate parts of their famous dream walk therapy using virtual reality, and I need the money."

Felix walks to the table, takes a pen and a piece of paper, and writes something.

"How about this?" He hands the paper to Itzel. "Would that be enough to help us?"

The gnome's eyes threaten to jump out and roll around. "Oh, yes, that would cover my debt and leave me with a good amount of spare cash." She stares at the paper reverently. "So many toys I'd be able to buy, so much—"

"So we have a deal?" Felix asks.

"You'll have to prove to me you actually have that much cc." She unglues her gaze from the paper and looks at Felix as though for the first time.

He puffs up like a peacock. "I can do one better. I can put the money into a quantum escrow for you. How does that sound?"

She looks at the paper again, then at each of us. "I don't think you know what this would mean for me. The debt—"

"It's our pleasure." Felix looks vaguely uncomfortable. "When do you think we can do the next test?"

"I can have the beta suit done tomorrow," she says eagerly.

"Tomorrow isn't a good day for Sasha to test

anything." Felix darts me a pitying glance. "We're going to a funeral."

My heart sinks. Somehow, I've blocked that factoid from my mind, and the reminder catches me like a gut punch.

"Just come back when you can." Itzel gives me a sympathetic glance. "I'll use the extra time to design my own suit, now that I'm going."

"Let me know if you need me to bring any parts from Gomorrah to make this easier," Felix says. "I've—"

"No!" She grabs Felix's forearm. "If someone catches you smuggling, you'll be questioned—and they'll know I was involved. I can't partake in anything that could get me banned from Gomorrah. You don't have enough money for *that*—not to mention ccs are useless outside Gomorrah."

"No parts from Gomorrah. Got it." Felix pulls his arm away and rubs the place she grabbed.

"If you don't need me, I'm going to head out," I say.

"I've got this," Itzel says.

"*Do svidaniya*," Felix tells me.

I repeat his Russian farewell, finding it easy to match his pronunciation.

"*Ne volnujsja*," Itzel says to me. "*Vsjo budet sdelano*."

"That's 'don't worry—everything will be done,'" Felix translates.

"I know," I say indignantly. My Russian may not be as good as his yet, but it's getting closer with every sleepless night.

"Your Russian is fluent," Felix says grudgingly to

Itzel. "The legendary gnome knack for languages must be true."

"It's probably better than my English," she says, still in Russian, then picks up a book in Russian written by Konstantin Tsiolkovsky. "If I didn't already know Russian, I would've learned it just to read this."

"Now you're just showing off," Felix says, switching back to English.

Figuring I already said my goodbyes, I leave them to bicker and head out.

———

THALIA DRIVES me back to the city.

When I get home, I update Fluffster on everything that's transpired and dive into my vision-assisted Russian studies—which culminate in me reading a short book I buy on Ozon.ru, Russia's online book superstore.

As I read, I barely have to look up any words. Either this book targets early grade reading level, or I'm making even more progress than I thought.

When it gets late, I don't even try to sleep, opting to rehearse the eulogy until I can't take it anymore, and then I switch back to Russian and start *War and Peace* in its original language. This time, I do have to look up some words—and yawning gets to be a real problem as the night goes on.

I finally drift off to sleep around five in the morning, only for my alarm to wake me in what feels like the blink of an eye. My head aches, and my eyes burn with grittiness as I throw on a robe and stumble to the bathroom to wash up.

At breakfast, Felix and Kit are as gloomy as I am.

"Are you going to wear the camera?" Fluffster asks Felix when we're almost done eating. "I don't want to miss Rose's funeral, but I don't want to force anyone to carry me."

I don't need Nero's powers to tell that my domovoi is lying through his rodent teeth. The reality is that he's been reluctant to even talk about leaving the apartment after the trip to Baba Yaga's restaurant, when she'd nearly killed him in the process of jolting his memory.

"It's all set up," Felix says solemnly. "I'll stream the live feed for you on the big TV, and it will be in Ultra HD. You'll feel as though you're there."

"Thank you," Fluffster says sheepishly. "I really appreciate it."

"Don't mention it," Felix says and leaves the kitchen, with the rest of us on his tail.

When I get to my room, I dress in all black. Coming out, I see that my friends are also wearing somber colors.

No one talks much on the way down to the limo, but a huge surprise is waiting for us downstairs.

Ariel.

She's standing next to the building, and even in her funeral clothes, she looks ready to shine in a Hollywood movie—or jump onto a runway.

"Sasha, Felix," she exclaims. "I missed you guys!"

Wow. She not only looks but sounds better.

When she gives me a huge hug, some tension in my chest eases, and for a moment, I almost forget what day it is.

Felix, on the other hand, turns beet red after his hug —Ariel's décolletage strikes again.

Releasing Felix, Ariel starts toward Thalia.

The nun steps back and shakes her head. She probably swore off hugs and kisses when she gave up speaking.

"What are you doing here?" I ask Ariel after she gives Kit a much more hesitant hug and steps back.

"I figured I'd ride with you." Her forehead creases. "You didn't think I'd miss Rose's funeral, did you?"

Thalia demonstratively gets behind the wheel, and we all climb into the car as I say, "I didn't know what to think. I just know Rose would've understood if you didn't show. She'd want you to focus on getting well."

"I had to come." Ariel sits next to me in the limo. "Besides, today will be an important challenge. There will be vampires at the event."

"I'm sure you can handle it," Felix says reassuringly.

"Besides, they won't pay you any attention at the Farewell Rite." Kit's face looks just like Ariel's as she says this. "Drinking or giving vampire blood is defined as a hostile act—and if anyone breaks the no-hostilities pact, the penalty will be swift death, with the whole Council there to enforce it."

"Oh." Ariel takes out a vape pen from her giant purse. "I didn't realize." She puts the smoking gizmo in her mouth, takes in a deep puff, and breathes out a cloud that smells suspiciously like cannabis.

"Should you be getting high?" Kit makes herself look like Cheech, then Chong.

"It's medicinal." Ariel takes another drag. "Carefully formulated and approved by the folks at rehab. It really mellows me out and is good for my non-vampire problems."

Felix and I exchange furtive glances. Not only is she becoming more comfortable talking about her PTSD, she's asked the folks at rehab to help her with it.

I'm happy with this development. Pot is not as strong as some of the stuff Ariel had previously been on.

"Speaking of therapy," she says, dipping her hand into her purse again. "I made you this."

She pulls out a pair of knitted mittens and hands them to me.

"What is this?" I hold the gift with my thumb and index finger, as I would a dirty diaper.

"I needed a hobby." Ariel takes out knitting needles, yarn, and an unfinished set of socks from her purse.

In the stunned silence that follows, Ariel demonstrates her newfound skills, calling out the types of stiches she's doing as her needles fly over the yarn.

"Dude," Felix says when he regains his capacity for speech. "I know time goes a bit faster on Gomorrah, but I didn't realize you'd turn eighty on us so quickly."

"Hardy-har-har," Ariel says without looking up from

the swift movement of her fingers. "Did you know these things are also great weapons?" Almost too fast to track, she thrusts one of the needles in Felix's general direction, then resumes the knitting as if nothing happened.

"When you put it nicely like that, I applaud your great new hobby," Felix says hastily.

"It's very soothing." She looks up at him. "These socks are for you, in case that's not obvious."

"It's obvious they're for someone with tiny feet," Kit says and looks at Felix's shoes with a smirk. "And you know what they say about—"

"I have normal-sized feet," Felix snaps. "And above average—"

"Hey guys, I have an important question." I look at Felix and Ariel. "You two are as old as I *think* you are, right? Felix's joke made me realize you might actually *be* eighty, given Cognizant longevity and all that."

Ariel grins. "I'm as old as you think."

"So am I," Felix says.

"Phew." I jokingly fan myself. "I thought so—given how immature you both are—but this knitting business made me second-guess myself."

"Anyway." Ariel focuses on her knitting again. "What's new with you?"

I make sure the partition to Thalia is sealed shut and whisper, "I made a breakthrough."

I proceed to tell Ariel about the recent attack in the restaurant, then about the map that leads to a world with (hopefully) my biological father.

Ariel turns to Felix. "You'll need to make me a spacesuit. I'm going with you."

"What about your recovery?" I ask, doing my best to suppress my excitement—and guilt over the excitement.

"I'll take a break," she says dismissively. "This sounds dangerous, and you might need me."

"I was going to invite Vlad." I grab a beer from the limo bar. "Are you sure you can be around him?"

Ariel puts down her needles and massages her temples. "I think so. Given how he behaved when I hit my rock-bottom, I think he's safe to be around."

With a shudder, I recall Ariel crawling on her knees and offering herself to Vlad in exchange for his blood. Pushing the memory aside, I smile at her. "Okay. Let's see how you feel when you see him and other vamps at the funeral."

"Yep." Ariel's answering smile looks forced. "Now, do you have a trick you can show me?"

"An effect," I correct her.

"Right," she says.

I check my pockets.

Luckily, I brought my deck of cards with me, as I usually do. I must've done it on autopilot.

Taking out the deck, I start shuffling. I want to try doing something I've been accused of doing—using my seer powers as modus operandi in an illusion.

A plan forms in my head. First, I'll decide/convince myself to perform a classic effect where I will ask Ariel to name any card she wants, but instead of actually asking, I'll see a vision where she does so.

This way, I'll know her card before she even thinks of it.

Thus determined, I convince myself to do the effect and instantly focus. Without much fuss, I end up in Headspace.

I assess my surroundings.

If I had a face in this place, it would be frowning right about now.

The default shapes my subconscious or whatever served up are much too frightening-sounding for anything to do with playing cards.

These are much more likely to show me how I'm going to die.

Crap. I hate it when magic needs to be rescheduled, but there's no helping it.

Dreading what I'm about to see, I reach out to the shape to start the vision.

CHAPTER FOURTEEN

I'M BODILESS, riding as a spirit in a moving vehicle.

Seems whatever this future is, I'm not there in person.

A man is loading a bazooka with a ginormous rocket.

His gloved hands are big—which makes them very familiar.

The weapon loaded and checked, the gloved guy reaches for the car's sunroof and exposes an also-familiar killer-clown mask.

The sunroof slides out of his way, and he gets his upper torso out while another large clown-masked dude holds him by the midriff.

Taking careful aim at something, the gloved finger squeezes the trigger.

There's a deafening sound of a bazooka firing, followed by a boom of an explosion.

———

I FIND myself back in my body, in the limo, staring at everyone with wide eyes.

"What's wrong?" Ariel asks. "Is this part of the trick?"

I leap for the button that operates the partition from Thalia and jab it impatiently until the thing slides down enough for me to be overheard.

"This car is bulletproof, right?" I yell at Thalia as soon as I can.

She nods.

"What about bazooka-proof? Could we survive a hit from one?"

Thalia emphatically shakes her head, and Felix mumbles that bazookas were designed to take down tanks.

"I just had a vision of a man firing a bazooka," I say. "Same guy that shot at Nero and me at the restaurant. I'm pretty sure that bazooka will be fired at *me*."

"Seatbelts!" Thalia barks and grasps the steering wheel so hard that her thin knuckles whiten.

I plop back into my seat and frantically buckle up.

Everyone does the same.

"Does she realize she just broke her vow of silence?" Felix whispers in my ear. "Again?"

The limo's motor revs, and we torpedo forward— Thalia must've floored the gas pedal.

The g-forces rip the cards from my hands and rain them through the limo.

The trees start passing us so fast I almost believe we can outpace a rocket.

"There's a turn ahead," Ariel screams at Thalia. "If you don't slow down, we'll skid off the road!"

Vein pulsing on her forehead, the nun yanks the steering wheel all the way to the right without slowing down.

There's a screeching sound, and everyone in the car turns white as we barely make the turn.

The next hour is like a racing-themed rollercoaster —leaving me on the verge of losing my breakfast.

But hey, at least we still haven't been hit with a bazooka.

Nor is anyone chasing us, come to think of it.

Maybe they didn't expect to have to chase us? Or we sped away before they could catch up with us?

Thalia doesn't seem to share my optimism. She doesn't slow down even for a moment, and as she pulls another stunt-driver-worthy maneuver, I start to ponder the irony of getting killed by her driving when that driving is a means to avoid a rocket.

Talk about a self-fulfilling prophecy.

Eventually, we barrel into a fenced-off area past a sign that says something very threatening to trespassers.

The dirt road soon becomes nicely paved, and in a few miles, we reach a fortified, tollbooth-looking blockade manned by pale, sunglasses-wearing dudes in black.

"Enforcers," Kit confirms my suspicion. Turning to

Ariel, she says, "You might want to focus on your knitting."

The vampires let us through, and Kit theatrically exhales and says, "No way anyone can shoot us now. This is Council territory."

Thalia seems to agree with this, because we finally slow down—which gives me the chance to catch my breath and focus on our surroundings.

Everywhere I look are picturesque forests and mountains, with a particularly large and impressive-looking mountain ahead of us.

As we approach it, I spot more Enforcers on patrol. Those signs around the property should say "trespassers will be exsanguinated."

Picking up speed, we ride over a creaky drawbridge.

"Is that a moat?" Felix asks Kit as he looks down at the dubious sludge under the bridge—a body of liquid that goes around the mountain as far as the eye can see.

"Indeed." Kit looks down into the muck. "You wouldn't want to swim in that."

A moat? Don't those usually surround castles instead of mountains? Then again, what I recall of the Council headquarters did have that vibe.

I'm about to ask Kit where the castle is hiding when I see it.

Enormous wide-open doors on the side of the mountain.

Most of the rock inside has been hollowed out, and in the empty space stands a medieval castle that could give the one on Disney's logo a run for its money.

Ariel lowers her knitting accoutrements to stare at the structure with openmouthed awe. "Did dwarves build this?"

"I think it was someone with the ability to control stone—a bit like my dad's powers with sand," Felix says, his eyes not leaving the castle.

"I imagine you're both correct," Kit says. "At least it's true of the Tokyo Council hideout. I was there when that one was built."

As we enter the mountain, I gawk at the gorgeous bastions, towers, and other castle sub-parts that I don't know the exact terminology for. We park in the castle's open area that Kit dubs "the bailey" and walk through the main doors that bring to mind Hogwarts.

"I just realized no one blindfolded us," I say, remembering my first trip to this place. "I guess it's not so secret after all?"

"The Enforcers can be overzealous," Kit says. "This location is kept on a need-to-know basis, and when you're invited to an event hosted here, you obviously need to know where to go."

As she explains this, we make our way to a ballroom that's teeming with people I know. Most of them, I've seen during my fateful encounter with the Council, while others—like Lucretia, Nero, Pada, Darian, Chester, and Isis—are more personal connections. Even the huge dude who performed my Rite is here—and without the weird mask, he looks just like my mental picture of a giant.

I look around. The décor is vaguely reminiscent of where Beauty and the Beast might live—after their happily ever after, that is.

"What's with the monks?" Felix asks.

I follow his gaze.

Here and there, the hooded monk-like figures I first met during my Rite are walking the perimeter. Something I couldn't have noticed before the Rite is that the monks have a Mandate aura—meaning they're Cognizant of some kind.

"The Brotherhood." Kit wrinkles her little nose. "I don't think they have much in the way of powers. But their weird religion jells well with the needs of the Councils, so they're tolerated."

"Yeah, quite a symbiotic relationship they have there," Ariel mutters.

Tearing my eyes away from the monks, I study the rest of the guests. Like us, everyone is dressed in somber clothes, but the vibe of the gathering is that of a cocktail party—an impression only enhanced when I spot a few monks walking around with trays full of finger food and drinks.

"If I'd designed this event, I would've stuck to the castle theme," I say under my breath. "The champagne glasses would be goblets, and instead of sliders, I'd serve one giant suckling pig."

Felix and Ariel chuckle as we walk deeper in.

"We're early." Kit grabs a cocktail from a nearby

server and takes a big gulp. "I'm going to go mingle. I suggest you do the same."

"Wait," I say. "Is this the wake? Does it precede the actual funeral?"

"I think she wants to know when her speech is scheduled." Ariel squeezes my shoulder. "Not a fan of public speaking, this one."

"Right." Kit downs her drink and puts it on the tray of a passing monk. "This is the wake. Afterward, Hekima will get the floor because he has something special planned. Next, the actual Farewell Rite will commence, with eulogies after that. If—"

"Kit," says an unfamiliar sultry voice from over my shoulder. "There you are."

Felix whistles under his breath as I turn and examine the newcomer.

If someone took all the blond bombshell celebrities, from Marilyn Monroe to Pamela Anderson, and then mixed them in a blender, this bleached, giant-breasted lady would probably be the result.

She looks at me with her icy blue eyes, and I move out of her way. Instead of walking, like a normal person, she pretty much leaps for Kit.

Kit moves with surprising speed, and the blondie misses her mark.

"So that's how it is?" The newcomer's bright red lips form the mother of all pouts. "First you leave me, then you don't invite me to this party, and now—"

"Listen, Lola," Kit says. "I was in rehab and—"

"You don't love me anymore!" The woman—Lola—

puts her hand on her forehead theatrically, acting so devastated you'd think she just learned all of the world's peroxide supplies dried up.

"You know things aren't that simple," Kit says, shooting an uncomfortable look in our direction.

Ariel clears her throat. "We need to go mingle."

"Yeah," Felix adds, blushing. "I want to say hello to a few people."

My friends run in different directions, so I mumble something about me also needing to go mingle and follow Ariel.

Behind us, Kit and Lola's conversation gets increasingly louder.

"I've heard of Lola," Ariel whispers when we're outside the earshot of even supernatural ears.

"Oh?" I grab myself a glass of champagne.

"We're distantly related, and my parents like to gossip," she says. "Lola is a nymph and has a reputation for being so obsessed with sex that she's notorious even among her kind."

"A nymph?" I look back and catch Kit and Lola making out. "Did you know that's where the word 'nymphomaniac' comes from?"

"It's fitting," Ariel says. "Out of the two of them, it probably should be Lola who's in rehab for sex addiction."

"Oh, crap." I almost choke on my drink. "This Lola must be the 'enabler' Kit was avoiding when she asked to crash with us. There goes that."

"That's scary." Ariel walks the long way around a

nearby vampire. "I hope I don't break my sobriety as easily as that."

I follow Ariel's gaze and see Lola dragging Kit up the giant staircase.

"You won't," I say confidently. "You're army strong, remember?"

Ariel straightens her back and gives me a grateful look. Then she looks over my shoulder and says, "Nero."

I turn to see him incline his head. "Ariel. Can I borrow Sasha from you for a moment?"

"Of course," my roommate says with exaggerated courteousness. "I'll go see what Felix is up to." With that, she surreptitiously winks at me and saunters over to the other side of the room.

Nero's blue-gray eyes study me with the intensity of an MRI machine. "How're you doing?"

"I've had better days," I reply, resisting the irrational urge to step closer in the hopes of getting a hug. "I had this vision earlier where someone tried to shoot me with a bazooka. I think Thalia saved the day, but—"

"Start over." His nostrils flare, and his limbal rings thicken. "Tell me every detail."

I tell him what little I saw, including the similarities to the restaurant shooters. "Did you get far in your investigation?" I ask when I'm done.

"No," he growls. "But speaking of my investigation, what was that about?" He nods in the direction I came from.

"What was what about?" I follow his gaze and see

no hint of what he might be talking about. "Can you be a tad more specific?"

"The blonde." He gestures to the staircase where Kit and Lola had gone. "She didn't look happy to see you."

"That's Kit's… girlfriend, Lola." I take a large gulp of my drink. "I don't think she cares about me. It's Kit she—"

"Is there anything going on between you and Kit?" Nero asks, and though he tries to make the question casual, his limbal rings grow even thicker.

I nearly choke on the bubbly. "No," I say when I stop coughing. "Not that it's any of your business."

Is it my imagination, or does he look relieved? In the next moment, however, his jaw tightens and he says grimly, "This Lola might think otherwise, and jealousy can be a powerful motivator."

"You think Lola could be behind the attempts?" I look at him for signs of mirth and find none. "She certainly wasn't the person behind the mask and gloves —too small. Also, even if she really is the jealous type, why single me out? She has just as much justification to feel jealous of Felix or Ariel. And, though he's not here, Fluffster had—"

"You have a way of making an impression on people," Nero says and looks at the staircase again. "I think Lola and I need to have a quick chat."

"But they might be—"

Without listening to my warning, Nero stalks after the reunited pair.

The chances of him interrupting a passionate

encounter are great, but why should I care? Nero can see as many naked women as he wants, with them in any kind of—

I spot Darian walking toward the exit.

Demonstratively holding a pack of cigarettes, he sneaks a look in my direction.

As soon as he notices my gaze, he speeds up his pace.

How interesting. He wasn't paying any attention to me until Nero left.

Without much deliberation, I let my legs carry me in the same direction. I can always find seer-related questions for Darian.

As soon as I go through the large doors, I spot him standing there, coughing his lungs out.

"You don't really smoke," I say on a hunch. "You just wanted an excuse to be alone with me, didn't you?"

"You're starting to think like a seer," he says with his signature British accent after he catches his breath. "Our window for privacy is rather small, so I must get to the point quickly."

"Hold on," I say. "How are you even here? Didn't Nero warn you to stay away from me?"

"I'm here to pay my respects." He somberly nods in the general direction of the wake. "Even Nero wouldn't be so gauche as to deny me this. I'd known Rose much longer than he had."

"I see," I say carefully, not thrilled at the idea of him using Rose's funeral to further his agenda. "There was an easier way for you to speak to me. You could've accepted my Headspace summons."

"I couldn't do that." He puffs on the cigarette and blows out the smoke without letting it reach his lungs —like an actor, or a cigar aficionado. "I need every ounce of my power to prevent the catastrophe you're working so hard to bring about."

I blink at him. "What are you talking about?"

"I saw the two of you in there." He tosses the cigarette on the ground and stomps on it viciously. "Very chummy indeed."

"Me and Nero? Chummy?"

"I've warned you." Darian's green eyes seem to stare into my brain. "You can't choose him. Death permeates every future where you do."

This again?

I don't need seer powers to know that falling for Nero would lead to a disaster, but having Darian put it like that bothers me on some deep, visceral level.

Whatever choices I do or don't make should be mine and have nothing to do with Darian's gloomy prophecies—or Chester's powers.

The door behind me creaks open.

Twisting on my heel, I gape at the newcomer.

I've heard of "speak of the devil," but this is "*think* of the devil."

"You," Darian grits out.

"Me." Chester walks out and stands between us. "You can never see me coming, can you?"

CHAPTER FIFTEEN

"THIS IS A PRIVATE CONVERSATION," Darian says, swiftly recovering his composure.

"Oh, boo hoo." Chester's lips curve in a devilish smile. "As luck would have it, I happened to be passing by the door when I got the urge to put my ear to it. You were in the middle of misleading Sasha." He nods at me. "Proceed."

"I'm not misleading anyone." Darian looks at me. "In the futures where you choose Nero, you die. No exceptions. The only future where you live is where you're with me."

"How romantic and noble," Chester says, every syllable dripping with sarcasm. "You risk Nero's wrath to let Sasha know all this so selflessly." He turns to me. "I'll eat my shoes if there isn't something in it for him. Besides gaining you as arm candy, of course. If I were a betting man—and I certainly am—I'd say the future with the two of you together is the only one where this weasel survives."

Darian's chin momentarily drops to his chest as he tries to avoid my gaze. Catching himself, he looks guilelessly at me, but it's too late. Having studied poker as part of my card magic education, I'm very familiar with "tells," and I think I just discovered Darian's.

"So it's true," I say, not bothering to hide my disappointment. "This was never about love. You're trying to save your own skin."

Darian opens his mouth to say something, then closes it again.

"Having trouble manipulating her with me here?" Chester sing-songs. Turning to me, he says, "Usually, he scans every future for a person's reaction to whatever he might say, then tweaks his words accordingly. That is the real reason he refuses your Headspace summons; he can't foresee what you might say there."

Darian's poker tell betrays him yet again—which means he *has* been looking into the future to find the best words to use on me, a bit like how I found the combination to Nero's safe the other day.

"Why are you here?" I ask Chester. "Don't tell me it's to look after my interests."

"Good question," Darian says, and trying to hypnotize me with his deep green eyes, he takes a step closer, invading my personal space.

The smell of bergamot hits my nostrils, and as I

stare at his lips, I can't help but wonder what it would be like, that future he so desperately wants.

"She's immune to your charms, such as they are," Chester tells him gleefully. "Nero is better in—"

"Shut your mouth." Darian's hands ball into fists as he spins around and takes a menacing step toward Chester.

"Go ahead." Chester turns his cheek. "Break the no-hostilities pact. End your miserable existence here and now."

Darian stops with a clear effort of will.

"I'm still waiting for your answer," I tell Chester.

He rubs his chin thoughtfully, giving me the impression that he too is trying to say just the right thing to get me to play ball.

The phrase "make a deal with the devil" loops in my head like a broken record played backward.

"Honestly, I'm just happy to spite him," he says after a moment. "But you're right. I do have a secondary agenda. I want you to do me a favor."

"What kind of favor?" I ask warily, remembering Baba Yaga.

"Sasha, don't do it. Don't help him with anything." Darian looks at me pleadingly. "He's tried to kill you while I've done nothing but watch over you."

Clearly, not seeing my possible replies has led Darian to make a huge mistake. I loathe the idea of being "watched over." It means Darian can meddle in my life whenever he doesn't like something I'm about to do—say, go rescue my father.

"Now now, Darian," Chester says, turning his cheek again. "Either hit me or leave so we can have some privacy."

Darian doesn't hit him, but doesn't move either.

"You might want to hurry up," Chester says, his grin stretching from ear to ear. "I have a feeling that Nero's about to get lucky and walk out to see you talking to Sasha."

Teeth clenched, Darian storms back into the castle, slamming the door behind him.

Chester waits a few seconds, then opens the door—probably to make sure Darian isn't eavesdropping on us the way Chester himself has done.

"So." He faces me. "I'd like to keep my daughter alive."

"What?" Is this a weird joke? He does seem the type to make those.

"You were there when Nero told me she submitted to you," Chester says. "Let's not play games."

"I'm not." I pinch the bridge of my nose. "I just don't know what you're talking about."

"You now have the power to make Roxy fight your battles for you." Chester looks uncharacteristically serious. "And you're a trouble magnet. It would be only a matter of time before you'd get her killed."

I finally begin to understand. Roxy did "submit" to me, but until he just explained it, I didn't know the implications.

Have her fight my battles? A teen? A teen who hates

my guts? That wasn't ever going to happen—but then again, he doesn't need to know that.

"Well well," I say, imitating his manner of speaking. "That is one huge ask." I mimic the way he rubs his chin. "I guess I can be amiable, but I want something of proportional value in return."

Chester's mouth tightens. "Fine. What are your terms?"

"I want to learn about your power," I say, even though what I really *want* to say is, "I want to learn how to thwart your power."

"Education." His brown eyes gleam happily, and I wonder if he expected to give away more than just this. "So long as we keep this a secret from Nero, I can teach you anything you want about probability manipulation." He pointedly extends his hand.

"And you will fight a fight for me," I blurt out instead of shaking his hand. "That is, if I need you to do so."

"What?" He drops his hand.

"This is a bargain and you know it," I say, feeling more confident. "Roxy would've fought as many fights as I wished, but you'd only owe me one."

"I'm far more powerful than my daughter," he says. "I was on the Council—"

"Which is why I'm asking for your help just the one time."

He looks at me intently, then relaxes slightly. "You drive a hard bargain. I agree." He extends his hand to me again.

I clasp his baby-smooth hand in a firm grip that I've practiced for interviews and give it a shake.

"If you don't mind, I'd like to put all this in writing later," Chester says when we both let go.

"I've heard written Cognizant contracts are unbreakable," I say warily. "How does that work?"

"Contracts piggyback on the magic of the Mandate." He nods toward each of our auras. "If you break them, you get the same fun effects as if you broke the Mandate."

That does sound pretty binding. I'll never forget Ariel bleeding from every orifice when she merely *tried* to speak about the existence of Cognizant to the pre-Rite me.

"All right," I say, "but I hope you can tell me at least a little bit about your powers before the written contract is in place."

"I can do that," he says. "Though the bulk of the lessons will have to wait until Bert and I return from our safari next week."

"Safari?" I raise an eyebrow. "Bert?"

"In Africa." Chester rolls his eyes. "As to Bertie, you've met him already. He so loves his—"

"You mean the lion?" I stare at him as though the lion might pounce on me at any second.

"Do you know any other Berts?"

"Okay. So you're taking your *pet lion* on a safari in Africa?"

"I know. I spoil him rotten." Chester grins. "You saw him, though. Who can say no to those—"

"How do you even go about taking a lion to Africa? Logistically, I mean. Do you walk through the Otherlands with him on a leash or—"

"Bertie doesn't like leashes and can't do gates," Chester says. "He walks by my side. We fly first class, a seat for me and a seat for Bert."

"Your lion just flies on a plane?"

"And walks around the airport without anyone being the wiser." He grins again. "Looks like it's time for the first lesson. See, I can make it so that, by lucky happenstance, not a single human will look in Bert's direction as we walk, or when he sits in his seat. As long as he behaves himself—which I've taught him to do—he'll be as good as invisible."

"Wow." I rub the back of my neck. "You do have a really cool power."

"I do. And here is another demonstration." He reaches into his pocket and pulls out a deck of cards.

At first, I don't react, but then it hits me: aside from magicians, it's not normal for people to carry decks of cards in their pockets like this.

"I was lucky to have those in my pocket in case I need them," Chester explains nonchalantly. "Here." He hands me the deck. "Shuffle, please."

I mix the cards with all the skill of a card shark as Chester burns my hands with his gaze.

"Now spread them," he says when I'm done.

I spread the cards and gasp.

The deck is in new deck order, from King to Ace,

with each suit separated as though the cards never got shuffled since their original printing.

"There are fifty-two factorial permutations of shuffled deck orders," I mutter. "The chances of actually shuffling the cards into this order are—"

"The same as for any other random-looking order of cards," Chester says. "And thus, my power can influence an outcome I desire—assuming I focus on it and am not distracted by—"

The door behind him opens, and a monk comes out with ceremonial robes draped over his forearm and two masks in his hands.

"Ah." Chester grabs the baby-chick yellow robe and the mask with a psychotic grin that reminds me of the Joker. "It's time."

I take the purple robe and the mask depicting a blind woman with an eye in the forehead.

The monk nods and goes back into the building. Chester starts to follow.

"Wait." I fish out my phone, create a new contact with Chester as the name, and hand the device to him. "Put in your number so we can arrange the lessons."

He types in the digits, gives me back the device, and puts on the mask and robe.

I do the same.

When we walk in, the room looks ready for an *Eyes Wide Shut* orgy.

"How come some people's masks are so bland?" I whisper to Chester as we pass a number of Cognizant in gray robes and nondescript masks.

"Some don't have the kind of powers anyone bothered to make specialized masks for," he replies. "And some—like your Mentor—just want to hide what their powers are."

I try to locate Nero to verify Chester's words, but telling people apart in this masked crowd is an exercise in futility.

Everyone is staring at the stage in the front of the room, and I join them.

An unmasked Dr. Hekima stands there, wearing a red robe that makes him look like a cardinal.

He looks somber as he stares at the back of the room.

We follow his gaze and see four monks approaching the stage, carrying something. Though a tall man in front of me blocks my view, I know what the object will be before they put it on a stone slab.

A baseball-sized lump blocks my throat as I step to the side to get a better view.

An intricate coffin made of polished redwood sits in front of me.

Moisture blurs my vision and anguish squeezes my chest as I contemplate the bitter finality of this moment.

Inside that box is the dead body of—

There's a crashing noise behind us.

As I start to turn, I realize two things, both related to my visions.

One: seeing that coffin has just gone down exactly

like in my funeral vision the other day, right down to my thoughts.

And two: the sound might be that of an exploding bazooka rocket.

CHAPTER SIXTEEN

INSTEAD OF A ROCKET, I see the ancient Hogwarts-like doors break into pieces and realize the cause of this destruction is far deadlier.

It's Vlad.

He's standing in the rubble with fists clenched and a savage expression on his face. He looks ready to kill and rip things to shreds. Then again, I wouldn't be surprised if he dropped to his knees and started sobbing.

A monk clutching a black robe and a mask with fangs bravely rushes forward. But when he sees the look on Vlad's face, the man simply tosses the clothing to him.

The objects plop uncaught at the vampire's feet.

"Vlad." Dr. Hekima's voice carries through the room as though he's speaking into a high-end microphone. "I'm glad you're here for this. Most of the words Rose left are for you."

At the mention of her name, Vlad looks like he was slapped.

"I'll proceed when you're ready," Hekima says. "Take your time."

Without saying a word, Vlad bends down to pick up the mask and the garment. Moving as though it all weighs a ton, he dresses and hides his face, then nods at Hekima.

"As many of you know, Rose left a will and testament, part of which is this," Hekima announces. "She wanted me to read to you her last words—only she wanted me to deliver these words using my power." He pauses—I guess to let the idea sink in. "Anyone not wishing me to use my powers on them, please raise your hands now, and you will simply hear me speak Rose's words."

Not a single hand goes up.

"So be it," Hekima says and raises his arms dramatically, like a symphony conductor. Pulsing red energy streams from his fingers into everyone's heads, and in the next moment, a much younger Rose is standing on the stage, wearing a beautiful summer dress. Her makeup is perfectly done, her jewelry is impeccable, and she radiates health and vitality.

She must've asked Hekima to turn back the clock by a few decades.

"Hello, dears," the illusion of Rose says in an achingly familiar breezy voice. "If you're hearing this, I must be gone." She determinedly walks to the front of the stage, a Mona Lisa smile dancing on her lips. "I've had a nice life. A full life." She stops at the very edge and looks around the room until she makes eye contact with everyone. "I appreciate each and every one of you here." Her gaze shifts to the back of the room, where Vlad is standing unmoving, as if turned to stone.

"Vlad, my love," she says softly. "I can't even imagine how you must be feeling, but I'm certain that this is hard for you." She sighs. "We've always known this moment would come, but I know that doesn't make it any easier. I don't know what I would've done if I had lost you first." Two fat tears roll down each of her blush-covered cheeks. "I need you to do something for me, my love. I need you to not grieve for too long. I need you to move on. I need you to—"

Vlad howls, like a wounded lion. Moving supernaturally fast, he rushes to the stage—and passes through the illusion of Rose as though she were made of smoke.

Neither she nor the hidden-by-illusion Hekima are Vlad's destinations, it seems. Instead, he beelines for the coffin.

Opening the lid, he stares inside as everyone recovers their breathing.

Bending down, he lifts his mask and gives Rose a farewell kiss.

The ever-growing lump in my throat makes it difficult to breathe, and my mascara is but a distant memory with all the tears.

A hand squeezes my shoulder. Despite the

nondescript mask, I know this is Nero, and I welcome his reassuring touch.

Closing the casket, Vlad jumps off the stage and heads for the broken doors.

I guess he's had enough of the funeral, and I can't blame him.

When he reaches the exit, he hesitantly stops, then turns and stares blankly at the stage.

Then his shoulders slump, and he sits down on the floor.

Following some intuition, I also plop down.

Nero and the other people next to me do the same, and soon, the whole room is sitting.

The illusion of Rose seems pleased at the sight of the sitting Cognizant. She walks to the middle of the stage and says, "If I could do everything over again, I'd chose only you." Her blue eyes are bright and intense as she stares at Vlad. "What about you?" she asks. "Would you have rather have *not* loved me?"

All heads turn to Vlad.

"If you could turn back the clock," Rose continues, "would you choose someone who wouldn't one day have to write this speech?"

Vlad shakes his head so violently I'm surprised his mask stays on.

I turn back to Rose and catch her smiling beatifically. "So there we have it," she says. "Councilor Albina, it's time for me to rejoin nature."

She steps to the side as a white-robed person stands up and walks onto the stage.

She (I assume) is wearing a mask that looks like the childhood drawing of a sun, with sunrays spreading in every direction.

Walking deliberately, the figure stops next to the coffin and points at it with both hands.

White energy streaks from her hands into the coffin, and as soon as the connection is made, the coffin and its contents seem to dissolve in a blinding flash.

Her work done, the Councilor slinks off the stage.

"Thank you so much," Rose says, and the illusion of her evaporates in the same way as the coffin did, leaving behind just Hekima holding a sheet of paper.

"It's time for some of us to say a few words," he says and locks eyes with me. "Sasha, please come up to the stage."

My heart plummets, and I can't move a muscle.

The crowd around me starts to murmur menacingly.

Nero squeezes my shoulder again, but that little bit of reassurance isn't enough to offset the terrifying reality of what's about to happen.

There are hundreds of people here, and I have to speak in front of them.

CHAPTER SEVENTEEN

"I CAN TAKE YOUR PLACE," Nero whispers in my ear, his warm breath wafting over my neck.

I numbly shake my head and shock myself by slowly getting to my feet.

That's right. I've done this successfully once before, when I faced the Council.

I didn't faint then, and I shouldn't faint now.

Ignoring the thunderous beating of my heart, I drag myself to the stage.

The crowd below me seems to have multiplied a thousand-fold.

I look at Hekima to see if he's messing with me, but he just has a kindly expression on his face.

I look back at the crowd.

Have these masks always looked so sinister?

"You can do this," Hekima murmurs as he walks past me to get off the stage. "I know you can."

In the fourth row, I spot a pale woman lifting her fanged mask.

It's Lucretia. She sucks air into her cheeks, then makes exaggeratedly pouty lips to let the air out.

Is she having a fit?

No. She's pantomiming breathing.

I inhale a deep breath and slowly let it out—just like Lucretia taught me after I fainted on a stage such as this.

"This is for Rose," I remind myself with the next breath. "Just pretend this is a big magic show, and they're the audience."

My back straightens.

"Thank you for coming to this Farewell Rite," I say, impressed at how well my voice carries through the room. "I don't know anyone more deserving of this honor than Rose."

Some of the masked people nod approvingly, and I continue. "You may know her as a powerful witch, but she was so much more than that." As I proceed to describe Rose's kindness and generosity, I marvel at the rehearsed words spewing out of my mouth.

I'm actually doing it. I'm delivering the eulogy without fainting.

Wow.

If I can speak in public while sleep-deprived, overwhelmed with grief, and worried about a rocket flying into the room at any moment, I can probably cross fear of public speaking from my list of phobias.

I deliver the rest of the speech without a hitch,

ending with a breathless, "So you see, Rose was not just a friend. She was family."

A few people start to clap, and the rest of the crowd joins them.

Hekima comes back to the stage to announce the next speaker as I return to the spot next to Nero and gratefully slump into a sitting position on the floor.

"Great job," Nero whispers, leaning in. "I'm proud of you."

If he says more, I don't hear it.

The post-adrenaline slump combines with the sleep deprivation to hit me like a truck.

"At least I didn't do it on stage," I manage to think to myself before I collapse like a fainting goat.

CHAPTER EIGHTEEN

I WAKE up from the most inappropriate dream about Nero. I was nude on the desk in my new office, and he was covering me in oil while talking about the stock market and—

Wait a second, what's with the loud noise? Is it the roar of motors?

Opening my eyes, I frantically look around.

I'm strapped to a seat next to Nero with giant headphones over my head.

Of course.

I'm inside Nero's helicopter.

Is he trying to *Fifty Shades* impress me again?

Looking at my boss, I press the prerequisite button on the headset and ask, "What happened? How did I get here?"

"You passed out," Nero says without turning away from the breathtaking view of the New York Harbor below us. "Isis was nearby, so I asked her to give you a restful sleep."

I examine myself.

Okay, so I feel better, but something about what he's saying bothers me.

"How did I get into this thing?" I ask, nailing the bad suspicion on the head. "Did you carry me out in front of all the funeral attendees?"

I also wonder if his carrying me was how I got the sexy dream, but I don't voice *that* question.

"Would you rather I have dragged you by your feet, like a sack?" Nero turns my way for a second, and I can see a hint of amusement in his eyes. "I can do that next time, if you insist."

"Where are my friends?" I look behind us and find no one. "Are they still at the funeral?"

"Thalia is driving them back." He fiddles with the gizmo I believe is called "the collective"—one of the primary controls in charge of lift.

"That's good." I can't help sneaking a peek at the Statue of Liberty in the distance. "They're probably safer riding without me."

Nero grunts something, but without pressing the button so I can overhear.

"How did your conversation with Lola go?" I ask. "Was she—"

"She said she'd only met you for the first time today." Nero adjusts the stick in front of his seat. "So there goes that theory."

"Any other leads?" I look at the only nearby patch of land on Staten Island and spot a tiny black van in the distance.

I could swear a tiny person is sticking out of that van, holding something.

I gasp as a wave of dread slams into me.

With a shaking finger, I press the speak button as Nero says, "No leads yet, but—"

"Swerve!" I shout, grabbing for the controls.

I have to hand it to my boss.

Without asking why or how, he jerks on the controls before I can get to them.

The helicopter lurches to the side.

A bazooka rocket whooshes by the front window.

This is it, what my vision had warned me about. And it's much worse than what I originally feared— getting hit while riding in a limo.

Another wave of anxiety hits me just as Nero violently yanks on the controls again.

My gaze snaps to the side window—and I see another rocket flying right at us.

CHAPTER NINETEEN

"ANOTHER ONE!" I shout at Nero, though he's already reacting, and every piece of monitoring equipment around us is going berserk.

We swerve, but not in time.

The rocket explodes with a sound of tearing metal, and our craft spins out of control.

CHAPTER TWENTY

"WE'RE GOING DOWN," Nero growls as we zigzag through the sky.

I look at the spinning world and the ever-nearing water below and try to swallow my heart back into my chest.

Nero unbuckles his safety harness.

The roar of the propellers turns unhealthy—the main or the tail rotor must be damaged.

Nero rips off my headset and unstraps me as though I were a doll.

"Are you planning to jump?" I shout over the roar. "Won't we be in danger of hitting the tail rotor?"

He doesn't reply. He must not have heard me over the nightmarish cacophony.

I pray to the helicopter gods that the tail rotor is the source of that horrible noise—or that I have my jumping-out-of-the-helicopter facts wrong.

Nero opens the door.

The harbor below us seems to be approaching so fast, you'd think we were riding a rocket toward it.

Then Nero pushes me out.

Without a parachute.

CHAPTER TWENTY-ONE

AS I FREEFALL, I scream like I haven't done since the time I went hoarse after accidentally swallowing a spider.

His face inhumanly calm, Nero glides after me like an expert skydiver.

Before I can blink, he has me in a tight hug.

I brave a look down over his shoulder and wish I hadn't. The harbor water is a high-rise building away.

I look back up and wish I hadn't done that either. Another rocket hits what's left of the poor helicopter square on—and it explodes into shards of metal and glass.

"Brace yourself," Nero shouts just as his back hits the water.

The impact knocks all my breath out of my lungs, and I see bright flashes of light.

Then the cold water surrounds me, and my consciousness slips away.

CHAPTER TWENTY-TWO

I COME to my senses as Nero pulls away from giving me mouth to mouth.

At least I hope that's what he was doing—until today he never seemed like the "sneak a kiss from a half-dead woman" type.

No. It must've been mouth to mouth. My lungs burn as though I breathed in salty water—and I probably did.

Still, though I'm cold and wet, I feel surprisingly alive for someone who just skydived without a parachute.

Did Nero's embrace protect me? What about him? That impact would've hurt anyone—

"Isis is on her way," Nero tells me soothingly.

I recover enough to notice the concern on his face, and warm fuzzy-wuzzies banish some of my discomfort.

Turning my head, I look around.

We're on the pier—the very one where I nearly drowned not so long ago.

Hey, one more drowning, and the next one is free.

I try to sit up, and Nero loops his powerful arm under my shoulders, helping me.

"I think I'm okay," I say when he carefully pulls away and I manage to remain upright. "Nothing hurts much."

Nero frowns at me skeptically. "You might be in shock. Something could be broken, and you wouldn't know it."

Shrugging, I glance at the water. There are pieces of the helicopter floating everywhere.

"Are *you* okay?" I ask, turning back to look at him.

It's dawning on me that Nero has saved me. Again.

He was willing to break his back against the water for me.

"I'll be fine," he says dismissively, standing up. "The fall wasn't as bad as it probably seemed with all that adrenaline coursing through your system."

Riiight. A normal person would've totally survived that—and there's a nice bridge I'm putting up for sale.

Whatever type of Cognizant Nero is, he must be extremely resilient.

Putting aside the mystery that is my boss, I resume looking around and spot people in Battery Park staring at the helicopter remains.

This is less than ideal. A few of the gawkers are even taking pictures.

"This will be impossible to hush up completely,"

Nero says, following my gaze. "It will be a high-profile case, but maybe that's a good thing. Maybe the humans will help us figure out who's behind this."

Taking out his phone, he swipes at the screen for a few moments. The thing must be waterproof, I realize as he pockets the device and lifts me with his signature bridal carry.

I debate whether I should act indignant as he walks, but I decide against it. I'm secretly enjoying the closeness and the warmth spreading through my body. Instead, when Nero shows no sign of slowing after a minute, I ask, "Where are we going?"

"That car." He nods at a silver Toyota Camry that's pulling up to the curb.

Lengthening his strides, Nero reaches the car with record speed.

"Is she drunk?" the driver asks when Nero puts me inside. "If she pukes—"

Nero takes out a wad of wet cash from his pocket and hands it to the frowning dude. "Get us to the address quickly, and I'll double that."

The driver looks at the cash in confusion.

"Waste any more time, and I'll throw you out of this car and drive it myself," Nero growls.

The driver wisely decides to do as the scary man asks, and we rip forward, nearly driving over a couple of pedestrians.

The AC in the car makes me shiver, and Nero loops his arm around me again, pulling me close to his incredibly warm body. Does he have a furnace pumping under his skin?

"Turn off the AC," he barks at the driver, and the man immediately complies.

My shivering abates, only to be replaced by an equally unsettling sensation—the kind that makes it difficult to even out my breathing.

"Any pain?" Nero murmurs, gazing down at me. "I have morphine at my place if you need it before Isis gets there."

"No." I reluctantly scooch away. "I'm doing better. Neither Isis nor drugs should be necessary."

"You're sure?" He looks me up and down, a frown creasing his hard features.

"Positive," I say, wanting to slap myself for being tempted to kiss that worried-looking mouth for some unholy reason.

When we park next to Nero's building, my boss tosses more money at our driver, then picks me up—of course—and carries me to his penthouse.

As he enters the elevator, I realize I've recovered enough to *really* notice the proximity of his muscular body.

Must not dwell on that.

In an effort to banish inappropriate thoughts, I take in a deep breath as we exit the elevator.

Nope, that made it worse. I can almost taste the hint of delicious spice in his cologne.

He carries me into the kitchen and carefully lowers

me into a chair, his movements so gentle you'd think I'm breakable.

I get a case of déjà vu as he then makes me a salad and potatoes with mushrooms—just like he did the last time I was here and distraught.

He even makes me drink tea again—chamomile with lemon balm.

As I start devouring the food, he leaves for a second —no doubt to set up the hot tub again.

By the time he comes back, I've put down my fork, and my belly feels like it might explode.

"You sure you don't want some pain medicine?" His eyes seem to peer into my brain, their limbal rings out of control.

"I'm fine," I say—and I am. My current discomfort has nothing to do with the fall from the helicopter and everything to do with the man pampering me. "No drugs necessary."

"Suit yourself. Now let's get you out of those wet clothes." He reaches for me.

Vivid images of Nero stripping my clothes sneak into my mind, but that's not why he's reaching for me.

Actually, the real reason is almost as bad.

He picks me up yet again and carries me into that spa-like master bathroom.

I was right.

He's set up candles and drawn a bath for me, just like the last time.

The images in my head evolve from stripping my

clothes to stripping off *both* our clothes, and progress to us naked in the tub—

Nero carefully lowers me to my feet. When I remain standing, he points at the huge pile of towels and says, "Use those when you're done."

He then walks over to a linen closet and riffles through it for a few seconds. "Also put these on." He drapes a bunch of clothes on the back of the tub.

I check it all out.

It's yoga pants and a sports bra that look about my size. Actually, who am I kidding? I bet they'll fit me perfectly—Nero has a history of knowing my measurements.

"What about you?" I touch his drenched shirt and feel his heart banging against his chest. "You're as wet as I am."

His nostrils flare as he grabs my wrist to pull me away. "I'm going to one of my seven other bathrooms," he says harshly.

I haven't been this disappointed since the ending of the second *Matrix* movie that Felix made me watch. The near-death experience must be messing with my brain because I don't want Nero to leave.

He steps farther out of my reach. "Did your phone survive?" he asks me.

Blinking, I fish the thing out of my pocket and check. Unlike my brain, the phone works as it should.

"It's all good," I mutter. "Waterproofing strikes again."

"Call me as soon as you're done changing." Nero turns to leave.

Would it be crazy for me to ask him to stay?

Before I can decide, he strides out and bangs the door shut behind himself.

Sighing, I undress and get into the bubbling water—which feels boiling hot.

In a minute, I realize the water wasn't hot—it was me who was freezing.

As I thaw out, I can't stop thinking about Nero.

Though I'm reluctant to do so, it's only rational to reassess some long-held notions about the man, starting with the assumption that he doesn't care about me. This takes many forms, though most frequently I swat away any good deeds of his as "he just keeps me safe because he needs me as his pet seer."

Is that valid anymore?

He now has access to the bannik, who is also a seer.

Yet despite the fact that I'm no longer a unique unicorn as far as seer abilities go, Nero is acting more protective toward me than ever.

Actually, that's an understatement.

There's "protective," and there's "risked his life not once but twice for me now."

Suppressing an unbidden yawn, I force myself to admit it: if actions do speak louder than words, Nero is showing me that he cares about me.

Or is that wishful thinking?

He could be just performing his duties as a Mentor, or fulfilling his contract with Rasputin.

Maybe I'm wishing for him to care about me because *I've* started to care about his bossy ass?

I increase the intensity of the tub's massage feature and let myself ponder if and how something between the two of us could work.

He saw me grow up—but that's not a complete deal breaker. I mean, I saw Daniel Radcliffe grow up in the *Harry Potter* movies, and I think he's cute as an adult. Besides, it's not like Nero has actually raised me; I only met him in my twenties. And he certainly doesn't *look* old, thanks to those Cognizant super genes.

He's also my Mentor—but so what? I haven't heard anyone say Mentor/Mentee relationships were frowned upon.

That he is my boss is a bigger obstacle but not insurmountable either. After all, work relationships are extremely common, and if other people can make it work, why can't two people as smart as the two of us? Besides, I can always get another job (assuming he doesn't block me from it) or—

I yawn out loud.

Like the last time I used this tub, the food coma conspires with the pleasure of the warm water to make me super drowsy.

I have to fight this.

The last time I fell asleep this way, I woke up naked in a bed—and it was obviously Nero who'd brought me there.

I yawn so hard my jaw joints hurt.

I guess that little nap Isis gave me didn't make that

big of a dent in my sleep deficit. Oh, and I'm crashing after having so much adrenaline swimming through my system.

Still, I can't bring myself to get out. The warmth is so nice, and the outside air is so cold. Surely I can stay awake for one more minute?

I close my super-heavy eyelids for just a second.

I'll open my eyes and get out any moment now…

———

I WAKE up to the feeling of motion.

I'm dry and pruney. Crap. Have I fallen asleep in the tub after all?

My eyes flutter open, and I confirm that I'm indeed not in the tub anymore.

Nope.

I'm in Nero's powerful arms yet again.

And surprise surprise, I'm nude… and an inch above a lush bed, which somehow makes this worse.

He lowers me onto the sheets, and I notice that he's not wearing much either—just a towel.

Also, the limbal rings in his eyes—and something under that towel—are out of control.

Flashing back to the last time he was wearing a towel, I recall the glory of it dropping to the floor, and the kiss that followed.

My hand reaches for the towel of its own accord.

As if possessed by a mischievous demon, I pull on it.

CHAPTER TWENTY-THREE

MY BREATH STOPS in my throat.

Holy pogo stick, that is *huge*.

A memory of something I heard in a half-sleep trance pops into my head. Nero was putting me to bed just like this, and Isis had implied I'd need healing if something were to happen between us. Is *this* what she meant? If so, she's a wimp.

I can totally handle this.

I mean, I'm pretty sure. It has been a while since I've handled anything.

Nero doesn't seem to notice the fallen towel. His eyes are too busy roaming over my body.

I lean up.

He leans down.

Our lips touch.

A melting heat moves through my body as his arms wrap around me, and the kiss turns hotter, rougher. We devour each other, our breaths mingling, our tongues tangling in an almost violent dance. My hands skate over the broad plane of his back, and I feel the incredible warmth of the muscles flexing under his skin as he presses me into the bed.

Moaning, I wrap my leg around his hips, pressing closer—and with an animalistic growl, he wrenches himself away from me.

Heart hammering, I stare at him.

"What's wrong?" I ask through bruised lips and look down at myself.

Spotting no discernible new deformities or pustules for him to be grossed out by, I look back at him.

Without a doubt, he still looks *very* happy to see me, so what gives?

Following my gaze, he uses his super speed to pick up the towel in the millisecond it takes me to blink.

"This can't happen." He does his best to wrap the tiny-seeming towel around his hips as he turns away.

I grab the blanket and pull it to my chin. "Why not?"

The muscles in his back tense as he stops to look over his shoulder. "I don't want to hurt you."

Is he talking physically à la the Isis thing, or is this something else?

"Hurt me how?" I blurt out. "Because I can handle—"

"No. You can't," he growls. "You don't understand what you're talking about."

I ball my fists over the blanket, fighting the urge to leap out and punch him in the towel.

Or kick.

Before I get a chance to do either, he strides out of the room, nearly taking the door off the hinges on the way.

Feeling like I took a dip in a polar ice hole, I leap to my feet and stomp into the bathroom.

"Asshole," I mutter under my breath as I dress. "How good does he think he is?"

No one replies—though I do hope he has a recording device here so he can hear the flood of obscenities spewing from my mouth.

Over the next two minutes, I set records for cursing, dressing, and how fast one can traverse a giant apartment.

An also-dressed Nero blocks the front door as I'm about to leave.

"Move," I snarl.

"Someone is trying to kill one of us," he says, his face so unreadable he might as well be wearing one of those masks from the Rite. "Or have you forgotten?"

"Right." I step closer. "And if they're trying to kill *you*, I'm in unnecessary danger if I stay here."

A hint of emotion breaks through the mask. "The limo isn't—"

"I can survive a single cab ride." I glare up at him. "It might even be for the best not to use something of *yours*."

"That limo belongs to a security company that—"

"I'll use the limo when it's available then. But it isn't now, so I'll make do with a cab."

He doesn't move.

Teeth clenched in frustration, I ball my hand to deck him in the chin.

He grabs my wrist before my punch can connect. "Without gloves, you'll hurt yourself more than you'll hurt me," he informs me coolly.

Huffing, I yank on my captured wrist, but he doesn't let go. "I can't stay here," I hiss.

He still doesn't move, nor let go of my wrist.

Spurred by frustration, I get an idea and start to breathe slowly, preparing to execute it.

The mental effort is on par with doing this in a fight, but I finally manage it.

I reach Headspace.

CHAPTER TWENTY-FOUR

I FLOAT among the shapes and enjoy not having to deal with Nero for a few moments.

Then I proceed with my plan—which is to get a vision of myself in the safety of my apartment.

Except, how?

Dwelling on the essence of the apartment doesn't bear fruit.

But what if I just focus on a person who's always home? Seeing the futures of people has worked pretty well for me thus far.

So, I try to summon Fluffster's essence.

I bring to mind his kindness, his thriftiness, and, most importantly, the extreme fluffy fuzziness.

A set of rounded pyramids show up, playing music so chill you'd think someone put them on Zoloft.

Good.

Metaphysically rubbing my ethereal wisps together, I touch the nearest shape.

———

"SO YOU'RE SAYING Hekima created a walking and talking illusion of Rose?" Fluffster says with undisguised jealousy. "All I saw from Felix's feed was him reading from a paper."

I feel my heart squeeze painfully at the memory. "Sounds like Illusionists can't do their tricks long distance," I say.

Fluffster's ears droop. He must've realized the topic is upsetting me. "What happened after Nero carried you out of the room?" he asks.

I sigh and launch into a highly edited, PG version of *that* story, ending with the huge fight I had with Nero in order to get him to let me take a cab home.

———

BACK IN NERO'S HALLWAY, I look at his hand on my wrist and pull once more—to no avail.

"I just had a vision," I grit out. "In this vision, I was perfectly fine when I got home." I lift my chin. "In that version of the future, we're about to have a big fight and I *make* you let me go."

Eyeing me with confusion, Nero finally lets go of my wrist.

"You know I'm telling the truth." I look him square in those hypnotizing eyes. "Why do *more* things we will regret?"

"You're not lying." He moves partially out of my

way. "But I can't believe I would've let you leave without the reassurance of the vision."

I squeeze past him, ignoring the rather heated impact his proximity has on me. "Perhaps you underestimate my persuasiveness," I say as I exit.

Whatever he says in return, I don't hear thanks to the door I slam in his face.

As I summon the cab, a million thoughts swirl through my head.

How could I have thought even for a second that Nero and I could be anything but boss and minion? Did hormones drive me completely insane?

Once inside the cab, though, I realize something slightly mind-bending—and worrying.

If I assume that the hypothetical fight with Nero that I saw in my vision took longer than a few seconds —which is a valid assumption—then I summoned *this* cab much sooner than the hypothetical cab in that version of the future.

Which means I have no reassurance that this cab is going to get me home safely.

CHAPTER TWENTY-FIVE

MY HEART HAMMERS throughout the cab ride, which seems to drag on forever.

Great. I'm scared unless I'm in a bulletproof limo. It's official. I've drunk Nero's Kool-Aid.

My phone dings.

It's a text from Nero.

Let me know as soon as you are home.

I guess he realized the same thing I did—that or he just misses bossing me around.

No one has tried to kill me by the time we pull up to the curb, which makes me feel relieved yet perversely disappointed.

It's not just Nero who doesn't want me; apparently, even the would-be assassin is over me by now.

Assuming it's me they were after.

Still, when I reach the new bulletproof apartment door, I exhale a big breath of relief.

Once inside, I take out my phone and send Nero a terse reply.

"Sasha," Fluffster says excitedly in my mind. "Where are Felix and the rest of the gang?"

I explain to him that I left the funeral early and that they're on their way home in the limo, and then we proceed to have a conversation similar to the one I saw in my vision.

"You should rest," Fluffster suggests after I tell him everything.

"Great idea." I go to my room and lock the door.

One encounter with Copperfield, my "massager," later, I take a nap.

———

BY THE TIME I wake up, Felix and Ariel are back, as evidenced by the loud conversation in the living room.

When I walk in, Fluffster is sitting on Ariel's lap and the cat on Felix's.

"Where is Kit?" I ask.

Felix blushes, then shrugs. "With Lola?"

"Speaking of reunited lovers..." Ariel wiggles her eyebrows lasciviously. "What happened after your knight in hedge fund armor carried you out of the evil castle?"

I cringe and give them the same PG version of the events that I gave Fluffster. It's obvious Ariel realizes there's more to the story, but she doesn't push in front of the others.

"I heard from Itzel," Felix says when I'm done. "She wants to do another test as soon as possible."

"How about now?" I suggest. "I just need to grab a bite to eat, and I should be as ready for suicide missions as I'll ever be."

We all go to the kitchen and snack. When we're almost done, I realize there's a problem. "Thalia works for Nero, and I don't want him to know about the Otherlands trip," I tell them.

"We can sneak out," Felix suggests.

"Or you can tell her the truth," Ariel says. "I need to return to rehab, and you're going to accompany me on the trip. You mentioned she won't go into the Otherlands because of her vow, so she won't join us on a 'trip to Gomorrah.'" She makes air quotes around the last couple of words.

"That's devious," I say with almost motherly pride. "On the day when we go for real, we'll tell her we're going to visit you at rehab. It will be close to the truth, assuming you're still up for joining, which you totally don't have to—"

"I'm joining," she says firmly. "Especially now that it doesn't look like Vlad is going."

I frown. I was hoping to invite Vlad, but given the way he was at the funeral, I don't think he'll be up for the trip—now or in any foreseeable future.

Kit might be out too—for Lola reasons.

"If you're sure," I say. "You can change your mind, though."

"I won't," Ariel says and starts to clean up around the kitchen.

"We better go," Felix says after we all help Ariel tidy up.

"Just be careful," Fluffster says mentally with grumpy overtones.

"Okay, Mom," Ariel and I say in unison, then chuckle.

———

"ITZEL, this is Ariel. Ariel, this is Itzel," Felix says when we enter the lab and the gnome greets us excitedly by the door.

"You look familiar," Itzel says in her Darth Vader manner, looking Ariel over from head to toe. "Are you a Gomorrah virtual reality actress?"

"No." Ariel smiles a Hollywood-worthy smile. "Not yet, anyway."

"I see," Itzel says, clearly disappointed. "I'm trying to get better at recognizing non-gnome faces. When I first got to Gomorrah, all human-looking Cognizant seemed the same to me."

"Racist," Felix says, making it sound like a sneeze.

Itzel doesn't show any sign she heard him.

"You said you help out at the rehab facility," Felix says when it's clear his earlier comment was ignored. "Maybe you saw Ariel there?"

"That sounds right." Itzel can't seem to peel her eyes away from Ariel's perfect features. "Even if I'd only glimpsed you there, you have the kind of looks that stick in the mind."

"Thanks." Ariel's smile is gone without a trace.

"Dude," I hiss into Felix's ear. "The rehab stuff is kind of Ariel's private business. You can't blab about it to every—"

"Can we see the suits?" Felix asks Itzel with overexaggerated excitement.

"A suit," she says. "Singular. If the test is a success, I'll work on more."

We follow her to the suit in question.

When we see it, Felix whistles, Ariel gasps, and even I—who thinks herself harder to impress than most—stare at Itzel's handiwork with a healthy mixture of awe and respect.

If someone was designing a Halloween costume and couldn't decide between cosmonaut and Iron Man, this might be the result. The impression is mainly driven by the back of the device, where Itzel trapped her ball lightning in a bottle-like contraption that crackles and spews energy throughout the whole suit.

There are extra gizmos all around the contraption, but the extra weight must not be an issue because Itzel also added hydraulic servos (or whatever they're called) at the joints of the device—making it look like something the military would pay dearly for.

"That's to make it easier to lift heavy objects and walk," Itzel explains when she notices me staring at the exoskeleton.

"It looks like the suit Batman wore when he fought

Superman." Ariel seems as excited as at one of my magic performances.

Felix unpeels his eyes from the spacesuit to glare at Ariel. "You're joking, right? If anything, it's like Mark I, the very first suit Iron Man had built. No doubt Batman's outfit was heavily inspired by—"

"It doesn't matter what it looks like," I say, knowing full well that if Ariel goes into her Batman-defending mode, we could be here a while. "The key is that I don't die while wearing it."

The reminder of the perilous journey seems to bring everyone out of comic book worlds.

"Let's get you geared up," Itzel says and readies the front of the suit.

I let her clothe me. Despite all the extras, the suit still feels like a straitjacket.

"Try lifting your hand," Itzel says when I'm fully in.

I do as she says. The motors whir and the joints creak—and my hand lifts much too quickly and easily for the effort I put in.

Before anyone prompts me, I take a step.

Just like with arm movement, the motors Itzel imbedded in the suit make my step unnaturally light and easy. Which is why I proceed to waltz around the lab like a hyperactive kid after a bag of cocaine-laced candy.

"Wearing this all the time would make me lazy," I say when I stop. "But I love it."

"Now that you've gotten acclimated, let's get you to

the gate," Itzel says, beaming with pride. "I'm staying here so as not to mess with your powers."

Ariel and Felix walk me to the gate in the hub.

I face it and do my best to get into the prerequisite mental state. But of course, knowing what happened the last time, convincing myself to want to step into that hellish place turns into a difficult project.

It takes a good half hour before I enter Headspace.

Hmm.

The visions that surround me feel safe.

Either I failed at my goal of convincing myself to walk into the gate, or I don't die in this new and improved suit.

Metaphysically shrugging my nonexistent shoulders, I touch the shape that looks most tempting and prepare for the worst.

CHAPTER TWENTY-SIX

MY STEPS as light as those of an astronaut on the moon, I prance into the bright yellow shimmer of the gate.

When I get to the other side, the post-apocalyptic landscape is the same—decimated theme park rides and all.

"Here goes another small step for a woman," I can't help but say as I walk forth.

No one replies.

The ground under my feet is once more covered with slime.

The contraption around me glows faintly with the same energy as that of Itzel's ball lightning. I guess it's creating some kind of a force field around me—which is encouraging.

I suck in spacesuit air.

No strange odor this time.

I breathe out as I walk. Step after step, I seem to be fine.

The stats in my peripheral view are acting as they should: the outside is still toxic and radioactive, but there's no penetration (Itzel's choice of words, not mine.)

Too eager for someone who'd recently fallen down and died in almost this exact spot, I rush for the gate that's my destination… and make it all the way without any stomach pains or even getting out of breath.

"Great," I say out loud. "Let's see if I survive whatever awaits behind gate number two."

I step into the next gate excitedly—

———

"IT WORKED," I say as soon as I find myself back next to my friends. "I made it through without any issues."

They—and Itzel through the headset—pepper me with questions. I patiently describe the speed of my gait, the environmental readings, and even my mood as I walked.

"What about the next Otherland?" Felix asks when the interrogation comes to a pause. "What did you see there?"

"The vision cut out," I say. "So I have no clue."

"Can you try again?" Itzel suggests in my headset. "Though I've made the suit pretty versatile, it would still be nice to be sure it can survive the next environment."

She's right, so I try the whole rigmarole again, finding it much easier to convince myself to step into the gate *this* time around.

Once in Headspace, I encounter nearly identical safe-seeming shapes as the last time—which is good.

I zoom out to make sure to get a longer vision, but not so long as to give up my weekly supply of seer juice in one go.

The jog through the toxic wasteland is as safe this time as the last, but the vision halts at the same point as the last time—just as I enter the next gate.

"Maybe it's hard to have a vision that spans too many universes?" Ariel says after I debrief them on what happened.

"Assuming the Otherlands *are* universes," Itzel mumbles under her breath. "For all we know, they could be planets in one very big universe."

"So what now?" I ask as we start walking back to the lab. "When can we head out on this quest?"

"Well," Itzel says, "if we consider the testing a success—which I guess it is—I can make more suits in a couple of days or so."

"Can you do it any faster?" Felix asks.

"I don't work well under stress and pressure," Itzel says. "And when it comes to suits, you don't want me to rush it, trust me."

"Agreed, no rushing," I say. "Just please make one extra suit for when we rescue my father. He'll need it to come back with us."

"Naturally," Itzel says. "How does Saturday morning sound? Do you want to head out then?"

"Saturday is good for me," Ariel says as we enter the lab. "There's not much going on at rehab on weekends anyway."

I take off my helmet and say, "If we have to wait until the weekend, can it be late Sunday afternoon? I might as well attend this week's Orientation."

"That works out well," Felix says without looking me or Ariel in the eye. "I'm having lunch with Maya this Saturday, and I'd hate to cancel on her."

I wriggle out of the suit and sneak a look at smirking Ariel. She's clearly on the verge of making virginity-related jokes at either Maya's or Felix's expense.

Felix must realize this too, because he gives Ariel a preemptive evil eye. "We'd better walk you to rehab," he says. "This way, if Thalia tattletales to Nero about our outing today, and he challenges Sasha about it, she can pass his lie detector test."

"My deviousness is clearly rubbing off on you guys." I grin. "Let's go."

———

THE TRIP through Gomorrah is as fascinating as every other time I've done it.

It's daytime, so the fire-and-brimstone-like nebula can't be seen in the sky, but the sprawling and never-ending metropolis is just as glorious as it is at night.

Maybe more so.

The feeling of being in a living and breathing cyberpunk movie comes over me as we ride the self-driving futuristic car. Only in addition to using fancy technology and wearing futuristic garb, the denizens of Gomorrah also happen to be a wide variety of shapes, sizes, and colors of Cognizant.

If Hollywood directors could travel through the gates, they'd shoot movies like *Ghost in the Shell* and *Blade Runner* right here—though I guess they'd need to hire more human-looking extras.

"Thanks for taking me," Ariel says, bringing me out of ogling mode. "I know it was to trick Nero, but it's still nice."

"Not just to trick Nero," Felix says. "That's a bonus."

"We can come get you on Sunday." I squeeze her shoulder reassuringly.

"Nah," she says. "Better if I meet you at the lab." She looks around the rehab facility's lobby. "We don't know how long your excursion to get your father will take, but if we're lucky, it might be as long as the trip here. If so, Thalia and Nero would be none the wiser."

"Since Felix doesn't need to take the stupid limo everywhere he goes, he can come get you while I'm at Orientation," I say. "I'll just meet the two of you in the lab afterward."

"That's a great idea," Felix says. "Let's do that."

Ariel looks happy too, so we hug it out and say our goodbyes.

Gawking at all the Gomorrah wonders on our

return trip, I decide that Hollywood can shoot movies like *The Fifth Element* here as well. It wouldn't take that much makeup to make elves, dwarves, orcs, and the like look like aliens—which is what they kind of are in any case.

I'm so fascinated by everything that I'm a little disappointed when we reach the skyscraper with the hub at the top. But I have to go back. We wouldn't want Thalia—and by extension, Nero—to get suspicious.

When we return to Earth, we update Itzel on the final plan and have Thalia take us home.

Then we fill Fluffster in on everything over dinner.

"Are you going to work tomorrow?" he asks as we clean up. "I bet Nero will expect you to."

"I don't want to, but I better." I stick a plate into the dishwasher with so much force it almost cracks. "I don't want to give him any excuses to interfere with our Sunday plans."

"That's wise." Fluffster puffs up his tail. "Now, how about we watch *The Diamond Arm*? It's an old Soviet comedy that you can enjoy even if you predict its plot, as usual. Most importantly, your Russian is now good enough to understand it."

———

THE NEXT MORNING, instead of simply dropping me off by the building entrance, Thalia guides the limo into the parking lot.

"Did he ask you to walk me to my desk?" I ask, eyeing her with suspicion.

She shakes her head, a smile playing on her thin lips as she takes out her phone and types out:

Nero wants us to resume your martial arts training.

I cringe.

She must notice that, because she types:

If you're uncooperative, he told me to tempt you with double work allotment.

She winks at me and types:

I'm happy to pretend you were uncooperative if you want.

"Thanks." I give her a wide grin. "I really appreciate that."

There's almost a bounce in my step when we get to the mat in the gym.

Thalia starts the workout less brutally than usual, but then she keeps amping it up until I'm sweating like a hyperhidrosis sufferer in a football mascot suit.

In a banya.

In hell.

Still, I don't mind the training today because of its therapeutic effects. I fantasize of punching Nero every time I hit Thalia's mitts. Also, the longer the workout, the longer I don't have to face him.

When the floor is a slipping hazard due to my sweat, Thalia calls it quits.

I shower and change, but instead of going to my office, I swing by the cafeteria and eat.

Then, when I can't postpone it any longer, I go to the top floor.

Though I *know* he heard the elevator doors open—and maybe my frantic heartbeat, too—Nero doesn't look up from his computer.

Of course.

Pretend like nothing's changed.

How mature.

As I walk to my office, Jason—the Venessa replacement—looks up and gives me a friendly smile.

I briefly contemplate flirting with him to see if that would get Nero to notice me, but decide against it. If by some remote chance, my flirtation makes Nero jealous, Jason could get fired. Or in a really extreme scenario, I might have to take another shower to clean off Jason's shredded entrails—and that wouldn't do.

When I take too many showers, my skin gets way too dry.

An email from Nero awaits in my inbox.

I glare at him through the glass wall separating our offices, but he doesn't look up.

Squinting at the screen, I read the email.

Nero wants me to research a few stocks.

Fine.

I do that until the computer screen is blurry before my eyes, and my stomach is rumbling. Then I email Nero my findings and check if that causes him to look up.

Nope.

Well, at least we can pretend he won't see me leave early.

Locking my computer, I head out with a confident stride.

Using the concept of a shiner from my bag of card-cheat skills, I sneak a peek at Nero's office in the reflection of the elevator.

He still isn't looking my way.

Jason, on the other hand, is checking me out with inappropriate-for-work appreciation.

Which might be why he isn't there when I walk in the next morning.

In his place is the kindest-looking old lady I've ever seen.

"It's nice to meet you, Barb." I shake her gnarly hand. "I hope you like it here." I look pointedly at Nero, but his nose is in his screen yet again.

When I get to my desk, an email requesting more stock research is there, as expected.

After I tire of working, I go into Headspace and check on Vlad. I find him still fighting at that arena place.

If he's still at it in a few months, I'll have to figure out a way to help him grieve in a less violent manner.

Somehow.

I resume researching stocks, then use my visions to drop in on Kit—and instantly regret it.

There's getting an eyeful, and then there's what I saw.

Leaving the vision, I clear my throat and shoot a

guilty look at Barb and Nero. I feel like that guy who gets caught watching porn at work.

Apparently, Kit and Lola will have an epic time in a bathtub in the near future. Kit will sprout not one, but four tentacle-like phalluses, and Lola will find the most creative uses for each of them.

Poor Kit. She's clearly going to end up back in rehab if this continues. I wish I could help, but I wouldn't even know where to start.

For the rest of the day, I act like a perfect employee and even stay late.

Nero doesn't look up as I leave, nor when I come back the next morning.

The rest of the work week is uneventful—that is, until I get an email from Nero at 4:59 p.m. on Friday, just as I was about to head out.

I need you to research the attached list of stocks for my Monday morning conference.

"Seriously?" I shout, staring at him through the glass wall.

He's looking at his monitor as usual.

"You realize you're asking me to work on the weekend?" I say out loud.

Why is he doing this to me? Is there really a conference, or does he want to keep an eye on me during the weekend? Or—and this is scary—has he gotten a whiff of my weekend plans and is trying to thwart them this way?

Could Kit have blabbed about the map? Did Nero sneak some surveillance equipment into my life again?

No. If he knew, he'd lock me up in the basement instead of using subtlety.

Maybe.

Another email hits my inbox.

Do this for me, and I'll clear the rest of the work allotment you owe me from the other week.

Mumbling curses under my breath, I open the list of stocks.

It's about a day and a half worth of work—which isn't that bad of a deal for the ungodly number of hours I still "owe him."

Okay. I'm on it, boss, I write back.

Then I notify Felix that I'll be home late and decide to pull an all-nighter in order to make sure my Sunday remains free.

A few stocks later, around 7:00 p.m., Barb offers to get me some dinner—an offer I gratefully accept.

After getting the food, she looks at me and Nero, shakes her head disapprovingly, and leaves for the day.

I eat the fried goodness she got for me and work tirelessly on the stocks.

At midnight, I begin to think Nero isn't going home today either.

By morning, I know it for sure.

Does he always work all night on Fridays, or is this a special occasion?

I pause for breakfast, get myself enough espresso to kill two zebras, a giraffe, and a horse, then keep working with bleary eyes and a sour feeling in my stomach.

I can't help but notice that Nero doesn't break even to eat—unless he snuck a meal of something like an energy bar when I wasn't looking.

By mid-day Saturday, I'm finally done. I email the results of my research to Nero and prepare to go home to pass out.

Another email arrives in my inbox as I get up.

I'm almost afraid to look, but like the proverbially deceased cat, I can't help myself.

Come to my office, the subject of the email says. My heart rate spikes, and I read the actual message.

We have to talk.

CHAPTER TWENTY-SEVEN

HE KNOWS.

The horrific idea circles through my mind, over and over.

When I see him, he'll lord the information over me, then lock me up in the basement cell until the Kobe cows come home to drink their beer and enjoy their massages.

I take in a deep breath, then another.

When I'm calmer, I realize I have a way to know what he wants without actually going into his office.

Of course.

I can have a vision of what happens if I go.

If he really intends to lock me up, I can try to run for it—though how I'll make it out is anyone's guess. Even if I make it to the elevator, he can pull that trick of already being downstairs, like the day when he fired Venessa.

I close my eyes and seek Headspace.

That I succeed is a testament to how good I'm getting at this process. With almost no effort at all, I find myself floating among shapes in the very next moment.

And the shapes around me are majorly frightening, which is odd. Is Nero planning to cut off my feet instead of merely locking me up in a cell?

Bursting from morbid curiosity, I reach out to the scariest shape and fall into a vision.

———

AS I WALK to Nero's office, I'm reminded of the venerable pirate tradition of forcing their victims to "walk the plank."

When I enter, Nero doesn't even look up at first.

When he finally raises his head, his blue-gray eyes are devoid of any hint of emotion.

I *know* whatever he's about to say is bad news. There's no doubt about it now.

Time seems to slow.

He says, "That can never happen—"

I stagger back. He knows. Somehow, he found out. He's going to prevent me from—

"—again," he finishes his sentence.

Wait.

What?

He said "*again.*"

But that means I got it all wrong.

He's *not* talking about my Sunday trip. This must be about our encounter in his apartment.

Though I should be relieved, this realization stings like a slap—and I don't know why.

Because he's right.

We shouldn't do *that* again.

But if I really believe this, why is my chest feeling so hollow?

"Is that all?" I force myself to say, and I feel proud of how evenly I deliver the question.

Nero nods. He looks like he's about to say something else when his gaze falls on something behind me.

I turn in time to see a woman exit the elevator.

She's dressed in a UPS uniform that's not unlike the one I once stole for an effect.

Not surprisingly, she's carrying a large package. Someone clearly paid through the nose for a Saturday delivery.

She waves at us and walks forward.

"Did you order anything?" Nero asks me, his forehead creasing in concern.

"No." I look back at him, wide eyed. "Did you?"

"Duck!" Nero shouts and launches into motion.

I don't even get a chance to follow his command. One moment I'm standing, the next I'm sprawled on the floor under Nero's muscular body.

Before I can inhale his scent or process how I feel about his proximity, the package explodes.

At least I assume that's what happens when my universe breaks apart with a deafening bang, and scorching pain envelops my whole body.

CHAPTER TWENTY-EIGHT

REELING FROM THE VISION, I find myself back in my office.

I sprint for the door.

"I had a vision!" I scream at the top of my lungs. "A UPS woman is about to come out of our elevator and blow us up."

Nero jackknifes to his feet. As I'd suspected, he can easily hear me over the glass walls, and his truth-telling ability must make him realize this isn't some perverse trick to avoid "the talk."

"To the window," he growls at me so viciously I can't help but start to obey.

Before I turn, I spot him grabbing something from the corner of his office and sliding it over his shoulders, like a backpack.

I run to the window as fast as I can, and I hear the sound of glass shattering in Nero's path.

When I'm by the window, I look back.

Nero is moving too fast to track with the naked eye, but judging by the state of all the tiny shards of glass between his office and the elevator, he didn't bother opening any doors.

Before I can blink, he reaches his destination.

His hands turn claw-like as he half slices, half grabs the elevator doors.

Eyes widening, I watch as his fingers reach into the metal as though it were clay and turn the doors into an inoperable mess.

Okay, so the doors won't open. Will that be enough to contain the explosion?

I'm not a demolitions expert, but I have strong doubts.

Nero then whooshes at me with that same blurry speed.

I swallow my heart into my throat as Nero grabs me in a steely hug and punches out the window behind me.

Shards of glass rain down as I get an inkling of what he's about to do.

Confirming my worst fears, he tightens his hold on me and jumps out of the window.

CHAPTER TWENTY-NINE

WE FREEFALL FOR A SECOND. Then Nero rips at the shoulder of his backpack—which opens up, turning into a black parachute.

Is he into BASE jumping, or did he decide to carry a chute around after the helicopter incident?

The wind resistance slows our descent straight away—which is when the bomb finally goes off.

The bang vibrates through my inner organs and devastates my eardrums.

Glass, metal, and concrete shards rain onto us, and I pray they don't slice through the chute.

"The elevator absorbed some of the impact," Nero breathes into my ear. "I got you. You'll be okay."

His reassuring words do little to quell my shaking.

Though it might be my imagination, I think I also hear him mutter under his breath, "When I find them, whoever's behind this will wish to have never been born."

We land on top of a yellow cab, in the middle of the street.

Terrified New Yorkers look at us as though we're aliens about to seek their leaders.

A limo honks at the stupefied people, nearly running over a few before they let it through.

Nero unstraps the chute and herds me into the limo.

I let him sit me down and don't say anything when he slides the safety belt across my chest.

"She's in shock," he says sternly to Thalia. "Take her home. I'll do damage control."

"Wait," I say, desperately clawing for some semblance of sanity. "There's something I wanted to tell you. Something important."

Nero eyes me with unabashed surprise, his limbal rings out of control.

"What happened at your place can never happen again," I say. "We have to keep things professional going forward."

There. This is what he wanted in my vision, but it's less devastating if I say it myself.

At least in theory.

In practice, I'm regretting the words even as they leave my mouth.

He looks like I just struck him.

No, that must be the shock from the explosion. There's no way Nero would be hurt by my rejection—not when he'd been about to do the same thing to me.

"If that's what you really want," he mutters.

Thalia clears her throat.

"Go," Nero tells her, the bossiness returning to his voice with a vengeance. "Text me as soon as she's safely home."

Thalia does as she's told, and it takes me the whole ride home to even out my ragged breathing.

When I enter the apartment, Felix, Fluffster, and Maya greet me by the door with varying degrees of concern on their faces.

Wait, *Maya*? Oh, yeah, Felix did mention something about a lunch.

She's here because they're on a date.

"Tell us everything," Fluffster says as Felix and Maya herd me to the kitchen table and put some yummy morsels on my plate.

I recount my story, which I have to expand on for Maya.

"If Nero recovers a piece of the bomb, I might be able to tell whom it belongs to with my psychometry," Maya says when I'm done.

I give her a tired smile. "That would be great. Thank you."

"I'm not against this trip to the Otherlands anymore," Fluffster states in my head. "Given all this activity, you might actually be safer *away* from Earth."

"I agree," Felix says. "If we're lucky, Nero will find and destroy whoever is trying to kill you by the time we get back."

"I'm sorry I ruined your romantic meal." I regretfully examine the mushroom julienne and the mashed potatoes with gravy—Felix's valiant effort to get at Maya's heart through her stomach. "Let me get out of your hair."

"Oh no, please. We're just glad you're okay." Maya puts a tiny hand on my forearm.

"Yeah, don't talk nonsense," Felix says.

"I need to get some sleep anyway," I say and yawn pointedly. "Sleepless night, food coma, adrenaline slump, and all that."

They lead me to my room and fuss over me until I kick everyone out—with the exception of Fluffster.

Hugging my fuzzy domovoi to my chest, I fall into the deepest and most dreamless sleep of my life.

———

"SASHA," a familiar voice says in my mind. "You'll miss Orientation."

I open one eye, then the other.

When I check the time, I see that the voice in my head is right.

If I don't get up now, I won't make it to class in time.

"Felix warmed up the leftovers in the kitchen," Fluffster—the owner of the voice in my head—states. "Hurry."

I rush through my "morning" routine and gobble down the food as Felix and Maya look on with amusement.

Did she stay over? No, couldn't have. She has

parents who wouldn't allow such a thing, and she's not wearing the same clothes. She must be back again, and I just slept through it all.

Still, these two are spending more and more time together—which means Felix and I might need to have a talk about what I'd do to him if he manages to break her tiny heart. And maybe a vice versa talk with Maya.

Thalia is waiting downstairs. Not for the first time, I wonder if she sleeps in the car. It's feasible. A hard, austere life is like the nun's hobby.

The ride to Orientation is uneventful, and when Maya and I enter the classroom, the werewolf clique pretends I don't exist—which is probably for the best.

"You will henceforth leave Maya alone," I whisper in such a way that I hope they can hear.

Without making eye contact, they all nod.

Wow.

I could get used to this awesome power. There are so many things I could make them do, like wearing frumpy outfits or not shaving their legs for a few years.

Then again, I made a deal with Chester to leave his daughter alone, so I guess I must.

Well, actually, all I said was that I wouldn't make her fight.

Dr. Hekima walks in, and everyone quiets down.

"Today's lecture is a student favorite," he announces with a smile. "I call it 'Fantastic Beasts of the Otherlands' because we'll talk about the varied fauna you'll find beyond the gates."

"Can you say copyright violation?" I whisper to Maya.

"I know," she whispers back.

Dr. Hekima clears his throat and gives us a stern look.

I drop my gaze to the desk, and Hekima says, "First, I want you to understand my goal for today is to stimulate your imaginations and broaden your horizons." I look up to see him pacing the room. "It's impossible to even fathom the numbers of creatures you'll find in the Otherlands." He stops and looks at us, eyes gleaming. "In fact, I could probably spend a few centuries in this room just talking about the millions of animals, bacteria, and plants you've never heard of that are native to this world alone. Since we don't have that kind of time, I'll just mention a few creatures that would seem exceptionally alien to this world, and touch on some that are interesting because they feature in human mythology—no doubt because of stories shared by the pre-Mandate Cognizant."

He raises his hands and streams pulsing red energy at us.

The classroom goes away, and we find ourselves standing in a field of flowers as colorful as a rainbow.

In the middle of the field stands a majestic cow-like creature that, on second look, turns out to be so weird that the whole class collectively gasps.

Countless legs, a head that has no eyes or ears, a coat of shifting colors, tentacles—the creature looks like something only CGI or a bad LSD trip should produce.

"They're called moofts and are the most intelligent herbivores our kind has ever encountered," Hekima's disembodied voice says. "The reason I show them to you is as a cautionary tale." He appears near a mooft and looks at everyone with a sad expression. "These creatures were common on Gomorrah before our kind came and built the giant city there—and now, because they turned out to be intimately linked to their habitat, moofts are on the brink of extinction."

He walks up to the creature and points at its colorful fur-covered tentacles. "This fur isn't part of the moofts," he explains. "It's actually another creature called a looft."

As I come closer to the gentle giant, I see that indeed the thing Hekima points at is a separate being that looks like a fuzzy bracelet—and there are countless similar creatures covering each of the legs and tentacles.

"The changes in color you see are due to the loofts," Hekima explains. "They can detect the mood of their host and show it—a behavior that helps the moofts socialize. Like their hosts, these are the most intelligent symbionts I've ever heard of, but I point them out because their fate is the continuation of the same lesson: with mooft populations dwindling, the loofts are disappearing with them."

I never realized Dr. Hekima was an environmentalist, but that seems to be the case. And looking at the marvelous creatures, I myself can't help but hope they keep existing.

"I know you've never thought about this before," Dr. Hekima says sternly, "but you should know that we Cognizant are no better than humans when it comes to crimes against nature." He waves at the peaceful moofts. "Keep that in mind if you get ideas that yours is the superior people—or other eugenics nonsense."

We're back in the classroom, and I don't know about the others, but I feel humbled and bummed out in equal measures.

"But do not despair," he continues after a theatrical pause. "Some species exist in more than one world—and before you ask, no one knows why that is."

He shoots us with his power again, and the classroom gets replaced by a forest meadow... with a twenty-foot-tall tyrannosaurus rex towering over us with hunger in its beady eyes.

Though I know this is an illusion, I want to run away screaming. I didn't realize this about myself before, but I have a serious fear of getting eaten by a dinosaur. Good to know. If someone builds the Jurassic Park for real, I'm definitely not going there.

"There are worlds where creatures such as this roam," Hekima says. "And worlds where these do as well." He changes the scenery to a snowy hill with a herd of giant mammoths.

He shows us more extinct-on-Earth creatures and says that while he personally doesn't know of any other places where moofts exist, they might be out there somewhere.

"Now let's move on to some of the legendary creatures, as promised," he says and shows us a familiar-to-me giant bird. "This is a roc." He switches the scenery again to what at first looks like a herd of grazing horses—except when you look closer, you notice they each have a giant horn in the middle of their foreheads.

"Unicorns," Hekima explains. "And you've already met a drekavac," he says as he shows us the nightmarish creature.

Removing the vile thing from our view, he changes the scenery to something reminiscent of the fiery depths of hell and points at a bird that looks as if it's made from pure fire. "Now this bird features in many human myths and goes by various names such as the phoenix, the firebird, the garuda, the simorgh, the paskunji, the anka, the Me byi karmo, the zhu que, and the hō-ō."

We return to the classroom.

"The legend of the phoenix teaches us the necessity of the Mandate," Hekima says somberly. "Without it, our kind clearly couldn't help but blab about the Otherland creatures to every human they met."

To drive in his point, he proceeds to show us more fairy tale creatures, from the giant squid-like kraken to animal hybrids like the griffin.

"That is all for today," he says when we find

ourselves back in the classroom. "Does anyone have any questions?"

I raise my hand.

"Yes, Sasha," Hekima says and sneaks a peek at his watch.

"Do all these creatures have the same basic biochemistry as us?" I ask. "Do they carry their genetic information via DNA, for example?"

"With the creatures we've been able to study, we've found that they do," Hekima says. "But when it comes to something like the firebird, your guess is as good as mine."

I raise my hand again.

He looks at his watch and gives me a regretful look. "I fear that will be all for today," he says. "Why don't you save your question for next time?"

Without waiting for my reply, he beelines for the door.

The teenagers around me jump up and jubilantly stampede after him—all except for Maya.

"Lies," I say to her as she grabs her bag. "Next time, I'll have a million more questions—and he'll be in as much of a hurry as today."

"You need to chill," Maya says, slinging her bag over her shoulder. "It's like you're here to learn or something—you make the rest of us look bad."

I chuckle as we head out of the building.

"We're driving Maya home and then going to JFK airport," I tell Thalia when we get inside the limo. The nun starts typing something on her phone, so I preemptively add, "I'm going to Gomorrah to visit Ariel."

Though my voice sounds calm, my muscles are locked tight.

If Thalia sees through my lie, she'll get Nero involved, and I can kiss our epic quest goodbye.

CHAPTER THIRTY

THALIA PUTS her phone away and starts driving.

We drop off Maya and head for the highway.

Phew. We're heading for the airport, not Nero's lair.

I feast on the snacks from the limo bar and force myself to relax.

Then, for good measure, I check the future—and see myself walking toward the lab under JFK. Exiting Headspace, I blow out a relieved breath. The vision means I definitely make it there. Still, I only fully relax when I enter the lab and see Felix, Ariel, and Itzel already wearing their suits.

At least I assume that's who these people are—with the visors down, all I can see is my own reflection in the reflective golden layer.

Judging by the height, the suit that's been painted black must be Ariel—no doubt the color is to make it look more like something Batman would wear.

Another tall, suited person lifts the visor, revealing

Felix's face. "She can't hear you through the visor," he tells the black suit. "Wait until she has her helmet on."

"I'm the only one who can speak like this," says Itzel's voice from the shorter-suited person. "I have speakers on the back of my suit."

"Figures." Felix rolls his eyes.

"Leave your gun next to your friend's," Itzel says and nods toward the desk. "The force field my power creates around the suit might make the gun powder ignite inside the bullets, and you wouldn't want that."

I reluctantly leave my gun next to the one already on the desk. Somehow, I'm not surprised Ariel brought a gun to a place called Tranquility. What's surprising is that she didn't bail on this outing altogether when she learned she has to leave her Precious behind.

"Are you all ready to go?" I ask as I begin to suit up. "Do you have the map memorized? Did you eat and use the bathroom? Did you get a good night's sleep? Did you talk to your shrink? Did—"

"We're ready," Felix says with an eye roll.

"I'm excited," Ariel says inside my helmet once I have it on. "Rehab can be boring."

Felix puts his visor back down and mutters, "You mean to tell me that knitting isn't fun enough?"

"Let's hope there's not too much excitement on this trip," I say.

"I concur," Itzel says as she runs some sort of diagnostic on my suit—which causes the display portion of my visor to flicker in and out like a rebooting PC.

"Let's go," she says when the visor's display is back to normal.

"Hold on," I say. "I want to make sure we didn't forget the extra suit."

Itzel walks up to Felix and makes a circle in the air in front of his visor.

"Yes, I'm the mule, obviously," he grumbles and turns around.

On his back is a backpack-like contraption that's much larger than the ones the rest of us are wearing, and there's a helmet attached to it that makes Felix look like he has sprouted an extra head from his lower back.

"You won't even feel the weight," Itzel says and heads for the door. "None of us will."

"What if we need to eat?" I ask as we walk to the hub. "Did you bring provisions?"

"The tube on the left is food, the one on the right is water," Itzel says as we enter the hub.

I dutifully locate what she's talking about and try sipping from both.

Right away, I grimace. "Eww. It tastes like someone made cough syrup from wood chips and chalk."

"Maybe, but it will keep you alive." Itzel heads for the fateful yellow gate. "We're not going on a picnic."

"Wait a second," Ariel says. "What do we do if we need to go to the bathroom in this thing?"

"I built advanced recycling into the suit so that no moisture or nutrients are lost," Itzel says. "Just—"

"Double eww," I say. I don't even want to think about this.

"Yeah," Felix says. "I think I'd rather die of thirst and starvation before I take full advantage of this clearly overdesigned suit."

"Well, we know there will be a habitable world out there where her father is," Itzel says sagely. "The squeamish can go hungry, thirsty, and with bursting bladders and bowels until that time."

She stops next to the gate, and we all quiet down.

This is it.

We're about to go in, for real this time.

"Ladies first." Felix gallantly gestures at the plasma-like surface.

"Chicken," Ariel says and confidently steps in.

I shrug and go after her.

On the other side, everything looks exactly as it did in my vision.

"Depressing," Ariel says. "Reminds me of Six Flags in New Jersey, but after a nuclear war."

"Your words didn't do this justice," says Itzel when she shows up. "I bet it was humans who caused this—or if it was Cognizant, I bet there were no gnomes on this world."

"Damn," Felix says when he finally turns up. "Let's get out of here pronto."

Agreeing with him, we all briskly walk over the slime-covered ground until we reach the next gate, and this time, I volunteer to walk in first—this whole trip being my idea and all that.

I step out in the next Otherland cautiously and look around.

Then do a double take and look around again.

Then look up until my neck strains.

Then around again.

"Are you seeing what I'm seeing?" I ask Ariel as soon as she turns up. "I just want to make sure Itzel's tech didn't fail to filter some hallucinogen from the outside air."

"I see the horizon sloping up, instead of down," Ariel says in an awed whisper. "If that's not what you're seeing, my trip is weirder than yours."

"Wow," Felix says, joining us. "I think we're on some kind of ring world."

I know what he's talking about. Instead of a planet, we must be on a wedding-band-like structure that loops around a star—and we're standing on the inside of the band. That would explain the upward slope of the horizon.

I squint as I focus on the dimmer-than-sun star the structure is circling.

Definitely not in Kansas anymore.

"The ring has to be spinning." Felix jumps up and down. "For centrifugal forces to generate the artificial gravity here."

I jump also.

Though the suit makes it hard to gauge, I think the artificial gravity must be similar to that of Earth because the jump takes about as much effort as when we were under JFK.

Itzel comes out of the gate next, and we can hear her excited exhale as she takes it all in. "This looks like gnome engineering," she whispers. "Had I known I'd see this, I would've joined you for free."

"Is this the world the gate makers gave your kind?" Felix asks. "I thought it didn't have gates leading to it."

"No," Itzel says. "I think this was built after that, by exiled gnomes like me."

"It reminds me of those generational spaceships at the end of *Interstellar*," Ariel says. "Only bigger."

"More like the Halos in the *Halo* video games," Felix says, still awestruck. "I thought these were impossible to keep stable. Whoever built these—"

"Gnomes," Itzel says.

"You don't know for sure it was gnomes," Felix says. "I wasn't—"

"Look," Ariel hisses at him. "She's not talking about the builders of this place. She's referring to our company."

Both Felix and I tear our gazes from the sky and realize Itzel indeed wasn't talking about the gnomes who may or may not have created this thing.

She was pointing out a disturbing fact: we're surrounded by armed gnomes.

CHAPTER THIRTY-ONE

AT LEAST, I assume these are gnomes—they have features similar to Itzel's. None are wearing breathing masks, all are male, and all are trying to look fierce—and succeeding admirably.

Also, they're holding odd-looking spears instead of something more appropriate for such an allegedly technologically superior people—like ray guns. Their clothes consist of tiny loincloths made of some shiny material, and they have war paint on.

The smallest—and thus likely the oldest—of the gnome tribe shouts something in a language that sounds completely foreign to my ears and gesticulates angrily with his spear.

"It's a hodgepodge of languages," Itzel tells us. "I think he said something like, 'You shall not pass.'"

Ariel takes a step forward. "Tell Gandalf to put that stick down, or someone might get hurt."

The small gnome thrusts at Ariel with his spear, stopping a quarter inch from her chest.

"If he pierces your suit, you won't survive the trip back," Itzel warns. Putting a hand on Ariel's shoulder, she says something through external speakers.

Hearing her talk agitates the tribe more than Ariel's threatening behavior, and they narrow the circle around us, spears outthrust.

The small one shouts something, and the gnomes stop.

"He either said, 'Don't hurt the nasty beast,' or 'Don't ruin the tasty bee.'" Itzel faces me, but all I can see is the reflection of my visor in hers.

"Can you ask them what they want?" Felix says.

"I think it's obvious," Itzel replies. "They want us to come with them."

She's right. The tribe herds us toward the middle of the hub, and as soon as we start walking, they seem less ready to turn us into kebabs.

"Where did they come from?" I ask belatedly.

"I think they hid behind the gates," Ariel says. "Speaking of that, isn't that our destination gate?"

It's true. As luck would have it, we're passing by the gate that we need, but we might as well be on the other side of this world for all the good it would do us. There's no way we can run for it without ruining our suits, and maybe some internal organs too.

"My best guess is that somehow these gnomes have gone feral," Itzel says.

"What gave it away?" Felix asks sarcastically. "Was it the spears or the lack of personal hygiene?"

We pass by a ravine, and they both shut up at the sight of the mighty hunt going on there.

A giant herd of mammoths is stampeding down a grass clearing. A small band of gnomes in garb identical to our captors is chasing the poor creatures to the edge of what must be an artificial cliff.

The mammoths realize their mistake too late, and a couple of them fall off the cliff with loud thuds.

The remainder of the mammoth herd turns and stampedes toward the gnomes in a panicked gallop.

The hunters disperse. The fallen creatures must be what they were after.

The small leader of our captors screams something.

"He said, 'move it,'" Itzel says.

"We could've guessed that much," Felix grumbles.

"Then walk faster," Itzel says. "I think he also suggested they might kill one of us to show the others he means business."

Itzel's motivational speech makes us walk in a brisk jog for a while—and thanks to the suit's help, I don't feel even a fraction of the tiredness I should, given the distance we end up covering.

"These gnomes don't seem to have respiratory problems," I say as we pass a herd of grazing bison sharing the field with the mooft creatures I just learned about.

"The air outside seems to have been artificially

formulated with extra oxygen," Itzel says. "Have you not looked at your readings?"

"I was too busy worrying about survival," I tell her. "And I still am."

Glancing at the readings in question, I see that the air composition here is indeed oxygen rich. Does that mean things are more flammable on this world?

"What do you think happened here?" Felix asks when our captors force us to climb up a tall hill. "Why build something so majestic and go feral?"

"Maybe not all of them did," Itzel says. "This structure is millions of times bigger than the surface area of your Earth. There could be millions of cultures and civilizations out here, some of which may be quite different from these savages."

"Wow." My head spins at the scope of what Itzel is saying. "If you're right, that's crazy. Alternatively, could it be that most of the smart ones went into space and left the dumb ones back here?"

"Or maybe these are the descendants of some back-to-nature cult," Ariel says.

"That seems unlikely," Itzel says. "But you might have the right idea." She scratches the top of her helmet. "Maybe the rest of the gnomes made themselves artificial bodies, and these guys are the descendants of the people who refused to undergo that transition?"

No one answers because we can finally see the view from the hill, and we don't like it.

Not one bit.

There are miles and miles of metal cages with a huge assortment of animals and Cognizant inside.

I see orcs, elves, and a ton of other types I've only previously seen on Gomorrah, as well as most creatures Hekima covered in our Orientation and some I've never heard of, in addition to a bunch of Earth species such as bison and elephants.

"I wonder if this ring world was designed to be something like a Noah's Ark for the Otherlands," Felix whispers. "Somewhere in this vastness might be every creature and every Cognizant type."

"And what's this, a zoo?" Ariel asks as she scans the place.

I don't say anything, but I doubt this is a zoo.

Each person and animal is in an individual cage, and they all look way more miserable than zoo denizens usually do.

"I'm afraid the truth is much worse," Itzel says, her voice hollow. "Look there, by the edge of the cell on the left side."

I see it right away, and my insides knot in terror and disgust.

What remains of an orc female is roasting on a stick over a giant pile of coals, and a bunch of feral gnomes are munching on chunks of the poor woman's flesh.

"This is a meat storage facility," Felix says, his voice barely audible over my panicked heartbeat. "They're planning to eat us."

CHAPTER THIRTY-TWO

I FIGHT the urge to throw up and faint at the same time. "How about we fight them here and now? I'd rather have a hole in my suit than become dinner."

"Hole in the suit is the best-case scenario," Itzel says dryly. "More likely, they'll spear us to death, and we'll end up as dinner anyway."

"Even so," Ariel says, sounding as repulsed as I feel. "I'd rather go out fighting."

"Violence might not be necessary," Itzel says. "The cages look high tech, which means they can be hacked."

"Hold on," Felix says, his voice quivering. "If by high tech, you mean the tech of the people who built this ring world, what makes you think it can be hacked?"

I'm impressed he's even able to speak coherently.

Or that any of us are.

"I'm guessing the gnome builders wouldn't have bothered to create these cages," Itzel says. "It must've been some other civilization."

She's clearly distancing herself from what we saw by being over-analytical.

"You're guessing," Felix says with uncharacteristic nastiness in his tone. "That's just great. I've always wanted to risk my life based on the guessing of a *gnome*."

I want to remind Felix how psyched he was when he first heard he'd be working with a gnome, but decide against it, as it would only highlight his inexplicable dislike of Itzel specifically.

"What does my being a gnome have to do with it?" Itzel's voice turns belligerent. "You'll risk your life even more if you fight."

"Can't Sasha look into the future and tell us if we'd win the fight?" Ariel asks.

"All the *gnomes* will mess it up," Felix says, pointedly facing Itzel.

Of course. That's why I didn't see a vision of myself entering this world—the presence of all the gnomes blocks my powers.

"I think Itzel has a point," I say. "But I think we should put this to a vote."

"I vote we fight," Ariel says.

"Fine," Felix says reluctantly. "Let's give hacking a try."

"You're the deciding vote," Itzel tells me. "I obviously vote for my idea."

"I vote for the hacking," I say after a moment of consideration.

I'm always up for the sneaky solution when one is

available.

"So be it," Ariel says. "But don't come crying to me when they eat you."

We keep walking, and as we get closer to the giant meat-locker prison, it looks like Itzel was right.

The cages appear to be operated by sophisticated electronics—so much so that I wonder if these gnomes might be less feral than they seem.

Turns out they *are* as feral as they seem.

A lady gnome dressed like a shaman spots us from the distance and starts dancing next to one of the empty cages.

"That thing she's holding as a staff looks like a device to open the doors," Itzel says.

Yep.

At the end of the ceremony, the half-naked shaman lady touches the screen-like lock with the wand, and the door opens.

As our captors herd us toward it, the shaman repeats the same rigmarole with a cage for each of us.

"You better hack us out of this place," I tell Itzel as I'm pushed into my cage. "If they eat me, I'll come back as a ghost to haunt you."

"They would eat me too," Itzel says. "So you won't get to haunt me for long."

"They might not eat *you*," Felix says. "Once they take off your suit, they might see you're a gnome—and we have no evidence that they're cannibals."

"We don't?" Ariel asks. "How about that cage on your two o'clock?"

She's right.

There's a miserable and naked gnome in the cage in question—which means that either these are cannibalistic gnomes or they use the same place for prison.

With another song and dance, the shaman locks us in and leaves with the gnomes who'd captured us.

I pace my tiny cage and see Ariel and Felix doing the same.

A giant orc male in a nearby cell looks us over and says something in an unfamiliar language.

Itzel replies to him in what seems like the same tongue, and they carry on a long conversation.

"He says they ate the rest of his family," Itzel says, and I cringe, recalling the sight of the orc female we saw getting eaten a few minutes ago. "It sounds like he's a native here and just as feral as the gnomes, the only difference being that his kind live far away from here. All he wants is to get revenge on our captors. In that, he seems to be just like the orcs I've met on Gomorrah—they're all about family values and vendettas."

"I can't blame the guy," I say. "If someone killed—let alone ate—my family, I'm sure I'd also be obsessed with revenge."

"Let's focus on escape," Ariel says. "I think the bad guys are now far away enough to try."

Nodding, Itzel walks up to the lock and fiddles with it for a while. "I don't see how I can do this without taking off the gloves," she says.

"The air outside might be especially designed for your kind," Felix says. "Besides, wouldn't you rather risk microbes than end up in fellow gnomes' stomach juices?"

Moving with reluctance, Itzel takes her gloves off and waits a few moments.

"I guess I'm fine," she says. "I'm going to give this a shot."

She reaches for the lock and messes with it for a while.

A long while.

"I'm much better at creating than dealing with other people's creations," she finally mumbles in frustration. "Maybe if—"

"Crap," Ariel says. "We're about to have company."

I look at where Ariel's helmet is facing and spot a familiar group of gnomes.

"They're the ones who ate that poor orc woman," I whisper when they get closer.

The gnomes examine the denizens of the nearby cages with the same expressions I've seen on people's faces at the all-you-can-eat buffets in Vegas.

"You're kidding me, right?" Ariel says.

"No, I think this is for real," Felix says, his voice unsteady. "I'm pretty sure they're choosing their next meal."

CHAPTER THIRTY-THREE

THE GNOMES WALK UP to the cage with the vengeful orc and seem to enjoy it when he futilely tries to attack them through the bars.

When they tire of watching him, they turn their gazes to me.

Oh no. If they're in the mood for something different, with the suit, I just might end up on the menu.

"Hurry," I hiss at Itzel. "What's taking you so long?"

"I told you before," she replies, her hands shaking. "I have trouble working under stress."

Grunting, Felix takes off his gloves and walks up to the mechanism.

"Silicon chips," he mumbles after the longest minute of my life. "Maybe if I—"

I don't hear the rest, my attention split between the gnomes outside my cage and the arc of magical energy going from Felix's finger to the lock.

The lock makes a chirping sound, and Felix's cage opens.

"Now do that orc," Ariel says tensely.

"Or better yet, all the cages at once," I say.

More energy streams from Felix's fingers, and the lock in the orc's cage shimmers—as does the lock in mine and all the ones in the neighboring cages.

"Never send a gnome to do a technomancer's job," Felix says triumphantly when all the cages open as one.

The freed orc jumps onto the nearest gnome and rips into him.

Ariel steps out of her cage, grabs a gnome, and tosses him at the rest.

The suit must greatly amplify her already-prodigious strength because the gnome fells his crew like a battering ram, causing screams of pain and severe injuries.

I see a bunch of armed gnomes racing toward us. "Run!" I shout.

My friends gladly comply, and we all scramble toward the hill we came from.

There are nightmarish screams behind us, and when I sneak a peek back, I see many former captives taking out their frustrations on the gnome gourmands.

As we keep running, Ariel takes the lead, and Itzel and Felix stay on my heels.

The suit lets me run much faster than I'd be able to do on my own, and when we reach the top of the hill, I spare another look back—and almost wish I didn't.

A whole squad of spear-carrying gnomes is behind

us—though it's unclear if they're chasing us or escaping their unwilling food stash.

"Head for the grass!" I yell, pointing at the waist-high brush at the bottom of the hill. "Our suits are powered; their legs are not."

Everyone follows my suggestion, and we find ourselves treading through the grass before our pursuers get off the hill.

When we're almost out of the bush, a spear whooshes by my shoulder.

"Crap," I pant. "They're getting pissy."

Another spear nearly pierces Ariel's foot and yet another almost hits Felix in the back, where it could've ruined not one but two suits.

"Itzel," I bark. "Shoot your lightning at the grass."

Her gloves still off, Itzel turns and does as I ordered. "I'm not getting paid enough for this," she chants under her breath, over and over, like a magic spell.

The mere sight of Itzel's projectile seems to silence our pursuers—that is, until the ball of plasma hits the grass and the oxygen-rich air helps the cellulose ignite like jet fuel.

"Felix, don't look back," I say as the first screams of burning gnomes reach us.

"How come these gnomes didn't shoot the same ball lightning stuff at us?" Ariel asks over panting breaths. "Not that I'm complaining, mind you."

"Their parents must not have taught them this, or anything else for that matter," Itzel says sadly. "All part of this horrific degeneration."

"Why don't we shelve discussions for when we're out of this hellhole?" Felix suggests. He then mutters a string of Russian curses before saying tersely, "More freaking gnomes ahead."

Ariel curses too, unwittingly translating what Felix just said.

At least a hundred armed dudes are streaming down a hill ahead, screaming at the top of their lungs.

"We can make it," I say breathlessly. "Follow me."

I push myself to the limit, squeezing as much speed out of my suit's motors and my own muscles as I can.

We zoom by the foot of the hill and leave the new group behind us, but they give chase.

A spear flies at Ariel.

She snatches it from the air and tosses it back.

The projectile goes straight through one gnome and skewers the next.

Wow.

Score two for Ariel's super-strength combined with the suit.

The gnomes must be equally impressed with what happened, because they slow down—which gives us the window we need to race for the gate and leap into it just as another round of spears flies our way.

CHAPTER THIRTY-FOUR

WE JUMP out on the other side and keep running. All I register at first is that the grass under my feet is green, and the sky has a yellow tint to it.

Then I see a purple gate—our destination—in the distance and realize that this hub is huge, with gates spread far apart. Luckily, each stride makes me fly through the air as though the suit's usual assistance has doubled in power.

"Weaker gravity here," Felix says as he takes giant leaps beside me.

"Shut up and keep running for that gate," Ariel says. "Gnomes are Cognizant and just as capable of traversing the gates as each of us."

"Except they didn't follow us," Itzel says, glancing over her shoulder. "I wonder why?"

I slow down and glance around.

The hub appears to be in a giant meadow, with a lush forest surrounding it on all sides.

Felix, Ariel, and Itzel come to a complete halt.

"Are you seeing what I'm seeing?" Ariel says, her helmet swiveling to the right.

I stop and follow her gaze.

No wonder the gnomes didn't chase us here.

Coming toward us is a creature the size of a truck, its dozens of legs shuffling back and forth like brushes at a car wash.

CHAPTER THIRTY-FIVE

"IS THAT A—" Felix starts in a horrified tone.

"Giant millipede, yes," Ariel says, sounding choked. "And I don't even want to know what the spiders here look like."

"You might find out," I say, staring at a bee-like creature the size of a helicopter that just landed on what looks like a giant fishnet between two dead trees.

"We should go around," Felix says as the millipede picks up speed. "It's coming right for us."

In that moment, an entire horde of giant insects appears from the forest, including a spider the size of Shelob—the one that almost ate Frodo in *The Lord of the Rings*.

Itzel mumbles something unintelligible about square-cube law under her breath, but I don't pay attention because that's when the screech reaches my ears.

Or more precisely, my bones.

The deep sound vibrates through me, shaking every cell in my body.

The millipede's legs blur with speed, and the bee frantically beats its wings, futilely trying to escape the sticky web.

And that's when I feel the ground shake.

Is this an earthquake? A volcanic eruption?

No.

It's what all these creatures are escaping from.

"Jump!" Ariel screams, and I realize the millipede is almost upon us.

We leap into the air, and the nifty gravity works with the suit assist to give us a jump worthy of Super Mario.

The millipede whooshes past us before we land back down.

As one, we face the fleeing horde of insects, and I see what they're running from.

It's an enormous dinosaur.

The creature is easily the size of Godzilla but looks more like a mix between a T-Rex and an ostrich.

As we watch in stunned shock, it casually shreds an RV-sized ant into little pieces, then snatches a couple of giant flies from the air, gobbling them down without even bothering to chew.

Then its radio-dish-sized eyes land on us.

"It must like shiny things," Felix says, his voice shaking. "That or something else about us looks appetizing."

As though in agreement with his words, the monstrosity heads our way.

CHAPTER THIRTY-SIX

"I'M SERIOUSLY NOT GETTING PAID ENOUGH for this," Itzel says in a panicked tone as she resumes running toward the purple gate.

Felix, Ariel, and I follow, taking giant leaps with each step.

I take the lead over my friends as the ground shakes more violently with each second.

When I'm a stone's throw away from the gate, everyone shouts something unintelligible inside my helmet.

Instinctively, I duck, and the huge claw reaching for me passes through the purple gate.

A chunk of the claw disappears, sliced off by the gate's plasma-like surface.

Right. The gates don't let this type of creature travel to other worlds—a smart design feature on the gate makers' behalf.

The pained screech of the monster is so loud that

the air pushes me closer to the gate—and I jump in as a river of blood from the severed claw sprays my way.

My blood-splattered friends land on the other side of the gate next to me, and we all stop, panting in relief as we look around.

We're standing on a patch of rocky ground between puddles of boiling yellow liquid, with smears of green and orange on their sides. They remind me of pools of acid in a geothermal park—except this park stretches as far as the eye can see.

The sky above is dark gray, as if a storm is coming, and the air appears to have a pinkish tint to it.

I take a step toward the next gate and feel a little lightheaded.

"Hold your breath and hurry," Itzel says, jumping over a puddle as she breaks into a run. "I don't know if the field I generated around these suits can withstand the exotic bouquet of toxins on this world."

I launch into a sprint as well, doing my best not to gulp in panicked breaths.

When we reach the destination gate, we all jump in.

CHAPTER THIRTY-SEVEN

IT'S night time on the world we end up in, with faint light from four differently sized moons illuminating a flat, whitish surface. It looks like a salt desert, with the crystals gleaming serenely in the moonlight.

"Now what?" Itzel asks.

Felix turns toward her. "Can you walk away from us? Sasha could then get a vision of what happens in our near future and—"

"No," Ariel says sternly. "It's too dangerous. We stay together."

"You don't want me to go, anyway," Itzel says. "These suits might need my power boost at any moment."

The brightest of the four moons dims for a second, catching my attention.

"Are you seeing that?" I wave at the sky. "Please tell me it's a cloud."

Before my friends can reply, I see that it is *not* a cloud.

Either the toxins from the prior world have powerful hallucinogenic side effects, or I'm looking at tentacles.

An impossibly large, ghostly squid-like thing is floating in the sky.

"Please don't let this be the Cognizant type that inspired Lovecraftian horrors," Felix says tremulously.

"Afraid so." Ariel's voice matches his. "It looks a lot like Cthulhu."

"Run," I say and put actions to words as salt crunches under my feet. "Our gate is just over—"

And this is when the mental assault—for lack of a better term—hits my brain.

CHAPTER THIRTY-EIGHT

THINKING BECOMES IMPOSSIBLE, and I stop, swaying on my feet.

The terrible noise reminds me of when Fluffster mentally shouted at Harper, the succubus who tried to kill me and Felix. Like that time, this sounds like death metal played backward and in slow motion—just a zillion times more intense.

I feel insignificant. Like an amoeba facing an angry elephant.

Fighting the desire to fall down and curl into a little ball, I ball my fists instead and take a step.

"I can't do this." Itzel's voice doesn't sound like her own. "I'm done. You go. Save yourselves."

Wow. The mental assault is affecting a gnome—beings immune from vampire glamour and things like that. What chance do our unprotected minds have?

"Shut up," Felix grits out, grabbing Itzel's arm. "Just

think of building some gadget or getting paid more, and keep moving."

He drags Itzel step after shuffling step, and they pass through the gate.

Faintly, I feel my seer intuition ring a distant alarm —just as the intensity of the mental assault grows exponentially.

My legs buckle under the onslaught, and I realize that this is it.

Whatever the thing in the sky wants, it's about to do to me.

"Oh no, you don't," Ariel shouts and gives me a rough push in the butt region of my suit.

As I fly into the gate, I hear her say, "See you on the other side."

I prepare to faceplant on the ground but float into a liquid instead, my feet sinking down into something solid.

This must be an ocean floor or the bottom of some sea because everything outside the faint glow of my suit is pitch black.

The only thing I can make out is Itzel and Felix, thanks to their suits' illumination, and the glowing plasma gate at my back.

"Where's Ariel?" Felix asks, his helmet swiveling from side to side.

"She should be out any second," I say.

But several seconds pass without Ariel appearing.

"Damn it," I say and take a clumsy step toward the gate. "I'm going back after her."

CHAPTER THIRTY-NINE

I CROSS the gate back into the sky creature's world and see Ariel walking away from the gate and toward a skyscraper-sized tentacle.

Ignoring my seer angst with all my might, I grab Ariel by her arm and drag her back.

She doesn't fight me, but the devastating mental attack explodes in my head again—and I'm not sure if I can take it.

On a hunch, I bite my tongue.

The pain keeps the mental shrieking at bay long enough for me to drag Ariel another step toward the gate.

But on the next step, I find it harder. The shrieking is growing in volume, and I feel like my brain is about to explode.

If I lose this fight, Ariel and I will hold hands as we skip right into that thing's mouth—and it's almost a certainty that I will lose before reaching the gate.

Suddenly, I hear a string of multilingual curses in my helmet and feel someone's hand grab my arm.

I clutch Ariel and let myself get herded into the gate.

As I'm recovering my wits in the watery depths of the new world, Felix lets go of my arm. "Are you okay?" he asks.

"Fine," I lie.

"I blanked out," Ariel says in a sleepy voice. "The last thing I remember is pushing Sasha into the gate."

"That creature must've broken into your mind," Itzel says. Under her breath, she adds, "I'm *so* not getting paid enough for this."

Felix faces the gnome. "Will our suits be okay with all this water?"

"The pressure is tolerable, and I'm not detecting any toxicity outside," Itzel says. "We should still get moving, though. I didn't design our oxygen tanks to resupply themselves from water."

She doesn't need to ask us twice. We head to where the gate should be, according to the map. We can't see it in the darkness, though.

Moving under water is extremely slow and nerve-racking, and my mind conjures up giant sharks and underwater sea monsters.

In my defense, after seeing a tentacled monstrosity in the sky, expecting one in this water is quite reasonable.

We've taken fewer than twenty steps when I see a cloud of tiny lights swimming toward us.

Crap.

I just had to jinx us with my imagination, didn't I?

"I assume everyone remembers that scene from *Finding Nemo*," Felix says, speeding up. "I doubt we'll like whatever those pretty lights are attached to."

"I have no idea what you're talking about," Itzel says, but like the rest of us, she doubles her clumsy steps.

The lights are coming closer.

"I hate it when Felix is right," Itzel says, swatting at a light that tries to attack her.

Whatever she swatted must've gotten hurt—because the light falls to the bottom.

A light dives in my direction, and I punch the creature just as I glimpse it.

It looks like it was designed by Hollywood's horror film CGI experts on acid. Its teeth seem to have warts, and the warts seem to have teeth. Something this ugly can only exist in these lightless depths. If the males and females of this fish ever saw each other in daylight, they would refuse to propagate the species.

Another monstrosity dives at my helmet.

Using the move Thalia drilled into me, I punch the thing in what I'll generously call its face.

Something cracks, and the broken thing floats down.

The deaths of their brethren don't scare the other monstrosities. Like sharks scenting blood, they dive for us in a killing frenzy.

I swat, punch, and kick, and so does everyone else.

The ocean floor around us starts to look like the night sky with all the lights lying around.

My arms are aching from swatting by the time we finally make out the shimmer of the gate.

We redouble our monster-hitting efforts, and when there's a lull in their attack, we speed into the gate.

CHAPTER FORTY

THERE'S no water on the other side, and it's bright—so bright that even with the visor, the sudden change momentarily blinds me.

When my eyes adjust, I see that our surroundings look like the inside of an active volcano—except even the sky is on fire.

Is this the firebird's home world or the inspiration for the descriptions of fiery hells?

Whatever the answer, I break into a run, and so do my friends.

"We need to move faster, or we'll risk igniting," Itzel gasps out, taking the lead.

Ariel and I overtake her and leap into the next gate just as my skin starts to burn.

Felix and Itzel join us a moment later, with Itzel berating herself for ever agreeing to help us and Felix panting inside the helmet like a dog.

As I catch my breath, I look around warily. This is

the last world before we reach our destination, so with our luck, it might be the most dangerous.

Not spotting any immediate danger, I begin walking.

Our surreal surroundings look strangely familiar.

There's a silver Grand Canyon-like mountain ridge in the distance that I could swear I've seen before, and same goes for the alien star formations in the sky. Ditto for the seven differently shaded moons.

When I see the magnificent aurora borealis, it finally clicks. "Nero has a painting of this place hanging in his office," I say, picking up speed as I head for our destination, the blue gate.

"He's clearly been here," Felix says, matching my stride. "Which isn't surprising, seeing how it's his map we've been following."

"Does that mean it's a safe world?" Itzel asks, taking the lead again. "I mean, would anyone stop to paint a landscape if it wasn't?"

"Nero might," Ariel says. "For all we know, he can waltz through the worlds we just passed without breaking a sweat. Maybe even the fiery one."

"Right." Felix slows down and looks my way. "Nero might be able to, but what about Rasputin? Did he also use a space—"

We don't hear what Felix says over the booming roar that shakes every root of my hair.

We break into a sprint.

Images of giant bear-dinosaur hybrids flit through my head, but as I throw a panicked glance over my shoulder, I spot something bird-like in the light of the aurora.

Whatever it is, it's massive, and it's diving for us.

I speed up.

The roar feels nearer.

I push the suit and my muscles to their limits once again.

When we're a few feet away from the blue gate, the roar shakes the ground once more, and—though it could be my adrenaline-overloaded imagination—I could swear there are human words embedded in the sound.

Ariel jumps into the gate, with Itzel and Felix following.

I'm about to follow them when I feel my seer intuition go into high gear. Almost on autopilot, I reach for Headspace.

———

FINDING MYSELF FLOATING WITHOUT A BODY, I congratulate myself on accessing Headspace under the most extreme circumstances yet.

When I metaphorically look around, not surprisingly, I find myself surrounded by shapes that exude music worthy of a Halloween soundtrack.

Not good.

Something truly awful must be about to happen, even worse than cannibal gnomes or the Godzilla-sized dinosaur—since I didn't get any warnings those times.

No, wait. That could've been Itzel's fault. Her nature messes with my powers. And since she left this Otherland, my powers finally got a chance to help me out.

Come to think of it, I felt a faint warning on the sky-squid world, too. It's just that the mental attack the monster hit me with made it impossible to go into Headspace.

All right. The good news is that it worked this time.

I wonder what it is that's chasing me. Another giant dinosaur, like a pterodactyl but much bigger? Or is this the legendary roc—the bird that Kit turned herself into on Buyan and that Hekima showed us at the most recent Orientation?

Actually, since birds are the descendants of dinosaurs, those two options pretty much boil down to the same thing.

Almost.

In any case, maybe this is the danger my visions are warning me about.

I examine the shapes in question and can't help but notice how unnaturally homogenous they all are. A lot like the time when I was trying to crack Nero's safe using my powers.

If I'm right, my best bet might be to see all these visions at once, just like I did on that day, and hope that one will contain the information I need to save myself.

Thus determined, I reach out to all of them at once and prepare for a bunch of visions in a row.

———

A TALON RIPS into my suit from the back, slices through me, and exits from the front with a fountain of blood.

It happens so fast I don't even get a chance to turn and see what did it. I just experience the mother of all pains in my chest, hear a bone-shattering crunch, and then my ripped-apart heart stops beating as I promptly die.

———

I TILT my body an inch to the left—and this time, when a talon rips into me, I get to feel the horrific pain for an extra second before I perish.

———

I TWIST my body even further to the left.

The talon still rips into the suit. I just get even more agony for my efforts.

———

A HUNDRED NEARLY IDENTICAL visions follow—the

only variables being how much I move left, how severe the pain is, and how quick my demise.

Then another set of visions follow, all identical to the first batch with only one difference—I try moving to the right this time, with the same results.

————

I FALL to the ground and roll a few inches to the right, then a few to the left. A claw pierces the ground but misses my torso by half an inch.

The roar sounds angry this time, but I ignore it, twisting my body once more before I leap to my feet and jump successfully into the gate—

————

I WITNESS a hundred visions where I fall to the ground, but roll the wrong number of inches to the right or to the left—with a deadly result each time.

————

I BACK AWAY FROM the gate—and right into a talon that rips into my back.

There's a searing pain in my chest, then blackness—

————

I'M BACK OUTSIDE HEADSPACE, in my body—at least my intuition tells me that I am.

My still-beating heart is hammering against my chest as I prepare to execute the only set of actions that might save me.

CHAPTER FORTY-ONE

I FALL to the ground and pray that my rolling is just the right number inches to the right.

When I find that I'm still alive, I roll a few inches to the left—again hoping against all hope that it's just the right number of inches.

The claw pierces the ground half an inch from my torso.

Yes!

The angry roar is music to my ears as I twist my body and leap to my feet.

Triumphantly, I jump into the gate—smack into Ariel's back.

"I'm alive," I mumble, over and over. "You guys, I'm alive."

"I doubt that will last long." Ariel steps away so I can see where we are. "We may want to go back."

My breath catches as I look around.

She's right.

If we stay here, we're toast.

CHAPTER FORTY-TWO

DESPITE THE MORTAL danger facing us, our surroundings are beautiful—especially the flying island that takes center stage among the clouds. No doubt supported by powerful magnetic fields—or magic—the floating chunk of rock would feel at home in the movie *Avatar*, especially if one ignores the medieval castle perched on its surface.

The castle looks like it was designed by the same architect as the one where the NYC Council meets, only scaled up to skyscraper size and painted crimson red.

Oh, and speaking of that color, there's a red river cascading from the floating island onto the ground. It looks like a literal river of blood, but I'm hoping it's just iron-rich rain water.

The ground we're all standing on has a reddish tint as well. At least I assume it's the ground. For all I know,

I'm standing on a floating island that stretches to every horizon.

"Are you gawking at our surroundings?" Ariel asks sternly. "We have to decide; do we go back into the gate or not?"

Her words refocus me on our impossible situation: an army that surrounds us on all sides.

I spot archers and swordsmen among them, but the majority look like the monks who work for the Council—except these guys are holding wooden staffs.

Every single man is staring at us with warlike ferocity, but I still hope they mean us no harm. That bubble bursts in the next moment.

The archers shoot a cloud of arrows our way.

We break into a run, and the arrows pepper the ground behind us, barely missing our suits.

"I think they're herding us away from the gate," Felix pants as he slows down.

"That's fine." I swallow my heart back into my chest. "We don't want to go back. The thing in the previous world is worse than this lot."

"I say we attack the monks," Ariel says and takes the lead. "The archers might be reluctant to shoot if we're close to their brothers in arms. We could fight our way to some other gate, jump into another world, and regroup from there."

"That might work," Felix says uncertainly. "I mean, how much damage can someone do with those sticks?"

That must cinch the deal for Ariel, because she

picks up her pace, heading right for the thousand monks that separate us from the nearest gate.

"Wait, let's analyze this further," Itzel says, but it's too late.

Ariel charges ahead with a fierce cry that only we can hear inside our helmets.

"That's that," I say and follow Ariel—who smashes into the sea of monks like a bowling ball into a rack of pins.

Four monks are knocked down right away. Another monk tries to hit Ariel with his staff, but she catches it mid-swing and crushes it into woodchips with her hand.

Seeing what happened to his weapon, the monk retreats—but not fast enough. Ariel kicks him, and he flies into the others, knocking them over.

"The sword guys are heading for every nearby gate," Itzel complains. "We need a new plan."

Ignoring the gnome, I pick a monk at random and punch him in the face.

The monk drops like a sack.

Damn, I love the boost the suit gives me. Also, Nero had better give Thalia a big raise for all the fight training.

A staff crashes into my helmet from the back—but all it does is irritates my ears with the resulting noise.

This fight might not be as hopeless as I feared.

Another staff rams into my shoulder, and that hurts, bringing my expectations back to earth.

Felix yells something, and I turn to see him tossing two monks to the ground.

Even Itzel is fighting now. She grabs a monk by his staff, rips it out of his hands, and bashes him on the head with it.

I kick one monk, punch another, then suck in a breath and rattle out, "Itzel, I assume the suits can't protect us from an arrow or a sword slice, right?"

"That's right," the gnome huffs. "They can't."

Then we're screwed, I realize as a staff slams into my midsection.

Gasping for breath, I punch the guy responsible, then dodge a staff-to-ankle attack—only to get hit on the shin two seconds later.

Definitely screwed.

Suddenly, someone blows a horn, and the monks in front of us scatter, as if to make way for reinforcements.

I wonder why they'd bother. They're probably minutes away from beating us to death with their staffs, and that's assuming the archers and the swordsmen don't get tired of watching passively and turn us into kebabs.

To my surprise, a single man is coming toward us. He's also dressed like a monk, but he's taller and much paler than the others. His robes are fancier, and he walks with the authority of a cardinal—which is what I mentally dub him.

Facing us, he says something in a foreign language and looks at us expectantly.

"Sounds like Hebrew," Itzel says. "But not one that's currently spoken. The H sound is throatier, like in Arabic and Maltese, and—"

"Thanks for the linguistics lesson," Felix says. "How about you tell us what he actually said?"

"I think it was 'heed my words, you false gods from hell,'" Itzel says. "Or something along those lines."

We all face the monk to show him that we're listening, and Itzel even says something in what sounds like a similar language through her external speaker.

Everyone but the big-shot monk steps back.

The cardinal theatrically raises his arms to the sky and says something else.

"The one true god is Lilith," Itzel translates. "Blessed be her name."

"Lilith?" Ariel says. "Why does that sound familiar?"

"I've heard her mentioned during a couple of Orientation lessons," I say, racking my brain for the details.

"Oh yeah," Ariel says.

"Right," Felix says. "She's a powerful Cognizant who once lived on the Otherland known as Earth," he says in a great imitation of Hekima's professorial tone. "She took over a world to force the humans there to worship her as a god, thus boosting her powers beyond—"

"That was it," I say. "Also, if I recall correctly, she has rare double powers—a vampire and a probability manipulator, I think it was."

"There was also the part about her being a jealous

god," Felix says. "Which might explain the welcoming committee by the gates. I doubt she likes other Cognizant showing up here."

The cardinal shouts something else at us as I examine the army with a new appreciation.

Yep. Those expressions can be explained by religious fanaticism—and that reduces our already poor chances of survival to zero if we continue to fight.

"Follow my lead," I say to the others.

Falling to my knees, I raise my arms toward the flying castle and shake them with what I hope looks like religious fervor.

Boy, do I wish Itzel wasn't here so I could use my powers to see how this will play out.

Though they don't move with as much enthusiasm as I fake, my friends mime my movements while complaining in their helmets the entire time.

The cardinal stops his tirade and looks at us with unabashed curiosity—as do the soldiers and the monks.

"Itzel," I hiss. "Tell him we came here on a pilgrimage to honor the mighty goddess Lilith, the one and only true god." I'm glad the visor hides my expression from the cardinal. I can't suppress a mischievous grin as I get into the spirit of my deception. "*She's* been recognized as the goddess among us, false gods, and though we're not worthy, before we are cast back into hell, we'd like to see her with our plebian eyes so that we can bask in the glory of her light."

"So that we can talk to *her* instead of her fanatical followers," Felix chimes in dryly.

"Don't translate Felix's part," I say just in case. "But that's the idea, yeah."

"I'm not sure that's such a great plan," Ariel says, but Itzel must like it more than our prior plan of fighting to the death, because she starts translating my words.

Given the cardinal's expression, my plan might actually work—at least part one, getting an audience.

With great pompousness, the cardinal says something to us.

"You must be bound," Itzel translates. "Like the beasts that you are."

"I really don't like this," Ariel says.

"This at least gives us a chance," Itzel says. "A single nick of an arrow or stab with a sword would mean we can't go back. Lilith is a Cognizant. Hopefully, she remembers that she's not really a god and will at least hear us out. Maybe we can somehow reason with her."

The cardinal yells at his minions, and four monks walk out of the crowd, holding ropes. One pantomimes putting our hands behind our backs, and I volunteer to comply first.

When he starts binding my wrists, I tense up and wonder if this was a grave mistake.

The others are tied up next; then the cardinal barks out a few orders and leaves the way he came.

The monks lead us through the crowd, and as they do, even Ariel must see the futility of our earlier fight.

There are literally thousands of soldiers here—and

behind the army, countless people are kneeling, no doubt worshiping Lilith.

We continue toward the floating island, and near the bank of the let's-hope-not-literally-blood river, I spot something Hekima just showed us at Orientation: giant birds of the roc variety.

Was this what attacked me on the previous world? Though huge, these birds don't seem nearly large enough. Then one of the birds produces a mighty squawk, and I become certain this isn't the culprit.

The roar I heard was completely different from this.

"The birds have saddles, like horses," Felix says warily.

"Do you see a ladder up to the castle?" Itzel asks him sarcastically. "Or did you expect to take an elevator?"

They bicker as the monks place us into the saddles and climb up behind each of us.

With a flap of giant wings, we launch into the air.

Wow.

Despite our prisoner status, I can't help but gawk at our surroundings.

I had the right idea earlier. What seemed like the ground turns out to be a floating island that's much bigger than our destination. It also appears to be some sort of pilgrimage destination for the citizens of this world, because all space not taken up by the army is covered by the kneeling people, their hands outstretched toward the red castle.

The magician in me is impressed with the scope of

Lilith's deception. She's no god. She's just a vampire like Vlad and a trickster like Chester, yet she was able to convince a whole Otherland of her divinity.

Then again, as a magician, I might be able to pull off the same feat even without my seer powers—provided I weren't the pillar of morality and ethics that I am. It would especially be easy in a less technologically advanced society like this.

As we approach the clouds, I daydream of performing fake miracles of all sorts to convince everyone of my godhood: from making tigers teleport from place to place to cutting people in half and then proving they're fine.

Yep. If I ripped off David Copperfield and Criss Angel's repertoires and threw in some real prognostications, I'd be worshiped as a goddess in no time.

But alas, as fun as that would be, I wouldn't do such a thing. Probably because, unfortunately, I'm not a sociopath.

I'm jolted back into the reality of the flight when we hit a patch of turbulence—though this could've also been caused by one of the bird's bodily functions… hopefully a sneeze.

There are some clouds around us, but they have gaps that allow me to see into the far distance. I spot more floating islands, a red-tinged ocean crisscrossed by large wooden ships, and a huge city that looks like how I've always pictured Camelot.

When we get higher, the clouds become less see-through, forcing me to focus my attention of our immediate surroundings.

There are dozens of people flying on the birds. Some of them are soldiers with their rocs wearing armor, and some are monks with less fanciful rides.

"What would be the collective noun for a group of roc birds?" Felix asks. "A brood?"

"That's for chickens," Itzel says. "I think it should be called a colony, like penguins, or a gaggle, like geese."

"A group of quail is called a bevy," Ariel chimes in. "Don't ask me how I know that."

"How about a murder, like crows?" I suggest. "Or a siege, like herons? Wouldn't that be more apropos given the rocs' fierce looks?"

"If we're just showing off, a group of finches is called a charm," Itzel rattles out. "While a bunch of pheasants is a nye." She inhales and adds, "A group of hawks is a cast, snipes a wisp, owls a parliament, swallows a flight, and—"

"Please stop," Felix says. "Let's just pretend that rocs are not social birds and never flock together; thus no one has bothered to name a group of them anything beyond 'a bunch of rocs.'"

Since we're already landing, I resist the urge to point out that we're about to step on a different 'bunch of rocks.'

When the monks yank us off the birds' backs, we recall our uncertain fate, and the banter ceases.

The captors lead us through the castle, and the

weirdness and opulence of the décor takes everyone's breath away.

First, we're shepherded into a botanical-gardens-sized display of what looks like carnivorous plants.

The next hall is clearly meant to serve as a zoo. It's full of predatory creatures: some from Earth, some mentioned by Hekima, and most I've never seen before.

An art gallery is next, with paintings, frescoes, and statues depicting bloody battles and sacrifices.

"What is she a god of? War? Blood? Death?" Felix asks when we enter the next room—one with such a huge selection of mummified remains of people and creatures that the folks at *The Bodies* exhibit might kill and mummify themselves out of jealousy.

"Let's just hope she hates all Cognizant equally," Ariel grumbles. "If she has a necromancer on staff, I give up right here and now."

I have to agree. If we'd fought Beatrice in *this* room, we'd have lost for sure.

The monks stop next to massive floor-to-ceiling doors made out of some reddish metal.

Two cardinals—each a seeming clone of the other—are standing on each side. They wave the monks away. Then, with maximum pompousness, they open the doors and gesture for us to go in.

Screams of either pain or extreme ecstasy emanate from within.

Mentally psyching myself to face a bloodthirsty goddess, I walk in.

CHAPTER FORTY-THREE

LIKE MOST OF THE CASTLE, this movie-theater-sized room has walls of red stone that look like they're sweating blood. I guess if it were a king's castle, this would be the throne room. To me, however, it looks like Christian Grey's Red Room of Pain on major steroids—thanks to all the whips, canes, chains, and crosses with naked people attached to them.

Beautiful naked people.

Equally beautiful are the few men and women who are using the various implements on each other. Same goes for the vast majority who are on their knees, prayer style. Some are wearing skimpy clothes and some nothing at all. As one, their eyes turn to us, and that is when I see *her*.

That is, assuming that's a woman. My eyes perceive a being of such beauty that the sight overloads my brain with both pleasure and pain.

The word "divine" swirls through my mind, and I

have difficulty gazing upon her without giving in to the desire to fall to my knees like the rest of the scantily clad worshippers.

If I were to take all the emotions I'd experienced when staring at a moving painting or a gorgeous animal or a postcard-like view of nature and cram them into one moment, that might approximate what the being before me is making me feel.

"How?" Felix whispers in awestruck fascination. "Is she *actually* a goddess?"

No one answers. We watch as a tall man walks up to Lilith, kneels, and tilts his head to the side, exposing his neck.

She bends over and rips into his neck, and somehow, even this brutal act has an otherworldly beauty to it.

The guy moans loudly in pleasure, then collapses on the floor.

"The addict in me doesn't perceive her as a vampire," Ariel says, her voice distant. "Usually, I'd already be thinking about my fix."

I make a mental note to keep Ariel as far away from the pseudo goddess's blood as possible.

Lilith finally looks in our direction—and begins to float off the ground.

I wish I didn't have my wrists bound or the visor down—because I need to rub my eyes.

"Are you also seeing what I'm seeing?" Ariel sounds as overwhelmed as I feel.

"If you mean seeing something that looks like an angel fly, then yes," Felix answers in a choked voice.

"No, more like a fertility goddess," Ariel says. "Or a—"

I tune them out, unable to tear my eyes from the majestic being in flight.

There are no wires that I can see, nor any other methodology to explain her gravity-defying feat. If I'm right about the lack of wires, the magician in me will be extremely disappointed with this turn of events. That would be like finding out that the Wizard of Oz was actually a wizard and not the man behind the curtain.

"She's just a powerful vampire," Itzel says without due awe in her voice. "They can all do glamour; hers is just more potent."

"So she's not flying?" I ask, remembering that gnomes are immune to things like glamour. "We're just seeing that?"

"No, she *is* flying," Itzel says. "Some of the oldest and most powerful of the vamps can gain that power, and this one has power in spades." Itzel looks up at the approaching creature. "She just doesn't look like an angel or a goddess, or whatever it is you're seeing. All *I* see is a typical-for-her-kind paleness, pitch-black hair, and symmetrical face. Her only distinctive feature is a tattoo on her right temple. The one that looks like a parenthesis sitting on top of a plus sign. She must be really into mathematics."

A parenthesis sitting on top of a plus sign? That sounds like the beginnings of an emoji.

I strain to see what Itzel is talking about but fail utterly. All I make out is a vague outline radiating sacredness—for lack of a better term.

Lilith starts to speak, and the sounds she produces do to my ears what her looks are doing to my eyes. I don't want her to ever stop talking. It's like heavenly harps playing all of my favorite music.

The urge to fall to my knees and worship intensifies. I stiffen my leg muscles and remind myself that this is just glamour.

"She demands to know what and who we are," Itzel informs us.

"Let me come up with a good tale," I say, wishing I actually had a plan. Still, when it comes to bamboozling a god, I have the best chance out of the four of us. "To start, tell her we're all gnomes, not just you."

Itzel says something, and the heavenly sound repeats.

"She said she's familiar with my kind and is glad our hands are tied behind our backs," Itzel says. "She also demands to know if I speak other languages because, and I quote, 'We don't want to pollute the divine tongue with your heretical ravings.'"

"See if she can speak Russian or English," I suggest. "She lived on Earth at some point, so there's a chance of that."

Itzel translates.

"I speak both," Lilith replies in strangely accented English, and the power of her divine voice impacts me even more now that I can understand what she's saying. "But I will speak thusly as that minimizes the odds we might be overheard and understood."

My pulse jumps with excitement.

She's concerned about being overheard and understood by someone who speaks Russian. Could it be that she's worried about my father glimpsing this exchange in a vision? Then again, isn't she a probability manipulator and thus able to shield herself from seer visions? Unless she figures we, as gnomes, will mess with her power? But that cuts both ways and would make Rasputin's vision just as impossible—but perhaps she only knows about gnome effects on her power, not on the others?

"I think she wants to speak another language so that her worshippers don't understand our conversation," Felix says. "Oh, and tell her that her English is great."

Itzel does as Felix suggests before I can remind her that I'm the one who's supposed to be doing the talking —using Itzel as my mouthpiece, that is, since she's the only one of us with an external speaker.

"Flattery won't get you anywhere, gnome," Lilith says. "Explain why you have come before I smite you."

"Tell her the four of us were born with exceptionally bad respiratory problems, even for gnome kind," I say quickly. "Tell her it's so bad that if we were to take off these suits, we'd suffocate in seconds." I pantomime grasping my throat. "Then say that we're on a quest through the Otherlands to find a world with enough oxygen to allow us to thrive without these clunky suits."

Itzel relays my words pretty well. She might yet make a good liar.

While she's doing that, I rack my brain for a name to give Lilith. I don't want to reveal my real identity given my connection to Rasputin, who may be Lilith's prisoner. I'm tempted to say Criss Angel, but that sounds too masculine and my suit has some curves. Maybe if I reverse it?

"Does Angel Criss sound like a girl's name?" I ask my friends. Then it hits me, and before they reply, I grin and say, "Never mind. I got it. I shall be Angelina. As in, Angelina Jolie."

"Then I'll be Brad Pitt," Felix says.

"You wish." Ariel chuckles. "You're more of a Billy Bob Thornton—assuming we entertain your fantasy of being a unit with Sasha, which is going to be hard to believe even in these suits."

"Let him be Brad," I say generously. "Besides, with that visor, I doubt anyone would question me dating him. Probably."

"In that case, I'm Jennifer Aniston," Ariel says. "She has Greek heritage after all. We can all pretend we're Brad's gnome harem."

"I think gnomes are monogamous," Felix says.

"I'm sure Ariel was kidding about the harem thing," I say. "And even if not, Itzel, please only relay what *I* say."

"Speaking of, we still need a name for Itzel," Ariel says.

"Gwyneth Paltrow," Felix suggests.

When Ariel and I chuckle, he defensively says, "She and Brad dated after the movie *Seven*, so I thought it would be thematically appropriate."

"Fine," I say, making a mental note to tease him about his encyclopedic knowledge of celebrity hookups. "Itzel, please introduce us when you're done. Just don't give her the last names in case she's actually been to Earth in recent decades, or she might catch on."

Itzel finally wraps up her explanation.

"How tragic," Lilith says, though she doesn't sound the least bit sympathetic.

"Yes," Itzel replies. "It is. This is Angelina, by the way." She points at me. "That is Brad." She points at Felix. "This is Jennifer"—she points at Ariel—"and I'm Gwyneth, the leader of this expedition."

"More like the only one with an external speaker," Felix grumbles softly.

"So, Gwyneth," Lilith says, seemingly tasting the name. "Did Tartarus send you?"

"Who?" Itzel asks, and I recall hearing that name during Orientation the other week. I quickly explain it to the others, and Felix confirms he's heard about him too.

Like me, he was horrified by what was left of the world Tartarus last ruled.

"I've never heard of Tartarus until today," Itzel says to Lilith. "No one sent us."

"Is that so?" Lilith says. "Now, tell me, would you truly die if we took you out of those gnome contraptions?"

"And quickly," Itzel replies before I can coach her on what to say. "So please don't."

"Oh, I don't mean for you to die quickly." Despite the words still sounding like beautiful music, I detect an undertone of malice that sends a shiver down my spine. "Though I suspect that you are telling the truth, I can't let you go without making sure of it. You might be spies from Tartarus or one of my other enemies." She floats closer to us. "I'm certain my torturers can devise a form of questioning that will leave your garb intact."

We all back away—and bump straight into a group of swordsmen, who seem to have appeared out of nowhere. Upon a command from Lilith, they start herding us out of the room.

"I will have you back here for dinner in the near future," Lilith says to our backs. "It has been a while since I've tasted gnome blood."

CHAPTER FORTY-FOUR

WE'RE mute with horror as the swordsmen drag us somewhere, with everyone processing the Hannibal Lecter-worthy threat Lilith has delivered.

"Do your best to remember the path to wherever they take us," I tell everyone, mostly to keep their minds off the upcoming torture and exsanguination.

They mumble in agreement and continue to sulk— which is reasonable.

A few minutes later, Ariel slides between me and Felix, and I see her straining with her bindings.

As a magician, I'm an expert at knowing what a group of people can or cannot see; in our parlance, it's called being aware of the angles. My sleight of hand and other secret maneuvers are usually angle proof— but Ariel's current efforts are far from it.

I cover her angles by stepping over to the right and adjusting my gait just so.

The guards remain oblivious to Ariel's efforts.

"Crap," she says in frustration, stopping the struggle. "I can't rip this stupid rope apart."

"Even if you freed yourself, they have swords at our backs," Itzel says.

"So what are we supposed to do? Go passively to our doom?" She looks at the nearest guard, then the one at his side. "I think I'll charge them with my hands tied behind my back. If I headbutt that one and slam my shoulder into—"

"You'll get chopped into pieces by the rest," Itzel says.

"That might still be a better fate than what Lilith has in store for us," Ariel retorts.

"How about we postpone suicidal missions for when we're really desperate?" I chime in.

"You don't think this is desperate?" Felix and Ariel say almost in unison.

"Let's just say we don't know all the variables yet," I say. "For example, let's say they use fewer guards when they take one of us to be tortured. That might give Ariel a better chance of surviving after that headbutting and shoulder charging."

"Oh," Ariel says disappointedly. "I thought you'd had a vision or something."

"She can't get a vision because of Itzel," Felix says accusingly.

"That's not true," Itzel says defensively. "I should only impact Sasha's efforts to see a future that involves *me*."

"And you're with us, so all our futures involve you.

Maybe we should get rid of you," Felix says. "How about *you* charge the guards and get killed for the good of the group?"

Itzel steps as far away from Felix as our current predicament allows. "My nature is not stopping Sasha from seeing a future where they torture *you*, Ariel, or her own self, assuming I'm not there when the torturer does it," she says flatly.

"Yeah, as tempting as it is for me to experience torture in a vision, I'm going to take a rain check," I say, suppressing a shudder. "But Itzel makes a good point. I haven't had the time to think more creatively about my visions. Maybe I could look at the future of whoever will be guarding our cell or something like that. Maybe he cheats on his wife, and I could use that as blackmail. Or he worships a god other than Lilith, and we could use that."

I wish I could be as optimistic as I make myself sound to my friends.

"Fine," Ariel says. "I won't attack anyone right now, but I have a feeling I'll regret this when I'm inside some spike-filled iron maiden torture device."

"They wouldn't use that," Felix says. "It would break the integrity of the suit. Something like the rack would work better. If they go slowly, the suit shouldn't rip at the joints—though our actual joints might—"

"Or they might stick the helmet into a fire," Itzel says with way too much enthusiasm in her voice. "Or—"

"How about we *not* apply our imaginations toward

possible tortures and save all the brain cycles for thinking up escape ideas instead," I cut in sternly.

Everyone quiets down. Hopefully, like me, they're keeping their eyes open for opportunities and in general brainstorming escape schemes.

Also, hopefully someone's having better luck at it than I am.

When we reach a winding staircase and start ascending, I rerun the conversation with Lilith in my head and wonder if it was the right move to pretend to be gnomes—or admit to it in Itzel's case. After all, if Lilith thought we weren't, she might've tried to glamour us to tell her if we were sent by Tartarus. With the right coaching from me, Itzel might've been able to fake being under Lilith's influence. But as things stand, we'll face the kind of painful questioning I saw in my father's memories, or worse.

Then again, when Lilith gets the answers she's looking for, she'll have us for dinner, so maybe the delay is a good thing.

Echoing my dark thoughts, our surroundings get danker and drabber with each step. The higher up we go, the more the interior design brings to mind dungeons custom made for the Inquisition.

Eventually, we stop at a floor that looks particularly rat-infested.

The guards lead us by a tiny cave-like cell adorned with rusted bars and a giant lock. Inside it, I glimpse a shadow of a person who makes the sorriest homeless guy in NYC seem like a healthy and thriving individual.

"Oh no," Ariel whispers. "Is that what's going to become of us in a few weeks?"

"Probably not," I say. "I doubt Lilith would find us as appetizing in that case."

Silently, we continue on our way, and as we walk by cell after miserable cell, I imagine I smell dirty bodies and decay—though it must be an illusion, given the suit's ability to filter out outside air.

When we turn the corner, I see two burly guards throwing a tall, limp man into one of the cells.

He's cleaner than the other prisoners we've seen, and his tiny room is a luxury suite in comparison to the rest of the cells. There's a bucket, a bed, a small bookcase, a table, and even a window.

The guards toss him on the bed, which allows the light from the window to fall on his face.

I gasp, recognizing him from our Headspace conversation.

It's Grigori Rasputin.

My father.

CHAPTER FORTY-FIVE

MY HEART IS BEATING WILDLY, and I want to jump up and yell that it's me, Sasha, that I've come for him, but I suppress the suicidal impulse. Instead, I check my angles, then adjust my body in such a way that none of the guards can see me wave my gloved hand at my father.

He has two black eyes and his face is swollen, so it's hard to tell if he saw my beauty-pageant-worthy maneuver or not.

Hoping that he did, I tilt my body once more to cover another gesture: using my extended thumb and pinkie, I mime answering a phone.

I think he lifts his head, but that could be my imagination.

Even if he did see what I did, I have no idea if he understood. Did they even have phones in Russia during the czar's reign?

The guards herd us into the corridor, preventing

me from any more gestures. We walk a few feet and stop next to a cell the size of a closet in a typical Manhattan studio.

The leftmost man unlocks the metal lock, and his colleagues push us in.

After locking the door, all but one of the guards leave, and I look around.

There's no window, no beds, and not even a bucket to use as a bathroom. The place feels haunted by all the prior occupants who died in it—likely of malnutrition or infection.

"Let me guess." Felix tilts his helmet toward Itzel. "You're not getting paid enough for *this*."

Ignoring him, Itzel does her best to nervously pace the room—which is hard to do, given how tightly we're crammed in here.

The guard paces also—and has more luck doing it, given the length of the corridor.

I focus and reach Headspace with ease.

The shapes that surround me play uncanny music, but I ignore that in favor of seeing if my surreptitious gestures to Rasputin have paid off.

I think of the essence of my father the way I did the last time—but nothing happens.

Crap.

He's not in Headspace. Maybe he didn't see my gesture? Or maybe he's low on power and/or badly hurt after his beating?

To keep myself sane, I decide to see what the visions that surround me are. To my horror, I witness Ariel getting brutally beaten with wooden staffs, which break her bones without messing with the spacesuit.

The torture seems to be taking place in a ruin of some kind, with cracked red rocks piled everywhere and the floor covered with soot. Was there an earthquake here recently?

Can there be earthquakes on a floating island?

When the terrifying vision ends, I get right back into Headspace.

Another set of shapes surrounds me this time. They look similar enough to the ones I just saw that I have little doubt they show my friends getting tortured.

No, thanks. One was plenty as far as extra motivation for escape.

What I need is to figure out when they'll be coming for us—and bonus points if I can figure out why the torture room was so damaged. Except when I try to access that, I fail miserably. Itzel's nature strikes again.

I change my tactics and do my best to learn something about the future of the pacing guard.

This also fails—probably because I need to know more about his essence. Alternatively, Lilith with her probability manipulation mojo might be protecting the guard from seer visions because she knows he's guarding Rasputin.

Speaking of my father, I try reaching him and fail once more.

Exiting Headspace, I ask Itzel to chat up the guard to see if we can learn something about him that would aid my seer sight.

She tries—but the guy ignores her so completely that I wonder if he might be deaf.

About an hour passes, and a new guard shows up.

Maybe I'll have better luck finding out something about *this* guy?

I don't, nor is Itzel able to chat this one up.

Frustrated, I return to Headspace and try getting in touch with Rasputin again. He's now had an hour to recover, and if he saw my gesture, he should accept my summons.

As soon as I make this new attempt, a familiar Headspace entity shows up in front of me.

It's Rasputin, and he's pulsing with eagerness.

We reach for each other in the Headspace equivalent of a hug.

The connection clicks into place, and we start to meld together.

Exhaling a metaphysical breath, I prepare to witness my father's memories.

CHAPTER FORTY-SIX

I'M FLOATING IN HEADSPACE.

Wait a second. Did I get kicked out of my connection with Rasputin back into—

No.

This *is* his memory.

It just so happens that the memory is of using Headspace.

Sure enough, I become aware of my father's thoughts, and it's a trippy experience because he's actually thinking about *me*. A three-year-and-eleven-month-old version of me, who is, according to his obviously biased view, "The cleverest, prettiest, most perfect little angel in all time—past and future."

I pay close attention and realize something extremely interesting. My father is using Headspace slightly differently from the way I've been doing. At least, it's not *just* the essence of the young Sasha that he focuses on, but his feelings toward her. Feelings that shock me, as he clearly loves the little me intensely. His love is so strong, in fact, that I don't understand how he could be the same man who abandoned me at an airport, leaving me to be raised by strangers.

His concentration pays off, and vision shapes surround him.

He must not like these shapes because he mentally swears. "Again the same," he thinks with anger. "Every future is the same."

He debates whether he should even see the visions, but then he decides to do so.

He examines the nearly identical shapes very carefully.

Unlike with me, his instincts help him when it comes to choosing the most useful of the shapes—or at least, he believes that to be the case. Then again, how do I know the same isn't true for me? Maybe when I choose one at random, I actually get the most useful one as determined by some nebulous intuition?

He reaches for a bunch of shapes that seem slightly different from each other. He clearly intends to see multiple related visions.

The first vision starts.

Rasputin is bodiless in a room made of white marble.

A six-year-old version of me is in this room with tears streaming down her face. She's naked and holding a dagger that looks like a sword in her tiny hand.

Also naked is the woman tied up at little Sasha's feet. She's gagged, but what can be seen of her face is very pretty—and terrified.

"Please don't make me do this again," little Sasha pleads in Russian to the ceiling. She then repeats the words in English.

No one replies.

Sasha sobs, her thin shoulders sagging, and looms over the woman on the floor.

The victim's eyes widen in horror, and she struggles harder against her bonds.

"I have to," Sasha says to the woman almost pleadingly. "If I don't, you will suffer." Her face twists in such an unnatural-for-a-child sorrow that I want to hug her and somehow steal her away from this horrible room.

The woman on the floor tries to slither away from the little girl, but her bindings don't allow it.

Sasha bends over her and gently moves her matted hair, exposing the white neck underneath.

Inhaling deeply, the child me slices down with the dagger.

The weapon sinks into the woman's throat, and blood gushes forth from the jagged wound.

The woman's body goes limp.

Sasha's stray tears turn into a stream that join the crimson puddle at her feet.

She kneels next to the woman—

The vision interrupts, just so that another can start.

It's nearly identical to the first, except this time

Sasha looks a little older—and she's killing a young man.

In the third vision, she kills a child her own age.

In the fourth, vision-Sasha is even older, and she doesn't seem as emotionally distraught after she does the horrible deed.

In the following visions, she kills her victims almost robotically—

The visions stop, and Rasputin and I find ourselves in what looks like a lake-side meadow.

"No." Rasputin is all but shaking with fury. "I won't let my angel become a demon."

Before I can figure out where we are, we're back in his Headspace.

He's thinking about how to prevent it. In every future where he takes the little me and runs, we get caught and the inevitable still happens.

He lets himself consider an idea, one that he'd thought about before but rejected.

It's a horrible one, but he sees no other choice.

What if he takes himself out of the equation?

What if he gives her to someone else to raise?

He thinks about my essence once again, but this time, he dwells on the idea he just had and he pictures me grown.

A bunch of shapes surround him, all very different.

He reaches for one, but I already know what he'd see. Me—the way I am now—being raised by Mom and Dad on modern Earth. A future much happier than that of the child soldier/serial killer in his visions.

Before I see if I'm correct, the memory short-circuits, and I find myself in a vacuum-like blackness, facing the synapse hologram of my father once again.

CHAPTER FORTY-SEVEN

THIS EPHEMERAL VERSION of my father looks a little better than his real-world self. His eyes and face are still swollen, but his posture is less defeated.

"What have you done?" he asks in rapid-fire Russian. "Why would you come to this deadly place?" He floats down. "You're as stubborn as your mother—and you can't even understand me. All my fault. If I left you with a Russian family, you wouldn't have forgotten how to speak our mother tongue. Maybe if—"

"I've re-learned Russian since we last spoke," I reply, my words halting and slow as I pull on all the knowledge I've drilled into my brain. "I came to save you. I had to."

He stares at me in shock, then starts speaking again, this time slower and enunciating every word. "It was a grave error to come here. I don't have enough power for a long conversation, but you have made a mistake." He rubs his temples in frustration. "I can't believe I didn't foresee your arrival. I would've avoided using my power for a week if I'd known. My visions help me temporarily escape my dreadful conditions, but—"

"Stop beating yourself up." I float closer to him and smile. "Using your power to make yourself feel better is understandable under the circumstances. Also, with me is a… how do you say it?" I rack my brain for the Russian word for "gnome" but don't find one and just say it in English.

His eyes light up, and he says a word that sounds a lot like "gnome."

"Yes, that's it," I say. "That's why you didn't foresee my arrival."

He shakes his head. "It's not just that. Lilith made my fate invisible to me long ago, and yours recently became too chaotic to keep up with. Still, I should've been trying. If there was some way I could've glimpsed it—"

"It doesn't matter. I'm here now, and I want to help you."

"You can't. I wish I'd taken your summons when you reached out to me. Maybe I could've—"

"So you *were* ignoring me?" I can't help my accusing tone.

"I was afraid I'd be weak and ask you to come," he mutters. "Or that if you got to know me, it would be harder for you to ignore my plight." He floats down. "It seems like it was all for nothing anyway. You came *here*, the last place you should be."

"Oh, please." I float down a couple of feet. "You've

been getting tortured for nearly twenty years. Did you really think I'd allow it to go on?"

"It's been less than a year since I left you at the airport." He floats to my level. "The time here passes nearly twenty times slower than on Earth, so it's been longer for you."

I look at him in confusion, wondering if my Russian skills are letting me down.

Twenty years of my life happened in less than a year from his perspective?

That's insane.

That means that in the hour during which I waited for the guard to change, a whole day passed on Earth. That—

"We don't have much time," Rasputin says solemnly. "Tell me how you got here, about the gnome, and why you are wearing that strange outfit."

I fill him in as quickly as I can.

"It's good Lilith didn't see your face and doesn't know your name," he says when I finish. "She's extremely vindictive and would follow you to the edges of the Otherlands if she felt slighted."

"I take it if I were to escape, she'd feel slighted?" I ask.

"Indeed," he says grimly. "Which is why it's critical that she doesn't get any of your hair or blood. As a vampire, she could use those things to locate you."

"Well, thanks to my lying skills, she thinks we'd die without the suits," I say proudly.

"Quick thinking and so great at deception,"

Rasputin mumbles under his breath. "So much like—" He stops abruptly.

"You were going to say 'your mother,' weren't you?" I say. "Who was she? Where is she? How come—"

He winces. "You have to understand, I didn't know who she was when we met." He looks at me pleadingly. "I was just a fool, in love and out of my depth." He shakes his head. "But at least it wasn't all bad. Just look at you." He examines me with paternal pride. "I wish I got a chance to see you without that suit just once in the real world."

"You'll see me without the suit so much you'll be sick of me," I say. "We're getting out of here together, you and I."

"No." He floats down. "If you get the chance to escape, you must leave without me. Lilith has my hair, so she can track me."

"So what? We'll get rid of it," I say with a confidence that I wish I felt. "Do you know where she keeps it?"

"Yes, but going after it will make the escape even less likely to—"

"Enough," I say. "When I make a bird call, I want you to create a distraction."

"What?" he asks, and before I can answer, the Headspace conversation interrupts, and I find myself back in my cell.

CHAPTER FORTY-EIGHT

"TWENTY TIMES SLOWER?" Ariel says incredulously after I bring my friends up to speed on my Headspace extracurriculars. "That's a pretty drastic time differential."

"My new client won't be happy." Felix looks glum. "Should've taken Monday off. Maybe Tuesday too."

"Yeah." Itzel's voice is dripping with sarcasm. "Next time Sasha asks you to go someplace, make sure to clear your schedule for the rest of your life—which might be short. Oh, and add many zeros to whatever she offers to pay you as well, not that you'll live to spend the money but—"

"She isn't paying you," Felix says. "*I* am."

I ignore the rest of their back-and-forth because something Felix said sparked an important realization.

If the time difference is indeed what Rasputin said, it's already Monday afternoon back on Earth.

Nero was expecting me at work.

By now, he would've called Thalia, and she would've told him we took Ariel back to rehab—meaning we should've been back long ago.

I close my eyes and focus, seamlessly entering Headspace once more.

Good.

It could've been mine, not Rasputin's, power that ran out. I guess I can thank Itzel for my extra reserves. And she's not going to thwart my attempts this time because it's not Itzel's future I want to glimpse.

It's Nero's.

I summon my boss's essence as much as I can, and even contemplate if I should add my emotions to it for good measure—the way Rasputin did when he wanted to see little Sasha's future.

The problem with using my feelings for Nero is that I find them very difficult to parse. I was ready to act on our mutual attraction, but then he went ahead and pulled that "you can't handle me" business.

Luckily, I don't need to figure out how I feel about Nero for this to work—a set of shapes surrounds me based on what I've done thus far.

If I had a heart in this place, it would be hammering right about now.

I can tell that these visions will be horrific. But surely nothing bad can happen to Nero, of all people?

Right?

There's only one way to find out. Using another trick of Rasputin's, I let my intuition guide my choice of shape and fall into the vision.

I'M BODILESS—MEANING I'm not there for whatever is to come.

My surroundings look familiar, though.

The flying island in the sky houses the red castle where I'm currently being held. The river of blood is here, and so is the army of soldiers and monks that are guarding the gates.

A masculine figure steps out of the gate we came through earlier today.

I recognize him immediately.

It's Nero.

A fully naked Nero. Did I fall asleep? Is this one of my inappropriate dreams?

No. This is a vision. Somehow, Nero must've figured out that I followed the map from his safe to Rasputin's location. I guess he lost his clothes on the way. Maybe he'd worn a spacesuit to get through those uninhabitable worlds and has just ditched it?

A few soldiers and monks notice Nero and attack.

Scowling as if his fund is losing money, Nero blurs into motion and turns everyone in his immediate vicinity into papier-mâché of blood, bones, and gore.

Though I've seen him do this to the orcs, it doesn't make the sight any less disturbing.

Once his immediate enemies are destroyed, Nero inhales a big breath, and a blinding burst of energy spews out from his body.

Nero is gone.

Well, not gone.

He's replaced with something that makes me wish I had eyes right now—because then I'd be able to not believe them.

A terrifyingly majestic lizard-like creature faces the army. It has a maw full of a sword-like teeth, claws that would look too big on a bulldozer, and scaly wings that could carry a giant Boeing jet.

If I didn't know mythical creatures existed, my first guess would be a dinosaur—a sort of flying T-Rex, just bigger and deadlier.

But I've seen enough since my introduction to the Cognizant world to call this what it is.

A dragon.

CHAPTER FORTY-NINE

ALL THIS TIME, I've wondered what Nero's nature is, and he turns out to be a freaking dragon?

Unless that dragon ate him?

No. Those claws remind me of the way Nero's hands sometimes look when he kills. Plus, there's no mistaking those eyes—assuming one ignores their current enormous size. They're the same blue-gray as always, with unnaturally (or perhaps totally naturally for his kind) thick limbal rings.

A dragon.

I thought I was done being surprised when a new mythological creature is thrown at me, but a dragon?

And Nero being one.

We kissed. We almost did a lot more than that.

Wait a minute. Is this why he said I wouldn't be able to handle him? Does his dragon nature make intimacy extra rough or something? If true, that would be a legitimate concern.

Then something else hits me.

When we debated who might be trying to kill us, Nero mentioned it could be one of *his* kind. No wonder he thought wearing masks and using weapons would be beneath them.

I don't get a chance to muse further because the dragon opens its massive maw and produces a booming roar.

There's something eerily familiar about the way the sound vibrates my inner organs—an extra impressive feat because I currently have no organs.

Then it clicks.

It was neither a bear-dinosaur hybrid nor a giant bird that chased us in the world just before we reached this one.

That, too, must've been a dragon.

Also, like the last time I heard the roar, I could swear there are human words in it.

"Give her to me or die," the roar seems to say.

The human army all pale as one, and the ones on the outer bands of the army skedaddle—along with all of Lilith's worshipers.

I think if they understood what Nero wants, they would give me to him, but as is, they have no choice but to raise their puny weapons.

The archers act in unison, spraying Nero with a giant cloud of arrows.

The sharp projectiles glide off Nero's scales as if he were made of tank armor. Not a single one leaves so much as a scratch.

With another, much angrier roar, Nero flies up and swats at the nearest group of monks with his massive claw.

What's left of the monks looks like it's been run through a food processor.

Despite what just happened, a brave group of soldiers throws spears at Nero.

Just like the arrows before them, the spearheads don't scratch a single scale.

They do seem to piss Nero off, though.

With a roar, he swoops down and lands in the middle of the squad. His claws shred the soldiers into baby food for cannibals.

A few swordsmen decide to take advantage of Nero's landing and charge at him, waving their swords.

His claws swipe around too fast to track, brutally killing each man.

More soldiers swarm to replace the fallen ones, which is when Nero gets bored with their suicidal tendencies and launches into the air with a single beat of his massive wings.

He roars with renewed ferocity, and his eyes narrow as their limbal rings thicken. Then his chest expands as he inhales enough air to fill up a large movie theater.

Is he about to—

Yep, there it is.

A stream of fire spews out of his mouth. It's directional, like that of a flamethrower, but with all the intensity of a small volcano.

Flesh sizzles, and hundreds of men scream in unison.

Nero dives and glides over the discouraged army, his maw agape. The fire covers the ground like napalm, causing armor, bones, and stones to melt and burn.

Happy with the damage to ground troops, the dragon turns his massive head toward the floating island—just in time to spot a squadron of solders riding on top of fierce rocs. Both the riders and the giant birds are heavily armored, and have long lances attached to a special holder in the bird's shoulder—as though they're about to do air jousting.

Nero swirls in the air, then spews fire at his attackers.

A huge chunk of the squadron bursts into flames, but some scatter.

Nero examines the figures around him, then looks down and spots a large bird and rider trying to flee to the ground.

Claws out, Nero swoops after them with a speed a hawk would envy.

The bird shrieks as Nero's claws rake its flesh, and the rider screams when Nero's talons peel his armor as if it were made out of aluminum foil.

The survivors swarm down at Nero, their lances ready.

A lance grazes his thigh. Another hits his shoulder.

The dragon's next roar sounds like it has notes of pain in it. Did they actually hurt him?

Then Nero's spiky tail strikes his leftmost

assailant's uncovered face, collapsing his skull into the helmet. The tail then strikes at the rightmost attacker—and at the same exact time, Nero's teeth crunch on another and his claws shred two more.

Meatgrinderfied chunks of bird and human rain onto the scorched ground below. Not surprisingly, the remaining roc riders lose their nerve and attempt to flee.

Nero has other ideas, though. He chases and destroys each one before flying higher, toward the castle.

"Give her up," the roar seems to say as he flies up to the base of the castle.

No one comes out to defend the structure or otherwise reply to the demand.

Nero angrily claws at the wall of the castle and—to my shock—rips away a room-sized chunk.

The rest of the building shakes as though hit by an earthquake.

Was this what happened to the room where I foresaw Ariel's torture? If so, I've got to question Lilith's priorities. I'd restore the castle first, torture prisoners later—

Nero sniffs the chunk of castle he's holding, then tosses it to the ground.

Was he sniffing for me?

As the broken red rocks rain down, I spot at least a hundred soldiers in the rubble, all screaming their lungs out.

Wings beating in the air, Nero flies up and looks

around. Zeroing in on one of the spires, he swoops down and rips it off. Sniffing this new catch, he discards it and looks for another piece to carve off.

A small figure floats out of the castle.

It's Lilith, and she's holding something in her hand —something like a sword hilt but with no sword.

"You're trespassing, lizard," she says in Russian in that heavenly voice of hers. "Did you forget about the accord I have with your kind? You stay out of my world, and I stay out of yours."

So there's a whole world of dragons? It must be the one where I was nearly killed by one.

Nero's reply roar is so intense that it blows Lilith back a foot.

Undaunted, she floats forward.

Nero swats at her with his tail, but misses. He tries to claw her—but misses again.

Is she that fast at dodging, or is she using her powers? I mean, she *is* a probability manipulator. Can that be used to reduce the chance of getting hit? If so, fighting a powerful trickster like her is going to be extremely challenging, even for Nero in this form.

The dragon's neck strains as he tries to chomp Lilith in half—but he somehow misses her body yet again.

"Feisty," Lilith says and extends her free hand at the sky above Nero.

A thousand birds of different varieties swarm at Nero out of a cloud with deafening squawking.

Is that part of her probability manipulation power?

I suppose there was a chance the birds would be hidden in that cloud, and an even smaller chance that they would want to attack a dragon.

Nero swats a few birds away, but they quickly cover him from head to tail. Though they're as small compared to him as mosquitos would be to me, the sheer numbers are overwhelming.

If that many mosquitos covered me, I'm pretty sure I'd be sucked dry.

With another roar, Nero spins in place, causing the birds to fly in every direction. Immediately, they fly back at him.

He sucks in air and spews fire at the birds.

As they go up in flames, Nero directs his fire-breath at Lilith.

She somehow manages to dive under the flames without getting singed.

The dragon lowers his head and shoots her with a new stream of fire, but she flies right above it.

Clearly angry, Nero torpedoes toward the pseudo goddess, but before he can reach her, the same cloud where the birds came from darkens and produces a lightning bolt, which hits Nero square in the snout.

I guess there's always a chance of lightning when there are clouds, so this might be Lilith's power again.

Nero looks momentarily stunned, but recovers quickly and resumes his onslaught.

Boulder-sized chunks of hail pummel Nero's head as he closes the distance to Lilith.

I didn't think hail ever got *that* big, but I guess it's

more likely than, say, a cartoon anvil or a Honda Civic falling from the sky.

Ignoring the ice blows, Nero lunges forward and snaps at Lilith with his teeth again—but misses.

Before he can get his head away from the tiny figure, she punches him in the snout.

To my shock, the impact causes the huge dragon to fly back a dozen yards. He shakes his head as if to clear it, then uses his wings to slow himself down and go on the offensive again.

With unshakable confidence, Lilith flies at him, uncaring that it puts her within reach of his deadly claws.

Nero swipes at her, his movements too fast to track, but he misses over and over.

He roars in frustration and intensifies his efforts.

In response, she hits him with lightning and hail again, but he ignores it. Somehow, he must hit her because Lilith is thrown back, toward one of the towers.

So there's a limit to her power, after all. She might've used too much of her mojo by manipulating the weather, and thus the odds finally did not go in her favor.

She smashes into the tower, and it explodes into pieces.

Whoa. Could anyone have survived that? Even someone with the power of luck?

As if answering my question, Lilith floats out of the debris, seemingly undamaged.

"What is it that you want, lizard?" She dusts off her clothes. "Out of respect for the lizard king, I'm doing my best not to kill you but—"

This must've been the wrong thing to say because Nero charges forward with renewed ferocity and lands another hit on her, destroying a castle wall but still not hurting her.

"Is this personal?" she asks, flying up from the rubble. "Because I'll have you know I've never killed one of your kind."

Nero doesn't seem to care and renews the attacks.

"Maybe you need a seer?" she shouts after she dusts herself off again and dodges another series of deadly attacks. "If it's Rasputin you're after, he's not as good as the legends will have you believe. Certainly not worth dying over—"

Nero's tail manages to strike her in the chest, and she flies backward—but recovers before she slams into anything.

"I can ask Nostradamus to make time for you. He's much, much more powerful," she says, flying toward Nero again. "You'd owe me a favor as a result, but he's worth it."

Clearly not impressed with that offer, Nero attacks her with renewed intensity and manages to swat her with his tail so hard, she crash-lands into a high tower of the castle—again breaking it into pieces.

"This is beginning to get on my nerves," she says and presses something on the sword hilt she's been holding.

A blade appears—a long blue blade made out of shimmering plasma that reminds me of whatever the gates are made from—and lightsabers from *Star Wars*.

"Leave!" Lilith waves the sword in wide arcs with a loud whoosh. "Last chance."

Nero's eyes narrow into slits. He must recognize this weapon.

I wish I had a mouth to tell him to leave. I should be able to figure out how to escape on my own, somehow. And even if I can't escape, there's no reason for us both to die on this world.

But he doesn't leave. Instead, he flies closer to her, and his tail strikes at her sword-wielding hand with the speed of an angry cobra.

She dodges his attack and slices at the same time—chopping off a tip of his tail.

The scaly bit of flesh falls to the ground, and blood pours from the wound.

Nero furiously roars and directs a thick stream of fire at Lilith.

She dives under the flames and keeps flying, going into a skydiving-like freefall. She stops a few feet above the ground—directly under Nero and the stream of blood pouring from his tail. Catching some of the red liquid, she floats away and makes a show of swirling it in her mouth.

"Atrocious bouquet," she comments after she swallows. "Tannic, rough, vinegary…"

Nero clearly doesn't like this blood-tasting

commentary. He dives down, his claws aimed at her sword-wielding hand.

Two things happen almost at the same time.

One of Nero's talons rakes Lilith's forearm, and her sword pierces his shoulder.

The plasma blade goes into the impenetrable dragon skin like a hot knife into butter. Then Lilith rips it out, and a fountain of blood gushes from Nero's shoulder.

Clutching her own injury with her left hand, Lilith lands on the ground.

Growling like a thousand wounded bears, Nero swoops down at a mind-boggling speed, the claw of his undamaged side extended.

His talon catches her shoulder this time, but her sword pierces Nero's chest.

I wish I could scream or help him somehow, but without a body, all I can do is watch helplessly.

Nero's claws strike the ground.

She yanks out the sword.

The blood is like a river now. It covers everything—including Lilith herself.

Nero clutches at his horrible wound with one claw, but it's like trying to soak up a whole lake with a sponge.

Lilith—whose own shoulder and forearm wounds are already closing—flies up and slices off Nero's right wing.

I can't bear to keep watching this, but I have no idea how to stop.

With a pained roar, the dragon collapses, the impact of his fall shaking the island like a mini-earthquake.

Lilith leaps on his back with her sword outstretched.

The plasma blade enters Nero's back.

Lilith pulls it out and runs up his back toward his head.

No. Please no.

Moving sluggishly, Nero tries to swat at her with the tail, but she dodges it as she makes her way to the giant neck.

Time seems to slow.

The shimmering sword makes a wide arc toward the dragon's powerful neck.

If I had a mouth, it would be gaping in horror.

The blade slices through the neck, and Nero's head drops to the ground.

Fire and blood explode out of the wound like a gory volcano, and the dragon's massive body slackens.

Lilith disables her blade, jumps to the ground, and looks over the now-dead dragon. "What a waste," she says in her heavenly voice.

CHAPTER FIFTY

I BEND OVER, gasping for air as tears stream down my face.

I want to wipe them off my cheeks, but my hands are bound behind my back—and even if they weren't, the helmet would be in the way.

"What happened?" Ariel demands. "Sasha, are you okay?"

My hyperventilating eases enough for me to realize that I'm back inside my body and that what I saw was a vision. Meaning *that* future doesn't have to come to pass. Maybe Lilith can still be stopped somehow. Despite how powerful she is and—

"Seriously, Sasha," Felix chimes in, sounding worried. "What's going on?"

I drag in a shaking breath and try to make words. "Nero is a dragon," I finally force out. "And... he's going to die."

In the silence that follows, I tell them about my

Headspace misadventures, doing my best to choke back my panic. When I'm halfway through my story, I calm down enough to start keeping an eye on the guard pacing the hallway, so I can count his steps and note his movement patterns.

"So *that's* what Nero is," Felix mumbles when I'm done. "That explains his super-deep voice and the eyes thing, plus the claws. Oh, and his lie detection abilities."

"How so?" I ask on autopilot, even as my mind keeps spinning, looking for solutions to our impossible situation.

"When I was little, my grandpa told me fairy tales about dragons," he says. "In those stories, dragons liked to play a variation of the Truth or Dare game. They would eat those who chose the truth option but then lied—and they would also eat those who couldn't do the often-impossible dares. I thought my grandpa made those stories up as a parable about telling the truth, but—"

"Right. It also explains why Nero likes making money so much," Ariel cuts in. "Even in human legends, dragons like treasure."

"You're right," Felix says excitedly. "I bet getting rich actually makes him more powerful. That's crazy smart and is like a loophole in the Mandate, if I'm right."

Could that be true?

When Nero first locked me up in the basement cell, I had confronted him about the pointlessness of getting wealthier when he was already rich as sin.

"It's not about wealth," he'd replied. "It's about power, and power is survival."

I hadn't understood what he meant, but in the context of a dragon hoarding his treasure, it makes more sense. Having a large net worth *is* just like sitting on a pile of gold.

Too bad Nero's wealth-boosted dragon power isn't enough to deal with Lilith, who's enhanced her powers by having a whole world believe her to be a goddess of luck or blood or whatever.

Or, more accurately, it *won't* be enough—future tense.

"When do you think he'll get here?" Itzel asks. "Do you have a plan?"

Instead of answering, I continue watching the guard and counting the seconds we're in his view.

Too many seconds for my liking.

Maybe I wait until another shift? The next guy might walk slower—or simply sit somewhere where he wouldn't see us.

No.

If I hadn't seen that vision, I might be more careful, but as is, I'll have to follow Felix's favorite Russian proverb: "She who doesn't risk never gets to drink champagne."

"Stand here," I tell Felix and position him near the cell bars.

"Why?" he asks.

"Because I said so, and you have nothing better to do," I mutter as I herd Ariel to stand next to him. Fear for Nero is like a living thing in my stomach, but I refuse to give in to it.

Now is the time to act, not freak out.

"Itzel, you stand here." I put the gnome next to the wall across from the others and wait for the guard to come our way.

To my huge relief, the guard doesn't question the new way everyone is standing. If I were him, I totally would have.

Mentally counting the seconds, I stick my head between Itzel and the wall and forcefully say, "Lean back."

Itzel does as I say, jamming my helmet between her butt and the wall.

Exhaling to calm my nerves, I twist my body until I hear the helmet's opening mechanism clank open.

"You still have your hands behind your back," Itzel says. "How—"

"Just make sure the helmet doesn't fall," Felix says. "I think I see where she's going with this."

Itzel keeps propping the helmet with her posterior, and I carefully remove my head from it.

The prison smells pretty much how I'd imagined it —like a mix between a morgue and a sewer.

Ignoring my gag reflex, I relax all my muscles.

Thanks to the fact that I tensed when the rope was put on me, relaxing now creates the slack I was hoping for.

I was right when I compared this spacesuit to a straitjacket. Drawing on that experience, I manipulate the slack toward my left shoulder and proceed to escape the suit as if I'm performing an effect.

My heart pounds as though I were on stage in front of thousands of people, but I free myself in a record-setting three seconds.

I then take the helmet from behind Itzel's butt and gently place it on the ground before untying the gnome.

The guard returns, and I freeze in place, using Ariel and Felix's strategically placed bodies to block me from his view.

He paces away, and I untie Ariel and Felix. I then have them face the hallway with hands behind their backs, so the guard won't see that they're now free.

Next, I pull out the lock picks that are pretending to be a stud in my tongue, but I don't go near the lock on the cell door because of the count in my head.

The guard passes by the cell just when I thought he would.

I hold my breath. If he questions Ariel and Felix's new stance, he can still raise an alarm.

He doesn't.

As he walks away, I push my friends aside and examine the lock.

It's as I feared.

There's no way I can defeat this thing before the guard returns.

There's something else I need to try, but it's risky.

Shrugging at my own reflection in Felix's helmet, I put my hands to my mouth and generate a bird call.

I do my best to imitate a roc, muffling the sound to create the illusion that the noise is coming from outside.

My friends' shoulders tense inside their suits, and I can picture their questioning expressions.

There's no way I can reassure them, so I don't. I need my father to do his part now, but I have no idea if he caught what I said before we disconnected in Headspace. And if he did hear me, does he know how to—

Something clanks in the distance. It sounds like someone upended a table.

My breath whooshes out in relief as I hear the guard run to check what the commotion is about.

Rasputin came through.

This is my chance.

I attack the lock with the picks as though everyone's life depends on it—and it very well might.

The lock is rusty and of unusual design, but this wouldn't have stopped Houdini. So, a few gray hairs later, I finally crack it open and exhale the breath I've been holding.

"Remember how you wanted to kick some ass?" I whisper to Ariel. "Now's your chance. Try not to make too much noise."

I then gesture at the door, and Ariel rubs her hands together menacingly as she walks through.

I follow her to Rasputin's cell.

The guard is there, inside, next to an overturned table. He's raising a fist to strike my father.

Ariel rushes in. Grabbing the guard's fist with her right hand, she locks his throat in the crook of her left elbow.

The guy slumps in Ariel's superhuman hold just as the bones in his fist break with a crunch.

Ariel tosses her victim to the side and lets me come through so that Rasputin can see me.

He leaps to his feet, his eyes greedily roaming over my face.

"Sasha," he whispers, his voice cracking... and in that moment, a roar shakes the walls of the castle along with my inner organs.

A very familiar dragon roar that seems to say, "Give her to me or die."

CHAPTER FIFTY-ONE

"WE'VE GOT to get out of here and save Nero," I say urgently, the fear gripping me again.

"Your mask and costume." Rasputin points at my head, then at Ariel's helmet. "You have to put them back on so that—"

"He's right," Itzel says through her external speaker. "You need your suit for our way back." Under her breath, she adds, "Assuming we actually make it off this world, which I doubt."

"Right." I grab Felix's shoulder and turn him so Rasputin can see his back. "I'll go put on mine, and you put on yours."

Rasputin looks at me in confusion, but then he realizes Felix has a spare suit strapped on, like a backpack.

As my father starts to gather his gear, I run back to our old cell and put my own suit back on.

"I'm Felix, and that's Ariel and Itzel," I hear my

friend say in Russian on the suit comms once my helmet is back on. "Do you want us to call you Rasputin, Grigori, Grigori Yefimovich, or Sasha's dad?"

"Since you're Sasha's friends, please call me Grisha," my father replies. "And thank you for—"

An outside roar interrupts him.

"No time for pleasantries," I say tersely. "That's Nero out there, and he needs our help."

"Nero," Rasputin says, pronouncing the name with a strong Russian accent. "He isn't bound by our contract to do this. Why is he here?"

"I think he came to save me," I say. "It's a long story."

"Itzel, can you translate to me what everyone is saying?" Ariel says in annoyed tone. "And can someone please tell me how I ended up as the only person who doesn't speak Russian?"

As I rush back to them, I can almost picture the parts of my vision where the archers and the spearmen attack Nero.

As though in confirmation, another angry roar shakes everything around me—vibrating my inner organs even in the suit.

"If you're in a rush, I can't join you," Rasputin says when he sees me. "She has my hair. Running with me would be pointless. I would lead her straight back to you."

"You said you knew where she keeps it," I say. "Take us there. Fast."

He nods and shuffles out of the room—clearly

unused to the boost in movement that the suit provides.

Ariel catches up with him, and the rest of us follow.

We turn the corner.

Four frightened-looking guards are staring out the window.

Under the cover of yet another roar, Ariel leaps for the guards and knocks them out before they know what hit them.

Not much can be seen from the window, but we hear hundreds of men screaming in unison.

"Nero just spewed out a stream of fire," I explain, my stomach clenching. "We need to hurry."

We reach the staircase and frantically run down, the suits enabling us to leap several stairs at a time.

Ariel chuckles mirthlessly as she runs next to me. "When they first took us up here, my first thoughts were, 'Great. I'll be a damsel locked in a tower. All that's missing is a dragon.'"

The sounds of Nero's napalm-like breath drown any replies.

Ariel speeds up to run ahead of us, and a floor later, she encounters a confused guard.

The man doesn't put up much of a fight as Ariel grabs him by his shoulders and unceremoniously tosses him down the stairs.

When we reach ground level, I hear the shrieks of wounded roc birds.

Nero must be fighting that squadron of flying soldiers—which means we're running out of time.

"Through here." My father sprints down a narrow corridor that's lit only by torchlight.

Five solders armed with swords block our way, and I curse under my breath.

Ariel leaps forward, and I follow.

She kicks the first guard's sword out of his hand, breaking his wrist, and then she smashes in another guard's face. The three other guards ignore their colleagues' screams as they surround Ariel—which is a mistake for the one who turns his back to me.

With a well-practiced move and all of my suit-enhanced might, I hit the soldier in the back of the head. He collapses in a heap of limbs.

Dodging two swords aimed at her, Ariel grabs the two remaining men by the backs of their heads and smashes their foreheads together.

The heads explode like overripe melons.

"Well, the hallway is clear." Felix sounds on the verge of fainting. "That's good news."

Rasputin jumps over the bodies and runs ahead, stopping next to a closet-like room the soldiers must've been guarding. Opening the door, he leaps in.

Outside, the dragon's next roar sounds like it has notes of pain in it.

I fight the temptation to take off my gloves so I can bite my nails. Instead, I rush after my father—just to bump into him as he comes out of the closet, holding something that looks like a hairball that a jaguar threw up.

My first thought is pubes, but then I realize it must be his beard.

"Got it," he says, holding it up triumphantly. Running up to the nearest torch, he tosses his disgusting score into the flame. "Finally, I'm free."

The hairball burns up in an instant, and I can imagine how it smells. Thankfully, the suit is airtight.

"Yay," Itzel says flatly. "Now we just need to figure out a way to get off a floating island while a dragon is trying to kill everyone and everything, including a god. Should be a piece of cake."

"This way to the exit," Rasputin says, ignoring the gnome, and we all hurry to follow just as the next roar rings out.

Crap. This roar seems to contain the words, "Give her up." Depending on where we are in the castle, we may be in danger.

Well, in a bigger danger.

A very specific type of danger, to be exact.

"Hey, Itzel," I say, trying to hide the panic in my voice. "A purely hypothetical question… can someone smell me when I'm encased in this suit?"

Itzel doesn't reply because we enter a large hall and face about a hundred soldiers—all armed to the teeth.

They look terrified by what's happening outside, but when they lay eyes on us—an enemy that *isn't* a dragon—they menacingly unsheathe their swords.

CHAPTER FIFTY-TWO

"DAMN IT." I swiftly take in the room layout.

Though I don't spot anything we can use to our advantage, something nags at me. I do my best to figure out where we are in the castle in reference to what I saw in my vision.

"There's no way we can kill them all without at least getting the suits pierced," Itzel says. "How—"

"On the ground," I shout as it comes to me. "Get down and scoot back. Move it!"

Matching action to words, I faceplant on the stone floor and start crawling backward on my stomach.

To my relief, my father and the others do the same thing.

I can't even imagine what the soldiers must think of our weird behavior. Then again, they're about to—

A world-ending crunch of rocks meeting claws deafens me.

If this were an earthquake, it would be a ten on the Richter scale.

People scream, and solid stone crumbles into pieces.

Bits of rock fall on my back, but none are big enough to harm me or my crew.

I chance a glance at the hall we just escaped. There's a gaping hole in its place. In that gap, I see the ginormous dragon sniff the chunk of castle he's holding, then toss it to the ground.

"We can get up now," I say and follow my own advice despite my shaking knees. "The next chunk of castle he rips out will be a spire, so we should be safe... assuming there's another way to the exit?" I extend my hand to help my father get to his feet.

"There is," he says, accepting my hand, and once he's upright, he leads us down a spiraling corridor.

We rush into a new hall—and come face to face with a dozen monks armed with staffs. Compared to everyone we've met thus far, and given the circumstances, they're surprisingly chill.

Heck, they even look calm when Ariel leaps forward, grabs the biggest one, and tosses him against the wall like a baseball.

"No doubt their faith keeps them so zen," Felix grumbles as he hits the monk nearest him in the face. "Lilith did a number on these people, that's for sure."

A monk hits me in the solar plexus with his staff, and I double over. My father yelps a Russian curse and hits the man in the jaw, knocking him out.

I catch my breath in time to spot another monk raising his staff to hit Rasputin in the back of the neck, so I kick his shin and, thanks to the suit's boost, snap his leg.

He cries out, but I punch him in the face, and he loses consciousness.

"Brace yourselves," I warn everyone when I estimate the castle will shake again.

Nothing happens.

I punch out another monk. Then another.

Finally, the earthquake comes. Nero must've ripped off that spire—which means Lilith is about to face Nero personally.

The shaking knocks a few monks off their feet, and the five of us take advantage of their position to knock them out before they can get back up. Then we effortlessly deal with their still-standing brethren.

"Grisha, how far to the exit?" I ask my father as we begin to run.

"A few minutes," he replies. "Also, could you call me Papa?"

"I don't think we have a few minutes," I grit out, my leg muscles straining as the Nero death clock in my head ticks louder.

"You're trespassing, lizard," Lilith's heavenly voice booms outside. "Did you forget about the accord I have with your kind? You stay out of my world, and I stay out of yours."

A chill streaks through my bones, and I speed up.

Rasputin follows closely behind, with everyone else on his tail.

"This way," my father pants over another roar.

The cardinal who was part of our welcoming committee and a couple dozen more monks block our path.

"Feisty," Lilith says outside, and I recall she's about to hit Nero with birds, hail, and lightning.

"No time to fight them all. Help me plow through them," I yell and leap for the cardinal.

With the same pompousness as before, the cardinal says something to me, his hands theatrically outstretched.

"We are on the side of righteousness," Itzel translates breathlessly. "Beasts like you cannot defeat—"

My fist smacks into the cardinal's jaw with great pleasure, stopping his tirade.

He falls like a garbage bag, and I jump over him, punching another monk in my way.

"Allow me," Ariel says as she passes me. Head bent low, she carves a path through the monks with the ease of an NFL player going through malnourished kindergarteners.

I follow, occasionally punching monks and dodging their staffs. Soon, we find ourselves running down a corridor with angry monks on our tails.

They can't keep up with our suit-enhanced speed, and before long, we leave the pursuit far behind.

Thunder booms outside. We're almost out of time.

Nero roars in frustration, and a tower explodes somewhere in the castle.

"Through here," my father says and turns left into another corridor.

"What is it that you want, lizard?" Lilith repeats. "Out of respect for the lizard king, I'm doing my best not to kill you, but—"

A castle wall breaks in the distance.

"Is this personal?" Lilith asks as we turn another corner. "I've never killed one of your kind."

"Just a little further," Rasputin pants and picks up speed.

"Maybe you need a seer?" Lilith asks. "If it's Rasputin that you're after, he's not as good as the legends will have you believe. Certainly not worth dying over—"

"So she doesn't know he came for Sasha," Rasputin mumbles under his breath. "That's good."

"I can ask Nostradamus to make time for you. He's much, much more powerful," Lilith says. "You'd owe me a favor as a result, but he's worth it."

"Does she mean *that* Nostradamus?" Felix sounds as out of breath as an overheated bulldog. "The one who predicted Hitler and—"

"He's not someone you or Nero ever want to meet," Rasputin says between his own gasps. "His prognostications caused a lot of grief."

I don't join in on the conversation, saving my strength.

We sprint through the carnivorous plants' display

we passed earlier into the large hall with the exit doors on the other side.

"This is beginning to get on my nerves," Lilith says.

Oh no.

This is when she activated her deadly gate-like sword.

"Ariel, grab Itzel and keep up," I gasp out as I torpedo forward. "There's almost no time left."

The sound of our suited feet slapping against stone rings through the large hall as I push my legs to their very limits, and a breath later, Ariel overtakes me, with Itzel slung over her shoulder like Santa's bag.

With her free shoulder, Ariel slams into the large doors, breaking them into shards in the process.

I'm a couple of feet away from the exit now, and I can see Nero and Lilith in the sky.

"Leave!" Lilith says as she waves the deadly sword in wide arcs. "Last chance."

CHAPTER FIFTY-THREE

"ARIEL, POINT ITZEL AT LILITH!" I shout. "Itzel, I need you to shoot her with your ball lightning as often as you can."

My plan is simple.

It's time Itzel's mojo messed up someone else's powers.

If I'm right, Lilith's luck will not apply when it comes to Itzel's projectiles.

Hopefully.

"I can only toss a few before I pass out from exhaustion," Itzel says as Ariel grabs her from her shoulder and points her head at Lilith as if she were a bazooka. "I also have trouble doing anything under this much stress—"

"Do your best," I say as Nero flies toward Lilith. "Now!"

With a grunt, Itzel shoots her ball just as Nero's tail starts to strike at Lilith's sword-wielding hand.

As the projectile flies through the air, I hold my breath.

Nero sees it and stops his tail just in time—which saves it from getting chopped by the sword, like in my vision.

The ball lightning hits Lilith in the back, spreading blue plasma energy through her. For a second, it looks like she has a force shield similar to the one in our suits.

Clearly, luck didn't help her dodge the projectile. Then again, she's lucky to be so resilient—I half expected, half hoped she'd go up in flames or at least fall out of the sky. At least she looks stunned, as if she got tasered.

Nero takes advantage of the assist and lunges at Lilith, his right claw aiming for her sword-wielding arm.

"Shoot her with another ball," I order Itzel, going on intuition.

Grumbling something under her breath, the gnome does as I say—just as Lilith recovers from the first hit and pierces Nero's claw with her sword.

The plasma blade goes straight through the dragon's palm, and Nero roars in pain.

Itzel's second ball lightning hits Lilith in the head.

Snarling, Nero reaches lower with his claw, impaling it further with the sword. Once half the hilt is in his flesh, he jerks the claw away, ripping the weapon out of Lilith's hand.

Flying up, he shakes the injured appendage, sending

the sword flying in a wide arc. It lands a sprint away from me as a fountain of blood gushes from Nero's wound, covering Lilith from head to toe.

Recovering from her stunned state, the goddess dives for the sword—and finally catches the sight of the five of us.

"Gnomes." She licks Nero's blood off her lips mid-flight. "You will pay for your intrusion."

"Itzel, one more hit, now!" I yell, running for the sword.

"I don't know if I can do it anymore," Itzel pants. "I'm lightheaded and—"

"Please try," Ariel urges. "I've got you, I promise."

Itzel grunts again, and out of the corner of my eye, I see another fireball hit Lilith.

It slows her down just enough to let me grab the sword and raise it above my head.

I have no idea if I can hurt Lilith with this thing, but I intend to try.

Except she might not be the only problem. Nero is swooping down, looking ready to kill me for the sword too. I guess he can't tell who I am with the helmet blocking my features and the suit masking my scent.

"Itzel," I say urgently. "Yell this in English through your external speaker: 'Hey boss, it's me with the sword.'"

Itzel's voice sounds extremely weak as she does what I asked, but Nero slows mid-dive, his enormous dragon eyes locking in on me.

Lilith recovers her senses and comes at me.

"Itzel," I bark, slicing at Lilith's outstretched arm with the sword. "Shoot her!"

Lilith evades my strike and zooms up, then comes at me again. This close up, her angelic glamour is almost painful. Instead of fighting for my life, I feel like dropping to my knees in supplication.

"I can't do it," Itzel gasps. "I'm out."

"Please try," Ariel begs. "I know you can do it."

Evading the blade, Lilith grabs the sword hilt right above my hand.

In desperation, I grip it with my other hand, and she flies up, lifting me off the ground.

In my helmet, my father sounds like he's hyperventilating with worry.

I cling to the sword with all my strength. I'm pretty sure she'll slice me in two if I let go.

"Itzel, she's going to kill her," Felix yells. "Shoot now!"

With the corner of my eye, I see Nero flying at us, but I doubt he'll reach us in time.

"Oh no," Ariel says. "Itzel just passed out."

Lilith's eyes lock on my helmet, and I kiss my life goodbye.

CHAPTER FIFTY-FOUR

SUDDENLY, Itzel's ball of light hits Lilith in the chest.

I could kiss the gnome right now. When Ariel said Itzel passed out, she meant *after* throwing this.

Lilith's grip on the sword handle loosens. If this were a cartoon, I'd hover in the air for a second, waving the sword in amazement.

Instead, I plummet to the ground.

Surprising myself with how clear my head is, I locate the off button on the sword hilt and press it, hiding the plasma blade to assure I don't accidentally chop off some body part as I land. I was not that high up, but I'm bound to at least break a leg or—

I land in someone's outstretched arms.

Rasputin grunts with effort.

So this is why he was breathing so loudly. It wasn't worry. He ran to catch me.

"You're not as light as the last time I held you," he says ruefully as he sets me down on my unsteady legs.

Letting the comment about my weight slide, I look around.

Felix and Ariel are running toward us with limp Itzel over Ariel's shoulder, and Nero has grabbed Lilith with his uninjured claw.

Leaving a trail of blood behind him, he loops in the air like a jet plane, then uses the momentum to throw Lilith at the side of the castle with all his might. He then dives for us as though he wants to eat us... but hopefully not.

Lilith's body rockets through the air as if she was shot out of a giant ballista. Flying head first, she crashes into the castle—and the impact sounds as though ten million tons of TNT went off at once.

The wall bursts into little pebbles, and I lose sight of Lilith inside the mess.

The rest of the castle seems to ripple out from the point of impact, then implodes like a building under a controlled demolition.

I guess the damage Nero had done earlier weakened its structural integrity.

A dragon roars right next to me.

I unpeel my eyes from the still-collapsing castle and focus on Nero.

Instead of eating us, he's landed a few feet away.

"Get on," the next roar seems to say.

"He's kidding, right?" Felix gasps.

"No, I think he means to give us a ride," Ariel says. "Sasha should go first. I bet she's dying to climb him."

Not dignifying Ariel's comment with a reply, I

dubiously examine the giant mound of scales, muscles, and teeth in front of me.

With what sounds like an exasperated sigh, Nero gently grabs me with his uninjured claw and deposits me on his back.

I stash the sword hilt in the crook of my elbow and grab onto the massive neck in front me of as Nero lifts a screaming Felix and plops him behind me. Rasputin gets on next, then Ariel—and she manages not to drop Itzel as she clambers up the dragon's giant body.

Nero roars again, and I think I hear the words "hold on" in there.

"Wait," I start to yell, but he extends his wings and leaps into the air.

Felix screams bloody murder and grabs onto me in a way I'd usually find inappropriate. I let it slide on the account of us riding my boss.

These are definitely extenuating circumstances.

Over Felix's screams, I hear Rasputin grunting curses, and though it might be my imagination, I think even the army-strong Ariel is squealing.

Movies like *The Neverending Story* make dragon riding seem fun, but it takes me all of two moments to realize that they're all propaganda pieces, no doubt commissioned by dragons.

In reality, being on a dragon is as much fun as riding a raging bull on top of a plane—during a hurricane.

Leaving the floating island with its broken castle far behind, Nero swoops down toward the gates.

Everyone's frightened screams gain in pitch, and I seriously envy Itzel in her unconscious state.

There is a small group of soldiers near the gates.

They look up and start to scatter, but Nero inhales a breath and spews fire in their direction.

I can feel the heat wave even through the suit, and our screams reach a crescendo.

Happy with the carnage he caused, Nero lands.

His giant claw puts me back on the ground.

"I'm alive," I say with genuine surprise in my voice.

"I think I inadvertently tested the suit's cleaning and recycling functionality," Felix mumbles as the dragon sets him on the ground.

"Is that what that was?" Rasputin asks. "It felt—"

He doesn't finish his thought on the account of a giant claw lifting him from his seat and gently placing him next to the gate we used to enter this hellhole.

I take calming breaths and examine myself. My hands are cramping from clutching at the scales on Nero's neck, and I'm drenched in sweat but otherwise okay.

Distracting me from further self-assessment, the claw goes for Ariel, setting her and Itzel down without a hitch.

Empty of riders, the dragon glows with a bright light and then shrinks into a naked—and definitely humanoid—Nero.

His right hand has a horrible gash in it that's still bleeding, but otherwise he seems okay.

Fine, who am I kidding? Nero looks much, much

better than just okay. With sweat glistening on every chiseled muscle, he looks good enough to—

"Into the gate," he growls, ruining the moment. Turning on his heel, he leads the way—and shows off his amazing backside in the process.

Ariel whistles low under her breath and slaps my shoulder. "You sure know how to pick them."

"Dude." I redden like a ripe tomato. "He has super hearing. I bet he heard that even with the suits."

Nero looks over his shoulder, and there's a hint of a smirk on his face. He waves for me to follow, then steps into the gate.

My face feels hot enough to cook an omelet on, but Ariel just shrugs.

Clutching my new sword, I go into the gate.

The Grand Canyon-like mountain ridge on the other side is just as breathtaking as before. Same goes for the borealis and the seven moons in the sky.

Ariel, Felix, and Rasputin step out of the gate after me.

"This way," Nero says in Russian and points at the gate that leads to the world of fire we passed on the way to this one.

He strides toward the gate, and I give myself a moment to enjoy the sight.

Ariel moves Itzel from her left shoulder onto her right one and follows him.

"Wait," Rasputin says. "Stop."

Everyone stops, and Nero gives my father a seething glare.

"We should go this way." Rasputin points at a green gate that's closer than the one Nero was walking toward. "That path is much too dangerous."

"It's the fastest." Nero crosses his arms across his chest. "With those suits and my help, you'll make it, old man."

"You're wounded," Rasputin argues. "Why take unnecessary risks?"

"We have to get a move on," I say. "This world is—"

A familiar dragon roar silences the rest of my sentence.

His face tightening, Nero looks at the sky.

"Fine, let's go to that gate," he growls. "It's nearer."

Turning, he jogs for the green gate.

I run after him, and everyone else follows.

"So," Felix pants. "You're telling me we didn't need to nearly get eaten by cannibal gnomes and all the rest of that? Do we even need the suits on this new route?"

"I haven't needed one there," Rasputin says, picking up his pace as another roar sounds in the sky.

"Itzel's going to have a fit when she learns about this," Ariel says, catching up with Nero.

"Well, we wouldn't have needed her if we'd known about a safer path." Felix is almost out of breath.

"Right, and we'd be dead now," I pant. "Her ball lightning was the only thing that stopped Lilith, remember?"

"She blocked your visions," Felix begins, but I don't hear what follows because the unknown dragon roars again.

Less than twenty feet from the gate, Nero stops, his back muscles tensing—and my friends gasp in horror as the source of the roar lands, blocking our way to the gate.

CHAPTER FIFTY-FIVE

THIS DRAGON LOOKS SLIGHTLY SMALLER than Nero was in that form, but that doesn't make him any less frightening.

"Cass." Nero spits at the ground in front of the dragon's massive claws. "Still guarding the gates like a dog?" he says in Russian.

The dragon shines with energy, and a naked man stands in its place.

Clearly, dragons don't choose what they look like in human form, as there's no way this guy would voluntarily look like this. His forehead protrudes far enough to allow him to star as a caveman in a GEICO commercial, and his upper body is much buffer than his lower body, making him look like a rooster.

Giving Nero a look that belongs in the dictionary under "fury," he says in a growly voice, "I knew I smelled a coward earlier, but you scurried by without saying hello."

Cass's Russian sounds a little strange, but I'm able to understand it—and since Ariel is not, I whisper a translation for her benefit.

"I'm going to give you a choice someone from your foul family doesn't deserve." Nero's fists flex at his sides. "Fly away now, and you live. Your uncle will never know that you met me and—"

"How about I give *you* a choice." Cass's limbal rings expand. "Once you're dead, your strange round-headed pets can pass through unharmed." He looks at the five of us menacingly. "I almost feasted on them when they last came through, but I can forego a good meal for the sake of glory."

Nero sneers. "You'd really fight me? I thought you and your coward of an uncle were only capable of hiring human thugs to do what you can't."

I translate Nero's words for Ariel's benefit, then add, "Sounds like Nero is accusing him or his uncle of hiring those people in clown masks who sent the bomb to our office and shot us with machine guns and the bazooka."

The warlike expression Cass's face gives way to confusion. "Humans?" He seems to taste the word and find it sour. "To kill *a dragon*? Why would I do something so stupid and futile?"

"Interesting," I say after I translate again. "I think the guy doesn't know anything about those assassins—or, for that matter, the modern weapons that can make a human dangerous even to a dragon."

"So it wasn't you," Nero mutters. He must've come

to the same conclusion as I did—and he has truth-detection abilities. "In that case, I will give you one last chance to live."

"I'm much more powerful than you remember." Cass puffs up his chest, increasing his resemblance to a cock. "I bet you haven't battled another dragon during your exile. And you're already bleeding. How hard would you be to slay?"

"Some of these are unfortunately valid points," I say in English and loudly enough so that Nero could hopefully overhear. "Let's take a chance and just run for another gate."

If Nero heard me, he shows no sign of it. Instead, he blurs into motion as he growls, "So be it. You *will* die."

Cass springs into action, his movements just as blurry as Nero's.

It's hard to tell what's happening at that speed, but I'm pretty sure Nero's uninjured left hand turns claw-like and slices at Cass's low brow. Cass ducks in time to avoid losing his face, and both of his hands also turn claw-like, slicing at Nero's face and torso. Nero dodges both strikes and throws a low kick that Cass sidesteps. He then claws at Nero's neck and right shoulder—but misses.

"Put Itzel down and let's go help him," I tell Ariel as the two men turn into an even faster blur of deadly claws and naked skin.

Ariel places the gnome on the ground and takes a step forward.

"Stay back," Nero orders in English as he dodges a series of attacks. "Don't move another inch."

"Then kill him already," I shout. I can't bear to watch Nero in danger.

"It's not that easy. He's lost a *lot* of blood." Rasputin points at the bloody streak that leads to Nero.

"I think Nero can take him still," Ariel says confidently, and as though to confirm her words, Nero succeeds at slicing a bloody gash in his opponent's cheek.

Now they're both bleeding—though Nero's injury is much worse than Cass's.

Growling, Cass headbutts Nero, causing him to fly back a few feet.

The vision in which Lilith sliced off Nero's head flits through my mind.

I can't risk him losing.

I can't risk losing *him*.

"This is bullshit," I grit through clenched teeth and press the button that activates the plasma blade on the sword in my hand. "I'm going to—"

Nero glances at me over his shoulder, and a bright shimmer surrounds his body as he turns into a dragon again.

"That's more like it," Cass growls and turns also. Then they both leap into the air and roar at each other like two bears fighting over a mate.

They then circle one another in the air, each studying his opponent with narrowed eyes.

"You shouldn't have done that," Felix mutters. "I

think Nero turned into his dragon form so you couldn't interfere—"

"Why?" I clutch the sword hilt tighter and wonder if I can throw it at Cass. I decide against it, worried that I might hit Nero instead.

"Notice how much more blood seeps from that claw wound compared to a human hand," Felix says. "He's bound to weaken faster this way."

"Shouldn't it all even out in the end?" I ask in desperation. "When he's big, he has more blood, right?"

"Sure," Felix says sarcastically. "Magical transformations like that always follow logic—"

Tired of circling, Nero zooms forward and swipes at Cass with his tail—landing a blow into the other dragon's chest.

Cass's tail wraps around Nero's damaged claw in return—and squeezes.

With a pained roar, Nero claws at the guy's tail, but Cass pulls it back just in time to avoid getting hurt.

Nero swats Cass with his undamaged claw, but the other dragon dodges and tries to sink his teeth into the claw—which Nero jerks back just in time.

Damn it.

Why hasn't Nero killed him already? With every moment, he's losing more and more blood.

"Can we wake Itzel somehow?" I poke at the still-unconscious gnome with the tip of my space boot. "One of her balls would be—"

Nero spews fire at Cass, and my breath stops in my chest as Cass spews fire back at Nero. In the blink of an eye, each dragon is enveloped in a thick stream of fire.

To my surprise, Nero looks as calm as if he were bathing in warm sunrays.

His opponent, on the other hand, roars in pain.

"Yes!" I pump my fist. "Burn him."

Cass looks at Nero in panic; then his eyes hone in on me, and he turns his fiery breath at me and my friends.

With an angry roar, Nero dives, blocking the fire's path with his body—which gives Cass a chance to dive at Nero's back with his claws.

Nero spins in the air—but not fast enough.

A claw slashes through Nero's right shoulder.

Dread and anger color my vision red.

"Ariel, throw me at that dragon," I order in English as Nero roars in pain and spins around to slice at Cass's chest, his claws leaving a shallow gash in the other dragon's hide.

"Are you insane?" Felix shouts as Ariel grabs me. "Those are dragons!"

"Do it," I insist.

She complies, and her suit-boosted super-strength doesn't disappoint.

Heart hammering, I launch into the air like a superhero.

"What did you do?" Rasputin shouts in Russian.

My fingers spasm over the sword hilt, and my heart pounds against my ribcage as I fly in a wide arc.

Cass's giant eyes widen as he spots me, and he extends his claw, ready to squash me like a fly.

Nero roars and chomps at the extended appendage.

Cass yanks the claw away—which is when I fly by him and slice his wing with my blade, cleaving it off.

Then, I begin to fall.

CHAPTER FIFTY-SIX

WITH A ROAR, Nero snatches me from the air with his claws.

Cass crash-lands on the ground, roaring in pain.

Nero swoops down and deposits me in Ariel's arms before zooming back into the sky.

Cass's body lights up, and he turns into a humanoid again.

Leaving a blood trail behind himself, he rushes at us.

I clutch my sword and try not to think of all the times I trained with Nero without landing a single punch. At least until I cheated using my powers—something Itzel is preventing me from doing now.

In the corner of my eye, I see Nero do a loop in the sky and dive at Cass, his undamaged claw extended.

Trying to leverage his currently smaller size, Cass tries to dodge, but Nero's talons tear into the man's midsection.

There's a gurgling sound, followed by a crunch. Nero rips his claw out and raises it for the ultimate blow.

"Wait!" Cass chokes out, spitting up blood. "I can lead you to Claudia."

Nero lights up and shifts back into a man—with a smaller claw still ready to strike.

The wound on his shoulder is gushing blood, and I don't need Ariel's background to know that it needs urgent medical attention.

"She's dead," Nero growls. "I saw—"

"You saw her badly wounded, but unlike the others, she survived." Cass coughs up a bloody chunk of mucus. "My uncle plans to marry her so that—"

With blurring speed, Nero's claw enters Cass's chest. Ripping out the man's still-beating heart, he tosses it on the ground and stomps on it with the heel of his foot, over and over, for a whole minute.

Then he starts stomping on Cass's face, crushing it with each blow.

At my side, Felix lifts his visor and starts puking his guts out.

A distant roar shakes the ground, sounding like it's coming from at least a dozen dragons.

Nero stops his grisly task and looks into the distance, his expression terrifyingly bloodthirsty. I'm pretty sure he wants to fight these newcomers; something about what Cass just said about this Claudia is fueling Nero's bloodlust.

"Nero," I say soothingly and lift my visor so he can

see the pleading look on my face. "We have to go. You're bleeding."

He glances at the sword in my hand, then meets my gaze.

"Please." I touch his uninjured shoulder. "I need you to walk into that green gate with me."

His fists clench as he glances at the sword once more, looks up into the distance, then returns his gaze to my face.

Jaw tight, he turns on his heel and strides for the gate.

Ariel grabs Itzel and rushes after him, with the rest of us hurriedly following.

We enter the gate and end up in some cavern.

Nero looks at Rasputin. "Which gate is next?"

"There." My father points at a purple gate a few feet away.

"We need to stop your bleeding," I tell Nero.

A muscle ticks in his jaw. "No time. They might come after us."

"And your blood trail will show them which gates we're taking." I unscrew my helmet and slip out of the suit to get at my shirt underneath it.

I rip off a sleeve as Nero stares, his expression peculiarly hungry. Ignoring it, I say, "Get over here, so I can do this and we can go."

He walks over, and despite our dire situation, my face heats at his nudity.

Ariel makes some inappropriate sound.

"Shut up and help," I tell her as I rise on tiptoe to get a good look at the wound.

Ariel joins me, and we do our best to bandage the shoulder.

Unfortunately, our work only slightly dampens the blood flow. Cursing under my breath, I rip off another sleeve, and Ariel wraps it over his hand. This works marginally better than with the shoulder.

"Now we go." Nero turns and strides for the purple gate.

I put the suit back on and follow, my eyes never leaving Nero's perfectly sculpted behind.

How bad can hooking up with a dragon actually be? Especially one who looks like *that*?

I mean, hypothetically, of course.

After the purple gate, we end up at an empty forest meadow in a world with stars that look much too bright—and illuminate Nero's body so that—

"We're going there," Rasputin says, pointing at the red gate nearest to us.

Nero walks where my father suggested, and I do my best to smear any blood droplets Nero leaves behind with my boot.

In the next world, the gates are standing in a crystal-clear shallow water that spans from horizon to horizon.

The water makes Nero's shapely calves glisten with—

"This is good," Felix says, kicking at the water with his booted foot. "Even if our pursuers are as good as dogs when it comes to tracking, they'll still lose our trail at this point."

Nero looks over his shoulder at Felix with a look that seems to say, "I'm going to pretend you didn't just compare dragons to dogs."

We go through the gate Rasputin points out and end up in a frozen wasteland, surrounded by what looks a lot like penguins—only they're solid white in color.

I close my visor in order not to lose my nose to frostbite and glance worriedly at Nero's naked feet.

He seems oblivious to the cold—with not a single goosepimple on that naked body... and I've checked thoroughly. When he stops to look at Rasputin for direction, I realize that even Nero's private parts didn't shrivel up in the cold—something I noticed purely by accident, of course.

The accident being that I'm a peeping perv.

"That way," Rasputin says, and without so much as a shiver, Nero strides to the gate in question.

I overturn the snow where I spot droplets of Nero's blood and follow everyone into the next world.

This world looks like a forest, but I don't get a chance to take in the details because of a naked Nero getting right in my face... with his face.

"You will *never* risk your life like that again," he growls, his expression furious.

"What are you talking about?" I ask, his lack of clothing messing with my concentration. "I've been walking safely, like everyone else."

"I think he means the stunt with the sword," Felix whispers.

"You stay out of it," I hiss at Felix, then unlock my visor and give Nero a narrow-eyed stare. "He had his claw in your shoulder. Did you want me to let him kill you?"

"I had him." Nero's limbal rings grow dangerously wide. "But even if I didn't, you are *not* to risk yourself on my behalf."

"Right," I say with as much sarcasm as I can muster. "So you can come rescue me from a goddess and get your head chopped off with this sword"—I lift the hilt —"but I'm not allowed—"

A gnome scream interrupts my righteous tirade.

Turning on my heel, I see Ariel setting a kicking-and-screaming Itzel on the ground.

"What happened?" the gnome demands after she realizes she's not in danger. "Where is Lilith? Where are we?"

"I'll explain on the way," Felix says to her. "But first, can you walk or do you want Ariel to carry you?"

Instead of answering, Itzel takes a few shuffling steps. "I'll walk, and you talk," she says, lifting her visor.

"This way." Rasputin points at a pink gate, and we enter it as Felix tells Itzel about recent events.

In the time it takes Felix to finish, we walk through a dusty world with too many moons, and through a place that looks like the surface of Mars—but with oxygen.

To his credit, Felix doesn't bring up the part where

Ariel tossed me at a dragon. No doubt he doesn't want Nero to start yelling at me again, and for that, I'm grateful.

For the next couple of worlds, Itzel fumes about the fact that there was a path that didn't need her or the suits, concluding with how she isn't getting paid enough for any of the events that transpired— particularly the part where she rode a dragon while unconscious.

"I'll add some zeroes to Felix's payment," Nero tells Itzel when she's done. "You were extremely helpful back there, and I want to make sure you're properly compensated."

"Oh." Itzel looks Nero up and down. I'm not sure if she realizes that he's naked or not, but I'd put my money on yes. "That's very generous—"

Nero waves his hand, cutting her off. "Don't worry about it. You'll get your payment."

"You're sure?" She looks him up and down again.

"Positive," Nero says. "I may need your particular skills in the future."

She nods, and her gaze stops around his crotch region. "I can't believe you're a dragon," she says without lifting her eyes. "I've never met one before."

"As far as everyone outside this group is concerned, you still haven't," Nero says silkily and looks at each of us. "Is that understood?"

"Yes, sir," Felix replies instantly.

"Who would I tell?" Ariel asks rhetorically.

Itzel bobs her head, and Rasputin mumbles something in Russian before pointing at the next gate.

Nero is first to enter, and the rest of us follow.

"Are we there?" I ask when I exit and look around. The hub looks almost identical to the one at JFK.

"Not yet," Rasputin says. "Unfortunately, the next gate is in another hub, elsewhere on this world."

"We have to trek through an Otherland?" Felix looks worried.

"That's the only safe way," Rasputin says. "We could go through these gates to more dangerous worlds, but—"

"I'm okay with this," Itzel says. "I'd rather hike than see giant insects ever again."

"Or cannibal gnomes," Felix mutters. "Or—"

"Just lead," Nero growls at Rasputin. "The sooner we leave, the sooner we get there."

"You might find this a rather depressing world," Rasputin says over his shoulder as he starts walking toward a regular door. "Just want you to be ready when you see all the bodies."

"Great," Felix mumbles. "Can't wait to see *the bodies*. Plural."

The mirrored floors of the hub reflect Nero's nakedness in an interesting way, keeping me occupied all the way to the corridors—which also seem to be clones of the ones at JFK.

Following the pattern, the door we reach also looks like a dead ringer for the one at JFK.

"This isn't warded," Itzel says, looking at the door.

"Hidden hubs like this are usually warded."

"You can see wards?" Ariel asks, sounding impressed.

"Of course," Itzel says. "I didn't realize others can't."

"What are wards?" I ask.

"A spell that keeps humans from even thinking about going into the hub," Felix explains. "There are witches who—"

"Spells? Witches?" Itzel's voice drips with disdain. "Did you grow up on a medieval world like the one Lilith took over?"

"Pedantic much?" Felix grumbles. "It's faster to say 'witches' than 'Cognizant with the power to make wards.'"

"It's unscientific," Itzel says. "We call them warders on Gomorrah."

"Sure," Felix says sarcastically. "*That* sounds so much better than witches."

"It's more specific." Itzel walks over to the door and opens it. "If you call mind manipulators, power removers, power boosters, and so on 'witches,' it makes it sound like they all have the same set of powers, which they don't. As to the term 'spell,' that's even worse. A ward is a perfectly good term for what a warder does; you just used it yourself. I personally prefer the term 'persistent psychological—"

She doesn't finish her thought because she sees the view outside the door.

Walking out in shocked silence, we stare at the bodies Rasputin warned us about.

CHAPTER FIFTY-SEVEN

IF YOU COULD TURN a human into a raisin, then suck some moisture out of that mummified corpse, it would approximate the dried husks of the people sprawled all over this very JFK-like airport.

Many of them have their suitcases lying right by them—as if whatever happened to them came without warning just as they were going through security or checking in their luggage.

"What happened?" Ariel asks in horror, and I realize I didn't translate Rasputin's "depressing world" warning for her earlier.

I translate Ariel's question and join everyone in staring at Rasputin, glad for a chance to tear my gaze away from the corpses.

"It was Tartarus." Rasputin raises his visor and massages his forehead. "He comes to a world, kills all other Cognizant there, gets the populace to worship him to get a boost in power, and then feeds on their energy to sustain his mockery of a life."

I translate the explanation for Ariel, and she shakes her head in disbelief.

His face pale, Felix looks at the husks again. "We were told about Tartarus during Orientation, but I didn't realize he was *this* bad."

"Oh, I knew he was bad," I say, remembering Hekima showing us a deserted world where humans attacked and ate a hapless Cognizant who came through the gate. "By the way..." I look at Rasputin. "Are you sure this world is safe?"

"Few, if any, humans survived," Rasputin says. "Developed technology worlds are particularly vulnerable to Tartarus at the stage when he chooses to reveal his power."

"I see," Ariel whispers after I loop her into the conversation. "He must've leveraged TV and social media to get worshipped by billions before he sucked them dry."

"Yeah." I look around again. "What kind of Cognizant is he, to be able to do something like this?"

"The type who feeds on human life energy," Nero says. "At some point, most of the other Cognizant deemed Tartarus's kind too dangerous and hunted them almost to extinction." He says this with a disapproval that makes me think dragons weren't among the killers—or that someone might've wanted to exterminate his kind for being too dangerous as well.

"However," Nero continues, "Tartarus himself was too powerful for anyone to slay, so he persists as the last of his kind to this day."

"Which explains why he starts his takeovers by killing all Cognizant," Itzel says. "Must be upset about what happened in the past."

"That makes sense," Felix says. "Racial cleansings do tend to bring out the worst in people."

We walk in silence for a few minutes, stepping over corpses as we go.

"Lilith thought *we* were Tartarus's spies," I say for Rasputin's and Nero's benefit. "I think that was why she wanted to torture us for information."

"Lilith has been obsessed with Tartarus for ages now," Rasputin says. "Nostradamus had made a series of prophecies for her, and one was that Tartarus will be Lilith's doom."

"That would mean that Tartarus sometimes accidentally does something good," Ariel says when I translate. "Not that it compensates for the bad." She looks around.

"No," I say and walk up to a husk that looks to be about Nero's height.

Crouching, I open the dust-covered suitcase lying by the corpse and rummage through it until I locate a black tracksuit with a logo that looks eerily like Earth's Adidas.

"Put this on." I toss a pair of pants at Nero. "You're making Itzel uncomfortable."

With an unreadable expression, my boss catches the

pants and puts them on.

Next, I grab the jacket and walk over to help him put that on over the bandages.

"Very thoughtful," Nero murmurs when I zip the jacket for him. "I'm sure Itzel is going to be much more comfortable now."

My face is overly warm, but I shrug and fish out sneakers from the same suitcase, along with a pair of socks, and give them to him.

"Let's go," a very sporty-looking Nero says and strides for the airport exit.

As I follow, I almost regret giving him clothes. Seeing Nero naked would've made this airport passing a lot less dreary—if anything could.

Oh, the sacrifices we sometimes make.

Doing my best to focus on anything but the thousands of dead bodies, I spot the airport sign, which states we're in New York International Airport instead of JFK. So we're obviously not on *our* Earth. Still, it's one where New York is actually called New York—and all the people's fashions are very similar, as are the uniforms worn by the mummified TSA agents.

Nero walks up to a corpse who might've been a tourist and snatches a map from his stiff, gnarled fingers. He studies it, then drops it on the floor.

"Where exactly are we going?" he asks Rasputin.

"This map is too small," my father says. "But it would be in this direction." He points to where New Jersey would be in our world.

"That's the equivalent of Newark Airport," I say, and

Rasputin nods, describing the long walk ahead of us.

"Can't we drive?" Felix asks.

"Don't you see that?" Itzel points at a huge pileup of cars blocking the nearest road.

Felix's shoulders sag. "Maybe the roads get better outside the airport?"

"It gets worse," Rasputin says, though I'm sure Felix could've guessed that much himself.

We start walking, and soon, we see the equivalent of Belt Parkway.

My father was right. There's a huge pileup of cars there, each with a dried corpse or two inside.

It's depressing to look at all the carnage, so we walk onto the road in silence, passing the pileup as we head south on I-678.

The farther we get, the more the scenery reminds me of different post-apocalyptic movies and shows—from *I am Legend* to *The Walking Dead.* Except there are no zombies anywhere, or even feral zoo animals.

"I hope a necromancer never comes here," Ariel mumbles under her breath after we've been walking for a while.

"I also hope Tartarus never comes to *our* Earth," Felix says with a shiver.

No one disagrees with him, and we walk on in dreary silence.

"Any chance we can take a break?" Itzel huffs when we're midway through Brooklyn. "My legs are killing me."

I sneak a peek at Nero. It could be my imagination,

but I think he's unusually pale. If he were human, I'd say he should eat lots of food with iron, but who knows if that's true of dragons who lose blood.

"How about we stop by that Key Food-like store?" I point at a supermarket just off the road. "They might have some cans that are still safe to eat."

No one argues, so we trudge over to the place.

It's dark inside the store, but the hardware section happens to be right by the entrance, so we manage to locate some flashlights and can openers straight away.

Deeper in, the store is just as bad as everywhere else, but it's somehow extra disturbing to see people sucked dry in the process of picking out their cereal or paying for groceries.

Nero nonchalantly grabs a shopping cart and fills it with twenty cans of organic tuna. You'd think he's planning to feed an army of cats instead of one man/dragon.

I grab pinto beans and peaches in heavy syrup for myself, and the rest of the crew get an assortment of other canned goods. We then go to the Hallmark-card section of the store because there are no corpses there, and make ourselves comfortable on the floor as we devour our selections.

Even though we can't see the dead, no one feels like talking, the corpses' presence in the next isle as oppressive as if they were right next to us. By the time we exit the supermarket, the sun has set, and like the rest of this world, the moon looks just like the one I'm familiar with, as do the stars.

"Are there many duplicate worlds like this?" I ask as we head for the highway.

"There are so many Otherlands that repeats are bound to happen," Felix says, but he doesn't elaborate—a sure sign this place is taking a psychological toll on him.

As we walk farther, the similarities to our Earth keep stacking up. The Manhattan equivalent has a nearly identical skyline, and the Brooklyn Bridge looks just like ours.

When we finally reach Manhattan, Itzel yawns demonstratively. "My legs hurt again. Also, I'm very sleepy."

"Are all gnomes such divas?" Felix says. "Or is it just—"

"Itzel makes a good point." I sneak a glance at Nero and wonder what's better for an injured dragon—some rest or professional medical attention?

"We'll camp out in a hotel," Nero says, deciding the matter. "I assume we need to cross the river, and it's not something we want to do in the dark."

"We can walk on a bridge if we take the longer way, but a boat ride would be much faster," Rasputin says. "And there are plenty of boats to steal if we can see what we're doing."

Thus decided, we look for a hotel that uses traditional locks that can be opened with a key—or picked. We finally locate one in this world's clone of Wall Street.

It takes us an hour to round up six rooms that have

no dead people inside, and by the time we do, I'm yawning as loudly as Itzel and thanking the stars we got proactive about this sleepover.

Once I actually try to fall asleep in my room, however, I find it impossible. There are too many confusing thoughts swirling through my brain.

I have to talk to my father, to learn more about the mystery of my origins, but he doesn't seem very talkative in this depressing place. I also want to talk to Nero, but I have no idea what to say or how to go about approaching him.

This whole trip, he's been distant, as if we're back to being an employee and her boss. Which is ridiculous, given that he's risked his life to save me.

Two sleepless hours later, I give up and get up.

Not sure where I'm going yet, I grab my flashlight and let my legs carry me where they will—and it soon becomes clear my treacherous legs took me straight to Nero's room.

I hesitate, then walk up to the door.

What am I doing here?

I turn and get ready to retreat when the door opens, revealing Nero, his blue-gray eyes bright in the glow of my flashlight.

"I couldn't sleep," I blurt out.

His limbal rings expand. "Me either."

"Can I come in?" I shock myself by saying.

He opens the door wider and gestures for me to walk in.

CHAPTER FIFTY-EIGHT

ONCE INSIDE, I set my flashlight down on a dresser and stand awkwardly in the middle of the room.

Nero studies me with an unreadable expression, and I realize that he's jacketless—as in, his chest is bare.

Well, at least he's not completely naked this time.

A part of me not drowning in hormones notices that he redid his shoulder bandage using one of the hotel towels, and that some blood has already seeped through the towel.

Then the hormones take over, and my eyes leave the wound to hungrily roam over his abdominal muscles.

Crap.

I force my gaze to his hand and notice it's doing much better than the shoulder.

"Dragon claws have enzymes that hamper healing," he says, following my gaze. "But I have a way to speed up my recovery when we get to Earth."

He probably means Isis—and the idea of her shooting Nero with that pleasurable healing energy bothers the currently overstimulated parts of my brain, the ones that make my eyes go to his abs yet again.

I can't help but wonder if it's customary—and even polite—for a rescued damsel to throw herself at her rescuer.

No. Bad Sasha.

Given what said rescuer is, that's a bad idea—for reasons still unclear. Also, if we're talking purely customs as defined by fairytales, the damsel is supposed to be rescued *from* a dragon, not *by* a dragon.

"I wanted to thank you," I finally blurt out, taking a step toward him. "For coming to save me and all."

His eyes narrow. "You left without a word."

"I saw a vision of what you would do if I told you what I planned," I retort, even as I take another step toward him. "You would've locked me in that stupid safe."

"And that didn't clue you in about the dangers you would face?" His nostrils flare. "You think I enjoy locking you up?"

"I think you might," I say, my hackles rising. "Not going wasn't an option. You know me better than that by now."

He steps toward me, stopping so close that I can smell hints of his spicy cologne. "I spent a day looking everywhere for you," he says in a dangerous tone. "Do you know what that was like?"

"Lilith *decapitated* you in my vision," I reply, matching his tone. "Do you know what *that* was like?"

"You got between two fighting dragons," he growls in such a dragon-like fashion, I can't believe I didn't guess his nature based on this alone.

Speaking of dragon stuff, can he spew fire in this form? He looks just about ready to do so.

Balling my fists, I lean in and hiss, "You—"

His lips angrily capture mine, swallowing the rest of my rebuttal.

Wow.

I kiss him back as though I need his tongue for sustenance.

His hands grip my hips and pull me impossibly closer.

The unburned adrenaline in my veins conspires with the years of abstinence to make this kiss a kind of out-of-body experience—one made that much stronger when he lifts me off my feet as if I were a feather and carries me to the bed.

Double wow. I don't think I've ever been this turned on in my life—and that includes my encounter with a succubus.

My practice in straightjacket escapes pays another dividend when I manage to slide out of my clothes without unlocking our lips.

His hands roam over my body, spreading tingles of heat everywhere he touches, and a flock of excited hummingbirds beat their wings in my belly as I reach to help him escape his stupid pants.

Except Nero catches my wrist in an iron grip and pulls away from the kiss with a pained groan.

"Are you kidding me?" I gape at my naked body and the impressive bulge being strangled by the pants.

"It's not safe." He pulls back, his gaze dark and tormented. "If I lose control, you could get hurt."

"I don't care," I pant, pulling him back to me.

His limbal rings leave no sign of the blue-gray in his eyes, and a very dragon-like growl escapes his lips.

A growl that promises pleasure but also maybe a dislocated pelvis and third-degree burns.

"Okay, so maybe I care a little," I whisper. "But surely there's something we—"

He silences me with another kiss.

The logical parts of my brain shut down again.

His lips trail over my jaw to my neck, which causes gooseflesh to cover me from head to toe.

I shiver with pleasure.

His lips draw a line to my right breast.

My shivers intensify.

His tongue generates waves of need that hit my core like a tsunami; then his mouth moves down my ribcage to my belly button.

With a sensuous inhale, I tangle my fingers in his hair as his mouth moves lower still.

When he reaches his target, I gasp, my back arching and my fingers tangling in his thick, silky hair.

Oblivious to me trying to scalp him, Nero moves his tongue faster.

The pleasure explodes through me with such intensity that I can't suppress a cry.

He further picks up speed.

The pleasure is almost too much.

If *I* were a dragon, I might hurt *him* at this point—besides pulling out his hair, that is.

His pace impossibly speeds up, and something inside me explodes as rays of pure pleasure pummel my every nerve. Moaning, I writhe against him, unable to control myself, my mind blanketed in sensations.

When my thrashing finally ceases, I realize that my throat is hoarse from screaming and my muscles have turned to mush.

Moving as though through molasses, I reach to return the favor, but Nero stops me again. Ignoring my objections, he forcefully puts me in a spooning position.

If he thought this would make things better, he was wrong. I can feel him pressing against my behind, and he's clearly frustrated.

Very frustrated.

He inhales deeply against the back of my head, as though smelling a bouquet of flowers, then exhales that breath slowly and deliberately, like someone trying not to let their temper take over.

"I want to make you feel good too," I protest—and feel rather proud that I can string so many words together in my gelatinous state.

"It's not safe," he growls and readjusts his hold on

me so I no longer feel his frustration. "You better go to sleep. You're exhausted."

Is he trying to hypnotize me? If so, it might be working. I yawn so hard that my jaws hurt, and my eyelids are starting to feel like they're made of lead.

I can't sleep yet, though. Turning over, I touch his shoulder, where more blood has seeped through the towel.

"Does this hurt?" I ask softly, and I see a shudder ripple through him as my fingers brush across his naked chest.

"It's fine." His voice is hoarse. "It's nothing. It will heal."

"Let me change it," I say and move to get up, but he tightens his hold on me.

"Stay," he orders, rolling over onto his back, and I obey, laying my head on his uninjured shoulder with a sigh.

For a few moments, we lie together quietly, and I feel myself starting to drift off when Nero asks softly, "So is he everything you wanted him to be?"

I pull back to gaze at him. "You mean Rasputin?"

Nero nods.

"I don't know yet," I say honestly. "It's been so crazy that we haven't really had a chance to talk. But I know now that what he did—leaving me at the airport and making a deal with you—was to protect me."

"Yes," he says, his gaze shadowed. "So does that mean you forgive him?"

I swallow thickly. Do I? How do you forgive a

father who's left you to be raised by strangers who aren't even your own kind? How different would my life have been if I'd been raised Cognizant?

Then again, given what I saw in his memories, maybe there was no other choice.

Nero is looking at me expectantly, and I don't know what to tell him. Instead, I ask, "What about you? What happened to your family? How did you end up living so far away from other dragons?" *And who is Claudia?* I want to add, but I don't. Because what if she's his wife, and he'd thought her dead all these years?

Could that be the real reason he doesn't want to take our intimacy further?

I recall a session with Lucretia the other day. She'd hinted that Nero fears feelings—more specifically, that he's afraid that another person he cares about might die.

Nero's face hardens, and he turns me around, arranging me back into the spooning position. Despite the tension I sense from him, his hand strokes my hip soothingly, and as far as distractions go, it's a good one.

I'm starting to yawn again.

To my shock, he says softly, "I was part of the royal family."

He falls silent, and I stop breathing, not daring to make a sound lest I interrupt him.

"A friend of my father's was an ambitious dragon who used a treacherous attack to usurp the throne," he continues after a moment. His voice is low and dark, as dangerous as I've ever heard it. "Afterward, he killed everyone I cared about. Or, as it turns out, almost everyone."

I suppress a shudder as his hand on my hip turns claw-like before returning to its human guise.

"I've been postponing my revenge, growing stronger, but if Claudia survived, it changes everything…"

He pauses again, and I wait for him to continue with bated breath. But he doesn't say anything else, and after what feels like hours of waiting, I hear his breathing even out, his tense body relaxing against my back.

He's asleep, the blood loss having taken its toll.

My heart clenching, I reach over, covering us both with a blanket, and then I join him in sleep.

CHAPTER FIFTY-NINE

THE RAYS of the morning sun welcome my corneas to wakefulness with smiling photons.

To my disappointment, Nero isn't in bed anymore.

Stretching like a cat, I sit up and look around.

Still no Nero.

Oh well.

The interesting thing is that I feel *great*. I guess doctors who deal with patients who almost get killed by gods and dragons should order said patients to sleep. Bonus points if that sleep can be done in the arms of a dragon.

I get up and look for the dragon in question—without any success.

Nero's not in the room, nor in the bathroom.

Maybe he woke up early and left quietly to let me have my beauty sleep? How nice of him to indulge me in this post-apocalyptic world.

I step out into the hallway to the sight of Ariel doing some kind of calisthenics.

When she spots me, her eyes widen and she stops mid-stretch.

"Isn't that Nero's room?" She stares at the door behind me.

"No, it's not," I lie.

"Dude. That *is* Nero's room. And you're glowing."

"It's not," I say but even less believably this time. "And I'm not."

"You're totally glowing," she says and jumps up and down in excitement. "What happened?"

"Where's everyone?" I furtively look around.

"Itzel is probably still sleeping, and Felix, Rasputin, and Nero left to get some food." She grins and adds, "I didn't get it at the time, but it seems like Nero wanted to bring you some breakfast in bed." She wiggles her perfect eyebrows lasciviously.

I bite my lip. I guess it's time to fess up. "I've been meaning to talk to you about this. It's just that you've had a lot going on, and this thing is pretty complicated."

"Is it though?" She winks. "Boy prances around naked all day, girl is flesh and blood—who could possibly blame you?"

"Right, but it's Nero we're talking about."

"Right. A friggin' dragon," she says. "Do you realize what that means?"

I shake my head, and she pitches her voice deeper. "You could literally become 'The Mother of Dragons.'"

I roll my eyes. "You know what? Forget it." I turn to head to my room.

"I'm sorry," she says like a not-sorry five-year-old. "Please, tell me all the details. I'll act like an adult from now on, I pinky swear."

"Fine." I wave for her to follow me as I enter my room.

As I put on my spacesuit, I tell her all about my recent encounters with Nero. When I get to certain parts, I fluctuate between blushing and grinning like an idiot. Mid-story, we exit out into the hallway, and I look around carefully before I continue.

"So, I still have no idea what would happen if he 'lost control,'" I say in conclusion. "Or if that is an insurmountable problem. Or who—"

"I doubt the insurmountable part," she cuts in, mirth playing in the corners of her eyes. "I'm confident that you, of all people, will find a way to *mount*—"

Male voices ring out down the hall, and Ariel theatrically covers her mouth with her hand.

Felix, Rasputin, and Nero walk toward us holding an assortment of canned food.

Is that heat in Nero's eyes when he looks at me, or is it just wishful thinking on my part?

"We rummaged through a convenience store downstairs," Felix says, looking from me to Ariel.

"Nero and Felix have told me about your various skills," Rasputin says in Russian, and I'm glad Ariel doesn't understand what he's saying. The idea of Nero telling my father about "my skills" would no doubt make her giggle right now.

Putting down his cans, Rasputin hands me a sealed deck of cards that look just like the ones in our world. "Nero suggested I give you this and ask you to 'show me something.'"

"Let's eat first," Felix says. "If Sasha gets going, this could take a few hours."

As though in agreement with his words, Ariel's tummy rumbles.

I grab the cards and help Rasputin with the rest of his cans.

"What about Itzel?" I ask.

"What about me?" a voice says behind me, and I turn to face the gnome dressed in full spacesuit regalia.

"Let's have breakfast in my room," Ariel suggests. "There's a table."

We camp out there and devour the food almost without chewing.

"The boats are in a marina there." Rasputin points out the window, and I realize we'll be passing right by this world's equivalent of our apartment. How creepy is that?

When we get there, it turns out that it *is* very creepy because our—or strictly speaking, Nero's—apartment building is there and looks identical to its Earth self.

As an icing on the creepy cake, some of the corpses around these parts look like our neighbors—though that could be my overstimulated imagination at work.

The Battery Park is also a dead ringer for "ours,"

and the marina Rasputin leads us to is the one where I like to trespass sometimes—and where an orc tried to drown me in the harbor.

An orc Nero—the dragon whose arms I slept in last night—hired to jolt my powers and later brutally killed in front of me.

Once we steal a yacht and set sail for New Jersey, I put on a card magic show for my father doing my "best of" effects, from the ambitious card—which always jumps to the top—to gambling demonstrations.

Rasputin keeps asking for more, and I oblige him over and over, until he remains the only person watching, and I start to dip into effects I haven't done in many years.

As I perform, I again let myself hope that one day I could have a show for the Cognizant. All I need is for everyone to stop trying to kill me so I can put together a good set, rehearse, and find the right venue.

"I have no idea how you did any of that," Rasputin says proudly when I have him miraculously cut to all four aces in a shuffled deck.

"And you can't use your seer powers to figure it out," I say with mock sternness. "That would be cheating."

"Cross my heart," he says. "I don't even want to know how it's done. It would ruin the mystery and the specialness of this moment." He puts his hand on mine and smiles so contentedly that something in my chest melts.

"Can you please tell me more about your life?" he

asks when I put the cards away. "I saw some of it in visions, but the time differential between our worlds made that difficult."

I smile and start telling him all about my obsession with magic, then about school, college, and my adoptive parents.

He absorbs the information greedily and asks countless questions about the most mundane details.

Eventually, I get to the most recent past that deals with zombies, vampires, and—as it turns out—dragons.

Rasputin hangs on to my every word and looks to be on the edge of his seat when I tell him the part about Baba Yaga.

"I knew her," he says when I finish. "You're lucky to be alive. You all are."

"Well, what about you?" I ask. "What happened to you in Russia all those years ago? Why did you have to leave? How did you meet my mother? Who is she? Where is she? Why—"

"I made powerful enemies in Russia at about the same time as I met your mother," he says and looks into the horizon with a distant expression. "She left with me when I escaped Earth. Then you were born, and—"

The boat jerks in that very moment, and I nearly topple from my chair.

"I'm sorry," Ariel yells from the port side. "It's my first time docking one of these."

I look back and realize I got so absorbed in our conversation that I missed our arrival in the glamorous state of New Jersey.

"We better go," Rasputin says and heads for the dock.

"Wait, you were just getting to the interesting bits," I say, but he doesn't seem to hear.

Once we start the second leg of our airport journey, I hang back with Rasputin, and when it seems we're out of earshot from normal people's ears, I say, "You started to tell me about my mother."

He walks in contemplative silence for a few beats, then says, "What's going on between you and Nero?"

I nearly trip over a mailman corpse and fight the urge to blush. "Nothing."

"You and I both know that's not true," he says sternly. "When did Nero—"

"This is none of your business," I snap, my embarrassment morphing into anger. I've known the guy for all of five minutes, and he's going to play overprotective parent all of a sudden? Where was he when my first boyfriend stole my underwear and passed it around to all his friends in high school?

If anything, it's been Nero who's been watching out for me all these years. And for my father to imply that Nero had been in any way inappropriate is—

"I'm just trying to look out for you," Rasputin says, giving me a confused look.

That he's surprised by my negative reaction pisses me off more.

"You know what he is," Rasputin continues. "I just want what's best for you."

"What's best for me?" I taste the words. "I'm not a

child anymore. You can't make life-defining decisions for me any longer."

He looks like I slapped him, and I feel a pang of guilt—but not enough to prevent me from storming off to catch up with the rest of my friends.

"Tell Sasha what you just told me," Ariel says when I reach them, and I can tell she's fighting to keep in a laugh.

"All I said was that there was something different about you today," Felix says to me. "That there's a bounce in your step or something—but I don't see why that's funny."

Ariel looks like she's dying from laughter, and I slide my helmet's visor over my face to hide my expression.

Nero—who clearly heard the exchange—smirks slightly, but it could be my imagination again.

In general, though, he doesn't seem to be acting differently toward me today. Maybe what happened wasn't as big of a deal for him as it was for me? I make a mental vow to rent *How to Train Your Dragon* as soon as I get home. Hopefully, it's a documentary with some practical tips.

"I also feel better today," Itzel chimes in. "A good night's sleep and a meal can do wonders."

"I bet Nero helped you sleep better," Felix says to Itzel, and Ariel and I nearly choke on our tongues.

Felix looks at both of us like we're crazy and says, "I meant Nero's offer to add all those zeroes to Itzel's payment. I don't know what's gotten into the two of you this morning. Did you smoke something when I wasn't there?"

I'm about to reply when Nero tenses and suddenly stops.

I follow his gaze.

A ragtag group of men is walking toward us. Their faces are covered in burns and tattoos, and one dude is wearing a necklace that looks suspiciously like dried human ears.

Matching their background perfectly, they remind me of the people Hekima once showed us during Orientation.

They look ready to rape, kill, and eat us, and maybe not even in that order.

Spotting us, they yell out a war cry, raise their clubs, and charge.

CHAPTER SIXTY

"STAY BACK." With a stern glare at me, Nero begins to strip. "I'll take care of this."

Before I can say anything, he's naked and leaping forward.

Ariel suggestively clears her throat.

I gape as Nero shimmers into a roaring dragon and tramples cars in our would-be attackers' way.

Seeing him in this form in a modern environment feels pretty surreal—and the newcomers must agree, because they stop as if rooted to the ground.

Tossing a truck with his good claw into the far distance, Nero shoots fire in their direction—but clearly as an intimidation tactic. His fiery breath melts the cars on the road and the road itself, but doesn't incinerate a single person.

The posse clearly haven't gone so feral as to attack an angry dragon. They run away screaming as fast as anyone would in their shoes—except none of them seemed to be wearing shoes.

Nero shimmers again and turns into the mouthwatering human form I much prefer, then dresses as if nothing happened.

"You said this world was safe," I say to Rasputin when he catches up with us, a huge look of surprise on his face.

"I've never had any trouble here before." He shrugs. "Never even seen danger in a vision."

"How are they even alive?" Felix asks as we walk around the melted asphalt and proceed down the highway. "Everyone else is sucked dry."

"For whatever reason, Tartarus's powers don't work on some humans," Rasputin says. "The criminally insane seem to be particularly immune."

"Then why is Lilith worried?" I mutter under my breath. "She's clearly in the criminally insane category."

No one replies, and we walk in silence the rest of the way.

———

THE NEWARK AIRPORT looks just as it did when I'd flown from it to Toronto—dead bodies notwithstanding, of course.

Rasputin leads us to the hub hidden here, and we take a turquoise gate, which leads us to an island on a world with two suns. The island is in the middle of a never-ending ocean that is teeming with millions of spawning birds that jointly squawk louder than a roaring dragon.

The next world has rings like Saturn, and the one after that looks like a hub under some airport once again—but not ours.

Next, we reach a hub on top of a building in a familiar world with a nebula that looks like fire falling from the sky. Judging by Itzel's excitement, I'm pretty certain the sprawling megapolis is what it looks like.

"Yes, it's Gomorrah," Rasputin confirms. "Earth is just through there." He points at the gate a few feet away—the very one we always take to get home. "Unfortunately, I can't go through that gate with you," he continues.

"You can't?" Felix and I say in unison.

"I can't risk going back. Especially with you in the picture." His shoulders sag as he looks at me. "My enemies from Russia could come for me, and you could get caught in the crossfire." His gaze drops to the surface under our feet. "I'm afraid I lost my Earth privileges a long time ago, and the last hundred years haven't changed that."

"But I just found you," I say in frustration. "We didn't even get a chance to—"

"I know." My father looks miserable as he meets my gaze again. "I could risk it, I suppose, and—"

"You'll stay in my club here in Gomorrah." Nero walks over to Rasputin and puts a hand on his shoulder. "It's under my protection, so the two of you can safely spend quality time there together." He looks at me. "Gomorrah is just a limo ride plus a gate jump away, and my club is across the street."

"Thank you," Rasputin says to Nero before I can raise a million objections. "That would be for the best."

"I'm sure you know this, but you'll want to go to a world with humans on a regular basis," Felix says to my father. "Else you'll lose your powers here over time."

"I'll figure something out," Rasputin says with a smile. "Thanks."

"How about we go, and I set it all up?" Nero says decisively and turns toward the elevator. Over his shoulder, he adds, "I can take care of Itzel's payment at the same time."

"That's great," the gnome says excitedly. "I'd love to be done with this adventure and never think about what happened again."

I shrug and follow everyone, and by the time we catch up with Nero, the elevator is already waiting for us.

The trip down is as fast as usual, and the lobby of the mega skyscraper is as awe-inspiring as always—as are the 3D holograms outside.

"I'm not going with you," Ariel says, looking across the street with a strange expression.

"You're not?" Felix frowns.

"Even just thinking about that club is—" She stops talking and shakes her head. "I think it's much wiser if I head to rehab instead. Right now."

"You do what you need." I give her arm a reassuring squeeze.

"It's just for a little bit longer," she says, chewing on her lip. "I'm doing much better, but—"

"Leave your suit with me before you go," Itzel butts in with all the social grace of a hippopotamus.

Felix and I glare at her, but she doesn't seem to notice.

"Here you go." Ariel wriggles out of her suit and hands it to Itzel. "I would look odd wearing this, even at rehab."

"We'll take you there," I say. "We can—"

"No. You should head home." Ariel glances at the bloody bandage on Nero's shoulder. "Just come visit when things slow down."

"I will," I say solemnly.

"We'll both come," Felix says.

"All right." She leans in to give each of us a hug. "See you later."

We watch her walk through the colorfully dressed Cognizant until she disappears around the corner.

Nero takes that as his cue to keep going, so we cross the street after him and walk up to the building covered by a collection of bulky neon signs in every language imaginable. The Russian and English versions of the sign declare, "Earth Club," strongly hinting that the rest do as well. In a smaller font, both also boast, "The best vodka in all of Otherlands."

Nero walks past the ever-present line at the entrance, and the bouncers look ready to bow or take a knee before him.

Waving at us, Nero mutters something like, "VIPs,"

and strides in. Ignoring impressed glances from everyone in the line, we follow.

Inside, the club is the same as I remember—with shiny floors made of glass and a vibe reminiscent of the *Star Wars* cantina.

As we walk through the gyrating Cognizant dancers, I see the wisdom of Ariel's decision not to join. The place is teeming with vampires, and each of them has an escort dressed in the kind of outfit Ariel once wore.

Ignoring the unpleasant reminder of my friend's addiction, I focus on elves, dwarves, pixies, and the rest as Nero leads us to the elevator.

When we get inside, Nero presses the button for the tenth level.

As we ride up, I can't help but think about the level just below our destination—the one that looks like a BDSM dungeon. I nearly got killed there by a succubus.

When the elevator arrives, we exit and walk down a corridor until we reach an office that looks suspiciously like the one Nero occupies in his fund building.

"Where did you find such antique technology?" Itzel asks when she spots his top-of-the-line monitor and keyboard.

Ignoring her jibe, Nero walks up to the "antique" and starts typing away.

"Here." He waves for Itzel to walk over to his desk.

The gnome approaches, and when she looks at his screen, she audibly exhales and her eyes widen.

"I decided you deserve this many zeros added to Felix's original offer," Nero says with a faint smile. "Is this good?"

"Yes." Itzel bobs her head so vigorously, I fear she might damage her neck in the process. "Oh, yes. That will clear my debt and—"

"Great." Nero walks away from his desk. "Now Rasputin and I need to go to another level to arrange his accommodations."

"Can I get his suit before he leaves?" Itzel asks. "For that matter"—she looks at Felix and me—"can I get both of your suits?"

"That's smart," Nero says. "You're not going to be allowed to wear those on Earth."

"Exactly," Itzel says. "And if you do wear them and get caught with gnome technology, I could get in trouble, so please, take them off."

We take off the suits. Itzel goes to pick them all up at once and ends up sending two helmets rolling in different directions.

"Let me help," Nero says and picks up my suit. "How about I also arrange for these to be taken to your place?"

Without waiting for a reply, he heads for the door.

Rasputin bends to pick up more suit pieces and follows Nero.

"I guess this is goodbye," Itzel says, looking from me to Felix.

"You help out at the rehab facility, right?" I say, shuffling from foot to foot. "Maybe we can say hello when we go there to visit Ariel?"

"I'd like that." She grins and gives me a hug. Much more coolly, she shakes Felix's hand and adds, "Just please, never, ever ask me to go somewhere with you again."

"That won't be a problem," Felix grumbles.

Itzel grins again and follows Nero and Rasputin.

When they completely disappear, I look at Felix and with a straight face say, "You know, if things don't work out between you and Maya, Itzel might be—"

"Don't." He narrows his eyes. "How would you like it if I joked about *you* hooking up with Nero or someone equally inappropriate?"

Boy, am I lucky Ariel has already left. She'd never be able to hide her expression. In her defense, I can barely do so myself.

"You know," I say when I recover. "This is a really good opportunity to snoop on a certain someone's secrets again." I pointedly glance at Nero's computer.

Felix pales and vigorously shakes his head.

"Spoilsport," I say with an eyeroll. "I doubt he has surveillance in his own office, and it's not like—"

"Please, no." Felix moves as far away from Nero's computer as the space permits.

"Fine," I say before he bolts out of the room. "But if you want plausible deniability, you might want to look away."

Felix looks away, sticks his fingers into his ears, and starts loudly singing, "Old McDonald had a farm..."

I fish my phone from my pocket and record his antics for a few seconds as blackmail material to use at a later time.

Then I walk up to the mouse and tentatively wake the computer up.

Score. Nero didn't lock his work station before he left, and it didn't auto-lock yet.

Some part of me feels guilty. I'm about to spy on a person who may or may not be my lover—an idea that requires digesting in and of itself. I decide to squelch the guilt. If I need a rationalization, I can remind myself how much Nero has spied on me throughout my life.

Deciding and actually getting rid of guilt are two different things, but as a magician, I'm pretty good at it. I had to learn to be. If you feel bad about an object secretly hidden in your hand, or about the bold-faced lies you have to regularly tell the audience, you won't cut it as a professional illusionist.

Without further complaints from my conscience, I start swiping the cursor across Nero's screen.

Except I'm not a hacker like Felix, and have no clue where to go from here.

I'm about to go ask him when an icon labeled "surveillance" stands out to me on the desktop.

I click it.

The screen fills with small windows—each with a camera feed of somewhere in this very establishment.

Color me not surprised. Nero is spying on everyone in his club.

Scanning the options, I see Itzel leaving through the front doors on one screen, and on many, many other screens, there are people performing all sorts of extremely private acts with each other.

Ignoring the temptation to click on one particularly enthusiastic orgy involving what looks like baseball bats and pineapples, I spot a window with Rasputin and Nero in it—and eagerly double-click that.

The window maximizes, revealing them standing in a plush-looking kitchen—hopefully, the apartment where my father will stay.

I can also hear them now, and I catch Rasputin saying, "—is really nice."

Then I notice something else. There's a timestamp in the corner of the feed, with the seconds ticking away. Something about it looks off, and I understand what it is when I look at the corner of the display where the current time is. The spy camera time is behind current time—meaning I'm looking at events that have already transpired, not something live.

Crap.

That means Nero might no longer be in that room —and could walk in on me at any moment.

I almost close everything, but then I hear Nero's voice say, "The reason I left the others behind is that I wanted to talk to you privately."

Well, I can't stop watching *now*. I'll just risk it and

hope that if he catches me, he won't eat me... in a bad, dragony way, at least.

On screen, Nero gestures for Rasputin to sit on one of the barstools.

"Interesting." My father sits down. "It just so happens that I have something I wanted to talk to you about privately. Of course, you, as the host, should go first."

I lean in closer—but not so close as to leave the telltale oil print of my nose on the screen.

"Right." Nero folds his arms across his chest. "Our old contract is now over, so in exchange for the lodgings and protection, I want you to provide me with a vision."

Rasputin reaches up, as if to stroke a long beard. When he grasps empty air where the beard used to be, he rubs his stubbly chin instead. "I'm not sure I have it in me to repeat the feat I did for you the last time, and, even if I were willing, my price would be much greater."

"I'm talking about a few short visions." Nero walks up to the fridge, opens the freezer, and pulls out a frosty bottle of vodka. "This would be a mere peek at the immediate future, that's all."

Rasputin leaves his chin alone to stare at Nero. "Of course. You're going to save Claudia. That's what this is about, isn't it?"

"Sounds like we have an understanding." Nero takes an enormous gulp of the vodka, then extends the bottle to Rasputin.

My father takes the bottle and gulps down a much daintier sip. "This is very fortuitous," he says when he's done cringing.

Taking back the bottle, Nero lifts an eyebrow.

"I was actually going to advise you to leave Earth as soon as you've healed, but it sounds like you're going to anyway," Rasputin says.

My seer intuition kicks in—no doubt telling me what I could tell by just looking at the timestamp. I'm about to get busted in my snooping.

But I want to know where this goes.

Then I remember that Itzel is now gone, and I can see my immediate future again.

Grinning, I easily convince myself that I'll keep watching the screen even if it means getting caught; then I focus and reach Headspace in record time.

The shapes surrounding me look promising, so I touch the one that feels right.

———

EVEN THOUGH I know I shouldn't, I keep watching the screen.

"Explain." Nero takes another massive gulp, then removes the towel bandage on his shoulder and pours vodka over the wound.

"You bled all over Lilith's world," Rasputin says, nodding at the injury. "If she's alive, she'll be able to find you anywhere."

Nero's jaw tenses. "That just gives me more reasons

to expedite my plans. Lilith mentioned some sort of an understanding with the soon-to-be corpse, so she won't follow me to his kingdom."

The sound of a door opening rips my attention away from the screen.

Nero barges in and gives me a baleful stare.

My father has disappointment in his eyes, and Felix—

———

I'M BACK in the room—and extremely happy that I've had the vision.

I *was* going to get caught—but now I don't have to be.

"Explain," Nero says on the screen, and I know what follows and how little time I have.

Exiting the surveillance app, I lock the computer and make sure the mouse stays in the position I found it in.

As an overkill, I use the bottom of my shirt to wipe away any possible prints.

Happy with my work, I rush toward Felix, remove his hands from his ears, and say, "Tell me the end of some dumb joke, right now."

Got to hand it to Felix. Without skipping a beat, he stops singing and looks at me with a sincere-seeming smile. "And the panda says," he says as the door opens and Nero and Rasputin walk in, "I have the right to *bear* arms."

I pretend to laugh, then pretend to be surprised they came back when they did.

"Felix," Nero says, smelling like an alcohol distillery. "Let's give them a second to say goodbye."

He herds Felix out of the office, and I stand there, staring at Rasputin with my emotions all over the place.

My birth father.

I've just found him, and I have to leave him.

There's a good chance he told Nero about the blood thing as a ploy to keep us apart—and it would've worked if I hadn't spied on them. Now I'll be able to counter the damage by having a serious talk with Nero, during which I also hope to learn who Claudia is.

Either because of that, or because the man in front of me *is* my father, I'm not nearly as mad at him as I should be. All I really want to do is hug him—so that's what I do.

"Thank you so much," he murmurs, squeezing me tight. "I can't believe you came for me after everything. I don't know where you got this compassion from, but I'm glad for it."

"Good. Because you owe me answers," I say, my voice thick as I step back. "And I mean a *lot* of them."

"Come visit me tomorrow," he says. "I'll do my best to answer anything you ask."

Nero and Felix return, and I take another step back.

"Go take care of that." Rasputin nods at Nero's shoulder.

"Right," I say. "Let's go."

"Just one second," Nero says and looks at the handle of the gate sword. "You can't use that on Earth either, so how about you leave it here?" He walks over to the wall and opens a safe that I hadn't noticed was there.

"But I can hide it and never show it to humans," I protest, clutching the handle like a kid with a new toy.

"You should listen to Nero," Rasputin says regretfully. "The Councils take their weapon bans seriously, and the Mandate would punish you if a human were to see you wield that."

I look to Felix.

"Better leave it if you ask me," he says.

I fight the urge to remind Felix about the fancy gun he brought from Gomorrah to Earth, but since Nero is on the Council, I don't want to say anything in front of him.

Besides, where Felix's gun could've passed for some gizmo or a toy, I know of no technology on Earth that could explain this kind of sword, so maybe they're right.

With great reluctance, I trudge to the safe and place the sword inside it.

"Now we go." Nero closes the safe, and the wall goes back to looking empty.

We leave, and Rasputin walks with us to the elevator, but he doesn't get into the car when it arrives.

"I'll take the next one," he says gruffly, and I see a suspicious shimmer in his eyes.

My chest squeezes. "That's fine. I will see you soon,"

I tell him as the doors begin to close. And right before they shut completely, I add softly, "Papa."

Rasputin beams like the sun, and I feel good that I said it, even if I didn't fully mean it yet.

Felix blinks rapidly and rubs his eyes, while Nero pretends not to notice another dude displaying emotions so openly.

I inhale a deep breath and wonder if I should confront Nero here and now about Claudia and the rest of it—right in front of Felix.

But no. Felix would hate to be in the middle of such a talk, and I'm not sure I want him to know about me and Nero yet—not until I myself have a good label for it.

The three of us walk through the noisy club without speaking, and we keep the silence as we cross the street to the super-skyscraper. Once there, we take the elevator to the roof with the hub.

I rush for the gate leading to Earth and step in first.

Nero and Felix join me on the other side, and I take the lead on the way out of the JFK hub.

They catch up with me as I turn the corner.

This corridor is wider than most, and the three of us have no trouble walking shoulder to shoulder.

We're halfway to the next turn when a massive seer warning slams into me like an iceberg.

It's the worst one ever, which can only mean one thing.

Someone's very imminent demise.

CHAPTER SIXTY-ONE

I FOCUS on Headspace and reach it instantly.

The shapes surrounding me confirm my suspicion. The music emanating from them would be at home at a funeral—not-so-subtly hinting that they'll show me something heinously bad.

My first impulse is to grab a shape at random, but given what I saw in my father's memories the other day, I let my intuition lead me to one that I think will be extra useful—even if I don't actually know what useful means in this case.

My ethereal wisp trembles metaphysically as I touch my chosen shape, and fall into the rabbit hole of the vision.

———

A MAN WEARING a killer clown mask rushes into the corridor in front of us, followed by a couple more.

They're all wearing those masks, and all but the first guy are basketball-player-turned-bodybuilder-big, and in general look extremely familiar.

Of course. They're the would-be assassins from my earlier visions, the ones who shot at us with machine guns and the bazooka. I'm sure they sent that bomb to our office too.

I'd tentatively decided they're not dragons, but seeing them live like this, all but one don't seem human either.

The smaller man—the one I've never seen in a vision before—raises a strange-looking weapon and shoots.

A dart hits my right shoulder. At first, there's a sharp prick of pain; then warmth spreads from the wound, making my legs buckle.

I start falling—but pass out before my body hits the ground.

———

I'M BODILESS, but I'm also watching my body fall to the ground from the side.

Am I—or my body—about to crack my skull on the floor?

No. Nero lunges for the unconscious me with super speed and catches her/me mid-air, then lays her/me by the wall like a sleeping princess.

At the same time, more of the huge masked attackers show up from the other side of the corridor—

meaning we're flanked on both sides.

"What's happening?" Felix mutters at the same time as the smaller masked guy aims the dart gun at him and squeezes the trigger.

Felix looks down at the dart in his chest and faints, hitting the floor hard. Nero didn't bother softening *his* fall—probably because he's too busy looking at the new group. His gaze jumps between them and the dart gun guy with his crew; he's clearly unsure which of them to start with first.

The dart guy uses Nero's indecision to his advantage and spears Nero's thigh with a dart.

Nero looks down at the dart, raises an eyebrow, and pulls the thing out as if it were a piece of lint.

If I had lungs, I'd exhale in relief. It looks like it would take a lot more than that dart to knock Nero out, even in his weakened-from-blood-loss and possibly drunk state.

"Go on," a familiar British-accented voice says from behind the small man's mask. "He killed Bogof and the rest of your kin."

The bigger masked people rush for Nero just as I realize whose voice that was.

Darian.

The very person who got me into the Cognizant world with his machinations—the man who is convinced the two of us will one day end up together in a happily ever after.

His trying to kill me makes no sense. Unless this is a weird, preemptive break-up?

"Remember," maybe-Darian shouts to the crew closing in on Nero. "The girl is not to be harmed under any circumstances."

Okay, so maybe he isn't trying to kill *me*. That makes it more likely this is indeed Darian, though it still doesn't explain why he's doing this. Although I may have an inkling as to his beef with—

The front wave of attackers reaches Nero, and I wish I had lungs so I could suck in an excited breath.

Nero blurs into motion and rips the first to arrive to shreds.

More victims rush forward, and Nero turns them into more chunks of dead meat.

Something about what's happening is familiar, and I'm on the verge of a realization when Nero turns back to deal with the next attacker—and rips the guy's head clean off.

When the head rolls past Felix, the clown mask slips, revealing the green face of an orc.

Of course. *That's* what's so familiar about this. I've seen Nero rip orcs to shreds before, and this reminds me of that day. I guess there's something particularly memorable about seeing orc insides become their outsides.

Then another thing clicks. Darian said, "He killed *Bogof* and the rest of your kin."

Bogof was the name of one of the orcs in that massacre. I even noted how it was also the abbreviation for "buy one, get one free."

That means these orcs are out for revenge, which

isn't surprising given what Itzel said about orcs having family values and being into vendettas.

In the time it takes me to realize all this, Nero dispatches a good dozen more orcs, but more stream from both his front and his back, replacing their fallen comrades.

One really fierce-looking orc rushes at Nero and—perhaps accidentally—steps on Felix's unconscious body.

My nonexistent heart leaps in horror as I hear the loud crack of bone breaking.

Nero's gaze whips to *my* unconscious body.

"It's not me, it's Felix," I want to scream at Nero, but I don't have a mouth.

Darian uses Nero's distraction to put a dart in his back.

The dart doesn't seem to affect Nero, except perhaps to make him angry. With a very dragon-like roar, he slices the orc who hurt Felix into halves, then rips those halves into smaller chunks before turning his deadly attention to another attacker.

More clown-masked orcs show up behind Darian—but the new batch coming from behind Nero didn't even bother with masks. That, or they ran out.

Seeing the pieces of their brethren makes this set of attackers charge more carefully. They get as close as they can to Nero, but stay out of the range of his claws.

Nero growls, his gaze snapping between the two groups, clearly deciding whom to kill first.

Darian shoots Nero with the dart gun again.

This time, Nero dodges the shot, and the dart hits one of the unmasked orcs. The orc looks at the dart very slowly—then just as slowly looks at Darian with an expression that seems to ask, "Why?"

Falling to his knees, the orc passes out.

How strong *is* the tranquilizer in those darts?

Finally making a decision, Nero leaps forward and starts slicing the masked orcs into bits.

When they're down, Nero glares at Darian, his gaze holding the promise of extreme pain—except more masked orcs show up and stand between him and his prey.

"Go!" Darian yells, and the extra-careful unmasked orcs shout a war cry and rush forward, forcing Nero to fight on two fronts yet again.

Nero focuses more attention on the unmasked ones, and I finally realize something: he's doing his best to stay in the spot where my body is.

Claws blurring, he slices off the arm of a particularly toothy orc and bashes him on the head with it. He then kicks the head of the knocked-out orc like a soccer ball. With a crack, the head disconnects from the orc's body and flies at another with devastating force, causing him to stagger—which is when Nero turns him into minced meat.

Darian shoots his dart again, and misses. Then he shoots once more, and it looks almost as though Nero walked into this dart.

Or more accurately, Darian shot where Nero would be.

Ignoring the dart, Nero wipes the blood from his eyes and renews his attack.

I wish he could shake off *all* the blood covering him as it makes it hard to tell how badly his shoulder is bleeding.

Another orc steps on Felix in his rush to get to Nero.

Felix spits up blood, and his breathing becomes uneven.

Oh, no. This is really, really bad.

The offending orc pays for what he did. Nero tears into him with such ferocity the leftover bits fly as far as Darian is standing.

Darian aims and shoots—again to where Nero ends up jumping.

He's clearly using his powers to assist his aim.

Nero kills the next orc, but another dart pierces his back. A few dead orcs later, yet another dart joins the others.

It could be my imagination, but it seems like Nero is beginning to slow. His hard-to-track attacks are starting to be more visible as he dispatches two more orcs. Confirming my fears, the next unmasked orc bites a chunk of flesh out of Nero's forearm before Nero squishes him into pulp.

The forearm gushes blood as Nero fights on, with more of Darian's darts hitting him. By now, even the orcs are noticing his slowing, and they get bolder in their attacks.

Darian reloads his gun while Nero kills five orcs.

He hits Nero with another dart when a particularly large orc walks out from the corridor leading to the hub.

This newcomer seems to dwarf the others—an impressive feat given the average orc's size.

"I'm the chieftain of the clan," the newcomer snarls, sticking out his chest like an elephant seal defending his harem. "Bogof was my brother."

Nero moves forward with a speed that's glacial for him, but impressive for even an elite martial artist. Without giving the chieftain a chance to take a fighting stance, he strikes his enemy in the chest.

The chieftain dodges the strike with surprising agility.

Perhaps he's the chieftain due to his fighting ability?

As he dodges, his giant fist flies at Nero's injured shoulder. Nero sidesteps—right into another dart from Darian's gun.

The rest of the orcs rush to help their chieftain, crushing my hope of there being a one-on-one fight.

Nero swipes at the chieftain again. Is he moving even slower now? The chieftain grabs Nero by the wrist. Nero swats with the other hand—and gets it captured as well.

Darian shoots another dart into Nero's back. Then another.

The horde of orcs closes the distance and starts pummeling Nero with punches and kicks.

Why doesn't he turn into his dragon form? That's

the only way I can see out of this situation, but he's not doing it.

Is he not allowed to turn on Earth? Because if there was ever a time to break the rules, it's now. Unless it's the Mandate that disallows it. Since Nero is on the Council, the Mandate is less restrictive for him, but maybe turning isn't on the list of perks? Alternatively, maybe he doesn't turn because the corridor doesn't have enough space to hold all that mass? Yes. This sounds closer to the truth. I bet if he turned, the whole underground structure would collapse on top of him and the orcs... but also on top of Felix and my unconscious body.

Four orcs grab Nero's right leg, and five more grab his left one. Three other orcs help their chieftain by latching on to Nero's right arm—which is when the chieftain lets go and smashes his fist into Nero's jaw.

Darian shoots a few more darts—some hit the orcs that are not holding Nero, but one pierces Nero in the neck.

The chieftain and the orcs not holding Nero keep punching him—and their hits, or the tranquilizer, make Nero sway on his feet.

Oh crap. This does not look good. Maybe Nero's just pretending to weaken so that they let him go?

That's what I'd do, at least.

A minute of abuse later, I strongly doubt Nero is faking. His body slackens in the grip of the orcs—but they keep pounding him.

Leisurely peppering Nero with more darts, Darian

approaches the orc pileup, and when he's a few feet away from the melee, he takes off his mask.

If I still had any doubts about his identity, they're gone now. This is definitely Darian—only for the first time I see a cruel expression on his face, one that looks quite at home there.

The orcs deliver another round of hits and kicks, but Nero fights unconsciousness to glare at Darian with pure murder in his eyes.

"You threatened a fellow Council member—and a seer at that," Darian says, pulling out a dagger from a sheath strapped to his back. "Did you think there would be no consequences?"

It's just as I suspected. Nero humiliated Darian by holding him by his neck like a kitten and forbidding him to talk to me on the pain of death. The seer clearly feigned his submission long enough to find allies in these orcs and strike when Nero would be at his weakest.

Nero grinds his teeth almost audibly, then sneaks a glance at my unconscious body with an unreadable expression on his face.

"Yes, *she* is why you can't risk turning," Darian says, noticing Nero's gaze. "And you're right to be afraid. In the futures where you dare it, she dies during the collapse."

If looks could be weaponized, Nero would kill Darian with his next glare.

"Hey now." Darian clicks his tongue in mock sympathy. "If you care about her as much as *I* do, I have a silver lining for you." Approaching Nero, he stops less than a foot away. "She dies in *every* future where she chooses you."

For the first time, I see pain on Nero's bloodied face —as if Darian's words accomplished what the orcs' fists couldn't.

I've never wished for a body as much as I do now. If I had one, I'd yell, cry, and, more importantly, use it to tear Darian into pieces for this.

"Ah, yes." Darian smirks. "You *know* what I just told you is the truth, and the truth hurts." His hand tightens on the dagger's hilt as he adds, "But not as much as this will."

With a wide arc, he stabs the dagger into Nero's throat.

I watch it go in but refuse to accept that this is actually happening.

Nero's roar is choked by the blood spurting out of his throat as he futilely tries to free himself from the orcs. But they hold on for dear life, and the free ones go into a blood frenzy as they frantically pound Nero, over and over—until he finally drops to the ground.

"We have to be sure," Darian mutters to the chieftain and points at the dagger in Nero's throat.

The chieftain grabs the hilt, rips out the weapon, then uses it to completely detach Nero's head—

CHAPTER SIXTY-TWO

I'M BACK TO REALITY, my heart jackhammering in my chest.

I feel sick, my body trembling all over.

"It was a vision," I remind myself, fighting the urge to vomit.

I can still prevent it.

I have to prevent it.

A modicum calmer, I leap back into Headspace.

———

THE SHAPES that surround me are identical to the ones from before—each no doubt ready to give me a vision just as awful.

For a few seconds, I allow myself the luxury of just floating there and letting my mind cope with the emotional overload.

Darian is behind everything.

Felix is about to get badly hurt.

Nero is about to be gruesomely killed—again.

And there's something else that bothers me—something I didn't get a chance to process in the vision.

"She dies in every future where she chooses you," Darian had said.

He's said this before. The last time was at the funeral. Chester had been there, and he'd cast some doubt on Darian's motivations, which made me more or less ignore his words. This time, however, Nero, with his truth-telling abilities, believed the seer—which means that this statement is somehow fact.

But what does that actually mean?

If it's the opposite of the future where Darian and I are a unit, I'm toast—because that's not happening, especially after this incident.

I'm in just as much trouble if by "choose Nero," he means I develop feelings for my boss. No matter how much I want to deny it, that's already the case—and my reaction to Nero's possible demise just makes me more certain about it.

I float there, letting that sink in.

I, Sasha, have feelings for my dangerous, manipulative boss and Mentor.

Who's a dragon.

Yeah, okay, I'm going to file that away and deal with it later—*if* there is a later.

Back to the whole "Sasha dies" business. The best-case scenario here is that Darian was talking about a future where I become Mrs. Nero Gorin, then perish as a result. Maybe in childbirth if I literally attempt to be the "Mother of Dragons" as Ariel was joking about?

Well, that fate is one that *can* be averted. I'd just have to stay away from Nero—an idea that fills me with dread but is, theoretically, doable.

Something else occurs to me. Is this why Rasputin seemed to be against the idea of me and Nero? Has he also seen the future Darian is talking about? Is that why he wants Nero to go away and reunite with whoever Claudia is?

Realizing I'm dwelling on this to stop myself from dealing with the much scarier reality of Nero's imminent demise, I force myself to focus on what needs to be done.

What if I were to break the big problem of having everyone survive into smaller, more manageable chunks?

Yes, that's it.

First, I need to figure out how to dodge the dart that knocks me out. If I'm not knocked out, I can surely save the day.

Somehow.

Examining the visions in front of me, I wonder if any of them contain a version where I dodge the dart, and if so, how to pick it out from the others.

Could using intuition—the way my father does —help?

Of course, I could just see all these visions at once, as a cloud, but that would eat up a ton of my seer juice, and I need to save as much as I can for what happens *after* I dodge the first dart.

Intuition it is. At least as plan A.

Another decision I need to make is the vision duration. These default visions will show me the whole fight—but I could just see the very beginning instead. The shorter vision would let me save some seer power and spare myself the pain of seeing Nero die at the end.

But no. What if, thanks to some butterfly effect, my attempt at a dodge helps turn the fight later—and lets Nero survive? I don't want to miss that.

So, I'm going with plan A and default vision duration.

Must dodge the dart, I convince myself, in case that helps my intuition. *He shoots me in the right shoulder, so I have to make sure he misses.*

Metaphorically chanting the phrase over and over, I reach out with my ethereal wisp and touch a shape that seems nearly identical to the others.

WE'RE HALFWAY through the corridor.

Darian shows up wearing a killer clown mask, followed by the orcs.

Knowing the dart is about to hit my right shoulder, I duck a moment before Darian shoots.

The dart whooshes by my shoulder and into the orcs behind us.

Darian lowers his gun—as if in confusion.

"Yes," I mutter. "I did it. This is—"

Darian raises the gun and shoots again.

I dodge to the left—and that action is what puts my thigh in the path of the second dart.

Because my leg muscles are tense, the pain from the needle is sharper, and my legs buckle even faster this time.

I start falling—but blissfully pass out before my body hits the ground.

———

I'M BODILESS AGAIN—AND I watch as Nero catches my body like before.

We get flanked.

Felix mutters, "What's happening?" and gets knocked out with the dart gun.

Everything else proceeds like in my earlier vision, with one exception—when he takes off his mask, Darian looks at my unconscious body and says, "I'm sorry, Sasha. I thought you'd be knocked out and wouldn't witness any of this unpleasant necessity." He looks at all the gore. "Alas, it looks like I underestimated your seer capabilities."

So, a butterfly effect did occur, but not what I wanted. Instead, Darian is now aware of my seer efforts, and might counter them.

No positive changes happen for the rest of the vision. Darian still stabs Nero in the throat; then the chieftain finishes the grizzly business with the decapitation.

CHAPTER SIXTY-THREE

I'M BACK in the real world for an eye blink, then get right back to Headspace despite my hammering heartbeat.

The shapes around me are all the same as before—but I feel even worse than the first time.

I dodged the first dart, but it was all for nothing. Darian realized that I used a vision to dodge; then he used a counter vision and shot me again.

Could I counter his counter? My head hurts even thinking about it, but I use my intuition and locate a shape that I hope is the one I need.

———

DARIAN SHOWS UP.

Since I know his first shot is at my right shoulder, I duck, but when he shoots, he aims lower than I expected, and hits my shoulder as in vision one.

My body passes out, and the rest of the nightmare proceeds unchanged from there.

———

I COME BACK TO REALITY, then leap back into Headspace—into the same cloud of shapes.

Damn it.

My third vision had gone even worse than the second. Now that Darian knows I'm using my powers, he's adapting.

Well, if he can do it, so can I. It's just a matter of perseverance. I'll just have to use up more seer power and utilize the trick with which I dodged the dragon— seeing a ton of possible moves and performing the best one.

With this, I reach out to as many of the shapes in front of me as I can—and fall into a multitude of visions.

———

DARIAN SHOWS UP.

Since I know his first shot is at my right shoulder, but the countermove to my ducking is to shoot lower, I bypass both fates by sidestepping to the left.

The dart misses me, but he aims again.

I know that dodging to the left put me in the path of the dart in vision number two, so I dodge right—but

Darian must've already corrected for this because he hits my thigh, and I pass out.

Then, as punishment for my failure, I watch the horrific demise of Nero.

———

I SIDESTEP FROM THE START—AND into the dart.

———

I DON'T SIDESTEP but drop my shoulder in the next vision. I get hit on the second shot.

In the vision that follows, I'm hit right away, and so on, failure after failure.

After countless permutations of basically the same vision, I manage to dodge the first two shots, just to get hit with a third dart a couple of feet later.

Frustrated, I return to my body and head right back into Headspace.

———

THE CURSED SHAPES taunt me once again, but I don't reach for any of them.

If I've learned anything from this multi-vision fiasco, it's that Darian is still the better seer when it comes to pure vision machinations. He's able to always get me within two, or in one case, three shots.

Now what? Should I let myself go into reality and

beg Nero to turn into a dragon so that at least *he* survives?

Something tells me he won't listen to me if I do.

Besides, that sounds like giving up, and I can't. It's not just my own life on the line here, but Felix's too. There has to be a way this can be done without anyone dying.

Then a dangerous idea comes to me. It hinges on a single question: do I have more raw seer power than Darian? Or more accurately, which of us has more seer juice in the tank at this very moment?

The answer to the latter question depends on many factors, like how much did we have to start with, and also on who used more prior to this showdown. Relatedly, did Darian need to expend as much power as I did when he countered my multi-vision attempt? Though my brain hurts to even think about counter-counter-counter moves, it does seem feasible he used less power than I did in his thwarting.

Still, dangerous or not, this idea is my best option, and it's pretty ironic that it was Darian who gave me the very information that's the basis for what I'm going to attempt.

It was during our Headspace conversation—the first time he raised the whole "don't fall for Nero" business.

"If one isn't careful, a more powerful seer can drain one's powers during an encounter in Headspace," Darian had warned me on that day.

If that's true, and if I *am* the more powerful of us, I

plan to do exactly that: drain him of his power. *If* I can figure out how to do so, that is.

I try to recall all the other pertinent information.

"Though willing participation is usually required, some very powerful seers can force the call to happen," he'd said that day. "The safest action is to leave Headspace when any hint of a call is about to transpire, which is basically when you see anything but the vision shapes."

That means my attack on him must be swift. I can't give him a chance to escape Headspace or give him a choice not to accept the call.

The good news is that Headspace conversations can't be foreseen with seer powers, so hopefully, he won't expect this.

He did underestimate me once already.

Yes, that's it. I will force a joining on Darian—except I need a less rapey-sounding term for it, like "a Headspace battle," for example.

To start, I'll need to make Darian accept my summons, then refuse to disconnect the call in order to drain his power. As he himself had told me, Headspace conversations can only end when both of the seers wish it, or one of them runs out of power, or if one of the seers is willing to give up a huge burst of power to disconnect.

That last scenario could cause a problem if Darian has a huge burst of power to give up and knows how to do it—but it's another of the million risks with this plan.

Obviously, the hope is that it's Darian who runs out of power, not me.

Which is far from guaranteed.

I float contemplatively for a moment and realize there's a chance that it's a set-up. Darian could've told me all that as a way to lure me into a power-draining trap—because he has foreseen this very moment.

Can he see that far ahead? I did hang out with Itzel for a while. Wouldn't that mess him up?

Maybe not.

He knew Nero would be here wounded, and that I'd be there too. The question is, how long ago did he know?

But wait, he'd said no one could predict what happens during a Headspace conversation. If that's true, how could he know he'd win the Headspace battle?

Of course, there's also a chance that he'd lied about everything to do with Headspace conversations. He'd definitely lied about the memories each seer witnesses when they make contact. He called those hallucinations. Perhaps he wanted to make Headspace conversations sound scary to prevent me from talking to other male seers, like the bannik, in case that upsets the future where we're a unit. Or maybe he didn't want me to talk to my father in Headspace for some reason.

Speaking of the bannik and Rasputin, if I'm willing to spend a little juice on it, I could consult one or the other to see if they think my desperate plan has any chance of success.

Deciding that the power expenditure would be worth it, I focus on my father's essence in order to initiate a conversation with him.

Except nothing happens. He's either dodging my calls again, is himself out of power, or is simply not in Headspace.

I focus on the bannik next—with the same lack of results.

Oh well. I guess I'll have to do this on my own.

I focus on Darian's essence with all my might— using everything I know about him, including the borderline-psychopathic ruthlessness I learned about today.

Nothing happens, but I don't give up. Instead, I bring my feelings into the mix the way my father does. In this case, they boil down to hate. Then I replay every conversation with Darian in my mind, his every gesture. I then go creepy and imagine I can smell the bergamot scent of his cologne.

That last bit is what cinches the deal, because a moving shape suddenly appears next to me.

It's a familiar entity-shape—the very one that represents Darian in this strange place.

Tensing my ethereal being, I prepare for the Headspace battle.

CHAPTER SIXTY-FOUR

I HAVE but a moment because given the chance, he'll either leave Headspace or float out of my reach.

Which is why I instantly grab him with my ethereal wisp as if he were a vision-shape I want to activate.

Only the joining conversation doesn't start as I had hoped.

I guess he needs to reciprocate to make this easy for me.

He exudes shock—for lack of a better term—then anxiety; then I feel him metaphysically writhing, like a giant fish on a hook.

Maybe it's not a set-up after all.

"You're not getting away," I think in case he can sense my words. Pretending he's a cloud of shapes a thousand strong, I reach for him with multiple wisps.

His anxiety pulsing turns into panic as he redoubles his efforts to slip by the imaginary hook—which tells me I'm on the right track.

I pretend he's an ever-bigger cloud of shapes. His efforts to rip away seem weaker to me, so I double down and rope him with a hundred thousand more wisps, then ten times that, then ten times that yet again.

When I lose count of the number of wisps I tentacle his way, something on Darian's end finally seems to break, and I reel him into the joining—his nebulous appendages metaphysically flapping each way.

———

I FIND myself in Darian's memory again—which makes me sure I succeeded in part one of my plan.

Standing in a forest, he/I look around at trees so tall they blot out the sky.

A familiar giant figure of the orc chieftain is standing there, looking at Darian/me intently, so Darian says, "I know who's responsible for your brother's death."

Darian proceeds to give the chieftain a more or less true version of what happened, but he makes Bogof look better by claiming he was hired to intimidate a fierce warrior, not little old me. He further claims that Nero killed the orcs in order not to pay them—not because one of them bruised me.

"You must take my best fighters to this Earth," the chieftain booms. "We must have our revenge."

"Things are not so simple," Darian says as he thinks uncharitable thoughts about orcs' intelligence. "There are humans on that world, so discretion will be of utmost importance."

Before the chieftain replies, the memory ends, and a new one begins.

———

HERE, Darian is still standing next to the chieftain, but there's also a huge crowd of orcs around them, including many wearing masks.

Though Darian is mentally stringing a rather creative chain of curses, he keeps his face placid as he says, "We agreed that the girl would be off limits. They"—he points at the masked orcs—"nearly killed her every single time they attempted your revenge."

"It's not their fault the bastard keeps his pet around," the chieftain says. "You're a seer. How about *you* tell us when to strike, and in such a way that she be safe?"

"If I could, I would," Darian says, then sighs. "There *is* a point in the near future where she can be easily taken out, but you have to swear on your honor to do exactly what I tell you to make sure she isn't harmed. That means no more bombs, no bullets, and no—"

———

THE MEMORY PART of the joining is clearly over because I find myself facing a hologram of Darian made out of the telltale green brain synapses.

Darian's transparent face is a mask of fury, and even the shape-entity representation of him is pulsing with rage.

"You've taken him to your bed?" he shouts and drops down at least seven feet. "Just walked into his hotel room, like a—"

"That is none of your business," I snap, realizing that Darian must've seen my memory of the other night. "You and I will *never* happen," I say with as much cruelty in my voice as I can muster, the violation of my privacy adding fire to my already boiling fury.

I realize I'm inadvertently plummeting down, so when my eyes are even with Darian's, I narrow them and add a finishing blow. "I'll choose Nero over you in every possible future from now on."

"Then you *will* die," he says mournfully and drops down another ten feet. "You're also not going to succeed with this—whatever it is you think you're doing." He waves around at the vacuum-like blackness around us.

"I call this a Headspace battle," I say, dropping so fast I feel like I'm skydiving. "And we'll see who's going to succeed."

"I'm more—"

I decide that I'm forever done with listening to anything Darian wants to say. Parroting Felix's childish behavior from earlier, I cover my ears, close my eyes, and start singing as loudly as I can.

If this is a trap, then I can at least annoy Darian before I lose.

When I tire of "Old McDonald had a farm...," I pick a random pop song and sing that as though I were in a shower.

After what feels like a week of karaoke nights and an infinite drop into the abyss, I peek to see Darian futilely attempting to grab me. His hands pass through me as if we were both ghosts, which isn't that far from reality.

Closing my eyes, I grin at his discomfort and keep singing until, a few more songs later, the Headspace battle finally terminates.

CHAPTER SIXTY-FIVE

I'M BACK in the real world.

This is the moment of truth.

If I won, then I still have seer juice to take advantage of, and will be able to return to Headspace. But if Darian is the more powerful of us and this was a trap, going into Headspace will fail—and Nero, Felix, and I are screwed.

Without so much as an extra breath, I focus my mind—and reach Headspace successfully.

———

FLOATING AMONG THE SHAPES, I let myself bask in my accomplishment for a few moments.

Soon, though, I realize I haven't won yet. I just took away Darian's ability to see the future for the time being. He still has an army of orcs at his disposal, Nero is still weakened, and I don't even know how to dodge the first three darts Darian shoots at me.

Then again, I can now do something about that last part.

I look at the surrounding shapes.

There seem to be fewer of them, but they otherwise remind me of the prior cloud.

Now I need to seek out a future where I do something that I haven't already tried in all the prior visions. Something Darian hasn't already countered or counter-countered.

A magician-worthy idea comes to me. It's bold, mean, and a little crazy, but those might just be the reasons why Darian wouldn't expect it.

Using my intuition, I guess which vision will show me what happens if I implement this plan.

Reaching out, I touch a shape that feels right.

———

LIKE IN ALL the other visions, Darian shows up in front of us.

Unlike every other time, I shout, "Nero, if you have to turn into a dragon, do so! Don't worry about me."

Nero doesn't reply, but that isn't important because his body tenses in my peripheral view, and I know he heard me.

Darian starts to raise his gun.

Instead of dodging or sidestepping, I grab Felix by his shirt and yank him toward me.

Felix gapes at me as though I've lost my mind, and I can tell when the dart hits him because his eyes widen to the size of quarters.

He slackens in my grasp and drops to the floor before I get a chance to soften his fall.

Crap. I'd hoped to prop him by the wall, but—

Nero blurs into motion, which is when Darian shoots *him* with the next dart instead of me.

The dart hits, but Nero doesn't even notice it.

I rush after Nero.

"Attack!" Darian shouts at the orcs by his sides. "He killed Bogof and the rest of your kin."

The orcs rush at us.

Darian raises his gun in my vague direction and squeezes the trigger.

I do my best to dodge the dart, but it hits my right breast.

I pass out.

———

BODILESS, I watch the rest of the fight unfold, and it's depressingly similar to all the ones that came before—proving once again how much the future likes certain patterns.

Felix gets stomped on. Darian has more trouble hitting Nero with the darts without the use of his seer powers, but that just means Nero gets to kill more orcs for a longer period of time. Eventually, Darian floods Nero's system with enough tranquilizer to slow him down.

Once Nero is partially sedated, the chieftain shows up like before, and his fight with Nero is identical to my other visions.

Despite my urging him to, Nero doesn't turn into a dragon even at the bitter end, and the beheading proceeds like before.

BACK IN THE REAL WORLD, I jump right into Headspace in record time, ignoring my distress.

Floating among the shapes, I push away the terror gripping me and consider my next move.

If I hadn't already used up a lot of my seer power, I'd do a whole cloud of visions at once, but as is, the more conservative approach is to keep having them one at a time—especially since Darian can't counter anything I do.

Thus determined, I seek out a future where I'm *not* shot in my right breast—and when I think I've pinpointed the shape I need, I touch it to see what happens.

DARIAN RAISES THE GUN.

Without wasting breath on telling Nero to turn, I use Felix as a human shield again—but this time, I strain with all my might to keep him upright.

"Go kill him!" I shout at Nero.

He blurs forward.

I decide to keep holding Felix upright—that's a surefire way Darian can't shoot me with a dart.

Familiar ripping sounds reach me from the front, and thanks to all my visions, I can picture Nero mass-killing the masked orcs—this time, a few feet away from my location.

As curious as I am, I don't dare peek out from behind my shield for fear of getting a dart in my eye.

Orcs begin flanking us from behind. To my relief, they pass right by me without raising an eyebrow at my unconscious shield or my own very conscious state of being. They'd told Darian they would let me be, and I guess a promise is a promise.

As soon as they pass by, I hear them get slaughtered by Nero up ahead.

This goes on for a few minutes, and I desperately strain my brain for something more active I could do. If Nero had let me keep my sword, then maybe I would kill the chieftain as a way to drastically change the future. Also, my gun is at the lab, but there's no time to run there for it.

In any case, if the chieftain doesn't deliver the finishing blow, some other orc might.

What I need is to do something truly random. Something Darian could not have foreseen back when he had his powers and concocted this attack. Something—

"Pick her up!" I hear Darian shout over the sounds of the massacre.

"Don't touch me!" I yell, but it's too late.

Giant green hands that belong either to the Hulk or the orc chieftain grab me by my waist and lift me into the air.

Felix slips out of my hold, and my captor savagely kicks his body, sending it crashing against the wall with a gut-wrenching crack.

Felix spits up blood, and his breathing becomes uneven, same as when he was stepped on—the cursed future and its fetish for patterns striking again.

"You bastard!" I yell at the orc, kicking and punching him as much as I can in my awkward position.

But I might as well be attacking the wall for all the good it does.

Why, oh why didn't I keep that sword?

From my high perch in the air, I see that the battlefield is covered with orc remains, but Nero is already slow to the point where his end seems all but inevitable.

Spotting me, Darian aims, and a dart hits my shoulder.

———

I'M BODILESS ONCE MORE.

The chieftain tosses my limp body to the side and stomps toward Nero.

Darian takes off his mask.

Why did he knock me out? Did he not want me to hear his monologue or watch him and the chieftain kill Nero? Doesn't he realize I might still hear those things in a vision?

More importantly, how do I stop this never-ending cycle of failures?

"You threatened a fellow Council member—and a seer at that," Darian says again and pulls out the dagger. "Did you think there would be no consequences?"

The rest of the vision makes me feel like I'm stuck in the worst possible *Groundhog Day*.

Nero and the chieftain battle it out again; then the rest of the butchery proceeds as always before Nero loses his head in front of my eyes for the umpteenth time—which doesn't make it any easier to witness.

———

I'M BACK in the real world.

Focusing, I eagerly await my return to Headspace so that I can attempt something else.

Anything else.

Using Felix as a shield is a good start. I can build on that.

Wait a sec. Why am I not in Headspace?

I focus.

Nothing happens.

I focus again.

Nada.

I try it again and again until, with a sinking feeling, I realize that the worst has happened.

I finally ran out of seer juice, so what happens next will be for the last time.

It will be for real.

CHAPTER SIXTY-SIX

JUST IN CASE, I desperately focus again.

Nothing.

And one more time.

Zilch.

Fine. If Headspace is outside my reach, I'll just have to act in the real world.

Except I have no idea how to act or what to do. I need something completely random, but what?

Maybe Darian would get confused if I started to dance a jig or sing a song in the middle of all this, like a court jester?

Somehow, that ridiculous thought sparks an idea. A plan that has almost no chance of working—only I have nothing else.

The strong point of this idea is that it will give us a chance. In fact, "chance" is the key variable here, so maybe—

Darian shows up—just as in my visions.

He raises the gun.

I grab Felix and use him as a human shield yet again, then keep him upright just as I did in the last vision.

Nero starts ripping the orcs apart.

More orcs rush by without hurting me.

Propping Felix with my body as much as I can, I free up my right hand and sneak it into my pocket to fish out my phone.

It takes me a second to locate the contact I need, then a few more to type out a text with just one hand.

My message is blunt:

I'm calling in my favor. Darian is attacking us in the corridors by the JFK hub, and I need you to thwart him right now.

I click send and hold my breath.

The chances of—

My phone dings with a reply text.

It's from the person I thought of when the word "jester" happened to pop into my head.

Chester, the man who sent a necromancer after me —and whom I've suspected every time something bad has happened to me since.

The last person I should bet my life on.

My eyes frantically skim over his reply:

As luck would have it, Bertie and I have just returned from our safari. We're a couple of minutes away from your location, so be a dear and keep Darian alive for me in the meanwhile.

I reread the text, my head spinning.

"Bertie" is the lion he took on an airplane to Africa the other day. The chances that they happened to fly back from that trip today and at just the right time are staggeringly low, but hey, so is shuffling a deck of cards into new deck order, and Chester had done it easily.

This is what I was hoping for.

Chester hates Darian, so there was a chance his powers might put him where he needed to be in order to cause his nemesis the most damage. Sure enough, his probability manipulation mojo didn't disappoint.

Then again, he could still get here too late to help *us*, the people his powers don't care about.

Hoping my desperate gamble will actually pay off, I listen for any change in the carnage.

Nothing different is happening.

Nero is ripping into orc after orc, with blood splatter occasionally flying all the way to my location.

"Pick her up!" Darian shouts again.

Oh no. Chester is almost out of time.

"Please don't kick my friend when you take me," I say as the familiar green hands of the chieftain grab me by my waist and lift me into the air once again.

When Felix slips out of my grasp, the chieftain kicks him even harder than he did in my vision—perhaps to spite me.

My stomach twists as my friend smashes into the wall, then slides to the ground. He spits up even more blood than before, making me fear for his life, but to my relief, he keeps on breathing unevenly.

For now, at least.

"You will pay for that," I snarl at the orc as he lifts me all the way up.

Just like in my vision, the battlefield is covered with orc remains, and Nero is already moving much slower than normal.

But something isn't happening like in my vision this time.

A bunch of masked orcs are supposed to show up from around the corner, but they don't appear.

Instead of them, two completely new players show up.

CHAPTER SIXTY-SEVEN

IT'S Chester and his white lion.

Darian aims at me.

The lion leaps into the air and flies in an impossible-seeming arc.

Before Darian gets the chance to press the trigger, sharp lion teeth sink into his arm. He screams—and misses the moment when Chester closes the distance between them and steals his dagger.

Chester holds the weapon in his hand for a moment, as if weighing it. Then, with a nasty smile, he plunges it into Darian's throat.

I almost clap. If the future wanted to have someone get stabbed in the throat today, it might as well be Darian.

"Nero," Chester says loudly enough to be heard over Darian's bloody gurgling and the sounds of Nero ripping orcs into pieces. "I know you wanted me to stay out of your sight, but Sasha summoned me to help." He elbows dying Darian in the stomach and adds, "I'm afraid I'll need to kill this Council member in order to save your life—the life of another Council member, I should add."

"Save Sasha," Nero barks. "And I'll make sure you're not only cleared of all blame, but also get back on the Council."

"This truly is my lucky day," Chester says and shouts something at his lion in an unfamiliar language.

Bertie lets go of Darian's arm and rushes in Nero's direction, attacking a small orc in his path.

Two of the orcs try to help, and instantly pay with their lives as Nero rips them into orc confetti.

"Move another inch, and I'll kill this bitch," the chieftain growls, shaking me in the air with such force my heart nearly flies out of my mouth.

Nero lifts his hands—and gets attacked by the surviving orcs.

In the corner of my vision, I spot something white streaking toward me through the blood and gore.

Grinning madly at the chieftain, Chester starts to also lift his hands, and on the way, his right hand grasps the dagger sticking out of Darian's throat.

Before I can blink, Chester rips out the weapon and throws it—seemingly right at me.

The dagger flies in the most improbable curved arc, only to land in the chieftain's right eye with a disgusting squelch.

Roaring in pain, the green giant throws me aside to clutch at the wound.

I hit the ground painfully, my breath knocked out by the impact.

Something large leaps over me, and I battle a surge of nausea to look up. I see the lion flying at the chieftain's throat before his teeth sink into it with an obvious relish.

The sounds of orcs being torn apart by Nero reach my ears, followed by a less familiar smacking noise— probably Chester's fists on orc flesh.

The chieftain grasps the lion by his sides and tries to rip him away.

Somehow, Bert manages to hang on, and the whole thing reminds me of a nature show where a particularly hungry pride of lions took down an elephant.

Sadly, though, *this* lion is alone, plus the chieftain might be stronger than an elephant. I doubt Bert can hold on for much longer.

I'm still out of breath from my fall, but I force myself to leap to my feet, ignoring an explosion of pain in my knee.

Remembering what he did countless times to Nero in my visions, and the way he hurt Felix for real, I grit my teeth, reach up, and yank the dagger out of the chieftain's eye. He roars, and I channel the movie *Psycho* as I stab him in his one remaining eye.

His new roar is so loud my internal organs shrink in fear.

He swats at me.

I dodge the hit.

He swats again, and this time, his massive hand connects with my chest, the blow cracking something within me and sending me flying through the air.

CHAPTER SIXTY-EIGHT

"I'M TOAST," I have a chance to think.

Then I land in Nero's blood-covered arms with a loud smack.

Whatever rib or internal organ I felt crack earlier sends angry pain signals to my brain.

Nero carefully puts me back on my feet by the wall —and I try not to vomit from the pain as I use my hand to steady myself.

Nero then rejoins Chester, and they brutally finish off the last of the orcs.

"Bert," I croak, wiping a gallon of orc blood from my face.

Chester looks where his lion is still trying to hold on to the chieftain's throat.

"Save him," I rasp and slide by the wall to check on Felix.

Chester leaps for the chieftain. Over his shoulder, he says, "You might not want to see this."

I focus on Felix as he suggests, then regret not also covering my ears. Whatever Chester does to the chieftain must be unspeakable. The orc screams over and over, like a thousand boars being barbequed alive.

Felix has a pulse, but I can tell he's in bad shape. He's going to need Isis, and quickly.

"Help me lift him," I tell Nero, but when I look over to where he was, I find him kneeling in a pool of orc blood.

The chieftain howls one last time, then goes silent.

I see that Nero is still conscious, but I guess the blood loss and the tranquilizer have finally caught up with him because he doesn't respond.

Ignoring the nauseating agony from my ribs, I shuffle over and rummage through Nero's pockets for a phone.

The chieftain's screams are replaced with the equally disturbing sound of a lion munching on something.

"You almost died," Nero growls tiredly as I finally remove the phone from his pocket.

"Well, you *actually* died countless times in my visions even though you could've turned into a dragon and prevented it," I reply in the same accusing tone as I locate Isis's number and dial it.

She picks up right away. "Hello. To what do I owe—"

"Nero is hurt, and so is my friend Felix," I say urgently. "Nero would like to procure your services." I thrust the phone his way. "Tell her."

"Whatever Sasha needs," Nero says dazedly into the phone. "Emergency rates apply."

I put the phone back to my ear as Isis says, "How badly is Felix hurt?"

I quickly tell her what happened and what he looks like to me.

"What about Nero?" she asks.

I detail his poor condition.

"Okay, I'm going to text you an address of a hospital near where you are."

Nero's phone dings with a text.

"Take Felix to the hospital, and a vampire friend of mine will make sure they put him on life support as soon as you arrive," she says. "Then take Nero to the basement in your work building, and I'll meet you there."

"Our work building? Why would—" I stop because the line goes dead.

Chester and the lion pass by me, covered in even more orc juices than Nero.

They walk up to Darian's body. Chester speaks that language again, and I manage to look away just before the munching sounds begin anew.

I know that Darian totally deserved what he got, and that lions aren't vegans, but I'll still need therapy if I dwell on this too much. So instead, I busy myself by texting Thalia to make sure she's waiting to pick us up.

To my relief, she is.

Then I call Pada to have him and his cleanup crew come deal with the bloody mess around us.

"We're done," Chester says, walking over with the lion. "What do we do now?"

"Can you lift Felix very gently, and I'll take care of Nero?" I say.

Chester does as I ask, but Nero doesn't take my outstretched hand. Bleeding profusely, he staggers to his feet, refusing to lean on me.

He does, however, lean on Bert's head, and we trudge through the corridors at a glacial pace.

My ribs are screaming bloody murder, but I feel like I've gotten away pretty much scot-free. Nero, however, seems on the verge of passing out, and Felix's breathing is barely audible as Chester carries him.

"Can you use your luck to help Felix survive?" I ask Chester.

He winks at me. "I don't like carrying corpses, so if there's any chance that he'll survive, he will."

We walk for another minute, and though it could be just wishful thinking, Felix's breathing slightly improves.

"Are there limits to your power?" I ask Chester when we reach the door leading out to the airport proper. "Like, can you keep using it on Felix but also do that trick you used to get the lion on the plane? Make it so that no one looks at our bloody clothes and the lion?"

"Limits?" Chester takes in everyone's bloody state, then looks at his lion again. "I can do what you say and still have plenty left over." Grinning, he adds, "It's a shame, though. I almost want to know what the TSA would think of this."

"We don't have time for any delays," I say, on the off chance he's actually curious enough to allow TSA to spot us.

"I wasn't going to do it anyway," he says, looking at the lion. "They'd want to hurt Bertie if they saw him."

With that, we enter the airport.

Though it's a normal, fairly crowded day, not a single person looks our way—not even a woman with a Cognizant aura.

What I wouldn't give for this aspect of Chester's power. If I could control attention in this way, I could make whole elephants—or tanks—appear and disappear under people's noses.

The limo is waiting for us as soon as we get outside.

Ignoring Nero's protestations and the yelps of pain from my ribs, I help him get inside. Thalia gets out to help, and Chester settles Felix on the seat opposite Nero.

Once Felix is secured, the lion waltzes into the car, perches on an empty seat, and licks his blood-covered paws.

"It's better if I drive," Chester says to Thalia after I briefly introduce them.

She shakes her head.

"Let him," I say. "He's a probability manipulator. He can probably make it so there are more green lights in our path."

Thalia nods reluctantly, then walks over to Felix

and sits in such a way that she can make sure he stays put and doesn't move around.

I sit next to Nero and cradle his head on my lap.

According to my phone's GPS, the drive to the hospital is supposed to be twenty minutes without traffic—but there's always traffic here, and today it's bad.

I stroke Nero's hair, and he closes his eyes, the pained expression on his face easing. His various wounds are bleeding, though, so I tell Chester to floor it.

The limo torpedoes forward, and I very quickly regret my words.

To call Chester's driving reckless would do a disservice to regular reckless driving. The insane speed with which we zoom through the traffic is closer to the suicidal side of the driving spectrum. Yet we're fine— by which I mean we're on the verge of an accident every single second, but through "luck," the collisions do not occur. Oh, and as I predicted, when there are street lights in our path, they turn green every single time.

Ten minutes later, Chester pulls up to the ER entrance.

"Watch them," I tell Thalia, nodding at Nero and the lion.

Chester and I drag Felix out of the car, and a pale woman with a Cognizant aura approaches with a stretcher.

Moving with super-speed and using her glamour

when she needs to, Isis's vampire friend gets Felix instantly admitted into the ER and hooked up to all the equipment, plus a morphine drip.

"I could just give him some blood," she says as Felix's irregular heartbeat shows up on the monitor.

"No," I say swiftly. It's bad enough I already have one friend in rehab thanks to a similar situation. "Can you please just observe him and only use your blood as a last resort?"

"Sure," she says. "That's why I'm here. I just wanted to see if we could save Isis a trip down here. The bill will be—"

"No need. She'll be here shortly," I cut in.

And she will be, even if I have to have the lion drag her down here by her neck, like a cub.

"Got it," the vampire says, picking up Felix's chart.

"I'll be right back," I tell my unconscious friend and rush back to the car.

———

NORMALLY, the drive to Midtown would take an hour and a half in the current traffic conditions. Even in the best-case scenario, the trip would take an hour if one followed the speed limits and was sane.

Chester pulls up to my work building in less than a half hour, then parks in a tow-away zone and helps me get Nero out of the car and on his feet.

Leaving Thalia with the car, we go inside, where no one questions our bloody clothes.

Chester must still be doing his luck misdirection thing.

"Stay here," Nero directs him when the elevator arrives, and Chester nods, not looking the least bit offended.

"Good luck," he says with a smirk as we get into the elevator, with Nero doing his best not to lean on me and failing.

I press the basement button, and when we step out, Nero guides us through a maze-like corridor.

We find Isis standing next to giant metal doors, her nose in her phone.

"Heal her," Nero barks, and Isis's head jerks up. Blinking, she quickly shoots me with her healing energy, and the pain in my ribs disappears.

"Thank you. Now heal him," I say, nodding toward the bloody mess that is Nero, but Isis ignores me.

Instead, she opens the doors with a flair.

I look inside—and can't believe what I'm seeing.

CHAPTER SIXTY-NINE

IT'S a room full of treasure. Actually, the word "room" doesn't do it justice. It's a stadium-sized vault packed to the brim with gold coins, gold bricks, platinum jewelry, diamonds, and other precious stones.

"Get him inside," Isis says, and I help Nero walk into the place.

Once we're in there, my brain has trouble coping with the literal mountain of wealth on display.

There've been rumors of something like this going around the office. Whispers of a room filled with gold. I always thought it was a joke meant to compare Nero to Scrooge McDuck, who was fond of swimming in a pool of gold.

But this is different. It reminds me of the treasure that Smaug—the dragon from the Hobbit—slept on.

As soon as Nero's foot lands on the nearest gold coin, there appears to be a spring in his step.

"I got it from here," he growls. "Let go of me."

I release him, and he walks farther into the room, then starts to pull off his shirt. For a brief moment, his eyes meet mine, and though he still looks on the verge of passing out, I can't help but recall our time in that hotel on the Tartarus-ravaged world.

It might be on his mind too, because his limbal rings thicken, and a certain softness appears on his face. In the next second, however, he grimaces in pain and resumes stripping.

Not wanting to ogle his naked body like the apparent pervert that I am, I turn an accusing glare on Isis. "Why aren't you healing him?"

"I don't need to heal him," she says. "Look."

With a shimmer, Nero turns into his dragon form and starts climbing the giant mountain of treasure.

The wounds that he had in human shape are still there on the dragon—just bigger and bleeding a lot more.

But by the time Nero is perched on the very top of his pile, those wounds begin to knit.

I blink once, twice, but he just keeps healing.

I sneak a peek at Isis to check if she's doing it somehow, but she's fiddling with her phone, and there's no energy flowing from her to Nero.

When the wounds are gone completely, Nero contentedly closes his giant eyes and relaxes, as if to sleep.

"Wait a sec." I spin on my heel to glare at Isis again. "Nero can heal himself?"

"When in this room, obviously." She pulls her eyes

away from her phone. "Just give him a few more minutes, and he'll be good as new."

"Then why did you meet us here and not at the hospital?" My voice rises with every syllable. "Felix can't do *that*; he needs your help."

"First, I provided you with a vampire, so I don't even need to go to the hospital," she says. "Second, Nero is the one who pays me, so I had to make sure he—"

"He's definitely going to be fine?" I look at the slumbering dragon.

"Better than fine," she says. "He'll be full of energy and won't need to sleep or eat for a while."

Interesting. Is that what's behind his incredible work ethic? He's literally super-charged by his wealth?

No time to dwell on that, though; we have to help Felix.

I grab Isis by the shoulder. "Let's go then. Now."

———

OUR DRIVE back to the hospital is even faster—and crazier.

"Bertie and I should go," Chester says when he spots the vampire nurse walking out of the ER entrance.

"Right," I say. "Thank you. You've more than fulfilled your side of our bargain."

"I did. And just so you know, after today, I'm very happy that Beatrice failed to kill you." He winks and adds, "Lucky how things can turn out."

Before I can ask him if he's implying all the craziness that's been happening to me is just to appease his luck, he walks toward a random-seeming car, opens the door without a key, and gestures for the lion to jump inside.

Shrugging, I attack the vampire with a bunch of questions, and she informs me that while Felix is not doing better, he's not in a critical-enough condition to have needed her blood.

She then takes us to his private room, where Isis shoots Felix with her mojo until he starts making disturbingly orgasmic sounds.

With a gasp, he jackknifes into a sitting position and looks at me. "You used me as a shield," he says dazedly.

I wince. "Sorry about that. I had no other choice."

"Sure," he says grumpily as I help him get to his feet. "So what happened after I passed out?"

I explain on the way to the car, and finish my tale when we get in and Thalia starts driving. We also eat most of the food in the bar and drink a couple of cocktails to calm our nerves.

When we park next to my building, Isis's phone dings, and she says, "Nero is well enough to text. He wants me to walk you home and tuck you in, so let's go."

We leave the car and go up to our apartment without meeting any of the neighbors.

"What happened?" Fluffster asks frantically when he sees all the blood covering us.

"We're fine," I assure him, shoving Felix toward the shower.

He needs it, badly, and so do I.

I then offer Isis tea, which she accepts, although she keeps her nose buried in her phone as she drinks it. Is she checking how many likes her selfie got or tweeting about how boring it is to be in my company?

"So, we survived the first world," I say, launching into the tale of our adventures for Fluffster. I'm about midway when Felix comes in wearing fresh clothes and looking like a new person.

"Now you tell him what happened after we almost got eaten by the sea monsters," I say to Felix and go into the shower to decontaminate myself.

An hour later, I come out all pruney. Isis is still there, waiting for me, and she walks with me to my room despite my protestations.

"Get under the blankets. I'm going to heal you some more," she says.

I'm already feeling perfectly fine, but I do as I'm told and she shoots me with her mojo, dropping me into the sweetest and most dreamless sleep I've had.

———

I WAKE UP FEELING AMAZING.

Isis has the coolest power by far. If I were as rich as Nero, I'd have her "heal me" like that every night.

Then again, if Fluffster learned how much her

services cost, he'd turn into his monster form and eat her, so maybe it's not the best idea.

Yawning and stretching under the blanket, I check whether my powers came back.

With no effort, I leap into Headspace, and for the first time in a while, the shapes that surround me play happy tunes.

Ignoring them, I attempt to reach Rasputin again, so I can tell him what happened. Also, maybe I'll get lucky and learn about my mother in his memories as we join.

I'm dying to find out who she was.

The call doesn't connect. Since I'm here, though, I decide to check on Vlad to see how he's doing.

I find him no longer in the colosseum. This time, he's actually training some young boys how to wield a sword—which I guess is an improvement on fighting to the death. Maybe he's moved on to the next stage of grief?

When my vision ends, I go back to Headspace and check on Kit as well.

To my shock, I see the shape-shifting Councilor talking to Ariel in a hallway. Ariel is knitting and puffing on her vaping gizmo as Kit tells her how she finally managed to escape Lola's sexual clutches and right away checked herself into rehab.

The vision completes, and I find myself back in my comfy bed. I'm about to get up and get on with my day when an idea occurs to me.

It's been a while since I attempted to see my

biological mother via a vision—and Rasputin has told a few tidbits about her recently, which could help.

Returning to Headspace, I dwell on every attribute I've learned about. He'd said she was stubborn, like me, and quick-thinking, also like me. Great at deception too—obviously like me as well.

Nothing happens, so I recall Rasputin hinting that she's not compassionate—in contrast to me—and add that into the mix.

Still no results.

I'm about to give up when I remember a memory of Rasputin that I gleaned the very first time we joined— one where he was brushing a lover's hair.

That was very likely my mother. She had black hair (like I do), pale shoulders (check), and a graceful back (not sure about the similarity on this one, as I'm not in the habit of staring at my backside in the mirror).

More importantly, in the memory, he'd called her unpredictable—and said that he loves that about her.

I combine all these facts together, then add my deep desire to know who she is, and something clicks.

A new set of shapes shows up in front of me— shapes that aren't exuding immediate danger but aren't all happy-go-lucky either.

Can it be?

Will I finally see my mother?

Using my intuition once more, I touch the most promising vision—and nearly explode with excitement as it starts.

CHAPTER SEVENTY

I FIND myself bodiless on a familiar New York street.

A beautiful woman is walking there, dressed in a strappy black dress.

She has the black hair from Rasputin's memory, and her shoulders—and her everything else—are vitamin-D-deficiency pale. What the dress reveals of her back is indeed graceful, but more importantly, if you took my face and removed any features I have in common with Rasputin, you'd get this woman's visage.

This is my mother.

I know this beyond a shadow of doubt—despite the fact that she looks too young to have a kid my age. Then again, the Cognizant don't age the same way.

The woman turns to walk into a building, and I realize why this street looks so familiar.

This is where Nero lives.

Is this some *Twilight Zone* "Meet the Parents"

episode? My father has met whatever Nero is to me and now my mother feels left out?

Then I notice something else, and it sends my mind *really* spinning.

With her face in a profile like this, I spot a tattoo on her temple.

A tattoo of a moon attached at the top of a cross.

It takes me a moment to understand the implications, and even then I refuse to believe it.

I must be wrong.

My mother cannot be who I think this is.

Waltzing into Nero's fancy lobby, the woman takes out a bloody rag from her dainty purse and gives it a surreptitious lick—though it could just as easily have been a sniff. She then frowns deeply.

Whatever she's just learned, she doesn't like it.

Spinning on her heel, she rushes for the front desk and faces the security guard sitting there. As she catches his gaze, her eyes turn into mirrors.

So she *is* a vampire. That supports my crazy theory, as does the bloody rag to some degree, but it just can't be—

"Did a man recently leave this place?" she says in a voice different from the one I expected, but with a strange accent that's still dead on. "A good-looking specimen with strange eyes and—"

"You mean Mr. Gorin?" the guard asks. "Nero Gorin?"

"I think I do," she says. "Where did this Nero go?"

She reaches out and grabs the guy by the collar of his uniform.

"He never tells me such things," the guard replies robotically, oblivious to the rough treatment. "His limo sped away pretty fast, so he's bound to be far away by now."

She lets him go, her frown deepening. "Did he have a man with him?" She proceeds to describe Rasputin—another piece of evidence to support my theory.

"No," the guard says. "I don't think I've ever seen a man with that description show up here with or without a beard."

"Fine," she snaps. "Do you have a key to this Nero's lair?" Under her breath, she mutters, "Since I'm here, I might as well see if he has any clues to Rasputin's location among all the gold."

"Do you mean his penthouse?" the guy asks in confusion.

"Whatever you call it." She peers at him more intently. "Give me the key. Now."

The guy hands her a key so fast he nearly dislocates his shoulder.

As she walks to the elevator, I cannot deny it any longer.

I now know who my mother is—and I wish it were anyone else.

Literally, anyone.

Unfortunately, reality doesn't care about my desires, and with a sinking feeling, I process the realization that I'm Lilith's daughter.

CHAPTER SEVENTY-ONE

I WANT TO DENY IT, but it makes too much sense.

On Lilith's world, she'd used glamour to look and sound like a goddess—which is why I didn't see our resemblance. Here on Earth, however, she looks like a regular vampire, just with that distinctive tattoo.

Itzel, being a gnome, was immune to Lilith's glamour on her world, and she'd mentioned a temple tattoo. Only instead of describing it as a moon on top of a cross, like a normal person would have, Itzel said it was a parenthesis sitting on top of a plus sign. Oh, and I can't believe Itzel told us about the tattoo but not the fact that Lilith and I look alike. Then again, she did mention she had trouble with non-gnome faces.

My mother is Lilith.

That explains the bloody rag she was holding in the vision. It no doubt contains some of the copious blood Nero had shed in her world. She's using the blood to locate him—the person who attacked her castle.

She's here for revenge.

That's what Rasputin said would happen, and he was right.

That she's also looking for Rasputin is further proof of her identity, as is the fact that she's a vampire.

And not just a vampire. Lilith is also a trickster— which is why Rasputin had said she was so unpredictable. He'd meant it literally.

A lot of other pieces start to fall into place.

Lilith's world runs about twenty times slower than Earth. A year there is twenty here. Three years and eleven months there is about eighty here—which explains how I was born in beginning of the twentieth century but grew up at the turn of the millennium.

Lilith's world must've been where Rasputin stole me away from—and now that I think about it, his visions of me slicing throats with that knife could've easily taken place in Lilith's castle.

My mother is Lilith.

That explains why Rasputin left me at JFK by myself. Lilith had his hair and could locate him at will. She did find him afterward, and this is why she was torturing him. She must've wanted me back, and he refused to tell her where he took me.

But if he's the father of her child, how could she treat him like that? What kind of a monster—

Wait. Who am I kidding? She made herself a god and uses people like water bottles. It was probably her who would've made the child version of me slice people's throats in the future Rasputin had prevented. No doubt she wanted me to grow up a psychopath, just like Mommy.

Then again, Rasputin had lived in the nicest cell of all the prisoners at Lilith's castle, and she didn't mutilate his body or drain his blood. Is that her version of loving care?

The elevator dings, and I examine this monster—my mother—more carefully.

Despite everything, I still want to know her.

But that's a bad idea.

Must think about something else—like the interesting fact I can now add to my list of vampire trivia.

Apparently, they can give birth. Or at least this one did—I must not forget that she's very, very powerful and a probability manipulator to boot. Maybe that combo lets her do things that regular vampires can't do. Like flying, for example. Or possessing the strength to fight a dragon.

Lilith exits the elevator and enters Nero's apartment.

"Honey, I'm home," she says tauntingly and sniffs the air.

Does she think Rasputin might be hiding here?

When no one replies, she walks around the apartment at random, first checking the kitchen, then the gym, then the spa-like bathroom I'd used the other day.

A minute later, she stumbles onto Nero's art studio, where a painting catches her eye.

A painting I'd also found interesting when I saw it.

It depicts me—or Nero's fantasy version of me—standing on a white-sand beach in a skimpy bathing suit. Nero drew this in the heyday of his stalking of me —long before we officially met.

Lilith rips the painting off the wall and stares at it, then walks over to a mirror and examines her own features.

"Could it be?" she mutters as she sets the painting down and steps back, staring at it with her head cocked. "She's much too old, but the resemblance is uncanny. Could this be where she was hidden all this time?" Then her eyes widen. "Of course. *That's* why the dragon came to save Rasputin. He's clearly infatuated with my beautiful spawn."

Beautiful spawn? If I'd had any doubts left about her identity or our relationship, they're now gone.

I'm Lilith's daughter.

"I need to know more about you, dear," Lilith says to my portrait and starts rummaging through Nero's place with the vigor of a DEA agent busting a heroin dealer.

Expensive furniture is ripped to shreds, and even the walls get torn apart in many places.

Eventually, she makes her way to Nero's office and locates the safe I was hoping she *wouldn't* find.

Instead of messing with the keypad as I did, she

simply rips the door off with her bare hands, then reads the same documents I discovered the other day: the contract between Nero and Rasputin, my birth certificate, and the map with the dangerous path to her own world.

"So, you go by Sasha Urban now," Lilith says, putting down the yellowing pages. "I can't wait to meet you—"

————

I COME BACK to reality with my heart pumping frantically in my chest. I'm glad I was lying down when I started the vision.

My legs feel so wobbly I could've collapsed.

Evening out my breath as much as I can, I try to organize my frantically spinning thoughts.

For the longest time, one of my biggest wishes was to learn about my origins. To find out who my birth parents are and how I ended up on my own at the airport.

Now I know most of it.

It's because my mother is Lilith. An evil goddess whose world they warn you to stay away from during Orientation… the boogeyman of the Cognizant community.

She's so infamous, in fact, that she's featured in the role of the "mother of demons," or something equally unflattering, in human mythologies all over Earth.

And she's the mother I've wished so desperately to find.

I guess the old adage is true.

Be careful what you wish for.

I'm Lilith's daughter, and she's coming for me.

SNEAK PEEKS

Thank you for reading! I hope you're enjoying Sasha's story. To be notified of new releases of my books, please visit www.dimazales.com and sign up for my mailing list.

Love audiobooks? This series, and all of my other books, are available in audio.

Want to read my other books? You can check out:

- *Mind Dimensions* - the action-packed urban fantasy adventures of Darren, who can stop time and read minds
- *Upgrade* - the thrilling sci-fi tale of Mike Cohen, whose new technology will transform our brains *and* the world
- *The Last Humans* - the futuristic sci-

fi/dystopian story of Theo, who lives in a
world where nothing is as it seems
- *The Sorcery Code* - the epic fantasy adventures
  of sorcerer Blaise and his creation, the
  beautiful and powerful Gala

I also collaborate with my wife on sci-fi romance, so if
you don't mind erotic material, you can check out *Close
Liaisons*. Visit <u>www.annazaires.com</u> for more
information and to get your copy.

And now, please turn the page for an exciting excerpt
from *The Sorcery Code*.

EXCERPT FROM THE SORCERY CODE

Once a respected member of the Sorcerer Council and now an outcast, Blaise has spent the last year of his life working on a special magical object. The goal is to allow anyone to do magic, not just the sorcerer elite. The outcome of his quest is unlike anything he could've ever imagined—because, instead of an object, he creates Her.

She is Gala, and she is anything but inanimate. Born in the Spell Realm, she is beautiful and highly intelligent —and nobody knows what she's capable of. She will do anything to experience the world... even leave the man she is beginning to fall for.

Augusta, a powerful sorceress and Blaise's former fiancée, sees Blaise's deed as the ultimate hubris and Gala as an abomination that must be destroyed. In her quest to save the human race, Augusta will forge new alliances, becoming tangled in a web of intrigue that stretches further than any of them suspect. She may even have to turn to her new lover Barson, a ruthless warrior who might have an agenda of his own...

———

There was a naked woman on the floor of Blaise's study.

A beautiful naked woman.

Stunned, Blaise stared at the gorgeous creature who just appeared out of thin air. She was looking around with a bewildered expression on her face, apparently as shocked to be there as he was to be seeing her. Her wavy blond hair streamed down her back, partially covering a body that appeared to be perfection itself. Blaise tried not to think about that body and to focus on the situation instead.

A woman. A *She*, not an *It*. Blaise could hardly believe it. Could it be? Could this girl be the object?

She was sitting with her legs folded underneath her, propping herself up with one slim arm. There was something awkward about that pose, as though she didn't know what to do with her own limbs. In general, despite the curves that marked her a fully grown woman, there was a child-like innocence in the way she sat there, completely unselfconscious and totally unaware of her own appeal.

Clearing his throat, Blaise tried to think of what to say. In his wildest dreams, he couldn't have imagined this kind of outcome to the project that had consumed his entire life for the past several months.

Hearing the sound, she turned her head to look at him, and Blaise found himself staring into a pair of unusually clear blue eyes.

She blinked, then cocked her head to the side, studying him with visible curiosity. Blaise wondered what she was seeing. He hadn't seen the light of day in weeks, and he wouldn't be surprised if he looked like a mad sorcerer at this point. There was probably a week's worth of stubble covering his face, and he knew his dark hair was unbrushed and sticking out in every direction. If he'd known he would be facing a beautiful woman today, he would've done a grooming spell in the morning.

"Who am I?" she asked, startling Blaise. Her voice was soft and feminine, as alluring as the rest of her. "What is this place?"

"You don't know?" Blaise was glad he finally managed to string together a semi-coherent sentence. "You don't know who you are or where you are?"

She shook her head. "No."

Blaise swallowed. "I see."

"What am I?" she asked again, staring at him with those incredible eyes.

"Well," Blaise said slowly, "if you're not some cruel prankster or a figment of my imagination, then it's somewhat difficult to explain..."

She was watching his mouth as he spoke, and when he stopped, she looked up again, meeting his gaze. "It's strange," she said, "hearing words this way. These are the first real words I've heard."

Blaise felt a chill go down his spine. Getting up from his chair, he began to pace, trying to keep his eyes off her nude body. He had been expecting something to appear. A magical object, a thing. He just hadn't known what form that thing would take. A mirror, perhaps, or a lamp. Maybe even something as unusual as the Life Capture Sphere that sat on his desk like a large round diamond.

But a person? A female person at that?

To be fair, he had been trying to make the object intelligent, to ensure it would have the ability to comprehend human language and convert it into the code. Maybe he shouldn't be so surprised that the intelligence he invoked took on a human shape.

A beautiful, feminine, sensual shape.

Focus, Blaise, focus.

"Why are you walking like that?" She slowly got to her feet, her movements uncertain and strangely clumsy. "Should I be walking too? Is that how people talk to each other?"

Blaise stopped in front of her, doing his best to keep his eyes above her neck. "I'm sorry. I'm not accustomed to naked women in my study."

She ran her hands down her body, as though trying to feel it for the first time. Whatever her intent, Blaise found the gesture extremely erotic.

"Is something wrong with the way I look?" she

asked. It was such a typical feminine concern that Blaise had to stifle a smile.

"Quite the opposite," he assured her. "You look unimaginably good." So good, in fact, that he was having trouble concentrating on anything but her delicate curves. She was of medium height, and so perfectly proportioned that she could've been used as a sculptor's template.

"Why do I look this way?" A small frown creased her smooth forehead. "What am I?" That last part seemed to be puzzling her the most.

Blaise took a deep breath, trying to calm his racing pulse. "I think I can try to venture a guess, but before I do, I want to give you some clothing. Please wait here —I'll be right back."

And without waiting for her answer, he hurried out of the room.

———

The Sorcery Code is currently available at most retailers. If you'd like to learn more, please visit www.dimazales.com.

ABOUT THE AUTHOR

Dima Zales is a *New York Times* and *USA Today* bestselling author of science fiction and fantasy. Prior to becoming a writer, he worked in the software development industry in New York as both a programmer and an executive. From high-frequency trading software for big banks to mobile apps for popular magazines, Dima has done it all. In 2013, he left the software industry in order to concentrate on his writing career and moved to Palm Coast, Florida, where he currently resides.

Please visit www.dimazales.com to learn more.